THE LOST CHORD

Music is the harmonious voice of creation; an echo of the invisible world; one note of a divine concord which the entire universe is destined one day to sound.

– Giuseppe Mazzini, 1805-1872,

Ian Thomas

Manor House Publishing

Library and Archives Canada
Cataloguing in Publication

Thomas, Ian, 1950-
The lost chord : a novel / Ian Thomas.

ISBN 978-1-897453-09-4

I. Title.

PS8639.H575L68 2008 C813'.6 C2008-905906-9

Printed and bound in Canada
First Edition.
384 pages.

Cover design: Romelda Morson

Published Oct. 14, 2008
Manor House Publishing Inc.
www.manor-house.biz
(905) 648-2193

We gratefully acknowledge the financial support of the Government of Canada through the Book Publishing Industry Development Program (BPIDP), Dept. of Canadian Heritage, for our publishing activities.

Manor House Publishing Inc.
www.manor-house.biz
905-648-2193

For my mother, Moreen Thomas,
And for the mothers of many species
who elevate us all through the metaphor
of giving so much to the next generation.

Acknowledgments

I would like to thank my brother and life long friend, Dave Thomas, with whom I kicked around a seminal idea for this book some twenty years ago. Writing, whether song or prose, is an exercise in isolation. When I emerge from my head, I am grateful for the presence of Catherine Thomas in my life and as the initial sounding board for anything I do creatively.

This existence would be a lesser place without the embrace of dear friends like Keith Reid, Stewart Farago and John Zaslow who read early versions of the Lost Chord. Book publishing is even more of a nightmare than the record business and so I consider myself very fortunate for the like of Michael B. Davie at Manor House Publishing for his steadfast support in these flights of fantasy. Catherine Marjoribanks provided invaluable feedback with a disarming sense of humour as well as some serious editing skills.

I am grateful for the exceptional artistic talents of Romelda Morson who designed the cover. My mother Moreen Thomas has consistently encouraged her two boys in anything we have ever attempted. *"Ye can do anything ye put yer mind to."* So she is in part to blame for this book, which she also proofread, leaving a trail of really tiny writing in the margins.

Origins of The Lost Chord

The Lost Chord originally appeared as the title of a hymn written by Arthur Sullivan on January 13, 1877 at the deathbed of his brother, Fred. The Lyric was from a poem written a few years earlier by Adelaide A. Proctor.

1

ORPHANS OF BELIEF

Hamburg
May, 1847

Far below the sanctuary of the Hamburg Cathedral, small chambers had been dug at great expense to house the remains of the privileged. The idea they had been sold was that one might, for a meaningful financial consideration, find a place of rest in the house of God in order to be closer, everlastingly, to the Almighty.

Sadly, there could not have been a place more devoid of anything of a divine persuasion. This was a stone gallery where the dust of fools craved the warmth of earth, and meticulously carved names longed to be read aloud by visitors who never came.

The dour face of an old priest flickered in the void from a torch that wept light onto the rough stone floor in front of him. He limped along on a badly deformed leg repeating obscure Latin phrases until an elaborate sarcophagus that jutted out into the passageway caught his eye.

"Put him down and remove the lid."

The priest placed the torch into a rusting iron sconce while three rough-looking men behind him lowered a body to the floor and began pushing on the heavy stone. With a slow grind, the massive weight scraped across the lip of the coffin before hitting the wall.

"That will do. Put him in and close it," the priest barked.

One of the men looked at him in horror. "But … but Father Luke … he … he breathes!"

"You will do as you are told or face eternal damnation! This one deals with the Devil himself. If he awakens in our world, we are all damned!"

"Forgive me, Father." The man cowered in the presence of such religious certainty and signalled the others to comply. They stuffed the body into an opening barely wide enough for the task, then grunted the lid back into place. The fragile promise of light fluttered away one step at a time as the burial party retreated up a stone spiral staircase and darkness flooded back in.

***

It was about an hour later that Brother Peter Verhoevan stirred. It felt good to feel the blood coursing through his veins again, though the view left something to be desired. He opened his eyes and stared into the blackest of black. An attempt to sit up ended abruptly with his forehead slamming hard into cold, rough stone.

"*Dummkopf*," he moaned in exasperation as he fell back. Blood trickled down the bridge of his nose as a familiar musty odour invaded his nostrils. He had the misfortune of knowing that fragrance, having come across the stench of decaying human flesh before. There had been a few occasions when, as a young priest, Peter had been ordered to reclaim bejewelled family heirlooms from the fingers and necks of the dead. He'd been told it was for the families involved but he knew better, as new chalices and crosses impregnated with very familiar-looking gems appeared at the altar soon thereafter.

Something hard dug into the back of his head. He reached over his shoulder for what he knew would be there—strands of decayed hair, and farther down, remnants of a nose … and farther still … teeth. "*Mein Gott*," he huffed as he squeezed himself over and came face to face with the carcass of an aristocrat of some importance. *Importance*—the word seemed silly given the journeys of the last few months, an earthly term meaning only the best fabrics and coffins in which to rot. The very idea of the word had on many occasions caused Verhoevan to shake his head in wonder at the stupidity of his own kind.

Everything in the material world had been turned upside down. A belief that had once defined the universe for Peter Verhoevan had been revealed as a frivolous comfort that now embarrassed him greatly for having once been its purveyor. Where no answers were forthcoming, well, that was where belief came in. It didn't have to be true, just appealing on some level … a drop sheet, nicely painted in floral pastels to hide the abyss of infinite possibilities on the other side. Men soon recognized the power of belief as a useful tool in the denial of reality. And so, Verhoevan concluded, belief had been repackaged under the more encompassing banner of "faith."

For most honest men there was honest doubt, or at least a temptation to wonder, to search beyond the boundaries of belief as new information became available. Faith, on the other hand, could be sold as an absolute, requiring the cessation of question, which effectively gave those in charge power over the faithful. How dare anyone argue with God! That any church would declare itself the voice and earthly manifestation of God was an assault to Verhoevan's common sense. It was simply preposterous for any man of conscience to presume to speak for the Almighty.

The fraternal twins of *fear* and *ignorance* were at the root of most human suffering, and he had no doubt they were behind his current predicament. He thought it odd how such fragile things could exact so much pain from humankind. Still, as a man of good heart, he felt a measure of sympathy for those who merely sought shelter in mindless surety. And it appeared that such surety might breathe easier now, with the likes of him dead.

Bracing himself on his elbows and knees, Verhoevan attempted to slide the lid of the sarcophagus with his back. He feared it would be a fruitless exercise, but anger at the cruelty of those who would put a living body in such a place drove him to an exhausting first effort. He caught his breath and heaved a second time … again with no reward. After a few more moments of rest he gave it one last try, with every ounce of strength left in his body. A searing pain ripped across his chest and his arms buckled, dropping Verhoevan hard onto the carcass beneath him.

"*Dummkopf*," he muttered again, in what would be his final spoken word. The corpse's teeth sank into his cheek from the pressure of his own dead weight. The pain began to dissipate quickly, more distant … more distant. He knew that when the pain was completely gone, he would be elsewhere … again.

Hamburg
One day later

The doors of Frau Hoffman's brothel on Lieber Strasse were not known for spewing sunny, fresh faces into the morning dew, and this day would be no exception. A shipment of Weisse beer had arrived from Munchen with the entourage of King Ludwig I the previous day, and somehow a "misplaced" barrel had found its way to Hoffman's seedy establishment.

There were few who could afford good beer in Hamburg, or for that matter in any of the Germanic states. Famine was reaching epidemic levels due to the potato disease and the failure of grain harvests. Typhus swooped down like a buzzard to pluck the last pathetic remnants of a painful life from the starved flesh of thousands. Peasants, demanding release from feudal obligations, were ransacking houses in the surrounding countryside.

The growing pains of moving into the Industrial Revolution to meet the challenge of British, French, and Belgian imports had planted the seeds of federalism. Growing ranks of people displaced by machines were the downside of industrial capitalism. Industrialization for many was nothing but feudalism in a mechanized disguise. In Prussia, there were already a couple of thousand mechanical looms, but well over one hundred thousand handlooms remained. Progress would not be easy.

The output from the looms of Dopp Textiles greatly exceeded that of the rest of the producers in the area. This was as much due to Herr Gert Dopp's keen sense of business as it was to the advantage of machine over man. His contacts in America had kept a steady stream of cheap cotton and other raw materials flowing his way to add to all the local wool he was buying. There was a sense of promise in Dopp Textiles, and the former weavers Herr Dopp employed to oversee the large looms were his best advertising. He paid them well, and so he was viewed by many as something of a saviour in an otherwise bleak economic landscape. Few realized his generosity was simply a well-calculated form of self-preservation.

The previous evening, Herr Dopp's son Matthias had decided to walk off the ringing in his ears – a side effect of hours immersed in the roar of his father's newfangled machines. To that end, his carriage had been sent on to the safety of the livery while he waited for the few remaining employees to leave. Once the head count was complete, Matthias reached into his trouser pocket and pulled out the large keys for the padlock and the cast-iron locking mechanism of the massive front door. After securing and double-checking, he spun around, free at last.

"*Guten abend*, Hans," he said to the night watchman, a man with tree-trunk limbs and but a few brown teeth left to lose to an unmanageable temper.

"*Guten abend*, Herr Dopp," the surly man snorted as he took up his position on a crude wooden bench thrown in front of the door.

Matthias, tall and full of his eighteen years, walked down the cobblestone street with a confident swagger fed by youthful good looks that caused more than a few women to smile in his direction. It was an unusually warm evening, and what began as a nice stroll quickly turned foul as he got farther away from the cool harbour breeze. Humidity and sweat soaked through his shirt and well into the lining of his jacket, like glue on gauze. He took a handkerchief and wiped the perspiration-soaked blond hair at the base of his neck. When he passed Frau Hoffman's establishment, the sight of the Weisse beer being offloaded from an oxcart was too much for a now desperate thirst. His eyes followed the barrel as it was hoisted onto the shoulder of a burly deliveryman, who stumbled over the uneven cobblestones under the weight. It was indeed a fair weight for any man to carry, but not enough of a burden to stop the brute from finding the necessary air for a lusty grunt at the fair-haired girl standing, quite fetchingly, in the doorway.

Matthias's focus was torn from the keg of beer by the intense gravitational pull of the young girl's green eyes, focused inquisitively in his direction. She had to be new, he thought … no more than sixteen. God, she was beautiful, and out of place at an establishment known for old cows that beckoned with burgeoning cleavage, rotten teeth, and far too much experience for even the most remote notion of romantic fantasy. It was terribly hot, he rationalized to himself … perhaps just one tall glass of cool beer. He moved towards the young girl in the long cotton dress—she was nearly his height—and, uncharacteristically, he found himself stammering, dumbfounded in her rose-scented presence.

"Uh, *guten tag, fraulein*. I see you have, uh … taken possession of a new shipment of Weisse beer."

She nodded a provocative affirmative and led him in by the hand, sensing that he might be coaxed into more than the beer.

Once in the dimly lit libido trap, Matthias became even drier in the throat as the young lass held his hand somewhat gingerly to her powdered cleavage. The power of forbidden fruit had caught him off guard and excited him to the core. *In for a penny, in for a pound*, as he had heard many a British sailor say. He assumed a manly stance beyond his years and slapped a handful of coins on the table, where Frau Hoffman sat drinking a cheap homebrew with some of her scantily clad employees.

"I should like the best room in the house, this fair young *fraulein*, and a large pitcher of Weisse beer, and don't try to pass off your own homebrew on me!" Matthias puffed, with a slight tremor in his youthful voice.

The proprietor's mouth curled up in one corner as she sized up the young buck in full swagger. She recognized the good-looking young man immediately, and saw an equally good opportunity.

"Nothing but the best for the son of Gertie Dopp," she rasped with a knowing smirk.

"Frau Hoffman, you would be better to show a little more decorum and respect for my father, Herr Dopp."

"I beg your pardon, Herr Dopp, I meant no disrespect. We all love your father here."

She had no sooner uttered the patronizing words than a barmaid chatting up the deliveryman popped her head over his shoulder and cackled, "And we all *have* loved your father here."

Laughter overtook the room, and a couple of snickers escaped from behind a curtain pulled haphazardly across the doorway to the back room. The space between the bottom of the curtain and the floor revealed the rolled-down trousers of a standing patron who apparently was in a bit of a hurry. It sounded as if he were blessing the woman kneeling at his feet as she hummed in what could have been mistaken for a well-rehearsed religious rapture.

Sensing that Matthias might be losing his purpose, and bringing her grin under control, Frau Hoffman swung into action. She was, after all, a businesswoman, and there was some business to be had from the son of a wealthy man.

"Follow me, Herr Dopp. And if you would be so kind as to join us, Anna."

Before Matthias could change his mind he found himself gazing into the dim light of a seedy third-floor room. He surveyed the cracked plaster, ratty furniture, and dirty-looking bed linens, wondering what he was doing in such a hellhole, until he completed his 180-degree sweep and found himself staring once more at the one called Anna. Her apparent nervousness held an innocence that Matthias found captivating.

"This is Anna's first week with us, Herr Dopp, and now that you know where she is we hope to see you again. I'll leave you two to discuss whatever comes up," Frau Hoffman quipped as she spun around and cackled at her bad joke all the way down the stairs.

The young girl closed the door quietly and her trembling hands began unbuttoning the embroidered cotton blouse, to the undivided attention of her captive audience of one. There was something about this girl that was far more interesting than the well-to-do daughters his father's friends were always forcing on him. They all exuded such uselessness that Matthias dreaded the day he might have to marry one and be responsible for her until his dying breath. There had been a couple of sexual dalliances, but those episodes felt like arranged traps to force a marital course. This was a moment of random passion with no such consequence, or so he tried to convince himself. He knew he was inventing ridiculous excuses for every inch of the slope he was sliding down, but he just couldn't stop.

What he didn't know was how hard Anna was working to hide her nervousness. In the last couple of days, she thought, she had seen and done it all. All the customers thus far had been filthy labourers and lonely old men, but this Matthias was young and handsome. She had observed him walking by two days earlier and was undeniably attracted to him. There were still a few girlish fantasies that she hung on to as a way of mental escape, but she had never expected one of those fantasies to walk so willingly into her hell.

The beer arrived moments later with a knock on the door, which opened just enough for two arms to slide a frothy pitcher and two beer steins onto the floor. With the click of the latch, the room fell silent once more to expectation. Any awkwardness was slowly discarded, along with their garments, as the young couple drifted away into what would be a longer night than Matthias had anticipated. He was indeed infatuated with the lovely young woman, but unbeknownst to him the beer had been laced with a substance used on special occasions by the canny proprietor to blur any lines of common sense. To Frau Hoffman, the appearance of anyone of substantial purse constituted such a special occasion.

The night disappeared into an unusual drowsiness that finally took Matthias under and delivered him like a castaway to the wreckage of the morning after. A monumental headache awoke him in such a disoriented state that it took him a disconcerting amount of time to realize where he was. His hand blindly floundered among the clothes on the threadbare upholstered chair at the side of the bed until it found the slit in his waistcoat. His index finger went on alone until the small, silk-lined pocket reluctantly spat out his grandfather's gold watch. An unwilling, pillow-free, blurry eye squinted into the burning light until the bad news, in Roman numerals, slowly came into focus … 8:25 a.m.

"On no!" He jumped off the lumpy feather mattress onto the rough planks of the floor and frantically grabbed at the rest of the crumpled clothing that lay strewn around the room. Anna didn't stir. He looked at her for a moment, mesmerized by her delicate, soft features, even though he had sufficient memory of his attempts to cure the fascination. Still, there was something different about this girl.

Such sweet thoughts were shattered when a quick inspection of his trouser pockets revealed that there was nothing clanking against his keys … the rest of his money was gone! There was no time to sit through what he anticipated would be well-rehearsed indignant huffs of innocence from the husky-voiced proprietor. He would just have to be grateful that Frau Hoffman had seen fit to leave him his grandfather's watch and his keys.

This was the day a new pipe organ would be dedicated at the Hamburg Cathedral in loving memory of Matthias's mother, Maria Dopp. She had died the year before in a fierce outbreak of cholera that had begun in the neighbourhoods worst hit by typhus, then spread like ground fire. His grieving father, seeking some kind of immortality for her memory, had taken over the financial responsibility of the new organ. The bass pipes were thirty-two-footers. The three manual sixty-note keyboards and two banks of ivory stops would be a testimony to state-of-the-art technology. It was to be one of the biggest pipe organs in Germany … nothing but the best for the wife of Gert Dopp, God rest her soul.

His best friends had begged Herr Dopp to hold fast financially for a few months, but there was something deep seated that stopped him from listening. He demonstrated a heart-wrenching remorse in the loss of Maria that he fruitlessly tried to sedate by throwing money at it. One year later, however, the only remorse he felt was in being considerably lighter of pocket.

The Church, on the other hand, was ever so grateful for Herr Dopp's generosity. In exchange for a good chunk of the Dopp fortune, a small brass plaque would be fixed to the polished oak cabinetry in memory of Maria Dopp and dedicated to the glory of God. Herr Dopp, at the time of the final and painfully large fund transfers, had remarked snidely to his son that apparently the God everyone worshipped was "only in it for the glory … according to that damned plaque!" The service of dedication was to take place on the day and time of his beloved Maria's death, 8:00 a.m. …twenty-five minutes ago!

How could Matthias have been such a libidinous fool? Well, the answer to that, he had shockingly learned the night before, was that apparently it ran in the family! He couldn't think of his father as a sexual being; it disgusted him. Had his father been frequenting Frau Hoffman's establishment even before the death of his mother? Was that the source of his remorse in her death? While engaged in condescending judgments, flashes of everything he had done the night before spat his own lust squarely back into his face.

Boots hastily laced, Matthias leaned over and gently swept a wisp of fine, fair hair from Anna's delicate face, then kissed her tenderly on the cheek. Even though he had satisfied his every fantasy, a part of him still didn't want to leave her.

He shook his head at the impossibility of it all, then spun around and flew down the stairs onto the busy street.

Anna hadn't stirred, even though she was wide awake. Unrealistic thoughts of life with her dashing young man crashed onto the filthy, cracked-plaster wall of the seedy brothel. She knew she wouldn't last long in Hoffman's business with such a frivolous vulnerability. Such feelings as she had for Matthias had to go … maybe even the ability to feel them. She had money to make, a father, mother, and siblings to feed with her meagre earnings. Matthias was for some other life, some other world, some place she might find in a tall tale from the imaginations of Jakob and Wilhelm Grimm of Frankfurt.

Carts and wagons of every shape and size had been bringing goods up from the harbour for a good few hours, feeding the street vendors and shops, who were well into their day's meagre take. Anna jumped out of bed to watch her gallant young man, three floors below, as he pushed his way through the crowded street towards the twin towers of Hamburg Cathedral.

His movements were like an intricate dance step, expertly avoiding the daily obstacle course of horse and ox droppings. An exceptional coordination of sight and reflex was a prerequisite for the well-dressed city dweller. One could hardly impress a soul smelling like horseshit, or, even worse, dragging the same onto the parlour carpet of some unfortunate host. As he began to run, Matthias became aware that his clothes held an aroma of dried sweat from the previous day. The odour, combined with a crushed and dishevelled appearance, would most certainly merit more than the usual words of disapproval from a fussy father who prided himself on his appearance.

There would be a gathering of local dignitaries at the ceremony, including the Lord Mayor of Hamburg and, rumour had it, the possibility of an ardent organ enthusiast in the person of none other than Ludwig I, who was visiting from Bavaria. Marcus Fricke, a musician of national note, had been rehearsing a short program of Bach that would showcase the power of this majestic musical instrument, and there would also be an original piece written for the occasion by Peter Verhoevan, a priest of the Franciscan brotherhood. Verhoevan was a brilliant composer whose music was the toast of local gossip for its powerful ability to move even the most monumental cynic to tears.

Matthias ran up the steps towards the giant, arched, weathered doors of the cathedral, quite expecting to hear the powerful new bass pipes rattling the foundations with their thunder … but the church was eerily silent. He must have arrived in a moment of prayer, he thought, as he reached for the large iron ring and hauled gently. The smaller inset oak door groaned, despite his efforts to open it ever so slightly that he might slide through unnoticed. The bright morning sun had blinded him to the dark and musty house of God. His feet slowly followed the stone squares of the centre aisle, worn from centuries of repentance and the salt of tears. A shaft of morning light now just high enough to engage the lower stained-glass windows fell in the direction of the altar.

Matthias gazed up at the high ceiling that attempted to contain Heaven, sensing something was definitely wrong … the great sanctuary was silent, deathly silent, with the exception of the gritty sound of his boot leather on stone. As his eyes slowly adjusted to the dark, a heap of purple satin on the altar steps came into focus. On closer inspection he could see that the clump of purple was in fact the Bishop of Hamburg in full regalia, flat on his back, motionless, face staring upward, frozen in a glaze of blank piety.

Matthias's head snapped back and forth to the pews on either side of the aisle. The occupants were slumped over as though sleeping, or were they … dead? He ran towards the front pew and recognized his father's expensive Italian leather boots sticking out from under the fine cloth of his tailored trousers.

"Oh, Mary Mother of God." He was unable to make any sense of the images that assaulted his eyes. He grabbed the pew with one hand and leaned down to turn his father over. He was dead … no, wait … he was breathing, eyes open, expression fixed, just like the Bishop's.

"Father … Father, can you hear me?" There was no response.

Matthias looked at the next pew, and the next, for signs of life. No one was moving, and yet he could now hear and see that most were breathing. What insanity was this? Was it the fever? There were nearly fifty people in the cathedral, all apparently in the same state. It had to be a new plague of some sort. And then Matthias realized that he had touched his father. Did he now have whatever it was? He fell to his knees and wept. Judgment Day must surely have arrived, and, like his father, he was to pay for his sins.

It was the Lord Mayor's coachman who sounded the alarm when he stumbled on the scene a few minutes later. The Lord Mayor was late for an appointment that would now most certainly be missed. Within the hour, police had cordoned off the building from a gathering crowd of the curious. An ornate carriage rumbled up to the front of the cathedral, barely missing a few irate onlookers. The driver jumped from his seat and ran to open the shiny, crested, black door after placing a small red-carpeted step onto the cobblestones. Two very dignified-looking men emerged and were briskly escorted by police through a sea of inquisitive faces to the great doors, where they were immediately granted entrance by the constable on duty.

Herr Reuter, physician to King Ludwig I, entered cautiously. He was a rotund individual of a good age and height with a meticulously coiffed beard. Reuter was attended by his ambitious and somewhat skinny young protégé, Rudy Bier, a studious-looking sort some twenty years his junior from the Vienna school of medicine. They both walked slowly down the centre aisle in a studied procession of scientific observation. Careful not to touch anything, they went directly to the Bishop, lying on his back surrounded by an abundance of purple satin, like a victim of a gaudy ballooning accident. Dr. Reuter held a small vial of smelling salts to the nose of the holy man, whose face gazed towards the ornate painting of his Maker on the ceiling above. They waited a moment and observed … nothing.

The two men turned to Matthias, who by this time was reduced to a mumbling madman, reciting over and over a mantra that begged forgiveness as he rocked gently with his father's head in his lap.

"I am told you are the son of Gert Dopp?" Reuters inquired sharply, bringing Matthias to a tentative attention.

"Matthias," the young Dopp mumbled.

"Yes, Matthias. What's happened here?" Reuters shot back.

Matthias looked up through his red eyes and shrugged his shoulders. "I was late, all is as I found it. Can you do anything for my father?"

Reuters tried the smelling salts, with no discernable response.

"Perhaps when we know what this affliction is, my boy, but for now I am afraid we shall have to close the cathedral for observation, and you will have to stay here with the afflicted. No one can come or go without my permission. We cannot allow whatever this is to spread. I am sure you understand, Herr Dopp?"

Matthias shrugged with indifference and returned to his grief.

"Rudy, ask the constable on the door to find some food and drink for young Herr Dopp, and then we must insure that all are instructed in appropriate precautions." His colleague reluctantly obeyed, huffing audibly, annoyed at his reduction to servant status. "Appropriate precautions" was a vague term that was subjectively determined by the man with the most power. In such matters as human health and disease, there was no one more powerful in Hamburg at that moment than the physician to King Ludwig I. Fortunately for Ludwig, he had made rather merry the night before and refused to get out of his bed that morning. However, when he was alerted to the state of those in the cathedral, he'd felt it prudent to send his physician.

After inspecting forty-seven bodies, the royal physician noted that all were breathing, except for one individual whose neck had been compromised when she apparently fell awkwardly onto the wooden kneeler in front of her pew. The cathedral would be sealed from the public and the breathing bodies would be observed, not touched. Some ale, bread, and spiced meat were left on the pew beside Matthias, and additional guards were placed at all doors, where entrance was *verboten*. By late afternoon, Herr Dr. Reuters had advised Matthias that if there was any change in the status of the afflicted he should inform one of the guards posted outside any of the doors and the doctor would come immediately. Otherwise, he would return again at dawn.

Matthias watched the doctors' cloaks take flight as they marched, in unison, down the aisle with the officious strides of authority. The door thudded shut with a hint of finality that echoed into the most minuscule reaches of the stone temple. As the echoes slowly died, silence moved in like a cold draft, sending a shudder that rippled up the spine of Matthias. He felt like an Egyptian servant buried alive with his master, entombed with the damned. After grieving the remnants of the day away, he finally crawled onto a hard oak pew and gave in to fatigue.

The sound of a crowd gathering in alarming numbers outside became a distant hum as he drifted towards thoughts of Anna and the sweet rose fragrance that cascaded from her soft white skin. A rustling of cloth suddenly pulled him back from his sweet escape … there was someone else in the great sanctuary, sounds in the foreground other than the eerie breathing of the living dead. He slowly lifted his head and observed a short, sturdy man in what looked like a robe of the Franciscan order. The priest was holding a leather-bound book and intoning Latin phrases over the bodies of the afflicted. Matthias felt a measure of comfort that the spiritual needs of his father were being met, and then he lowered his head to sleep. As he fell deeper and deeper into Anna's arms, he felt a loving hand on his forehead and a gentle voice in the distance.

"Worry not for thy father. He will return if he so wishes. God be with you, my boy."

"And with you, Father," Matthias whispered in automatic response as he fell back into the warm memory of Anna.

All night long he slipped in and out of consciousness, not wanting to believe where he was. Every so often he thought he heard the painful sound of a man weeping. It seemed to emanate from the sad, chiselled faces of the Apostles who looked down at him from every corner of the cathedral.

***

The next morning, when the royal physician returned, the carriage driver was forced to whip his reluctant black gelding through the throng of people who now flooded the streets outside the cathedral. Anxious fears of typhus and cholera fluttered through the air, amplified by frightened calls to burn the bodies of those inside before a new plague spread. Most of the city's available constabulary were posted on site and quickly created a pathway to the great doors, while the driver, now on foot, jostled by irate onlookers, struggled to accomplish his duties.

Carriage door ajar, Herr Dr. Reuters leaned forward and looked with disdain into the crowd. He finally got up and stood on the carpeted step, instructing an armed constable to fire his pistol into the air. The crowd was startled into a moment of silence that Reuters quickly claimed for his own purpose.

"Ladies and gentlemen, please go to your homes. There is nothing you can accomplish here! If this is, as some of you think, a new plague, then surely your safety lies in distance, not gathering here in proximity to the source!"

"It *is* a new plague!" a voice from the crowd shouted.

"A pox!" another voice threatened.

"They should be burned!" came yet another bloodthirsty cry, barely audible above an escalating cacophony of hysteria.

Reuters knew his moment was gone, and he quickly put leather to cobblestone moving down the path cleared by the police, protégé in tow.

"Perhaps they are right," Bier said sheepishly as they were escorted into the Cathedral by a police captain. "Burning might be the prudent thing to do, for the safety of the public at large."

"Perhaps, Rudy, but I will decide when it is time for such action."

Rudy's face was red, but not with embarrassment. He turned away to conceal his anger at what he felt was another condescending dismissal. He was, by his own estimation, better educated in the latest science than the old man and deserving of far greater respect.

Matthias stood inside the door with a look on his face that was now fully conscious and anxious with fear.

"Is my father to be burned? What about the rest of the people here? Surely you would not burn the Bishop of Hamburg or the Lord Mayor?"

"Please, Herr Dopp, control yourself. No one is going to be burned." Reuters strode down the aisle towards the stricken. "Has there been any change overnight in anyone?"

"No sir. Only ..." Matthias wasn't quite sure what to say. Herr Dr. Reuters and Rudy Bier stopped abruptly and faced him.

"Only what, Herr Dopp?" the royal physician inquired.

"Well, it might be nothing …"

"Let us be the judge of that, boy. Spit it out!"

"There was someone else here, a priest who was ministering to the afflicted … and there was weeping, loud, painful weeping."

"And where is the priest now?"

"I … I don't know, sir."

"Captain?" Herr Reuters stared at the tough-looking policeman who had heard every word.

"I assure you, no one has entered or left this building since you were here yesterday, sir," the policeman replied officiously.

"Then someone is still here. Please conduct a thorough search, including the chambers below!"

Reuters and Bier proceeded to inspect the bodies again, and all was as before … only one dead, while the remainder curiously breathed as though all was as it should be. There was no fever, no discoloration of the skin, no rashes, no indication of ill health other than a complete lack of consciousness. The unruly crowd now worried Herr Dr. Reuters more than the afflicted people in the cathedral. There would be no answer to this medical riddle if the fearful mob had its way and burned the poor souls.

A good hour later, the police search had found no sign of the curious monk that Matthias had described. Matthias offered the explanation that perhaps he had been dreaming, which seemed to appease all but Herr Dr. Reuters, who called the police captain over to discuss a plan to move the bodies to a more secure location for observation. If they were not allowed to get to the bottom of this it could occur again, and perhaps place even more lives in jeopardy.

Two large wagons were commandeered and sat a block from the rear of the cathedral, where they would wait until dark. Dr. Reuters needed time and room to manoeuvre, and to that end, he sent Rudy out into the crowd to spread words of reassurance that all were recovering nicely and the crisis was over. Stretchers and crude wooden planks to move the bodies were smuggled in. It was arranged that the bodies would be taken to an empty barn on the outskirts of town for further observation. If worst came to worst, the entire site could be burned and the contagion, whatever it was, contained with no public threat.

By dusk the crowd outside of the cathedral was even larger and more unruly. Reuters thought this odd, given that he had sent word that the afflicted were recovering. Even more curious was the fact that Rudy had not returned. The warm evening had encouraged above average levels of alcohol consumption, leaving good numbers of the inebriated spoiling for some kind of altercation.

Interesting phenomenon, inebriation, Herr Reuters thought as he listened to the crowd. It reduced some to sentimental fools and others to belligerent monsters; some achieved an annoying state of giddiness, while yet others lost all sense of morality. He had seen fear manifest itself in equally strange ways. The thought that he was facing a double-edged sword—a crowd of people both inebriated and fearful for their own lives—gave him no sense of security in his current authority. And what of young Matthias, who had pawed his father for hours in grief? Was he to be burned with the others? Would he succumb to the same illness? And where was Rudy? What could have happened to him? Reuters's mind stirred through horrid possibilities, among which a sad wish emerged that Matthias might also lose consciousness before all options had been exhausted and orders were given to light the fires of purification in the public interest.

The front door slammed, startling all within. A harried-looking constable began rattling all the locking bolts into their cast-iron yokes. The captain ran to him for a brief exchange, then back to Dr. Reuters.

"It is time, we must act immediately."

No sooner had the captain spoken than the sound of thumping on the main doors began. The crowd, determined to have its way, was becoming increasingly bold.

"Bring the wagons to the rear entrance," Reuters barked.

Stretchers and wooden planks were hoisted one by one, transporting their catatonic cargo to the back of the cathedral. Reuters looked sadly at the faces of the afflicted: some he knew, from various social functions over the years, and all were of a privileged class, as demonstrated by their expensive clothing and jewellery. One middle-aged baroness he knew very well as a former patient and family acquaintance of many years, and then there was the Lord Mayor of Hamburg. The back of the cathedral was unusually quiet as the wagons arrived—too quiet, Reuters thought. All but four of the bodies had been loaded when Reuters called for the police captain.

"Is my assistant, Herr Bier, outside with your men?"

"No, I have not seen him for some time."

"Have one of your constables look down in the vaults below. Perhaps an idle curiosity has caught his imagination."

Reuters headed towards the back entrance to oversee the loading of the last few bodies. As he stepped outside into the warm evening, an odd sound assaulted his ears, one that he soon recognized as the clatter of hundreds of feet heading his way. He turned to face a wall of angry-looking people being led down the street by … Rudy Bier!

"There they are!" Rudy screamed.

The crowd roared and broke into a faster pace, swarming the rear entrance and the wagons. The constables were overwhelmed and cast to one side as the crowd converged, staring curiously at the human cargo, until a large man yelled, "Burn them! Burn them, or we all will die!"

Voices in the horde repeated the call—"Burn them! Burn them! Burn them!" — until the words bled into a loud cacophony of insanity. After the horses were unhitched, thatch and lumber appeared from nowhere and were instantly stoked underneath the old beer wagons. Dr. Reuters screamed in vain, his words consumed by the roar of the large organic mass that no longer held any semblance of reason. He was pushed back inside the rear entrance and his exit blocked by two surly men who threatened to put him on the wagons with the damned if he didn't co-operate.

The fires were lit and the crowd cheered as the flames quickly took root, caressing the floorboards of the wagons that had once held barrels of beer. More and more wood was thrown onto the blaze, until the tops of the flames moved heavenward, like the spires of some hideous cathedral of death.

An elegantly dressed woman whose body had lain lifeless moments before in the front wagon suddenly stood up and began to scream. Reuters looked with horror at his former patient, the Baroness, her eyes terrified in a newly regained consciousness as she tried to climb over the side rail, only to be harshly pushed back by pitchforks and poles. Her eyes cut deeply into Dr. Reuters's with a look of panic wrapped in a pitiful plea for some kind of explanation. She began to cough, overwhelmed by smoke. Flames ate into her petticoats, and then, with an explosive *whoomph*, she was transformed into a screaming human fireball that twisted and turned, writhing in agony, before falling onto the other bodies in the wagon.

As the crowd cheered with ugly delight, Reuters looked back into the shadows of the rear entrance of the cathedral. Tears streamed down Matthias's face as he held the end of his father's stretcher, watching as, one by one, the bodies caught fire to the roars of the crowd.

A familiar voice began once again to dominate, slowly drawing the attention of the crowd. Dr. Reuters recognized it as the excited voice of Rudy Bier, his dark task not yet accomplished.

"There are more inside. And don't forget the young Dopp boy, who is most surely infected!"

Angry citizens pushed through the narrow Gothic archway into the once dark vestibule, now well lit by the wall of heat and dancing light of the fire.

Matthias had dropped the stretcher to defend himself when he was suddenly pulled off of his feet sideways by a sturdy arm in a rough woollen sleeve. Reuters saw him disappear and attempted to follow, but when he finally made it to the corner where Matthias had disappeared, he saw only an empty alcove with a statue of the Holy Virgin.

One by one, the remaining bodies were thrown on the fire. Gert Dopp was thrown into the air and onto the flames, stretcher and all, like a pile of refuse. The oily, sickening stench of burning human flesh began to permeate the air as Reuters made his way back to his carriage, defeated, and betrayed by one whose professional kinship he had severely overestimated.

Bier had no desire to follow in the footsteps of Herr Dr. Reuters; in fact, he loathed the wealth and unearned respect of the aristocracy. He had seen doctors die from caring for the sick and had made a pact with himself that he would never engage in such heroic stupidity. In fear of his own life, he had calculated that the only way to avoid the wrath of the crowd was to join them—or, even better for his own egomaniacal self-importance, lead them.

"Get us out of here," Reuters said to his driver in a barely audible rasp. The footman closed the door behind him, a door that Reuters wished could shut out the sound and stench. As his carriage pulled away, he sat, stunned, until his usually stoic front cracked into a steady stream of tears. They were tears of failure, of plundered responsibility … of the deepest sadness he had ever felt. And what of young Matthias? Had he been thrown onto the flames, or had he somehow survived? Would he ever have an answer to the illness that affected those in the cathedral? The Baroness had actually recovered from the mysterious affliction; would the rest have done the same, if they had been allowed the time? The images and mysteries of that night would frequent his fitful sleep for the rest of his life. The cries of an old acquaintance burning alive would call to him relentlessly, until he achieved the welcome silence of his own grave.

2

INTERSECTION

The Airport Holiday Inn, Toronto
October, 1989

A sign in the lobby read:

This week in The Treetop Lounge
The Danny Blum Experience
A fabulous tribute to the Eagles and the music of the Seventies!

The eight-by-ten colour picture on the bulletin board was a little faded and dog-eared … for good reason. The promo shot was from their *up-and-coming* period, which had moved gradually into their *still-not-up-but-hoping* phase, which had slid with no mercy into the present … *down and on the way out.* The four-piece band had been on the road far too long, playing to dwindling audiences on a circuit that was all but dead. What had started out as fun for a bunch of young musicians had become a monotonous drone of an existence.

In 1979, when Danny had put "The Experience" together, the club circuit had been booming with venues and women aplenty. They had played to packed houses, and band members had bet on who would get lucky most often in a week. The "groupie" phenomenon had treated them all well.

That phenomenon was a curious cultural anomaly to Danny. He concluded that no matter how bad or ordinary a guy looked, no matter how bad the band, how seedy the dump he played in, no matter how small the town ... no matter, no matter … if you were on the stage playing rock 'n' roll, there was some female out there who wanted to sleep with you, or at least give you a blowjob in the parking lot. The only rationale he had ever heard was on a local talk show, where a psychiatrist (who looked as though he hadn't been laid in years) offered lame psychological spew involving theories of power or the like. Nonetheless, it was undeniable: after joining bands, some of the ugliest, least powerful guys on the planet suddenly and very gratefully found women. The true beneficiaries of such a phenomenon in a capitalist world were, of course, the manufacturers of antibiotics.

But all good things must come to an end, and now when the Danny Blum Experience rolled into town the pickings were as slim as the audiences. If band members scored it was usually with someone they had met on a previous pass through town. This was becoming a comfort to a couple of the guys, who were now actually forming relationships with some of the old groupies, who turned out to be real people with real lives. Danny, for one, had finally found a trophy blonde who even had some money to boot. He knew he couldn't do any better cosmetically, and the financial bonus held additional security appeal. Danny, at forty years of age, was beginning to worry about a future that was, statistically speaking, shorter than his past. He had two more weeks to go before he'd pack it all in. He was going to get married and move to Nashville to try his hand at country music. It wasn't for love, but Danny was resigned that looks and friendliness would have to do.

He and his childhood friend and keyboard player, Joel, had been setting up mini-studios in Joel's hotel rooms for the past couple of years, writing and recording songs. Joel was a bit of a gear-pig with an eight-track Fostex tape recorder, multi-timbral synthesizers, Atari computer with a midi sequencer, and a few pieces of outboard effects like compressors and digital reverberation units. The two bandmates made great little demos, and in fact had sparked some interest from a minor music publisher in Nashville.

Nashville was where Danny had met Karla Rose. Her real name, he'd found out, was Karla Rosen. There were still more than just traces of anti-Semitism in Nashville, causing Karla's family to legally change the family name years before. When she'd come through her parents' door a couple of years back with a musician who didn't wear a cowboy hat and was actually a Jew, Danny was welcomed with open arms. Of course, Mr. and Mrs. Rose were always telling Danny he needed a regular job in order to be home more with their Karla. A band was no place for a good Jewish boy. To which Danny replied, "Well, Nashville is no place to be wearing a yarmulke! Yarmulke and cowboy boots, now there's a cultural train wreck!"

Danny's religious upbringing had been very relaxed. He struggled to reconcile his heritage with who he felt he was. Like any proper religious upbringing, though, his made him feel guilty for not wishing to join the rank and file in the drone of ancient words. Simply being ancient gave the words no special significance to Danny if he felt they were irrelevant to his life and time. Most ancient religious teachings, to his way of thinking, had been a colossal failure to humankind. He felt that maybe it was about time humanity sought a new, more inclusive curriculum, one that connected all human beings rather than causing them to hole up in the tribal enclaves of one religion or another.

Years of Seder dinners had left him only with the notion that a few thousand years should have been enough time for his people to get over Egypt and move on with their lives. The God of that time seemed to be a bit of a low-ball deity, really … a nasty fellow who killed innocents whose only crime was being first born.

For some, traditions were to be worn like armour or medals commemorating battles past, but Danny couldn't go there. He was just a regular Canadian guy. The logic was simple: where he was born, that's what he was. He felt no affinity for the Middle East or other points of tribal origin and subscribed to the theory that his ancestors had left for good reason.

It was a bonus that the girl he was to wed was Jewish, which would of course thrill his mom. Funny, but even at forty, pleasing his mom still mattered to him. Maybe this was the key to a greater understanding of the whole tribal thing—parents, in order to feel validated, need their beliefs validated by their children, and so begins the pressure and guilt.

The band had rolled into Toronto early Sunday morning after a long drive from a bar gig in the northern mining town of Sudbury, Ontario. They were setting up their equipment on stage when a polite but officious hotel manager with a thick Pakistani accent gave Danny an urgent message to call home.

His mom broke the news in words halted by short sniffles. Her father, Sid Feldman, had been sliding down the slippery slope into the silent waters of senile dementia until finally he had drifted completely away from a body that was no longer capable of supporting even the most basic level of life. When Danny had last seen him, on the band's way through Montreal six months earlier, there hadn't been even the slightest hint of anything cognitive in the man. Danny's grandfather was then nearly eighty-nine, and the thought of what the old man had been reduced to had become more painful to Danny than the idea of him being no more. In the tradition of his people, the body would be buried as soon as possible. For his mother, that meant the following morning.

Once the band van had been emptied, Danny hit Highway 401 east to Montreal. The foliage of fall always surprised Danny with its beauty, particularly around Kingston, Ontario, where the stunning rolling countryside was ablaze with colour. As Danny thought of his grandfather's demise, his mind wandered to the mortality that surrounded him. The death of vegetation in the fall offered a glimpse of undeniable beauty, unlike *Homo sapiens*. Humans looked just plain bad in death, and many stiffs benefited greatly from makeup. Once thriving green leaves now floated down to the ground on soft currents of air in stunning oranges, yellows, and shades of red. Their bright colours were like the nova of a dying star, a last attempt at attention … a plea to be seen and known before being reabsorbed into the great cycle. Snow would soon consign their demise to the black muck of nutrients so greatly anticipated by the soil. Of course, humans would deny the soil even this small gratuity with cement-vaulted coffins—heaven forbid the thought of giving anything back to Mother Earth!

Five hours and three cups of strong roadside coffee later, Danny arrived in Point Claire, on the outskirts of Montreal, and pulled into his grandfather's driveway. His mother was standing in the open front door by the time Danny got out of the van and she walked calmly towards him, inspecting her son with a mix of pride and undeniable love. It was only when she stroked his face that her eyes began to fill. She wrapped her arms around him and muffled a few quiet sobs into his sweatshirt while her body shook. Danny held her lovingly and stroked the greying hair of the generous soul who had given so much to him. As far back as memory could reach, he had known only praise and love from this woman who always called him "my lovely boy." He felt her anguish subside and knew it was coming. Her head tilted up, a crumpled smile crossed her teary face, and Old Faithful erupted. "How's my lovely boy?"

They sat in the kitchen reminiscing for most of the evening and answered a pathetically small number of calls of sympathy for the end of such a long life. Myra saw her son's eyelids starting to droop, and the good mother led him to the guest room as he half-heartedly protested. There was another hug, a few more tears, then she kissed him goodnight and resumed her watch, staring out the kitchen window as darkness passed though the glass and played into her thoughts of the man she called Dad.

He hadn't been much of a father. She knew that at some level, beneath his self-possession, he had loved her, but he'd been unable to express it. She shook her head as she thought about how little talent Sid had had as a businessman. In fact, Myra had watched her father fritter away a successful textile business, one that had been in the family for generations, with his lame ideas on how to make money, all of which had inevitably failed. Somehow in his death the pathos of the man's life now grew as a monumental hurt in her chest. On his sixty-eighth birthday, the bank had foreclosed on business loans, forcing the family company to go under and leaving Sid with nothing more than the few good investments that his wife had made and the family home. When his health had begun to wane, Myra had seen her mother, Ida, thrust into the role of health caregiver. Stress from dwindling resources and the strain of a demanding patient had ended Ida Feldman's life in the kitchen one winter's morning. Myra had found her mother face down at the kitchen table in a puddle of spilled coffee. Sid sat staring as Myra's attempts to revive his wife disintegrated into uncontrollable weeping and a frantic 911 call. Myra saw only one tear roll down her father's face, and she wasn't sure if he was sympathizing with her grief or if that one lonely tear had been summoned from a dying spark of awareness that the love of his life was gone.

Myra Blum was Sid and Ida's only child. She and Danny's father had parted ways when he'd found a young hottie who was in love with the idea of a lavish lifestyle with a successful judge, even though he was twenty years her senior. He had used his legal expertise to do Myra out of pretty much everything. Of course, it didn't hurt that the judge in their divorce hearing was a golf buddy.

Myra had been economically forced to move in with her parents for the last year of her mother's life, and after a couple of years of attempting to care for her father she had been talked into a reverse mortgage on the Feldman house in order to place Sid in a full-care facility. Sid Feldman had come into this world as a physically and mentally helpless baby and left the same way.

The funeral the following morning was modest, and to add to the pathos, poorly attended. Danny was hoping to see his father, but instead he received a heartfelt phone call from one of those "A" islands in the Caribbean … Aruba or Antigua … didn't matter where he was so much as where he wasn't.

After the few funeral guests left, Danny's mom appeared from her room with the family photo albums. They flipped through tears and laughter in captured moments of lives lived. After a coffee they combed through some of Sid Feldman's belongings, dusted off and brought up from the basement. Danny stared with curiosity at a tattered leather suitcase with a rusted brass lock.

"Where's the key for this?"

"No idea."

"Do you mind if I open it?" Danny asked.

Myra was lost in a few stray photos and responded with a shrug.

Grabbing a kitchen knife, Danny assaulted the cheap lock, which gave up its charge in a matter of seconds. Inside, wrapped in a delicate and very old shawl, lay a beat-up and even older looking leather-bound book. It was written in Latin, the text illuminated, and it seemed to be a Christian book of some sort, given the number of ornately painted biblical-looking characters. The opening page held a huge, ornately painted crucifix that caught Danny's imagination.

It seemed odd to Danny how such an ancient tool of death as the cross had become the symbol of a religion. If a modern-day messiah were put to death, would his followers wear mini electric chairs or syringes of lethal injection around their necks? Or maybe a little gold necklace depicting a firing squad? It was all somewhat ghoulish to Danny for people to wear such things, or to place them on the altars of their churches. It reminded him of the cheesy movie *Beneath the Planet Of The Apes*, where the mutants sing hymns of praise to the Golden Bomb on the altar of their sanctuary. Each to his own whacky traditions, he thought, while mulling over his own aversion to many such things in his own tribe.

Myra glanced over at what he was holding and froze.

"I remember that! Dad showed me that once when I was a kid. I think it belonged to his great-great-grandmother. Do you think it's worth anything?"

"Who knows, but the illuminated writing plus the age of the thing must give it some kind of value to the right buyer."

"Would you look into it for me, Danny? Don't sell it without talking to me first … it is a bit of a family heirloom, I guess. Maybe just find out what it is?"

"Mmm," Danny responded, still curiously flipping through the yellowed pages of the old manuscript. " Somebody went to an awful lot of trouble to create this." He looked at his watch and placed the book back into the case. He had just enough time to get back to the gig in Toronto, and it was time to kiss mom goodbye.

As Danny got into the van, he turned to see his mother standing in the doorway, looking somewhat smaller in her grief. When he rolled down the window to blow her a kiss she found that smile of unconditional love and closed sweetly with, "Goodbye, my lovely boy."

Her words held pain instead of praise, for the first time in Danny's life. He had left her alone before, but somehow the daily tasks for her father, even after he was institutionalized, had always given her purpose and distraction. Now, that nurturing, motherly heart had no one to look after. The drive back to Toronto was a pensive one, full of memories that all led back to one sad, lonely soul in Montreal.

As Danny's mind zoned out into the drone of snow tires on asphalt, something of Myra's loneliness followed him, drafting in the wake of his van.

3

THE DAMNED

Hamburg
May, 1847

Matthias was being hauled down a damp corridor, past a series of crypts, under the sanctuary of the Hamburg Cathedral. The cries of the mob in the street rang off in the distance like an echo of a horrid nightmare. Matthias dug in and broke the fierce grip of the sturdy man who pulled him along like an errant child.

"Who are you? Where are you taking me?"

"I am Vasquez, a fool who is taking you to your life, if you will let me. There is only death back there."

"I … I don't understand."

"If we don't get you out of Hamburg they will find you and most likely seek to burn you, as well. The fools think they are fighting a plague, may God forgive them. Come quickly, we have no time to stand about!"

There was just enough light for Matthias to identify the frightened face of the priest he had seen blessing the afflicted the first night in the cathedral. He was a short, unkempt man in a rough wool robe with a leather shoulder bag that he clutched tightly. Matthias sensed only good intentions and followed his only hope of not being thrown on the fires of fear.

They came to a cast-iron door that barely opened wide enough for the ample belly of the clergyman. Once on the other side, he hauled Matthias through and strained to push the door shut, an action that resulted in the painful shriek of metal on stone. Pitch-black, accompanied by a musty silence, filled in around them like cold water.

"Hold on to my robe!"

Matthias did as he was told and felt oddly secure in his new blindness. The two men stumbled over a floor covered in refuse that felt like broken bits of wood. It was a good five minutes later when they turned a corner and a dim light from the distance sprinkled a modest dusting of visual capability on the scene. The walls around them were stacked with bones, and what Matthias had thought to be bits of wood on the floor were now revealed as more bones … everywhere bones, bones on piles of bone. Some had been feebly sorted by size, most randomly strewn.

A dank stench grew in intensity as they moved towards dim light, segmented into distorted dark rectangles from a cast-iron grid. At the source, the priest, Vasquez, stopped and pushed the heavy grate out of his way, stepping onto a narrow ledge on the side of a bricks-and-mortar sewer tunnel. Light from the moon fell onto the fetid water through an opening in the street above, and yet more light came up to meet them in the mist from the end of the tunnel. Matthias stepped gingerly after the priest, and minutes later they stood overlooking a short drop to the waters of the harbour.

"What now?" Matthias asked.

"I understand you are Matthias Dopp, the son of a wealthy man with business connections. Is there any way you can use these resources to get out of Hamburg?"

"To where?"

"Where nobody knows you, and you may need to stay away for some time."

Matthias's mind raced in any direction connected to some kind of survival. He came to the thought of his father's warehouse, where a considerable amount of what his father called "emergency funds" lay stashed behind a false panel in the oak wall near his desk. It was money in the form of gold coins set aside for the occasional load of contraband merchandise. This was how his father had survived the really rough times. There was also a ship, one that Dopp Mills regularly leased, sailing back to Savannah, Georgia, the following morning. Matthias knew the owner and captain to be a good and decent man. Captain Harding had been to the Dopp home and dined with Matthias and his parents on many occasions over the years.

"I must get to my father's warehouse."

"Is there money there?"

Matthias looked slyly at the priest, his face giving away his distrust.

"Oh, don't be silly, boy, I have no need of your money. But you should not go there, it's too dangerous. Tell me what to do and I will get it for you."

"They wouldn't let you past the front door. Though I believe you to be a priest, the night watchman has been told to let no one pass, and I know he is not a God-fearing man. He will see only a man in a robe who claims to be a priest."

"Will those who guard the front door let you pass, or give you away under the present circumstances?"

"I don't know."

"Not good enough."

As if to underline the severity of the situation, a distant roar erupted from the crowd at the cathedral. Both men turned towards the sound, only to see the spires of the great temple silhouetted by flames that licked the night sky. A cold shiver of horror went up Matthias's spine, followed by deep sadness.

"I should have died with my father." Matthias's words burst out of his mouth accompanied by a flood of tears.

"Don't be silly, boy! None of those souls deserved to die, so why should you have needlessly thrown yourself on the flames?" The priest, feeling the boy's anguish, softened his tone but knew any such indulgence could cost them both dearly. "There will be plenty of time to grieve, Matthias, but for now you must show a measure of the devious in order to survive. You must live the days your father has been denied in this physical realm so that his life will have had the purpose of continuity."

The two men sat on the ledge, and as the young man's tears subsided they slowly began to devise one bad plan after another, until Matthias stumbled on a suggestion that the priest found disgusting. Matthias reminded Vasquez that it had been his instruction to be devious and this plan held the promise of being just devious enough to work … knowing Hans Bertrand, the warehouse guard, as well as he did.

Two hours later, as the streets of Hamburg began to fall silent at last, the plot was put into action. The priest put his arm around the boy, who held his head low and staggered like a drunk. Within minutes Vasquez was inside the door of the brothel talking to Frau Hoffman while Matthias hid in the shadows. Negotiating for sexual favours with a blatantly wicked and sinful woman was almost more than the priest could manage. Matthias was shocked when Vasquez emerged with Anna, and when she saw Matthias she froze.

"You! You have the pox! The whole town looks for you, Matthias!"

"There is no pox, girl!" the priest scoffed. "We are saving a perfectly healthy young man."

"Why did you have to get *her* when any old hag would have sufficed?" Matthias asked with obvious embarrassment.

The priest looked confused for a split second, then a look crossed his face that said he didn't care and time was of the essence. "She was the only one not indisposed by, what do they call them, customers?" the priest snapped back at Matthias as he started on the move.

"How are we to save a perfectly healthy young man?" Anna said snidely, following behind at a quick pace.

The answer to that question was revealed with great discomfort as they headed towards the Dopp warehouses. As she was told of the plan, Anna looked into the cowering eyes of Matthias, whose demeanour she found curious. When they neared their destination, she went on ahead as instructed, turning a couple of times to look back at Matthias with a sad expression of betrayal.

Hans Bertrand was sitting on a wooden bench by the front door, sliding the edge of a rather large knife along a sharpening stone, when he saw the fair-haired girl approaching. She was an eyeful, and as Matthias had expected, she won Hans's full attention. Small talk began, and soon the man's hands were fondling the young girl's breasts until, at Anna's planned insistence, they disappeared around the side of the building and into a stairwell.

Matthias cringed at the thought of what Anna was doing for him, but he knew he must move quickly. Pulling his key from the pocket of his trousers, he opened the padlock, then the door mechanism, and quickly went inside. The office was dark, but he knew every inch of the building he had played in as a child. He slid his hand along the corner of the oak panelling on the wall behind the desk and pushed in a small piece of dowelling that rewarded his effort with a metal click. A small section at the base of the panel swung open as the lock mechanism released. Matthias removed a heavy leather bag with brass rings that held its wooden handle, then clicked the panel shut.

Seconds later, after locking the front door, he slipped down the street to the shadows of the doorway where the priest waited. He looked over his shoulder in the direction of the stairwell with concern. The priest saw the worry on the boy's face and spoke gently as he placed his hand on the young man's shoulder.

"We must move now, Matthias, or all the indignities we have inflicted on that poor girl will have been in vain."

Reluctantly, Matthias moved down the street towards the harbour. Within minutes it became apparent that somewhere along the way they had picked up a shadow ... someone was following them. It was Matthias this time who pulled the priest out of harm's way into a courtyard. The air sat heavy with the smell of manure and damp hay from the stables behind them that housed many of the city's draught horses. Whoever was following passed by them, only to stop and double back. Matthias's heart pounded, and he became aware that the priest's laboured breathing indicated that he, too, feared for his life. They ducked down behind a pile of hay as they heard footsteps approach and then fade away, until a familiar, horrid voice rang out from behind them.

"My pistol is cocked and I would suggest you turn slowly. Believe me when I tell you I am a good shot."

The two men turned to face Frau Hoffman, who stood in an archway that framed her like some macabre shrine of a not-so-blessed Virgin. She looked Matthias over pretty seriously before speaking.

"The entire town looks for you, boy. I am sure there could be some business we might conduct for your freedom."

"You would extort money from this poor soul who dies of the pox as we speak?" the priest said, playing the guilt card that built a church.

"Well, if he is indeed going to his Maker he will have no need of money, priest!" Hoffman scoffed.

"How did you know it was me?" Matthias asked.

"Don't flatter yourself, boy, I have no interest in you. I simply followed the priest. It isn't often I have a man of God seeking the services of one of my girls. It had to lead to something fascinating like … what might be in that bag you are holding so tightly?"

The words had no sooner smacked from her lips than the handle of a pitchfork came out of the darkness and cracked down hard across the back of her neck, sending Frau Hoffman sprawling to the ground. The priest wasted no time and kicked her hard in the side of the head, rendering her unconscious. Matthias looked at him with startled wonder.

"We must be devious to survive. She will awaken with only a sore head for her sins!" Vasquez said, apologetically.

"Perhaps the meek will inherit the earth after all, even if only out of fear," Matthias countered.

They both looked towards the figure standing in the shadows. Something was out of place in the air. In amongst the ripe smell of horse manure and hay was the distinct fragrance of a rose-scented perfume.

"Anna?" Matthias inquired.

The girl emerged through the archway into the silver moonlight that glistened on the cobblestones of the courtyard. Her blouse was ripped and her face was smudged with dirt.

Matthias was overcome. "Oh God, what did Hans do to you?"

"You know very well what Hans did to me. You paid Frau Hoffman so he could do it to me! God in his mercy at least granted brevity to the deed."

"What is it you want, girl? We have little time to stand about with this boy's life in the balance!" the priest said in a frantic whisper.

"Take me with you, Matthias."

"Don't be silly, you don't even know me!" Matthias responded coldly.

"I thought we got to know each other fairly well the other night."

"What?" A look of realization grew on the priest's face. "That's how you know the boy? Oh, mercy, my son, have you no morals?"

"Forgive me, Father … there were no lies, only honesty and a business transaction agreed upon by two people. If that is immoral, then I fear we have a problem with the world in general." Matthias stared sheepishly at the priest for a moment, then turned back to Anna. "I don't know where I'm going and cannot promise you anything other than running with a fugitive."

Anna reached for his hand. "Then we will be fugitives. I can't stay in Hamburg. I can't continue with the life my father has put me to." Anna's eyes welled up and she took to Matthias's shoulder and wept. He instinctively put his arms around her and was surprised how good it felt to hold her in the midst of all of the confusion.

Vasquez was incredulous and tried to bring everyone back to reality. "A priest travelling with a boy and a whore? Are you possessed, woman? We would draw curious eyes like a circus, to say nothing of ridicule!"

"She is no whore!" Matthias snapped.

The priest's eyes flew back and forth between the two until a look of realization crept across his face. "Matthias? Surely you are not really contemplating taking her with us?"

"I … well … yes, sir, I am."

The words were out, and the looks between the two young people seemed to surprise them both. The priest, on the other hand, stood shaking his head in wonderment. He had seen affections emerge in the strangest places, but these circumstances really won the prize.

"You would have her, Matthias, after what she has done?" the priest inquired.

"I did it for him, priest, not the money you paid Frau Hoffman!" Anna shot back angrily. "Don't you teach the words of one who gave of himself for others?"

"Oh, God forgive me, a whore who thinks she's the Messiah."

"Stop it, stop it! Don't call her a whore again!" Matthias didn't want to talk, let alone think, about what she had done, but he knew with gratitude that it had indeed been done for him.

"Perhaps, priest, it is best you do not travel with us. I'll need someone back here in Hamburg to put my business affairs in order for me, if I could so impose."

"I am no businessman … I am a simple priest."

"You insult me, sir! You are no simple priest!" The words had caught up with the thoughts that now emerged from the machinery of Matthias's mind. "You are somehow knowledgeable of what happened in the cathedral in a way I am not privy to. How did you know there was no pox or plague? Why did you save me?"

"I will not say. It is better you should remain ignorant of it all." The priest's face revealed a heavy sadness.

Matthias grabbed the holy man's hand and pressed the keys to his father's business into his palm. "If you require my ignorance, then I will require of you the small favour of keeping these until further instruction. I promise I will not burden you with my affairs for long, but now we must find Captain Harding, who sleeps tonight at the Harp Inn by the harbour. He sails in the morning."

"Are there no family friends or businessmen more suited to this charge than me, young man?"

"My father didn't trust anyone, and that was the key to his success. My first day in charge I will play by his rules, and that, sir, makes you, a man with no interest in worldly possessions or business, the safest person to hold these keys."

Matthias grabbed Anna's hand and strode down the cobblestone street. This girl wanted to be with him, and he had felt something for her the first time he laid eyes on her. There was no one else like that in his life. His mother was dead, and now his father. She was it, a touchstone, someone to hang on to in order to avoid drowning in the vastness of the uncertainty surrounding him.

The priest looked at the keys and shook his head with the realization that somehow he was no longer in charge. When he looked back up, Matthias and Anna were well on their way towards the shipyards. His short legs scurried beneath his robe as he ran to catch up with the boy for whom he felt a pressing sense of responsibility.

There was an eerie mist hovering a foot or so off the still water of the harbour. The Harp Inn stood feet away from the wharf that would be bustling with commerce in a couple of hours. The priest, perspiring from the brisk walk, talked Matthias into hiding with Anna in the shadows while he banged on the door. An annoyed voice called back from within, and soon a weathered old innkeeper's face appeared inquisitively out of a crack in the door.

"I have urgent business with Captain John Harding!" the priest stated, as authoritatively as possible.

"It is a little early to be about the business of saving souls, is it not, Father?"

"My business is none of your concern, sir. I would ask you to open the door and show me to Captain Harding's quarters immediately!"

A voice with a distinctive southern drawl spoke calmly in English from behind the innkeeper. "What business does he have with Captain Harding?"

The innkeeper was about to translate the Captain's words into German, only to be cut off after a deep breath.

"It is a private matter, sir," Vasquez interrupted in perfect English.

"Ah, you speak English," the voice said from the shadows. "That will be all, Herr Freeman. As you can see, I am quite awake."

The innkeeper eagerly went back to his bed. A man moved slowly into view, wearing a nightshirt tucked hastily into his trousers, a pistol in his hand.

"I am Captain John Harding. What is it that cannot wait until morning?"

"It is more, Captain, that it cannot wait until the revealing light of day, for there is a life to be saved and …" Matthias moved towards the door with Anna in tow.

"Matthias?" Harding said, squinting at the shadows.

"They have killed my father, and they would burn me as well for an affliction I most surely do not have."

"I've heard much that saddens me this night. Is your father's death a certainty?"

"I fear so, Captain Harding," Matthias replied.

Harding's face dropped briefly in sadness, but he was soon sizing up the situation. His ability to assess and act was what made him an exceptional captain. He swung the door open.

"The lot of you, get in here before we draw attention to ourselves."

Once the door was locked they huddled around a whale oil lamp. Their distorted shadows mingled on the walls as they conspired in a hiss of whispers.

Captain Harding sent the innkeeper's son on an errand, and in twenty minutes a large rowboat manned by four weary-looking American sailors met them where they waited, at the bottom of the wharf. Matthias had written letters of introduction for the priest that included instructions as to the running of the house and the business in his absence. As they were about to leave, Matthias gripped the priest's hand and the two exchanged the look of an unspoken promise.

"I will send instructions when I know what to do. Until then, you may rely on the foreman, Jorge Hacker, to keep things running smoothly."

Matthias assisted Anna into the boat and climbed down after her. At Harding's signal, the men cast off lines and the rowboat jerked to life with the crew's full attention to the oars.

Vasquez stood on the wharf as the sun began to nose up over the rim of the horizon. He ignored the clatter of the day's business awakening around him, eyes fixed on the *Southern Belle* as her sails went up and she slowly drifted away. When the mast of the *Belle* was but a distant pin on a crest of brine, the sturdy Franciscan brother turned towards town. Faint wisps of smoke drifted up from the direction of the cathedral, and tears formed in the corners of his eyes. The events of the last two days were like a bad dream from which there would be no awakening.

4

THE GLAMOUR OF SHOWBIZ

Toronto, 1989

The drive from Montreal went by quickly as time disappeared into thoughts of his mother with nothing but sad memories to keep her company. Danny wheeled the long Chevy GMC van into the parking lot of the Holiday Inn with an hour to spare before the band's first set was to begin. Gathering his belongings, and Sid Feldman's old suitcase, he headed towards the lobby. The rule of thumb, after everything from guitars to personal belongings had been stolen from that van, was to never leave a damn thing in it other than candy wrappers and empty pop cans. Joel, keyboard player and Diet Coke junkie, was beating up a machine at the end of the hall for yet another can of the aspartame brew when he saw Danny walking down the corridor towards his room.

"Hey, Danny, everything okay with your mom?"

"It's all pretty sad, Joel. You know the drill."

"Sorry, man. Well, if the timing's not too insensitive, I have some good news."

"I'll take good news any time. What is it?"

"I nailed a great idea for a song this morning. I've been itching to play it for you."

"Great, let me hear it."

Danny followed Joel down the hall to his room. A master keyboard was set up next to the road cases that carried all the gear. The Atari computer screen was up and displaying a song sequence.

Joel plugged an extra set of headphones into the junction box on the floor and passed them to Danny. This was the world the two lived in when they wrote. Due to the noise restrictions in most hotels, Danny and Joel spent hours every day lost inside headphones in a soundscape of synthesizers, samples, delays, and digital reverberation. Joel hit the play button on the transport display with the mouse, causing the sequencer to run. After a four-beat click, the midi lights on his multi-timbral synthesizers came alive, flashing with programmed data.

Danny listened, nodding his head to the drum groove and the beginnings of Joel's song.

"It's great!" he yelled so Joel could hear him.

"You think so?" Joel screamed back.

This was the flaw in their supposedly discreet hotel room recording system: unless they were doing vocals and there was an open mike to communicate through, they would yell back and forth rather than remove their headphones.

When the song kept repeating on what would be a fade-out ending, Joel stopped the sequencer. Danny looked at him with approval.

"Man, they're gonna love this in Nashville!"

"Feels okay, huh?"

"More than okay, Joel. I'll try and get going on a lyric after the show tonight."

The door, which had been left ajar, burst open and Ron the drummer flew in. "Man, did you see the hooters on the blond bartender in the. . .? Oh, sorry Danny, how was the funeral?"

"Like most funerals, Ronny, sad and depressing … glad to see life goes on with you, as always."

"Hey, fuck you, no need to get snotty, man! Anyway, the manager wants us to start a half hour early so they can close up earlier if it's a typical slow Monday night. See ya on stage." Ron huffed out of the room spinning a drumstick in his left hand.

Joel gave Danny a knowing look. "Just a couple of weeks, Danny, and we won't have to listen to Ron's moment-by-moment updates on hooter watch."

"On stage in fifteen." Danny grabbed his bags and headed out the door to his room "Great-sounding track, Joel," he called encouragingly over his shoulder.

Danny got to his room and put on his tight pants and a loose-fitting shirt to hide the bulge hanging over his belt. He looked in the mirror and messed up his hair, undoing his mom's request for a "more sensible" appearance at the funeral. Now it was time to go on stage, and even though he was at the damn Holiday Inn, it was time to appear as though he represented some kind of alternate lifestyle to the people caught in the Land of Humdrum. He topped off the tuning on his old Fender Stratocaster, pulled the guitar cord out of the strobe tuner, and headed down to the club.

The Treetop Lounge got its name from a phony tree that sprang upwards from the middle of the floor, exploding in a display of fine plastic foliage that looked in need of a good power-wash. The room held about 150 at a combination of tables and booths, each festively appointed with a small candle in a red fishnet bowl. It was a typical Monday night: a couple of businessmen away from home hoping to pick up a little action, a guy with an alcohol problem, and one awkward-looking woman in a business suit who was probably an easy mark for Ron, who in fact was already eyeing her from the stage.

The bartender was a good-looking young woman with a couple of readily noticeable features, as Ron had so eloquently observed, but she was young. Danny concluded that Ron had tried all of his best stuff and knew she was a lost cause or way too much work, which was why Ron was making such friendly faces at the businesswoman. The "way too much work" thing used to be a common topic of discussion. It was simply a territory of economy that all band members had arrived at in the years of plenty. There had been occasions when an entire week was lost working on a "hard to get" case while surrounded by "sure things." Sometimes the chase was worth it, but more often than not it really wasn't.

There was something about "hard to get" that went against human nature. When one added to this the pace of the world, "how much time to get" became an even greater factor, and this was where McDonalds fast food and bulk consumer outlets offered the best metaphor for what earthlings had become, by and large, in the affluent West. Cheap volume satisfied the "shortest distance between two points" nature of the average human. So, why waste a week on one "hard-to-getter" who might not pan out anyway, when you could have two or three "sure things" in the same time period, which might prove more satisfactory in the appeasement of physical want?

Danny took to the stage, turned on his amp, and looked at Joel, Ron, and then Brian, the bass player, who no one really understood. At least everyone knew that Ron was pretty much about getting laid. Brian, on the other hand, appeared to be passionless about pretty much everything. He was a brilliant musician but lacked any real drive or ambition. It seemed all he wanted from life was to sleep all day in his hotel room surrounded by Chinese food cartons and come out at night to play the music of his youth. He didn't appear interested in any forward movement, like improving his craft or his lot in life. Danny thought Brian probably didn't dream. Maybe life was more enjoyable with no dreams. Then again, maybe Brian had it all figured out and simply refused to be driven by ambition, which usually resulted in disappointment anyway.

Joel hit the introduction tape. "Ladies and gentlemen, sit back and enjoy the sounds of the Seventies with the fabulous Danny Blum Experience." The band launched into the old Eagles classic *Take It Easy* and rolled through their forty-minute set on autopilot, ending with the old Orleans classic *Still the One*. Nothing could have looked more ironic to the point of comedy than those four guys that night singing, "We're still havin' fun, and you're still the one."

In the first set break, Ron made a beeline for the woman in the business suit. He had to establish contact in order to get the ritual underway. There would be a follow-up visit after the second set, and by the time The Experience launched into their final set, that poor woman would probably be the only person left in the club. Out of habit, at the end of the evening Danny thought he would suss out the bartender, but she was exactly who he had thought she would be—she really enjoyed hearing all that *old* stuff her *dad* listened to. The generation gap was too great to overcome, so Danny turned to retire and caught Ron leaving with the woman in the business suit, presumably to *her* room.

Back in his room, Danny checked in by phone to see how his mom was, then flipped the TV on and began watching an old Gregory Peck war classic on the local PBS station until his grandfather's tattered suitcase caught his eye. He opened it and gently lifted out the leather-bound book from its protective shell. The illuminated Latin writing was amazingly vibrant, given what Danny assumed to be the volume's ripe old age. In the centre of the book, two pages were stuck together from the pressure of the book being shut for so long. Very carefully, Danny slid a guitar pick along the edge of the pages and they began to separate. They were still stuck—he needed something longer to pull the pages apart, so he padded down the hall to knock on Joel's door. Joel was up watching the same movie and invited Danny in while he searched for his pocketknife.

Shortly thereafter, the two men managed to carefully pry the pages apart. They appeared to have been stuck together by smudges of a black substance resembling aged blood. Ornately painted angels centred around four stanzas of music. Each stanza contained one chord and no apparent melody. There were references to what appeared to be organ stops, and at the bottom of the last stanza was a notation that looked as though it was intended for a bass pedal.

"What do you think, man?" Danny asked.

"Dunno, looks more like score than linear music … you know, where you have violin parts over viola parts over cello parts as though they're all supposed to be played together, like the opening chord of a symphony? You want to leave it with me? I feel like something to do rather than gawk at the damn TV. Mind if I fire up my gear and see what this stuff is supposed to sound like?"

"Yeah, okay, I'm a little whipped. Be careful with the book, huh? It might be the only thing of material value my grandfather left my mom."

Danny patted his friend on the shoulder and headed off down the hall to his room. It had been a long couple of days.

5

THE CRUCIBLE

Somewhere in the Atlantic Ocean

They were a good five days out to sea when the swells began to rise with brutal frequency. The structure of the *Southern Belle* groaned as water, weighted down with tons of stinging salt, flew over the gunwales, crashing onto her decks. Atlantic rollers soon towered over the mast as the ship sank into troughs, only to rise again up the sides of angry mountains bent on humbling all in their path. Captain Harding ordered all but essential crew below decks as they attempted to get through the worst of the storm. He reckoned it was hurricane status and must have started somewhere in the warm waters of the Caribbean a good week earlier.

Matthias stroked Anna's soft hair as she retched in dry heaves towards a porcelain thunder-mug from under her berth. She was raw from hours of the forced contractions resulting from an inner ear constantly seeking balance where none existed. Then, without warning, Anna jumped to her feet and circled the cabin floor.

"What is it, Anna?"

"Air, I need …" She bolted to the door and Matthias ran after her. She was standing at the open cabin door, holding the frame and breathing deeply.

"You'd better get back in!" Matthias yelled over the roar of the storm.

Anna had just turned to face Matthias when behind her a monstrous shadow rose up, and kept rising.

"Anna, look out!" Matthias screamed as he reached to grab her arm.

The rogue wave broadsided the ship, ripping her arm from Matthias's grasp as it swept her away. Matthias was thrown back into the cabin, hard against the wall, as the ship keeled heavily. Struggling to his feet, he pulled himself up the sharp angle of the floor towards the door until the ship suddenly righted itself, throwing him out the open door onto the slippery deck. His feet slammed into the spindles of the deck rail. Frantically, he grabbed onto a line of loose rigging and squinted through eyes stinging with salt water for any sign of Anna. She was gone.

"Man overboard! Man overboard!" he screamed in anguish as he attempted to stand on a deck that twisted and groaned to the limits of its timbers. Matthias desperately looked over the side, only to catch a torrent of stinging salt water in his eyes. Within moments a few crewmen had stumbled on deck, and Harding appeared out of nowhere, barking out orders.

"It's Anna!" Matthias screamed over the roar.

"Tether yourselves to the masts or gunwales! No man walks freely! Pair up!" the Captain barked.

Harding's men were already tying ropes around their waists in order to begin a methodical search over the sides of the ship, looking for any sign of the young woman in the raging brine. Harding grabbed Matthias by the scruff of the neck and threw him into the cabin.

"Captain, she's gone! Anna's gone!" Matthias screamed frantically.

"I told you to stay off deck," Harding snapped. "Now stay in your cabin, if you know what's good for you! Let experienced men conduct this search! Lord have mercy on the girl!" Harding slammed the cabin door and screamed more orders that disappeared into the thundering walls of water that surrounded them.

Matthias sat trembling in a heap where Harding had thrown him, chilled to the bone by fear and the icy water that permeated every fibre of his clothing. He strained to hear the faint sound of men yelling and more men scrambling by the door, shouting at one another over and over as the roar of the sea made the transmission of sound all but impossible.

"Someone's aloft! Someone's aloft!" an excited voice bellowed outside Matthias's door, causing more feet to scramble by.

On deck, Harding looked up into the tangled rigging of the mainmast a good twenty feet up, where something hung down in shreds like a tattered white flag. On closer inspection, Harding saw feet underneath wet petticoats and a frightened young lady hanging in breathless fear, completely entangled. At the bottom of a trough, for a brief moment, he was able to hear her wispy voice calling pathetically for help.

A crewman climbed the web of rigging like a spider while his crewmate released more tether line. Just as the crewman reached for her, Harding gasped at the sight of a wave that crested over the ship and crashed down like the rage of a malevolent god. The ship was pushed under the brine with the massive weight of the Atlantic. Water rushed through every crack on board and underneath the door of Matthias's cabin. A porthole hatch cover ripped open, allowing a torrent of cold sea in for a closer inspection of the ship's interior. Harding held on to the deck rail, submerged for what felt like the limits of his aching lungs. When the ship bobbed back up to the surface, he frantically began a crew count, looking where he had last seen his men, then aloft to where Anna had been hanging moments before. There was no sign of her. He moved his eyes down the mast and at the bottom he saw a crewman, tied off on a deck cleat, holding onto the end of a taut, vibrating rope. Harding's eyes followed the rope over the port gunwale and yelled.

"Port gunwale! PORT GUNWALE!!"

By the time he'd made his way there, two more crewmen had appeared and they began hauling on the rope dangling over the side of the ship. In moments the legs of a man appeared, and after the next pull on the rope Harding saw that the man was holding onto a bundle of wet cloth with a flaxen mop at the end … Anna.

"Secure the forward hatch, then everyone below decks!" Harding screamed. "Matheson, see to the bilge pumps, we're heavy in the water! Ferguson, give me a hand with the girl."

The door in front of Matthias's face flew open and Harding appeared with his first mate holding Anna, who didn't appear to be breathing.

"Let's get her on the floor and push the sea out of her!" Harding instructed.

Ferguson gently laid her face down and ripped open her corset. He began pushing on the young woman's ribcage, forcing a torrent of salt water from her mouth. On the second push, Anna began to cough.

"Good work, man," Harding said, patting his first mate on the shoulder.

"We were fair lucky wi' this 'un, Cap'n. That wee lassie had more sea in her than I've ever seen anyone spit out," Ferguson responded.

"All right, Mathias, look after her this time, and don't leave your cabin again or I'll throw you overboard myself! Get her out of those wet clothes and as dry and warm as you can! You're with me, Ferguson. We'd best help with the pumps or the depths will have us!"

The door slammed, and Matthias turned Anna over. She was trembling and trying to speak. He looked around the room and ran over to a trunk, hoping the contents might be dry. To his great relief he found dry linens and blankets. Back to Anna, he stripped her of clothing while she just stared in shock. Matthias towelled her wet body with a dry bedsheet, then removed his own wet clothing and quickly wiped himself down. He pulled the wet sheets and mattress from the bed, then threw a wool blanket on the bed boards. The ship lurched, and Anna's naked body squeaked across the wet floor towards Matthias, white and silent as a corpse.

Matthias picked her up and began wrapping them both in the cocoon of the last remaining sheet and wool blanket while holding onto the side of the bed. He slid them both onto the bed slats and rubbed Anna's skin wherever he could. Her soft skin was hard with the cold, robbed of warmth by a sea that moments earlier had been welcoming her for a more permanent stay. Pulling the blanket over their heads, Matthias hoped their breath might help establish some baseline of heat, as he wedged his feet against the bed boards to stop from rolling out.

Anna began to shake as Matthias rubbed her skin, weeping in the realization that he was clutching his lifeline. Thoughts of his dead parents and an acute awareness of being alone in the world were overwhelming. He gently held Anna in his arms as though he was the keeper of the most precious thing on earth.

***

The brunt of the storm took another two days to pass through. leaving all on board the *Belle* wrung out from facing grim thoughts of being unceremoniously commended to the deep. Thrust together in such a life-and-death struggle, Matthias and Anna embraced each other constantly for reassurance, immigrants in a strange, precarious environment that was even stranger for Anna, who spoke no English. She relied on Matthias as her connection to the small, bobbing world they clung to. Dependence and circumstance pressurized a natural attraction for one another into a deepening sense of affection. Hundreds of miles from anyone who even knew them, they became each other's only security. When they made love, it held more meaning than they had ever felt in their lives.

After a few more days of driving rain, drizzle, and damp, the sun finally and somewhat shyly poked its head through the clouds and lit up the sails. Spirits on board began to lift as the seas calmed and items of every description were dragged out on deck to dry out. Real warmth was finally achievable.

On the second day of sun, the young lovers knocked on the door of Captain Harding's cabin. Upon hearing his usual gruff command to enter, Matthias and Anna did so, closing the door sheepishly behind them.

"Well … what is it, you two?" Harding barked as he continued to write his daily entry in the ship's log. After a few moments of silence he glanced up at Matthias and Anna, and a fatherly smile drifted across his face.

"Am I supposed to guess what's on your mind, Matthias?" the Captain asked.

Matthias finally found the courage and spat it out in one breath. "Well, sir, we were thinking that, being as everyone on board thinks we are married, we wondered if you, being captain of this vessel … and having the power to do such things … if you would bestow some dignity and honour to our current situation by binding us in holy matrimony?"

"Slow down, boy. Are you sure this is what you want?"

"We feel we are already married in the eyes of God, Captain Harding."

"Oh, so we know what God is thinking about our current situation, do we?"

"I hope I have not offended your religious sensitivities with my statement, sir. That was not my intention. I only meant … " Matthias began to retreat respectfully, and Harding cut in to save the proud youngster any feelings of humiliation.

"I know you meant no disrespect, my boy. I must confess to you that I have felt somewhat compromised by the extraordinary circumstances of late that you have now inadvertently helped me to clarify. As a civilized man, I must confess it is indeed honour and dignity that have been lacking in your behaviour, and if this is what you seek, I shall be very happy to comply with your wishes for the same. The young lady will bunk in your current cabin and you may bunk in a spare berth below. It might serve you well to cease living in sin and take some time to think about recent events, and even to reflect on what your father's wishes might be in such matters."

"Might I remind you, sir, that I am paying my passage and that of my companion and will not be told what to do?" Matthias said with a shaky courage.

"I am not speaking to you as a hired captain, Matthias, I am speaking to you as the son of a friend. I strongly suggest that when we reach port, you and your betrothed stay with my wife and me, and after an appropriate time of betrothal, if you still so desire, you might consider a proper wedding in the eyes of God, as would befit the son of Gert Dopp. I believe your father, a man who prided himself on proper appearances, would wish such consideration. I ask you to do this for your father, for yourself, and for the honour of the girl. Think on it, then let me know of your decision!"

The Captain's words were final, despite all protests. Matthias sensed Harding's earnestness, and indeed his proposal did sound like something his father would have wanted. After explaining it all to Anna, Matthias could tell by the expression on her face that she was flattered by the dignity afforded her in the Captain's plan. And so Matthias and Anna were separated and allowed to be together only on deck or in the presence of a chaperone, which usually meant the Captain or Ferguson, his first mate.

Captain Harding had dealt with all rumours on board in a matter of hours, and young Anna was given the respect befitting a woman of nobility. In the matter of her less than noble and all too revealing attire, Harding found a prudish dress amongst items purchased for his Quaker wife. It was expertly altered by a crewman skilled in the art of sail repair to fit the girlish figure of Anna.

Even though the two young lovers hadn't been granted their immediate wish, it soon became apparent that Harding's gift to them both was providing their desire to be wed with a resonance that exceeded anything they had imagined. In her newly acquired poise and growing sense of dignity, Anna blossomed into even more of a stunning beauty to Matthias. There was something wonderfully normal about the formality of their new situation, to say nothing of the excited anticipation of a wedding. The Captain enjoyed the restoration of decorum on board and delighted in presiding over the young lovers like a doting and advising father. It was how he thought he could best honour the memory of his friend and business associate, the late Gert Dopp.

In the remaining days of the voyage, Anna and Matthias dined together in the Captain's quarters, where Anna received respectful instruction in English, the art of table manners, posture, and other ladylike behaviours. This was all done in the spirit of preparing for the New World. Excited discussions ensued about what life might hold for them in America, as well as what business options Matthias might consider given his new status as owner-manager, in absentia, of the Dopp textile empire. These conversations were not entirely selfless on the part of Captain Harding, whose livelihood had been closely connected to the fortunes of Matthias's father.

Increasing debris, human waste, and garbage was the giveaway of land ahead, and more obviously of a sizeable population. Soon, boat after boat, plying the coastal waters in every direction, appeared on the horizon. The *Southern Belle* glided into the welcome retreat of the Savannah River a good week behind schedule. With surprisingly little effort, thanks to compliant winds and the assistance of three tethered rowboats, she was soon secured to one of the main docks with huge hemp mooring ropes.

There was a welcoming sweet warmth in the air of Savannah. Anna and Matthias gazed at the shores of the New World. Word had travelled to Mrs. Harding once the *Belle* was spotted off shore and she'd hired a carriage, as she always did, to take her down to the docks to greet her husband. Every Atlantic crossing was a lifetime of worry, though she would never burden the Captain with such information. By the time the gangway was swung into place, Mrs. Harding was waiting on the wharf. She was surprised to see a young blond woman run down the ramp and fall to her knees a few feet in front of her … the *Belle* was, after all, a cargo ship, not a passenger ship.

Anna kissed the ground, then looked up into the pained face of the first black man she had ever seen. With the sweat of his burden, his body glistened in the light, and Anna saw that he was just one in a long line of enslaved blacks bent from the weight of the loads of raw cotton in the huge bundles that compressed their spines. It was an unsettling sight for one who had been trying to forget the sting of her life in Hamburg. This wasn't such a new world, after all. She was frozen in the thought that wherever man went, it seemed, he carried the same old sickening need to inflict suffering on others in the pursuit of his own comfort and power.

Anna heard the laughter of Matthias and the Captain behind her and suddenly became aware that she was creating a bit of a scene with her backside in the air. She stood up, red in the face, and curtsied as she and Matthias were introduced to Mrs. Harding, who immediately took Anna under her wing and escorted her towards the carriage. Anna tried to be polite but couldn't pull her eyes away from the line of black men, slaves, bent over like beasts of burden. One of them looked at her and attempted a faint smile that registered as a humiliation she had known.

Mr. and Mrs. Harding had offered only polite hellos to each another on their reunion, which seemed odd to Matthias for a man and wife who had been separated for months. But he realized it was the Quaker way. If there were any warm moments to be shared between the two, it would be only where no one from the outside world could see them.

Within minutes of arriving at the Harding house, the Captain prepared a room for Matthias in the back kitchen, while Anna was escorted upstairs, by the lady of the house, to the guest bedroom.

Anna walked into the room and burst into tears at the sight of bright bed linens, flower-patterned draperies, and luxurious carpeting. She had never seen such a room, let alone slept in one. Mrs. Harding thought at first the room was beneath the standards of her European guest, until Anna looked at her and, with a thick German accent, said, "*Das ist zo* beautiful, Frau Harding," only to burst into tears again. By the time Matthias ran up the stairs to see what the problem was, Anna was sitting on the edge of the bed as Mrs. Harding held her to her breast, stroking her hair with reassurance. "There, there, child, this is your home for a while." Matthias was fairly sure Anna didn't know what was being said but fully understood the warmth of it. He sneaked back downstairs and left the moment alone.

The Hardings welcomed Matthias and Anna with open arms. Having no children themselves, they delighted in assuming a parental role in the marriage of young Matthias and Anna. Matthias enjoyed the sense of family they imparted, but his agenda would prevail … he was, after all, his father's son, self-directed, self-assured, and now beginning to think about ways to run his family business from America. Anna shone in the affection and tutelage of

Mrs. Harding and she soon began to exude a confidence she had never known in Germany.

And so it was, in the middle of their second week in America, that Matthias was forced to leave the Harding house early in the day to dress at the home of a neighbour, while Mrs. Harding put the finishing touches on a beautiful but plain (in Quaker tradition) wedding dress. Captain Harding walked to the altar of the small church overlooking the harbour where he gave the bride to a stunned young Matthias. His bride was gorgeous, the most beautiful girl he had ever seen. Anna was breathless in seeing her wildest dream become a reality … she was dressed in fine clothes, marrying her handsome prince in a foreign land.

The service was a little long as Pastor McLean, a pious and somewhat self-important man, insisted on reading the entire service in English followed by his hopeless version of German, from a translation provided to him by a member of his congregation. Though this was for the benefit of the young German bride, Anna appeared to have an easier time understanding the English version. As she turned to face the congregation, having been pronounced married, she wept tears of joy. To the people of Savannah, she was simply a beautiful young woman from Europe married to a well-to-do businessman.

There was a modest get-together over tea and pastries where a few of the Hardings' friends and fellow church members gathered to help celebrate the marriage.

"You know, there is nothing I can say to fully express my gratitude," Matthias said, moved by the Hardings' generosity.

"Matthias, I have never seen my wife so happy as she has been these last two weeks, so let me thank you. Before you retire, though, I would like to see you in the back kitchen to toast a friend of mine who can't be with us."

Matthias knew of whom he spoke, and once the guests were gone the Captain stood and faced his wife and Anna.

"My dear, if you would wait here with the new Mrs. Dopp for a couple of minutes, there is something I must do with Matthias."

Mrs. Harding glared at her husband, knowing full well that spirits were involved, but she said nothing.

Once in the back kitchen, the Captain reached into the back of the pantry and produced a bottle of whisky. He poured two small glasses and handed one to Matthias.

"On this, your wedding day, I have had the distinct honour of walking your bride up the aisle and witnessing your vows. I couldn't help but think of the man I was standing in for. To the memory of your father, Gert Dopp."

Matthias thought sadly of his father's horrible demise as he raised his glass, and he couldn't help but think of the unknown complicity of Vasquez in the matter. Words that he had heard the night he spent with the damned in the cathedral played over and over in his dreams: "Your father will return if he so desires." What did Vasquez mean?

"Matthias? Are you well?" Harding's voice returned Matthias to the moment. "Perhaps we should return to the company of our wives."

The glasses were wiped and stowed along with the bottle, and the two men returned to the parlour. There were a few minutes of polite banter and "good night"s were exchanged. Anna and Mrs. Harding embraced, then Anna turned to her husband and they headed upstairs, while the Captain and his wife began a stilted conversation. They talked about the weather and the nearly completed refit of the *Belle* while they clattered the dishes to create enough noise to cover any undignified sounds of newlyweds in the throes of passion.

But there were no such sounds emanating from the guest bedroom that night where the young couple slept … apart. One carefully planned formality remained. Even though they were wed in the eyes of their Quaker hosts, Matthias and Anna were good practising Catholics. As they searched for themselves as adults, the religious tradition they had grown up with began to represent the presence of an absent family. And so, after breakfast the following morning, they excused themselves and went for a walk.

Once out of sight they made their way to the church of St John The Baptist where they were wed and given communion in a Catholic ceremony. In the cadence of familiar Latin pronouncements, Matthias and Anna finally felt truly married. Although the Quaker ceremony had been more understandable, the Catholic ceremony in Latin was one Anna had fantasized about since she was a little girl. Somehow the dead language that she scarcely understood was a metaphor for all things spiritual. To a peasant girl, it had become God's tongue. For his part, Matthias felt he was honouring his family's traditions, which had the effect of a blessing from his dead mother and father … a rite of passage.

On their way home, they stopped to let a carriage pass in front of them. Anna looked up at her handsome young prince and reached to kiss his cheek. Matthias was about to welcome her gesture when he became aware of a man who had stopped across the street and was staring at him. He wore the familiar black suit and hat of a rabbi, and he continued to stare at Matthias, even though Matthias glared back at him as if to call him on his rudeness. The man crossed the street and stopped in front of him.

"Pardon me for staring, young man, but are you not zeh son of Miriam Lieberman from zeh Hamburg Temple?" His German accent was thick.

"I fear you have mistaken me for someone else, sir," Matthias replied. "Though I am indeed from Hamburg, I am the son of Christians, Gert and Maria Dopp."

'Yes, yes. I knew it vas you. Miriam left us for your father and sacrificed her faith in order to marry him. She vas Miriam Lieberman, a lovely girl. I vas saddened by her death. I sat shiva for her at zeh home of her sister Esther, who now lives here in Savannah. Are you visiting Esther while you are viss us in Savannah?"

Matthias looked at the man and saw he was quite serious. "You are suggesting to me my mother was a Jew?" Matthias didn't know where it came from but he spat the words out with audible disgust.

"I thought you knew of your people. I can see now that I have offended you and I am most sorry."

"Good day to you, sir," Matthias shot back.

The rabbi was about to speak again but decided against it. He bowed politely to Matthias and Anna, then walked away.

Matthias was clearly rattled. What had started off as an exciting day was now entirely ruined. If this man was to be believed, he was part Jew? Many well-positioned people of Hamburg harboured distaste for the Jews, and it was a distaste, Matthias realized, that was woven into the way he thought. He knew thousands of Jews had emigrated to America to get away from a prejudice he had never admitted to having.

Anna looked at him with her eyebrows raised. "Does this mean I am now part Jewish?" she asked, expecting some kind of confirmation.

"Don't be so silly. It doesn't matter what he thinks. We are Catholic!" Matthias said, dismissively.

Anna stared at her husband with something resembling disapproval. "You were mean to that man. I have been treated like that, Matthias. I was spat on by church-going people in front of Frau Hoffman's. You owe that man an apology."

Anna was more than serious, and it rattled Matthias. He looked at his wife and realized she not only spoke passionately but she was right. Somehow he felt he was losing his footing in a marriage only minutes old in the eyes of the Catholic Church. His wife was demonstrating a stronger character than him.

"If that man is to be believed, I have family here in Savannah, and they are of a faith that is completely strange to me. At this moment, I don't know what to do with any of this."

"But you will at least apologize for your rudeness?" Anna pressed.

"Yes. And I can also tell you no one will ever spit on Mrs. Dopp as long as I live." Matthias replied.

Anna loved the protective sound of his bravado almost as much as the sound of her new name. She embraced Matthias, and after promising to say nothing of the conversation with the rabbi they hurried back to the Hardings' home.

Anna spent the rest of her wedding day helping Elizabeth Harding with shopping and the running of the household. The Captain went down to the *Southern Belle* on business while Matthias wandered around Savannah and his mind. He pondered the rabbi's words and his certainty that the one he called Miriam was actually Matthias's mother, Maria. He also couldn't help but ponder his stunningly beautiful bride, who had demonstrated an extraordinary sensitivity to injustice. This was new information, and as he was concluding that he had married an exceptional woman indeed, another thought began to trickle back into his consciousness, one that stole his imagination completely. It was his wedding night.

After dinner that evening, Mr. and Mrs. Dopp retired to their matrimonial bed conspicuously early and eager. Captain and Mrs. Harding found it necessary to go for a long walk.

6

AGAIN

Toronto Airport Holiday Inn, 1989

It was an hour before show time and no one had seen Joel all day. His keyboards weren't on the stage, which was very unusual. He was Mr. Nitpicky over his set-up ritual, and more than punctual. Danny had knocked on his door at lunchtime but there had been no answer. He'd assumed Joel had gone somewhere to look at gear or software updates for his music programming. Going to music and computer stores was a ritual for a gear-pig like Joel.

Ron was wandering down the hall, returning from a long night and morning with his latest conquest. When Danny asked him if he had seen Joel, all he got was an unwanted and overly detailed report of the night's sexual escapades.

Danny and Brian, the bass player, finally decided something was wrong and went to the front desk. Mr. Dahliwal grudgingly gave in to their requests to open Joel's room, but only, as he repeated a few times, because he "sensed" an emergency. There might have been generations of Dahliwals who all "sensed" things they were already being told, or perhaps just this one idiot. But, technically speaking, hearing was, after all, a sense. Danny figured Mr. Dahliwal was one of those people who talked so much that they never really heard or learned anything from anyone else.

Danny and Brian were now joined by a curious Ron in the lineup behind Mr. Dahliwal as he opened the door to Joel's room.

"Good God!" the manager gasped as Danny pushed by him. Joel was slouched over, face down on his keyboard, with a pair of headphones strapped to his ears … eyes wide open.

"Has he overdosed?" Dahliwal whispered, assuming this must be the end all musicians eventually faced.

"Not unless you can overdose on Diet Coke," Danny responded in his friend's defence.

The manager was on the phone immediately dialling 911 while Danny and his two bandmates looked at their friend, dumbfounded. How could he be dead? He was too young, and he didn't have any bad habits that they knew about. Joel refused to spend money on drugs or alcohol, saving it for his only true habitual affliction … studio gear.

Within minutes the paramedics had arrived and Joel was on a stretcher. Before he was rushed out it was established that not only was he breathing, but also all vital signs were completely normal, with one little exception: consciousness. As the paramedics loaded him into their truck, Danny grabbed Joel's phone book on the table by the bed and flipped through it for Joel's parents' home phone number.

Joel's mother, on hearing the news, spoke in halting stabs, as though she was gasping for air, saying that she and her husband would be on their way from Pittsburgh within the hour. Though Danny and Joel had grown up in the Montreal area, Joel's father, a chemical engineer, had been promoted and transferred to Pittsburgh a few years earlier.

As soon as Danny was off the phone, Mr. Dahliwal, with a deeply sympathetic posture, began dancing between his heartfelt concern for Joel and, of course, his real worry.

"What on earth are we going to do?" he huffed. "This is all so sad, but of course we do have a contract and we are all professionals here."

Danny caught the drift—no show, no dough.

That night, The Danny Blum Experience became a trio. The Eagles tribute sounded a little Gregorian, though, without Joel's voice adding the third interval to the harmony mix.

It was a typical lame Tuesday night turnout that wouldn't even have noticed a no-show from the entertainers. The same lonely woman was back for Ron. Attention was rare for her, and so she'd extended her trip for one more day. For his part, Ron was wishing she had left town, primarily because he had pretty much used up everything and anything charming he had in his limited repertoire the previous night. There were a few businessmen and a couple of heavy-drinking stragglers. The audience didn't appear to care about, or even notice, the huge holes that Joel's absence had left in the arrangements. In fact, everything Danny had worked so hard for when it came to keeping his band top-notch now appeared to be a complete waste of time. It was time to pack it in, all right, he thought. People would probably prefer a damned karaoke machine.

The term "disposable pop culture" found a greater than usual resonance in Danny that night.

At the end of their last set, Ron and the lonely woman made a beeline to her room for what Danny assessed as another assault at defeating the loneliness of empty lives with the erotic stimulation of sex. Ron's usual relationship trajectory was a well-oiled machine: Night One, exciting sex with a stranger; Night Two, almost as exciting sex with an almost stranger; Night Three, strained conversation with very little excitement and TV after some relatively boring sex; Night Four, some excuse for either why he couldn't make it that night or had to leave right after sex for some personal matters that needed attention. If Night Four didn't send a strong enough signal of waning interest, he would draw from an arsenal of blatant lies about a death in the family or heart problems.

Brian appeared concerned for Joel and offered to buy Danny a drink. They wondered out loud over what was to become of Joel until the bar closed a few minutes later and Brian headed off to his room with a transparent profession of great fatigue. Five minutes had been a longer than usual display of concern for anyone other than himself. Danny knew that Brian's fatigue was really the call of the Chinese food he would order as soon as he got back to his room. The Sci-Fi channel would be on until the wee hours, when Brian would drift off as usual amongst the security of cartons reeking of deep-fried everything and soggy bean sprouts.

Danny sat down on the phony-leather loveseat in the lobby and caught his reflection in the window: a middle-aged guy with big hair, tight pants, and that increasing waterfall of flab hanging over the beltline. "Pathetic," he hissed out loud, causing the young Asian girl on the night shift at the front desk to glance his way. The rest of the thought-stream involved a certain recipe for depression, beginning with being in a cover band at his age, and sporting a look that used to be cool back in the early Eighties but by 1989 was as over as *Saturday Night Fever*. He added in a few immediately obvious items to his recipe for the blues: he was playing in an airport Holiday Inn to a handful of sad souls, some even more pathetic than he felt he was. Fortunately, before the list got too long, his thoughts went to Joel, which saved him from a complete meltdown.

Joel, what of Joel? He went over to the lobby pay phone and called St. Michael's Hospital and got the lowdown, or as much as they would offer. Joel was under twenty-four-hour observation in Intensive Care. Danny hung up and stood staring at the phone. He would head over in the morning and hopefully see Joel's parents, who might have some of the nitty-gritty. Then Danny's mind went to his grandfather's book.

"Shit."

For the second time the night clerk glanced his way, but now with a look of disapproval. Danny sauntered over to the front desk and managed to talk the clerk out of the key to Joel's room.

The room was as they'd left it. The computer screen saver was running through its "fish tank" loop, the audio effects rack was on, as was the keyboard. Danny turned off the power bar everything was connected to. The leather-bound manuscript was sitting on the music stand of the master keyboard as though Joel had been playing it. Danny grabbed the book and sat on the edge of the bed, staring at the bad floral painting on the wall. Tears appeared. They were for his friend initially, but then they were for his grandfather, and his mother, and there were a few thrown in for himself.

***

A car door slammed outside in the hotel parking lot, jolting his eyes open. The night had vanished. It was 7:14 in the morning, according to the bedside clock, and he was sprawled on the familiar patterned quilt of a Holiday Inn bed. He had no recollection of falling asleep or how much the previous day had taken out of him until he scanned his surroundings and realized he was still in Joel's room. He grabbed his grandfather's manuscript and headed down the hall to his room, where he shed his grogginess into the drain of a soothing hot shower.

By the time he got downtown in rush-hour traffic it was close to nine o'clock, and the portico of the Emergency entrance to St. Michael's Hospital danced in a macabre festival of flashing red lights. A line of ambulances backed up onto Shuter Street while Emergency staff instinctively employed the protocols of triage. More serious victims on gurneys were rushed through the thicket of teenagers costumed in the various trappings of first aid. Danny sat for a few moments illegally parked in his van, eyes glued voyeuristically to the cast of a disaster in arm slings, neck braces, and bandages, while others displayed the vacant stare and shivers of shock.

After parking the van in a city lot, and despite some serious rubber-necking, he finally made it to the information counter in one piece and asked the receptionist what was going on. The volunteer worker with the blue hair and matching jacket excitedly informed him of the high school bus accident that had two area hospitals hopping. The driver of the bus, so the story went, had suffered a heart attack while approaching a ramp onto the highway. A student had seen him grope at his chest before he lost consciousness, leaving the bus to continue on through the guardrail. After rolling over the steep embankment a couple of times, it managed to go up the side of a shallow ditch right into the generous grille of a transport truck. The death toll was a work in progress - two or three were already pronounced, and an equal number of students were fighting for their lives with injuries of various descriptions. The local television stations were all over the entrance, capturing what scenes of carnage they could to titillate the viewers. Of course, no names were being released, to be courteous to next of kin, but the media showed no restraint as footage of bloodied bodies was broadcast live. Much like war coverage, blood and guts were somehow more acceptable so long as the bodies were nameless.

Danny made his way to the ICU, where he found Joel's mom curled up on a cold vinyl couch in the waiting room. As he walked towards her she opened an eye and bolted upright.

"Oh God, Danny!" She stood and burst into tears, seeking the comfort of his embrace. "They've done all kinds of tests and they still don't have a clue why he's unconscious." She burbled on his shoulder.

She and her husband had been taking turns on watch at Joel's bedside. It had been pretty much a sleepless night, between driving up from Pittsburgh and standing vigil. Joel's dad came out a few minutes later and also embraced Danny as if he were the son they couldn't hold at that moment. Joel's mother took Danny by the hand into the ICU, then, to look at Joel. His eyes were still wide open, his breathing seemed normal, and in fact he looked very much alive in every way, with the exception of any cognitive abilities. This was more painful to observe than someone with an obvious affliction, Danny thought. At least if there had been some evidence of trauma to a body part, loved ones could have a kind of understanding, or at least an idea of where to focus any thoughts of healing or prayer, if they were so inclined.

After an hour in the ICU with Joel's mother and another half-hour reassuring his father that Joel didn't use drugs, they all sat in silence in the waiting room. The elevator doors opened and attendants pushed two teenagers from the bus accident towards Intensive Care. The first gurney went by and Danny glimpsed the pretty face of a blond girl whose beauty still shone through, despite a half-shaved head held together by a crude assembly of stitches. A second gurney followed, transporting a black youth whose athletic build couldn't be disguised by the sheet that attempted to cover him. The two gurneys went through the doors into ICU, where patients were wired into monitors and IV lines were double-checked.

It was around noon before Danny bade Joel's folks farewell and went on his way, assuring them both that he would return the next day, and once again repeating firmly that Joel was definitely not a drug user. He walked to his van at a brisk pace and, before starting the thing up, he quickly scanned a road map to his next stop, the University of Toronto.

The campus parking lot was a fair distance from the arts buildings, and Grandpa Feldman's old suitcase was getting heavy. After leaving the Philosophy Department and finding the History Department, Danny was finally directed to another building where, in the Department of Religious Studies, he located the office of someone who could translate Latin. The name on the wall next to the open door was Dr. Alison Truman. Danny looked in on a rather nerdy-looking individual with short, mousy brown hair wearing a button-down shirt, khaki pants, and penny loafers that stuck out from under her desk.

"Dr. Truman?"

Truman had her head buried in some scholarly paper and didn't look up. "I'll be with you in a moment," came the curt response. Danny's presence in the room was a distraction from her work, and so, it was a somewhat irritated Dr. Truman who finally looked up to see a rock 'n' roll love god with an out-of-date hairdo, squeezed into pants that were just far too tight for anything that might be called normal circulation. She nearly laughed, but then the overt sexuality of it all made her blush.

Danny saw he had her attention and stared at her face. It had a freckled gentleness to it that seemed out of place with her gruff presence. He looked a little too long and caught himself attempting to assess her bust size.

"What can I … are you sure you're in the right place?" Alison Truman inquired.

"God, I hope so. I've been running around the halls forever trying to find someone who can translate Latin."

"Why don't you get a book and work it out for yourself? It isn't rocket science … Mr. …?"

"Blum, Danny Blum. I guess you're right, I could give it a shot, but I am equally interested in knowing what the hell this book is … you know … how old, what it was for … that kind of stuff?"

Danny rested the suitcase on the corner of Dr. Truman's desk and opened it up. He reached in and grabbed the leather-bound manuscript and placed in front of the impatient academic.

The obvious age of the book piqued her interest. She carefully opened it, with a well-practised reverence for scholarly records of days gone by. Alison Truman loved old books, and touching old, leather-bound manuscripts was nearly a religious experience for her. She moved her fingers respectfully over the old cover, then opened it carefully, inspecting the first page of illuminated writing. Her face took on a look of fascination as she turned the page.

"So, what do you think it … ?" Danny began, but he was stopped dead by a dismissive flick of her hand, followed by a finger pointing at the chair in front of her desk. The motion clearly said, "Sit down and shut up."

Danny sat uncomfortably in his tight pants for a moment looking around the room, then stood up and walked over to the window. Everywhere below, students milled around, socializing in clouds of smoke, in between or en route to classes that held the wonderful promise of fulfilling futures. He realized in a flash that he was old enough to be the father of some of those kids. A darkness of spirit fell in behind that deepening awareness. These young kids were studying to be doctors, lawyers, teachers … whatever … and on the other side of the glass was an idiot in tight pants who had devoted most of his life to screwing everything that moved on the bar circuit. Only moments before he had breezed confidently through the halls like a strutting peacock, past academic dweebs and nerds. Now he suddenly felt a measure of his own ignorance, accented by how silly he began to feel in his dated rock 'n' roll costume. *I'm a fuckin' cartoon*, he thought.

"Where did you get this? This is incredible," Dr. Truman muttered, face stuck in the manuscript.

Danny stared out the window, lost in self-abuse, and answered in a distracted tone. "It was my grandfather's. I'm just trying to find out for my mother if it's worth anything."

"Well, I couldn't tell you what this is worth, but someone has either gone to a great deal of effort to create a fantastic fairy tale or this manuscript is the find of a lifetime … make that the find … of *all time*."

"What is that supposed to mean?" Danny turned around, curious, and waited for an answer as Truman turned the page onto the four stanzas of music and the illuminated writing and floating angels that surrounded them.

"Let me finish this page … fascinating!" she muttered, losing herself in discovery.

"What?" Danny's interest was now more than just piqued. Another minute passed before she finally responded.

"Well, according to the literal translation of this page, and the direction of some of the preamble, these musical symbols—or I guess that would mean notes—when bled into the next four and the next four and the next four after that … in a great house … which presumably could mean a temple or church, no, very probably a cathedral … these notes collectively create an arch to the Kingdom of Heaven through which only the spirit or soul may pass."

Danny turned pale and sat down on the chair. "Joel."

"Who?" Now it was Dr. Truman's turn to be curious.

"Joel played those notes," Danny muttered.

"Who's Joel?"

"He's in my band. Actually, he isn't in my band at the moment, he's in Intensive Care at St. Michael's Hospital."

"What do you mean he played those notes?"

"When we found him last night in his room he was still sitting at the keyboard with his headphones on, breathing and everything, but he was unconscious … and that manuscript was in front of him."

Dr. Truman got up and closed the door to her office, then went right back to the manuscript. "Any idea of what 'notes when bled' means?" she asked, with serious interest.

7

BACK TO BUSINESS

Savannah, Georgia
October, 1847

> *Matthias, there is now proof that any training I have had in my life leaves me wanting in the field of business. Though your family enterprise has been doing splendidly in spite of me, I fear it is now facing an approaching downturn. I find that even with the present orders to complete, we are, for some reason unknown to me, facing a shortage of funds and might not be able to bridge the gap between operational expenditures and materials until delivery. Please advise or send help. Is there no one else here in Hamburg who can assist?*
>
> *With the greatest of sincerity,*
> *Vasquez*

Matthias replaced the letter in the envelope and sat back in the kitchen chair, deep in thought.

"Trouble?" Harding inquired.

"Vasquez appears to be sinking the business."

"What can you do from here?"

"I am not sure. I think I have to go back to Hamburg and hope I am not too late."

"Take me with you, Matthias." Anna appeared from the hallway, having overheard her husband.

"Why on earth would you want to return to Hamburg? You begged me to bring you here. I thought you loved it here," Matthias said, with an expression of genuine surprise.

"I am worried for the well-being of my parents … and my brother and sister."

"Why haven't you mentioned this before now?"

"I have been selfishly enjoying this dream I have been living with you. I was angry at my father, angry that he consigned me to the business of … you know … to pay off his debts. Oh Matthias, I must help them, though. I cannot live so well while they suffer in squalor. My father drinks whatever money comes his way leaving my mother and siblings with nothing. I don't even know if they are alive. What if my little sister is forced to do what I …" Anna began to weep.

Harding excused himself and went through to the parlour.

"Let's go up to our room and talk more privately." Matthias said quietly.

It was a long night before they finally agreed to some sleep. Anna's heartfelt and compassionate need to help her parents was great, but Matthias's fear for her safety was greater. It was finally agreed that he would go alone, find her parents, and see to their well-being. If he could sort out his father's business in a satisfactory manner, and if Anna's family was amenable to the idea, he would then pay for their passage and bring them back to America.

Harding's services as captain were procured, and the *Belle*, though not totally finished with her refit, was deemed seaworthy and provisioned for the journey immediately.

***

A good week later, a warm fall breeze gently pushed through the curtains of the open window, caressing Anna's face. It wouldn't be light for another hour but the crackle of wood in the fire downstairs nonetheless signalled the beginning of the day in the Harding household. She reached over for Matthias, who had already gone to fetch a pitcher of water for the basin on the washstand, as he did every morning. The hushed tones of her husband's voice engaging Mrs. Harding filtered up through the floorboards, followed by the squeak of the hand pump in the back kitchen. Moments later, the bedroom door was opened and closed in an effort to be quiet that failed in its conspicuousness. Anna turned to see Matthias smiling affectionately at his young wife as he carefully placed a large flower-patterned water jug in the matching bowl on the washstand. She loved that look. It was a look she had never known until Matthias, and she blossomed in the nourishment of such loving approval.

"*Guten morgen*, Frau Dopp," he cracked with a smirk.

"And to you, my young prince," Anna answered sadly. Within moments Matthias was back to bed and they were embracing, while Anna collapsed further into tears.

"I pray my family are all right ... I wish I were going with you. You men think all women are helpless," she said, as a rare shard of anger shot out at Matthias.

He stroked the fine fair hair that fascinated him so and held her close. "Captain Harding fears enough for my life that I will not add my wife to the burden of his charge. And what of Frau Hoffman? That witch is still owed the money she loaned your family, and she is capable of anything. No, I must go alone, my love."

Not wishing to prolong the discussion, Matthias hopped back out of the feather bed onto the pine-planked floor and poured some water into the basin. He splashed himself the rest of the way into the morning of goodbyes with bracingly cold well water.

Anna resigned herself to the thought that the secure joy of married life in the New World, a joy she had known till that day, was really too much for any human being to ask for. It was what she had imagined Heaven might be ... no want or suffering, only love in the most ideal of circumstances.

After disappearing to dump the dirty water, Matthias, now scrubbed and dressed, returned with a clean bowl and a pitcher of warm water for Anna. He sat on the edge of the bed to enjoy the privilege of watching his beautiful bride bathe herself, committing the images to memory, and a few minutes later they headed down the stairs towards the fragrant smell of burning hardwood in the kitchen fire.

Captain Harding, dressed in his finest, sat with his left wrist on a clean white tablecloth, drinking a cup of hot tea from his wife's best china. She always insisted on the best china before seeing her Captain disappear on the horizon. On sailing days, they dressed well for each other and employed gracious formalities that might befit a social gathering of the finest dignitaries. It was a ritual begun, as Mrs. Harding had explained, when they were first married, to ensure only the finest of memories should they ever be parted through mishap.

"Good morning, you two." Mrs. Harding sensed that Anna was on the verge of tears and grabbed her hand. "Perhaps you could help me with the fresh biscuits and preserves, my dear."

Matthias sat at the table with the Captain, aware that this breakfast would be nothing if not formal and uplifting. Mrs. Harding chatted away in cheery tones until Anna caught on to the idea that no sadness would be tolerated that morning.

"You worked late last night, sir," Matthias began.

"Some provisions were tardy in arriving, and I tend to triple-check everything before an Atlantic voyage. The seas this time of year will seek advantage in the slightest flaw of preparation."

The *Southern Belle* would sail with the morning tide. She was heavy with raw cotton that Matthias had acquired through some fairly astute bargaining that left the seller with only the slimmest of profits. He had learned many lessons in business from his father, and not only in the area of negotiating for raw materials. As a manufacturer, he also had the job of marketing his product, and to that end Matthias had secured orders for finished fabrics that could be run off in his father's mills and sold with a good margin to some of the best textile suppliers in Georgia on their return. Anything European had appeal in the upper social circles of the South, particularly when one factored in the additional status of having a custom order.

***

Matthias stood on deck staring at the figure of his wife, which grew smaller as the ship pulled away. The rising sun made her fair hair glow golden, and he wondered how he could ever be leaving.

Mrs. Harding stood on the wharf with Anna as the *Belle* left the harbour, but she soon spirited the girl away from a parting that was beginning to be too pathetic to observe. It was bad luck for tears to touch the wharf … water was not to touch board.

As they turned the corner towards town they saw a black man, overburdened with a large box hoisted on his shoulders, lose his balance. The box smashed open onto the street scattering pieces of shattered china.

"You goddamned fool!" The words shot from the mouth of a tall, red-haired man who ran to the slave and laid into him with his riding crop. The slave begged his master for mercy, but the red-haired man would have none of it and whipped the slave over and over until he bled profusely.

Something in Anna snapped. She bolted towards the red-haired man, yanked the whip out of his hand, and struck him in the face with it while cursing him in German. It all happened so suddenly that at first the man's reaction was simply a stunned silence. Then anger made his face flush crimson. He was enraged to the point of madness that a woman would dare speak to him in such a manner while humiliating him in public with his own whip. He lunged to strike at Anna with his fist when Pastor McLean appeared out of nowhere and stepped in the way.

"Jacob Smitherim, have ye no shame, man? Ye have taken the Lord's name in vain with your curse. Ye have beaten a servant who lives through your Christian generosity, and now ye would strike a woman. I know ye to be a God-fearing soul who minds He who walked amongst us showing mercy to even the lowliest leper. It would serve ye well to think on the words of our Lord Jesus Christ as more than just hollow sounds, or your faith is no faith at all!"

Smitherim looked around, aware that everyone on the street was staring at him, and even though he was seething he forced a smile. He bowed to Pastor McLean and then turned to Anna.

"My humble apologies, my dear," Smitherim seethed through clenched teeth.

Mrs. Harding took her cue and spirited Anna away, taking care to hide her proud approval of Anna's actions. Anna's sympathy for the plight of slaves, she thought, just might be put to good use.

***

Two days out of port, the *Southern Belle* caught an unusually swift push from the North Atlantic drift bringing warmth up from the Caribbean. The breezes were not overpowering for the square-rigger and she didn't have to tack nearly so much to make forward progress. It appeared at first that the crossing would be effortless, but such wishful thinking ended with slow swells that soon began to grow. Harding didn't like the look of it. A weather front moved in from the north, and all hell broke loose a few days east of Newfoundland. The seas on this trip were designed to test even the most tempered of Harding's crew.

The *Southern Belle* made her final tack from the North Sea towards the sanctuary of Hamburg's harbour and soon lowered anchor near shore. The air was fresh and invigorating to Matthias as he anxiously awaited the lowering of the rowboat. Harding was to arrange for a berth at the wharf for the cargo to be unloaded, while

Matthias needed to see how badly his business was faring, or if indeed he was too late.

Captain Harding saw Matthias had an uneasy look about him and worried, like a father, for his safety.

"Are you sure you don't want me to go with you?"

"I'm fine, sir. You see to the barges for the cargo and I will go on ahead to make sure preparations are made to offload the barges at warehouse … if I still have one." With that, Matthias stepped out of the boat and up the steps onto the landing.

Harding smiled at the forcefulness of the young man's instruction and watched him as he disappeared into the crowd. The workers on the docks bustled as ever with the day's chores, paying no notice to the man in the billowing cloak who strode purposefully away, or to the two American sailors who followed closely behind, having been dispatched by Harding to watch over the boy.

The walk up from the harbour was a haunting one for Matthias. The streets he had walked for so many years no longer felt welcoming to him. His home, now, was where his love was waiting. It was happiness and a new beginning, free of the hideous memories painted in melted flesh on every cobblestone under his feet here. He kept the hood of his cloak up, afraid to reveal a face that, months before, the town had wanted to burn.

As he approached the door of his father's warehouse he shuddered at the sight of Hans sitting at his post. Matthias could not forgive himself for what Anna had been asked to do in his escape, and he also could not abide the sight of the filthy man who had pawed over her. Hans remained a formidable sight, however, and Matthias assumed that was why the priest had kept him at his post on the front door.

"No one passes," Hans grunted as he stopped Matthias with his tree trunk of an arm across his chest.

Matthias pulled back his hood, causing Hans to gasp, "Herr Dopp … you are in the New World … you have the plague … you?"

Hans's limited brain was attempting to process too many thoughts simultaneously. Matthias knew the man's only real fear was what people with money and social position could do to him. He certainly feared no man physically.

"I can't tell you how good it is to see you again, Hans. As you can see, I have no more plague than you do, and I am not in the New World. I am glad to see you remaining splendidly effective at your post. There shall be a *bonus* this week for such a display of loyalty."

Matthias breezed by, leaving him stunned. Hans was fixed on the idea of a bonus that, of course, meant a good drunk, and maybe even a wench or two. "*Danke*, Herr Dopp. *Danke*." He stood there staring at the door that closed in his face.

A pang of sadness ripped though Matthias's chest as he entered and saw the painting of his father hanging on the wall of the vestibule. Behind the tall oak door of his father's office he heard voices speaking in calm, businesslike tones. He might almost have guessed that nothing had changed in his absence. Business went on, he supposed, long after the businessmen were dead and buried … or burned. He opened the door and saw Vasquez behind his father's desk, flanked by Schmidt, one of his father's old associates, and Heinz Beckman, one of the wealthiest bankers in Hamburg. Beckman gingerly held a pen.

"Matthias, oh, thank God you are here," the priest blurted.

"Herr Dopp?" Herr Beckman's look was one of disbelief, while Schmidt, his father's old friend, appeared to cower with disappointment. Matthias knew immediately what was going on.

"Vultures giving a man of God a few lessons in the greed of the material world, perhaps?"

"On the contrary, Matthias. I am here out of respect for your father, to pay off his debts," Schmidt offered, with the speed of a sly fox.

"Debts? We have no debts!" Matthias shot back, but the look on the priest's face indicated all was not well. It was obvious he needed to talk with the priest and buy some time.

"Perhaps, gentlemen, we could meet tomorrow to conclude this transaction, as I have just returned from America with a tidy sum in deposits for a new run of fabric. If you please, I am quite fatigued."

The businessmen appeared somewhat reluctant to leave, having been so close to the kill, and they left like a pair of unfed gluttons pulled from a buffet. In parting, they made it quite clear that their offer was good only until the next day, at which time all of Dopp's holdings would go to those owed money.

As they left, Matthias looked for the first time in broad daylight at the man who had saved his life. He still wore the rough robe of his order, and the straps of his crude leather sandals dug into the puffy flesh of his dirty feet. His physical strength stuck out of his robe in the form of two well-muscled forearms ending in thick hands accustomed to hard work.

"You look well, my son," he said affectionately, but Matthias wasn't having any. He had questions, questions he'd had plenty of time to brood over, about his father's death, about Vasquez's role in it.

"I was Gert Dopp's son, and they burned him alive, but that shouldn't sadden me, should it, priest? After all, he can return *if he so wishes* … isn't that what you told me?"

The priest fell back into his chair. He had known the questions would come. "I feared you would need an explanation."

"*Deserve* an explanation, Father Vasquez—that would be a more appropriate wording."

"Forgive me, Matthias. When I spoke those words to you it was still possible for your father to return. And you must believe me, I had no way of knowing that the power of Verhoevan's work had fallen into the wrong hands."

"Verhoevan?"

"Brother Peter Verhoevan. Your father commissioned him to write some music for the dedication service, and unfortunately Verhoevan passed into the hands of God only one day before your father. He was a good man, may he rest in peace," the priest said, as though burdened with sadness.

"What do you mean, the power of his work?" Matthias snapped impatiently.

"That day in the cathedral, at the service for your mother, Herr Fricke, the organist, was to end his program with Brother Verhoevan's postlude, but Fricke's assistant took the wrong manuscript from Verhoevan's desk. His life's work was contained in that manuscript. It made no sense to Herr Fricke, but your father insisted he play it anyway. It consisted of only four chords, found in the middle of the manuscript, which we assumed were designed to demonstrate the majesty of the organ. But something amazing and … unfortunate happened."

"Unfortunate? Amazing? Do such words not diminish the deaths of innocent people?"

"Enough, boy!" The priest stood up, beet-red in the face, and stepped angrily towards Matthias with his hand raised to strike him. With evident difficulty, he stopped himself and regained his composure. "I had nothing to do with the death of your father or the others. When I realized that Herr Fricke's assistant had taken the wrong manuscript I rushed to the cathedral, but I arrived too late. If you wish to speak to me, you will do so with respect for the man who saved your life and ran this God-forsaken business of yours in your absence! I have done my best for you, Matthias, as any father might wish to do for his son. I have only tried to help."

Until that moment, Matthias had assumed that Vasquez had agreed to run his business inspired by a feeling of guilt, of responsibility for his father's death. But now it appeared the priest's actions had been motivated not by a responsibility for Matthias's loss, but simply by a feeling of … compassion? Matthias realized that he had been thinking narrowly, like a suspicious, self-serving businessman … the very sort of man he had just ushered out of the office. To act out of the goodness of one's heart was a motive, he was ashamed to admit to himself, that he was only now beginning to learn, from Anna.

"Forgive me. I am confused. I thought …"

"It's all right, Matthias. I understand. And you are, indeed, entitled to answers, but the only answers I can offer are … too incredible for most men to comprehend." Vasquez sank into a wooden chair behind the desk and dropped his face into his hands. "Matthias," he said, looking up at him intently, "do you believe that the spirit lives on after this earthly life?"

"Is this not what the resurrection of our Saviour promises us? I confess I have wondered about such things, but of course I bow to the knowledge and certainty of clergymen like you," Matthias answered sheepishly.

The priest smiled. "You are a good Catholic, Matthias, but I confess I am no longer a priest of such certainty. My own understanding of Heaven — and God, for that matter — has been shaken by the circumstances of your father's death. What I am about to tell you requires only an openness to the possibility of a life beyond this one... for I have seen it, and returned!"

8

READING THE MANUAL

Toronto
October, 1997

Alison Truman couldn't believe what she was doing. She had only just met this man, who wore ridiculously tight pants with his primitive parts bulging out for all to see, and now here she was sitting next to him in a van on the way to the Airport Holiday Inn. Either the manuscript was authentic, or she had just been fished in by one of the most elaborately staged come-ons of all time.

Danny was equally uncomfortable, but due to a different set of criteria, arising from an entirely different socialization. He was uptight about being seen with an academic nerd, nothing like the trophy blondes he thought were more befitting a rock 'n' roll performer of his stature. But just what the hell *was* his stature? His stature was based on playing in a freakin' Holiday Inn band to a handful of lonely alcoholics … crunch! Yeah, well, newfound perspective notwithstanding, there was still a major nerd sitting next to him with her hair cut short, dressed like a man.

Alison Truman's translations of the text were frightening, if they were to be believed, Danny thought. But so too was Joel's catatonic state, and the possibility of how he'd got that way. The pieces did appear to fit. For her part, Alison was just plain fascinated by the words of the manuscript and keen to find out if they could be connected, even remotely, to Danny's friend's loss of consciousness.

When they turned into the parking lot, Ron was kissing his businesswoman plaything goodbye through the window of a beat-up K-car. The car pulled away, and Ron saw Danny getting out of the van carrying his grandfather's old suitcase with a nerd in tow. Ron coughed rather demonstrably and gave Danny a knowing look with all the subtlety of a school kid.

Danny was embarrassed for a split second, but he realized that the embarrassment wasn't for himself. He was embarrassed that Alison might learn too much about the way he and his bandmates lived and further assess him as a reject from the waste pile of humanity. He led her at a fast pace to Joel's room and quickly closed the door, which left Alison with an obvious look of discomfort.

"You have nothing to worry about from me, Dr. Truman. My intentions are, uh, well, you know, honourable."

"You must admit, this is all a little weird," Alison said.

"Oh yeah," Danny replied emphatically.

He flipped on the power bar and Joel's rig fired up. The computer was loading; the keyboard came on immediately, as did the bank of rack-mounted synthesizers and effects gear. The whir of a CD ROM drive indicated that a disc library was loading sound samples, and in moments a menu came up on the screen. The computer screen popped on seconds later.

"He was using a pipe organ sample and, according to the sequencer memory, it was this one." Danny clicked on the same sample number that Joel had stored in his sequencer on the arrange page and the drive started to load.

"You know, it would be prudent for us not to attempt anything until I read a little more of the manuscript … if I may."

Danny opened the beat-up suitcase and gently placed the leather-bound curiosity in Alison's hands. She placed it on the oak veneer table, flipped on the lamp, and pulled up a chair, immediately absorbed.

"Could I get you a coffee or something?" Danny said, feeling somewhat useless.

"That would be nice, and maybe something to eat, I'm starving. Do you want some money?" Alison didn't look up until she heard the door close and realized Danny was gone. She thought nothing of it as she scanned the manuscript.

When Danny returned, Alison was standing, looking out the window. *She has a nice backyard*, he thought, but he immediately took himself to task for Ron-like thoughts.

Alison turned and caught him as his eyes came up. She realized she had somehow been sexually assessed, which made her blush, even though the voice in her head said, *Give me a break, rock 'n' roll boy*.

"Well?" Danny opened.

Alison was caught totally off guard and stumbled into words she didn't want. "Well what? Did you get a good enough look at my bottom?" she shot back angrily.

Danny was now embarrassed and attempted to cover his tracks. "I meant, well … did you finish the manuscript?" he said, steering out of awkward waters.

"Oh, excuse me, yes, I did." Alison's face was even redder, if that was possible, but she snapped back, grateful for the change of subject. "It's really rather bizarre. The final two pages are the author's last will and testament." She went to the book and read the last page: "*... and so in the event I do not return, I, Peter Verhoevan, a brother of the Franciscan order, leave all of my earthly possessions and the safekeeping of this, my life's work, to my friend, Brother Vasquez of Hamburg. I ask forgiveness for the loss of my assistant who entered with me for a time a few months back, but did not return in a timely fashion. This is a pain I will carry with me for eternity. As warning to all who may travel this way, know that the body will not carry breath more than the passing of two days without its own light. But beware in other cases; the soul can reside in the body for much longer periods of time without consciousness. In physical form we have no way of separating one case from the other."*

Alison looked at Danny, who sat stunned on the edge of the bed. Then she broke the silence.

"I was so curious about this that I had to go back and reread some pages from my initial glance. Up to that full page of music with the four stanzas, this book reads like a manual devoted to the science of music. It is a dissertation on harmonic combinations that evoke emotional responses. Get a load of this: *When we are moved to tears or feelings of great joy by music, we possess a connection to that which is unseen yet known internally. The harmonic structures of music can resonate with us in such a manner as to convey the sensation or awareness of something greater than ourselves. This is evidence of a spiritual kind that music may far exceed our crude understanding of it. As new music moves us with that which resembles emotional familiarity, this suggests that the spirit knows what it has not yet heard. How is this possible unless the spirit has either travelled or has some origins in the harmonic tones to which it responds?"*

"So this guy Verhoevan's life's work was to find out why music moves us. If this manuscript is to be believed, in the process of pursuing these ideas Peter Verhoevan stumbled onto a combination of notes that were the culmination of years of research and luck."

"What was the luck part?" Danny asked, cynically.

"Well, over here ..." Alison flipped forward a few pages. "Remember that stuff about notes bleeding together and creating an arch?"

"The stuff you read at the university?" Danny answered.

"Yeah, he goes on here to say: ... *the notes themselves have no power. I realized this only when I discovered by pure accident that the notes became one when bled together through the pipe and the lingering effect afforded by the organ in the great sanctuary of Hamburg. As the notes lingered in the sanctuary, they escalated in the most beautiful and intricate weave of a harmonious nature that I have ever heard, until there was a power unleashed, momentarily deafening to the mortal ear. In the aftermath of the sonic deluge, there emerged serene sounds that affected the soul, in as much as it was freed to move where it wished. Even then, I was not aware anything had occurred until* ... And this is where it gets spooky, Mr. Blum, ... *until I fortuitously turned and saw myself in a vacated corporeal state.* A vacated corporeal state? Wow, just think about seeing your own body and you're not in it. Apparently his assistant somehow was not so lucky. I wonder why he thought it good fortune to have turned and seen himself. Maybe that realization was the key to survival that escaped his assistant. So, how do you bleed notes?"

"I dunno ... he does use the word 'lingering,' so maybe reverberation is the contribution the great hall makes. Maybe each chord, given the decay time of sound in the cathedral, caused each stanza to sustain into the next, creating one massive piece of harmonic information."

Danny walked over to Joel's recording rig and looked at his effects rack. In the rack was a digital reverberation unit with a list of preset decay times. The list read: "Small Room," "Small Tiled Room," "Small Concert Hall," "Large Concert Hall," and "Large Cathedral." The latter, "Large Cathedral," held an asterisk in the margin meaning it had been selected and loaded.

"Well, look at this." Danny pointed to the unit, and Alison looked on, a little puzzled, while Danny filled in the blanks. "It simulates what something would sound like in a large cathedral." He moved the edit cursor to view the parameters. "See? It has a decay time of three and a half seconds, which is pretty long, and a one hundred millisecond pre-delay that would help simulate the refraction of sound off the walls in a very large hall. Maybe it doesn't have to be an exact setting … just long enough for whatever happens to happen."

Danny picked up the manuscript, opened it to the four stanzas of music, and placed it on the wire music stand of the keyboard.

"So, if these four chords were played, I guess the reverb would cause them to momentarily overlap sonically, or bleed into one another."

"Then what?" Alison inquired.

"I don't know … let's see." Danny put on the headphones and played the four chords and … nothing. He pulled the phones off and shook his head. "I must being doing something wrong."

"Or what happened to your friend is unrelated," Alison responded, ever the academic.

"You must admit, Dr. Truman, this manuscript appearing and Joel's condition are eerily coincidental."

After a few more tries Danny looked at the professor in defeat, then unintentionally glanced at her breasts, which he assessed as small but firm. Alison was immediately uncomfortable with his penetrating inspection.

"I wonder if you might take me back to the university. I have a fair workload to plough through."

"Sure." Danny headed to the door and opened it. "After you."

The two of them walked silently down the hall and out the side door to the parking lot. As they were getting into the van, an odd look came over Alison's face.

"What if you just didn't play the chords fast enough? I mean, you have to use both of your hands for each chord. For the decay of the first chord to reach the last chord, you would have to start the last chord within, what did you say the decay was, three seconds?"

"Mmm, well, my sight-reading isn't as good as Joel's. I wonder if the trick is to make the sound of each chord intersect at a certain point in the waveform. The sound is more potent the closer it is to the crest of the wave," Danny thought out loud.

"I can sight-read, I've played the piano since I was a little girl. Let's give it another shot."

Back in the hotel room, the two excitedly plugged another set of headphones into the junction box so they could both listen. They took turns sitting in Joel's chair, trying the chords, while the other timed how long it took to get to the last chord. After a good hour of effort they came out of the phones.

"Are you sure everything is the way Joel left it?"

"Well, the organ patch he was using is the same, because he did make note of it … see, the preset is here on his arrange page."

"What about that reverberation decay thing?"

"The verb unit? It loads what was last used or stored."

"Can you increase the decay time?"

"Sure but … mmm, you could be right. Maybe Joel increased it but didn't store his edit as a preset."

Danny hit the edit cursor and moved the decay time up to four seconds. He put on his headphones and looked at Alison, who quickly followed suit. After their previous efforts Danny was well rehearsed, but then something dawned on him. He took his time, hit record, and played through the four chords very slowly.

Alison looked at him curiously. "What are you doing? That's way too slow."

"Duh! I'm such an idiot. I'm loading the chords into the computer as midi information so we just need to hit the play icon."

"Why didn't you do that before?"

"Joel usually does all the programming. It just dawned on me that the computer can do the work for us with a midi file."

Danny finished programming the last chord, dragged the mouse to the tempo icon, increased the speed of the sequence, then hit play. The computer ran the sequence of chords and the sound appeared to be slowly dying off. Alison pulled her headphones off, but Danny kept his on.

"Now I'm going to increase the tempo on the arrange page even more so it will play the four chords in a faster sequence."

Alison put her phones on, and again the sound appeared to be dying out. Once more she took her phones off in defeat and was about to theorize when she noticed Danny still listening closely.

"It isn't going away, something's happening … put your phones back on!"

She did so and listened to the distant sound. It seemed to be interacting, folding in on itself, as though notes were setting off other notes sympathetically in random cadences. The thick mixture of harmonic information slowly began to increase in intensity. The louder it got, the more the timbre of the massive chord morphed, as different constituent harmonics and partials usually inaudible to the most acute human hearing revealed themselves.

As the chord increased in density it began to reach Alison's pain threshold when all of a sudden all sound abruptly dropped in volume to an incredibly delicate sound, like the tinkling of wind chimes. Behind the wind chimes were traces of human voice and birdsong. It was an incredible tapestry of sound that was gentle, yet oddly powerful. It was sweet yet sad; something they had never heard, and yet somehow it was familiar. It made Alison feel warm, as did an intense light behind her.

She turned to see Danny silhouetted by light, looking at her rather oddly. She stood and faced him for what seemed like a long time. He looked back at her with a bizarre expression on his face.

"What's the matter?" Her voice sounded as if she were speaking into a velvet curtain, devoid of any room ambience, and from Danny's perspective her lips barely moved.

"Plenty," Danny whispered, as if gasping for air.

Alison walked slowly towards him, concerned. He was clearly overwhelmed.

"You don't look well."

"Oh sure I do."

"What do you mean?"

"Turn around."

Alison turned, and what she saw would have scared the hell out of her if she hadn't felt so inexplicably calm.

"How can this be?"

Danny's body was slouched over in the chair in front of the synthesizer. The left side of his face was on the keyboard; his eyes were fixed and glazed. Alison's body had fallen backwards onto the bed, eyes open and gazing towards the ceiling.

"Good grief, that's us," she whispered.

"So are we having an out-of-body experience? That's what it's called, right?" Danny walked over to his body and tried to touch it, but his trembling hand disappeared into the shoulder. "Did you see that?" He looked at Alison, who followed suit, passing her own hand into her thigh. The two of them stood frozen, trying to process what was going on.

"So, uh, how do we get back?" Danny asked.

"I am trying to remember what the manuscript said about returning. There was a passage that didn't make any sense to me but maybe …"

"Maybe what? Don't leave me here by myself." Danny's tone was one of childlike fear that caught Alison by surprise. She saw a little boy, a sweet little soul looking at her, and felt an odd affection towards him. She sensed an innocence that was unquestionably endearing.

Danny felt her affection enter him immediately with an overpowering warmth. "Sorry, Alison, I don't mean to make you feel responsible for me."

"That's okay, Daniel," she said softly. "Do you feel all right?"

"Never felt better, actually, but I think … it's coming from you."

"What do you mean?"

"I just feel like you don't … like you … well … like I don't disgust you any more, which is pretty much what I have felt from you all day until now."

"I'm sorry, Daniel. And if it's any comfort, you didn't disgust me. I think I was just afraid of you. What is interesting, though, is why we are saying all of this now."

"My mother calls me Daniel."

"I know."

"How do you know that?"

"I have no idea, and that fascinates the hell out of me."

"You said there was a passage about returning that made no sense to you? What was it?"

Alison went to the manuscript, and the pages one by one became transparent until she lingered on the one she was looking for. Danny felt a little spooked.

"How did you do that?"

"Do what?"

"You made the pages dissolve."

"I don't know … it felt like I was turning them."

"Well, you weren't." Danny watched her expression change as she found what she was looking for.

"Here it is … *to look through one's eyes is to be as one*."

"What does that mean?" Danny asked.

"I'm not sure. You passed your hand through your shoulder, right?"

"Yeah, so?"

"So maybe put your head into your head until you look out of your eyes … your physical eyes. Sounds creepy, but what else could it mean? Just climb back into your body, but make sure you look through your eyes. It might have something to do with perceptions of body and spirit needing to be synchronous."

Danny went behind his body and slowly leaned over until the outline of his face disappeared into the back of his unconscious head.

"Is this supposed to hurt? The side of my face hurts." Danny's questions sounded distant to him. Then he realized why. He felt the pressure of the headphones on his ears and sat up, looking at Alison's body on the bed, staring at the ceiling. He was back. His face must have hit the keyboard with a reasonable impact when his body lost consciousness.

"Alison?" There was no answer. He felt an odd sensation, as if there was a presence beside him. "Is that you?"

The computer flickered. Danny waited, expecting Alison to come back … but … nothing. Fifteen minutes went by as he sat motionless, mind racing through horrific scenarios, all converging on a dominant feeling of guilt. Now he had two deaths, or zombies, or whatever the hell was going on that he was responsible for. He looked at poor Alison's face and saw a plain beauty that he hadn't noticed before … or maybe it hadn't been allowed to shine through her defensive posture.

Why hadn't she been able to come back? Why only him? He stroked her hair and felt a strange compulsion to kiss her, but she was defenceless, which made Danny feel vile and opportunistic. He began to pull away when Alison came to life, catching him totally off guard. He was so startled that he flew off the bed and hit the wall before tumbling to the floor.

Alison sat up and pulled off her headphones. She rubbed her face with her hands as though shaking off sleep, and then a look of realization came across her face.

"Don't you dare touch me! Nobody touches me!" she screamed.

"You're back! Where the hell have you been?"

"Don't change the subject."

"I swear, I wouldn't have done anything … I don't even know why I thought about … I …"

"Just don't ever touch me again. I can't stand it when someone touches me!" Alison was livid, and Danny was taken aback by how different and sweet she had seemed when they were outside their bodies. Now she looked insane with anger. She stood up and was hyperventilating ... and just from the thought of being touched?

"I … " Danny began an apology but was cut off when Alison held her hand up to stop him. *This chick has some serious baggage*, he thought to himself as he sat down on a chair, more than a little unsettled by all that had just happened.

"God, this is so bizarre. We *did* have an out-of-body experience, didn't we?" he asked himself quietly.

"That'd be my guess, but don't ask me to swear to it because I can't exactly say I'm an authority," Alison replied as she slowly calmed down.

"What took you so long to come back, Alison?"

"How long was I gone?"

"I dunno, about fifteen minutes or so."

"You're kidding!"

"No. I've been in this room going nuts by myself while you were probably floating around like Casper the freakin' friendly ghost!"

"Maybe time has no relevance there, or maybe time here is ridiculously slow. Anyway, I was briefly distracted," Alison mused.

"Distracted?"

"I wanted to see if there was more to this thing than standing outside of your own body and staring at yourself."

"So?"

"So when I looked away from myself, I was aware of others looking at me."

"I saw them too, when I first entered … I just couldn't deal with it," Danny admitted.

"Why? I didn't sense they meant to harm anyone," Alison continued. "Couldn't you feel that? I spoke to them and asked them who they were. A familiar-looking one said they had heard the sound and were drawn to it. It's as if this sonic . . . event, I guess it is … opens a window, creating some kind of draft. One fellow asked me if I was going back, and if not, would I mind if he went back in my place? I'm not sure, but I think what he asked must be possible.

Maybe when someone is in a coma or unconscious, sometimes others come back in their place. I remember a friend whose brother was knocked off of his bike in a hit-and-run. He was in a coma for two weeks, and when he came back everyone was incredibly relieved, except his brother, who confided in me that he was not the same man. He said his brother seemed normal in many ways, but he had a slightly different personality and a new sense of humour. The thing that first made him curious were changes in his vocabulary, words that his brother had never used before. He said everyone chalked it up to brain trauma, but now … I wonder if, in fact, another soul came back in his brother's body? All of the genetic and chemical stuff might remain in the brain and body, maybe even some talents, like a predisposition to math or athleticism. Just think … some other soul might occasionally get to ride in the talents of a vacated body!"

"How the hell could you possibly know any of that?" Danny snarked.

"Couldn't say … just felt it, and so much more that was … amazing, to put it lightly."

"So what do we do about Joel?" Danny muttered sadly.

Alison went to the manuscript and flipped a couple of pages.

"Maybe there's still time to get him back. Verhoevan did say the body would live for two days without its own light, which must have meant the soul. When do you think Joel left?'

"I don't know exactly, but I left him with the manuscript around two in the morning and he was going to look at it then. I mean, there's not much to those four chords. A reasonable guess at the outside would be within a couple of hours of me leaving.

"So we have until somewhere between two and four tomorrow morning. That isn't much time."

"Much time for what?"

"For you try to find him and bring him back. But we're going to need help." Alison was way ahead of Danny. "We have no idea what's out there or what the rules are. Before you even think about going back for Joel, if you go back, you will need some more information." Alison headed to the door. "Let's go, you're driving. I'll get directions." Alison knew the most they could hope for was anecdotal information, and she had an acquaintance with plenty of that. She made a few calls in the hotel lobby and got the address.

Twenty minutes later, Danny turned the van onto a street lined with mature trees in the Forest Hill area of Toronto, and Alison began to scan the houses for numbers.

"Left here, it's this one." She pointed to a modest, red-brick bungalow. Danny swung into the driveway, and by the time he got out, Alison was halfway up the flagstone path. The garden on either side was overgrown, though it looked as though it was once the pastime of an avid gardener. Alison was already ringing the doorbell by the time Danny caught up, and a good minute or so later, a frail old man appeared in the doorway.

"Hello, Dr. Walters," Alison began.

"I'm sorry, you have me at a bit of a disadvantage," the old man said, squinting in Alison's direction.

"My name is Alison Truman. I lecture in the Department of Religious Studies at the University of Toronto. I met you at the Elisabeth Kubler-Ross lecture at Convocation Hall a few years ago? We spoke at the reception afterward. I wonder if we might have a few moments of your time."

"Well now, I do remember your face, and you're the best prospect I've had for a decent conversation today. C'mon in, the coffee's on, and you can bring that straggler in as well, if you'd like."

"Blum, Danny Blum," Danny offered, not wishing to be so marginalized.

"Well, you're welcome to come in too Blum, Danny Blum. That's a bit dramatic, like Bond, James Bond, don't you think? Next I suppose you'll want a martini, shaken not stirred," the old man quipped over his shoulder.

Danny followed them to the hall, past a living room that looked like a decaying set for "The Brady Bunch." The house was clearly in a state of decline not unfamiliar to many old widowers. Dr. Walters led them down the dark, narrow hallway and through the kitchen to a bright sunroom in the back of the house. It was clearly the room he lived in. There was a game show playing on a TV with the sound turned off. The couch to one side was faded and a little past its prime, as was the comfortable leather recliner facing the TV. In front of the bay window sat a large mahogany dining-room table strewn with a mountain of papers and books, flanked by two large, gray, metal filing cabinets. On the cabinets, the desk, and even the TV set were pictures of the same kindly looking woman at different ages. A more formal and expensively framed picture of the old man and the woman hung on the wall.

Dr. Jeremiah Walters was a professor emeritus in cardiology at the university's medical school, Danny learned. His true passion, however, was the gathering and study of anecdotal evidence of a spiritual nature. Much like Elizabeth Kubler-Ross, who had devoted herself to research into death and dying, Dr. Walters had meticulously documented hundreds of out-of-body experiences from patients in his long medical career. He had published a couple of books on the subject.

Dr. Walters had come to what he believed was a logical conclusion, based on tons of irrefutable evidence from around the world. The conclusion was simply that there appeared to be such a thing as an extracorporeal consciousness. There were far too many examples of patients who had died on operating tables, been somewhere, seen people they'd never known existed until the out-of-body experience. Many had observed their own bodies and what was being done to them from a position not consistent with lying on an operating table looking up. There was documented case after documented case of people coming back with information from friends or relatives who had died.

Such a body of evidence, according to Dr. Walters, was not to be brushed aside with fear or ignorance. To him, the empirically minded naysayers who chalked up out-of-body experiences to chemically induced hallucinations were quite possibly members of the latest Flat Earth Society. If they didn't know about it, or couldn't measure it, then it couldn't possibly exist. This, of course, didn't allow for the obvious: that as instruments improved with advances in technology, so did scientific discovery. The stupidity of scientific fundamentalism, much like religious fundamentalism, he said, was an egomaniacal presumption of knowing all that was to be known. The great Copernicus, after all, with scientific proof of a heliocentric cosmology, feared the wrath of other scientists nearly as much as the Church. And the world hadn't known that Jupiter's moons even existed until Galileo developed a lens to see them. Of course, Dr. Walters pointed out, Galileo was threatened by the Church to recant his support of Copernican heliocentrism for the more biblically acceptable geocentrism. What an affront to humankind that the universe didn't rotate around man's self-importance!

The two guests had coffee mugs filled with warm coffee, and Alison had the floor.

"Dr. Walters, what would you say if I told you we are about to go on a journey to another plane of existence?"

"Are you planning on killing yourselves?"

"Not if we can help it."

"So, how are you hoping to do this?" The old man looked at Alison with genuine concern.

"Music," Danny muttered sheepishly from behind. "Four chords, to be exact."

The old man's face lit up. He turned around with a smile on his face, went to his file cabinet, and grabbed a manila folder.

"Four chords … when bled? You mean the studies of brother Pietro Brebeuf?" He scurried down the hall, and a few minutes later he returned with an old book, speaking excitedly before he even entered the room. "Now this fella, from nineteenth-century Germany, started off as a priest in the Franciscan brotherhood, but he was also a well-known organist by the end of his life. He claimed that as a young man he had seen people move freely to `Heaven' without body, and this was the result of the brilliant work of a Franciscan colleague, a brother many years his senior, a—"

"Peter Verhoevan." Alison signalled Danny to open the suitcase and produce the book.

"Why … yes, I believe that was his name. How did you…?"

The old man's jaw dropped at the sight of the leather-bound book Danny placed on his desk.

"Oh my goodness …" He stroked the cover reverently, then opened it. "Verhoevan's manuscript! I thought this a flight of brother Pietro's imagination . . . a work of fiction, the proverbial one that got away… a holy grail. He said he buried it with the body of Verhoevan, to protect others from falling victim to its power."

"Yeah, well, it isn't buried. I have a good friend whose body is in the ICU at St. Mike's, and God only knows where his consciousness, soul, or whatever you call it is. We need your help, sir, and we need it fast." Danny spelled it all out.

The old man fell back into his chair with a look of wonderment that slowly turned into a wide, boyish grin as he considered the possibilities.

"I am at your disposal."

9

HIS FATHER'S SON

Hamburg

January, 1848

A fire roared in the huge stone hearth of the Dopp warehouse office, attempting to counter the cold, damp day. Matthias sat in his father's chair with a look of incredulity on his face. He wanted the priest to be a madman; to think otherwise meant he would have to seriously entertain what he had just been told, that there was another life — a Heaven, of sorts — and Vasquez had been there.

"I know how my story sounds, my son. The only way I can prove myself is to cross over briefly with you so that you know what I speak is truth. Perhaps there is even hope of seeing your father there … I don't know, but I think it might be possible."

"Hope of seeing my father? Are you saying that his soul crossed over to some kind of afterlife, leaving his still-breathing body behind to be burned? It sounds ridiculous, and yet you speak of it so calmly, as though he simply went out for a morning stroll." Agitated, Matthias stood and began to pace the room. "Well, I have no need of Heaven now, for surely this is my time for more earthly pursuits. And what if, like my father's, my body was burned while I crossed, as you suggest?"

Matthias looked genuinely scared, and the priest laughed. "A wise position, Herr Dopp. It is indeed your time for earthly pursuits. So, what of the young whore who sailed with you?"

"I will ask you to never use that term again, because you are speaking of Frau Dopp, my wife."

The priest shook his head. "Please accept my apologies. You are an exceptional young man, Matthias."

"No sir, I am not, but one day I hope to have a heart as good as the exceptional woman I have wed. However, we can speak of these more spiritual matters again soon. Right now my thoughts are on the sins of the living. These men you have been entertaining will have everything I own if we don't move fast. I need the names of every person we owe money to, no matter how insignificant the amount." Matthias's tone was firm, his purpose focused.

The priest looked inquisitively at him. "But surely these colleagues of your father will back down now that you have returned?"

"Nothing is sure but the letter of the law, which, at the moment, they can use to acquire considerable wealth for a minimal investment."

"Disgusting!" the priest huffed.

"Business," Matthias replied calmly.

The two men got to work, and within the hour Matthias had the list of those he was indebted to. He pored over the books, and then the invoices and receipts, until only one document remained. He went back to the books and a smile of relief came across his face. He grabbed the document, folded it, and placed it in his pocket.

"We now have a plan."

As his carriage crossed town, Matthias couldn't rid himself of the thought of seeing his father again, even though merely entertaining such a possibility frightened him to the core. However, as they rounded the corner and turned down the narrow alley to Jorge Hacker's home, he slowly pulled himself together for the task at hand.

The hovel consisted of two rooms behind a tailor's shop. Matthias had given Hacker a lift home in his carriage on a few rainy occasions. He was a good foreman and oversaw the operations of Dopp Mills in a very orderly, disciplined fashion. Matthias knocked on the door, and a very plump Mrs. Hacker answered. She took one look and ran back into the poorly lit house to fetch her husband. Jorge appeared in a soiled undershirt and spoke very coldly.

"Matthias, I heard you were alive. I am glad of it."

"Well thank you, Jorge. Might I come in? I have business to discuss with you."

Jorge's face turned like that of a schoolboy caught in an act of mischief. His demeanour confirmed what Matthias had already deduced. He reluctantly bade Matthias enter with a shake of his head before closing the door quietly.

Once seated on a wooden chair in front of the fireplace, Matthias placed his valise at his feet and wasted no time.

"Jorge, if you and your men wish to be paid in full and remain employed I will need your co-operation. Stop me if I have misconstrued what I believe are the circumstances before me. Schmidt, I think, has probably offered you a partial payment for what is owed you, and with the mill shut, you considered that suggestion better than nothing, so you organized everyone and made a deal. But now things have changed. I have returned from America with a shipment of raw material and orders for manufactured cloth. I can offer you a future, but … I will need to know everything you know if I am to turn this around tomorrow morning."

"And what if you can't, as you say, turn this around, Herr Dopp? Will I be forfeit the balance of the money I was to receive when the acquisition of the mills was complete? Your papist friend has done us all in, I am afraid!" Hacker was not mincing words.

Matthias recognized this as the speech of a desperate father. When the priest had approached Hacker to reopen the mills for Matthias after the death of Herr Dopp, it was Jorge's hungry children who had made the decision an easy one. Matthias picked up his valise, removed a small wooden box, and handed it to Hacker.

"Here is payment in full of all that is owed you and your men. You may keep this whether you help me or not, for it is what is owed you, but what Herr Schmidt has advanced you I must ask you to deduct, as it should be reimbursed."

"But I have signed his papers. They'll throw me in prison!"

"No one goes to prison in business if they have a better proposition."

Jorge felt the weight of the gold coins in his hand, but that wasn't all. Underneath the fear for his family's well-being sat the warm glow of something else … loyalty.

The following morning, both Herr Schmidt and Herr Beckman, the bank manager, were waiting in the large, ornate bank office with the mosaic marble floor. Clearly, Schmidt was as annoyed at the sight of Jorge as the manager was surprised. Extra chairs were brought in and everyone was seated, with comments about the weather and inane pleasantries soon exhausted. Beckman, a tall, aristocratic, impeccably dressed man, loved the superiority he felt sitting behind his huge, imposing black desk, and he began the play as he thought it was written, in a commanding tone.

"So, gentlemen, in the matter before us we have outstanding debts to your employees, which Mr. Schmidt has paid on your behalf, and —"

Matthias interrupted. "Actually, Herr Beckman, he hasn't paid my employees in full. He has advanced only a quarter of what is owed, with a half-hearted suggestion that he might pay out an additional quarter if and when business picks up, which of course it never will, as liquidation of the assets is more Herr Schmidt's style, I should think."

Beckman looked surprised, and Matthias read his face well. He knew Schmidt to be a crafty one, indeed—his plan had been to partner up with a bank, get them to front half of a buyout, then negotiate with labour behind the scenes for even less and pocket the balance. The bank would simply appear as a neutral intermediary, even though it was, in fact, a silent partner, nicely removed from the light of day. That way, should a businessman who has fallen on hard times ever make a comeback, the bank could again nuzzle up for business as usual. Gert Dopp had told his son about Schmidt's tactics, and even though Schmidt was considered a family friend, Matthias had been warned repeatedly to be wary of him.

Beckman regrouped and began again as he attempted to distance himself from Schmidt. There might, after all, he thought, be more money to be made with a Dopp in charge, if the son was anything like his father.

"Perhaps you have a better proposal to bring to the table today, Herr Dopp?"

"Perhaps I do, Herr Becker. First of all, here is the full amount, in gold, paid thus far to our employees by Herr Schmidt." Matthias placed a valise on Becker's desk. "My men go back to work. It is only 25 percent of what is owed, and as there appear to be no other partners in Mr. Schmidt's acquisition attempt, we will consider his advance paid back in full."

Becker grimaced, but caught himself, not willing to be revealed as the unseen partner Matthias knew him to be. The gold, however, served Matthias's immediate purpose, as it showed he was a man of considerable means.

"I will also pay a bonus fee to the bank for negotiating in good faith the paperwork for all necessary arrangements. Furthermore, I will keep my business at this bank, as I have returned from America with lucrative new contracts and a shipment of raw materials to be manufactured into fabrics for which I have buyers in America."

"But … what of the debt to Herr Schmidt, who provided raw material that your mill might remain open an additional two weeks? This was the basis of his financial claim."

A smile crept across Matthias's face. The priest had seen that same smile at the Dopp warehouse, and his interest was piqued. Matthias pulled the folded piece of paper from his pocket.

"Oh yes, the matter of Herr Schmidt's generosity." He unfolded the document and slapped it on the desk in front of Becker. "As you can see, this is an invoice dated the day before my father died. It is made out to Herr Schmidt for a sizeable order delivered to him that day, and it remains unpaid. I am sure this was just an oversight, given the sincere grief Herr Schmidt must have suffered in the unfortunate circumstances of my father's death. In actual fact, after taking into account the money advanced to labour and for raw materials in my absence, you will note that it is Herr Schmidt who still owes the Dopp Company money." Matthias removed the valise from the table.

Becker scanned the document before him and looked infuriated. Schmidt, for his part, attempted a poor cover.

"I loved your father, Matthias, and was meaning to factor that invoice into my offer today. I …"

Matthias wasn't interested in lies and he stood, signalling to the priest and Jorge that it was time to leave the thieves to squabble amongst themselves.

"I will issue you a new invoice for the balance, Herr Schmidt, and as you are such a dear friend of my family I'm sure that prompt payment would be your wish, as well as mine, in these difficult times. Should payment not be prompt, procedures will begin to liquidate your assets until payment in full has been met." He brushed the arms of his coat, demonstrably indicating that he was ridding himself of dirt, and gave Becker a knowing look.

"Our business is concluded, Herr Becker, but I believe the two of you may still have much to discuss. Gentlemen?"

Becker was taken aback by the young man's poise. Matthias strode out of the room, with Jorge Hacker following in step beside him. The priest, however, stood frozen, clenched fists at his side and an icy glare of disgust chilling in the direction of Schmidt. As the tall door closed behind them, Matthias and Jorge stopped, realizing that they had lost their associate. The sound of crashing furniture, followed by a muffled scream, came from Becker's office. Moments later the priest appeared at the door, closing it quietly in the wake of the silence he left behind him.

The three men walked from the bank in synchronous strides, like troops in a victory march. Once outside, Matthias looked inquisitively at the rotund holy man, who rubbed blood from the knuckles of his right hand.

"Schmidt?" Matthias asked.

"Fell like a bag of bricks, may God forgive me," the priest muttered under his breath as he crossed himself.

Matthias tried to suppress his laughter but it would not be stopped.

As they walked down the street Hacker looked at the priest, and his face crumpled into a smirk. "Well, if your God doesn't forgive you, I'm pretty sure mine might."

The priest maintained a straight face for a good twenty yards until he blew up in an explosion of jackass-like grunting and gasping. It took a second or two for Matthias and Jorge to realize that the priest was not in some kind of distress but in fact was laughing, which made them laugh all the harder.

"Poor Schmidt! It was quite a disappointing day for the fox in the henhouse!" he gasped in a fit of hysterics.

Poor Schmidt indeed, Matthias thought - the money he had to pay back to Becker, a huge invoice he'd thought had slipped through the cracks, and a black eye, to boot. Matthias had played his hand well and was grateful no one had looked into the valise that now held only two small brass bookends and a few knives and forks for sonic effect.

***

Captain Harding arrived at the Dopp home later that afternoon, having concluded his own business at the docks. He handed his coat to the old housekeeper, who lived in the servants' quarters downstairs. The priest, at the invitation of Matthias, had been living in the Dopp home for some time while providing the old woman with enough money to run the household. Her husband had served as valet to Gert Dopp until his life ended abruptly in an effort to climb the stairs with a travel trunk. Gert had kept the old woman on, even though her best days of service were well behind her. Somehow, though, she managed to keep everything rolling in the house … everything, that is, with the exception of cooking. In that regard, a cook had been hired by Vasquez, primarily to ensure that the old woman, who was becoming a little forgetful, didn't burn the place down. Fire had exacted enough of a toll on the Dopp family.

When Harding entered, Matthias was sitting in the parlour, staring at a painting of his parents dressed in their finest that hung above the marble mantle of the fireplace. The Captain observed but respectfully said nothing. After re-stoking the waning coal fire, he poured two snifters of brandy and handed one to Matthias. He stood warming his backside until Matthias wiped his eyes and looked up at the Captain, who gave him a concerned, fatherly smile.

"We fared well at the bank today," Matthias told him.

"I thought you might. Beckman think there was more future with a young Dopp than an old Schmidt?"

"My father would have loved it." Matthias drifted to a place of pain momentarily, then shook it off with a smirk. "And how did you do this day?"

"There is a merchant from New York who is seeking passage back to America for a cargo of European furniture and art. Even though your lease on the *Belle* is up, I would not commit until I was sure of your plans."

"It is best you look after your own interests, my friend. I'm not sure how long I will be here. I will certainly need more raw material from America, though, which can pay your way back, and by that time there will be fabrics completed for a return journey."

"I am afraid I can't leave for at least three weeks myself, until we are assured of spring's intentions and some repairs are completed on the *Belle*. She took quite a pounding on the crossing. I wonder, Matthias, if I might impose on you for a roof over my head until I make the return journey."

Matthias looked at Harding with great affection. "If I may be so bold to say, sir, and with no desire to offend, I think of you and Mrs. Harding as family now. My house is yours." The look that passed between two men contained a stream of unconditional trust.

"Any idea how much time you'll need?" Harding inquired.

"As long as it will take to find Anna's family and restore my father's business. It was his life."

"And what about your life, Matthias?"

"I know my life is in America now … with Anna. I will conclude matters here on terms of my own design. I will not be robbed or devalue the legacy of my father's life. I will be paid in full measure for my business and holdings and not a beggar's wage less!"

Harding nodded in agreement and waved the brandy snifter in front of his nose.

It was an unusually quiet dinner that evening, given the events of the day. The venison was splendidly cooked in a delicate pastry, and Harding tucked in. Matthias and the priest would look at one another as though something was up, and Harding could not help but notice that his young friend barely touched his food. After dinner, as they sat in an odd, strained silence, Harding did his best at feigning fatigue with a poorly acted yawn. He excused himself to his bedchamber, where he snuffed out the candles and took up a comfortable position in a well-padded French Provincial chair a few feet back from the window.

Some time later, having inadvertently dozed off, Harding was awakened by the vibration of the front door closing beneath him, and he looked up to see the priest and Matthias walking down the street at a brisk pace. The mystery of Matthias scurrying off at such an hour with a papist had the better of him. He feared for the safety of the boy he had come to think of as his own. If he were to err, it would be on the side of prudence. Harding grabbed his cloak and headed out in pursuit.

There was an eerie fog wafting up from the harbour that made following difficult. Not only was it hard to see his quarry, but also his feet sounded unusually loud on the cobblestone streets, causing him calf pain from walking in such an awkward manner as to avoid detection. Harding did feel a measure of guilt over his idle curiosity but nonetheless stalked his quarry for another ten minutes before sinking into the shadows of a shop doorway to avoid being discovered.

Matthias stood in the dark square where his father had been burned. The fog in the air was reminiscent of the aftermath of a fire that sent a shiver up his spine. He heaved uncontrollably in sorrowful convulsions as he relived the horror forever seared into his memory.

The priest had continued across the cobblestone market square to the back entrance of the cathedral and stood waiting for a few stragglers to pass. As the sound of their feet echoed off in the distance, the square was enveloped in silence, broken only by the sniffling of Matthias tending to his tears. Looking around his perimeter once more, the sturdy little man of God pulled a key from the satchel he had over his shoulder and plunged it into the cast-iron lock.

"Hurry, before I change my mind!" the priest half yelled, half whispered. Matthias looked over towards the hooded shadow and obeyed.

Harding watched the two ghostly figures vanish into the giant cathedral, then strolled over to the great oak door. It looked shut, but on closer inspection he saw that it remained slightly ajar. He pushed it, expecting far more resistance, and had to grab on to the iron handle to stop it from slamming into the stone interior wall. Once inside, he carefully closed the door just short of engaging the lock. The corridor was black, with the exception of the flickering of candlelight ahead in the distance.

Harding moved towards the hushed whispers of Matthias and Vasquez. A shudder moved through his bones as he bumped the stone sarcophagus of a wealthy nobleman. He looked up at the reclining, sculpted outline clutching a huge broadsword as if to protect this last claim to privacy and something moved in the perimeter of his vision. The priest appeared out of nowhere, heading back towards the rear entrance. Harding ducked in behind the sarcophagus and squatted.

"I have changed my mind. This is too dangerous," Vasquez said with conviction. Matthias appeared behind him and grabbed his sleeve. If they had taken one step forward, the light from the candle in Vasquez's hand would have revealed the top of Harding's head.

"I too fear danger, but I must know. You said you would show me, and if you oblige me in this one attempt to see my father … to allow me the chance to at least say goodbye . . . I will never trouble you again."

"And what if you don't see your father? Will your curiosity continue to place us all in jeopardy? What happened to the young man you were yesterday who had no desire to look beyond this life?" Vasquez shot back.

"I implore you, Vasquez, to accommodate me only this once. Whether I am successful or not, I will never ask you again."

Vasquez turned and looked at the boy. "I know not why I feel such guilt over your father's demise, for it was not my doing. If you never ask me again, and if you promise to do as I say in this matter ..."

"I will never ask again."

Vasquez turned and headed back towards the sanctuary, with Matthias in his wake.

Harding emerged with a puzzled look on his face. Was his old friend Gert Dopp alive? Was he held in some kind of religious exile in this huge Catholic cathedral? He crept into the left wing of the transept that created the cruciform of the cathedral's architecture and there he saw the shadows of Matthias and the priest walking up the steps of the altar. They were stopped by the appearance of a third man. Harding darted behind a large statue of the Virgin Mary and looked under the elbow of a marble arm that clutched a rather well-fed and highly polished infant.

"Brother Vasquez, the bellows are ready for you, but we must not remain here long."

"Of course," the priest answered as he reached into his satchel and produced a leather-bound manuscript. He handed it to the other man.

"You know what to do, Pietro. You have wax for your ears?"

Pietro nodded in the affirmative.

"Come, Matthias," Vasquez barked.

All three men disappeared from view, and Harding began to stir when he was stopped in his tracks by a blast of sound from the huge array of pipes he had not seen directly over his head. He dropped to the stone floor and held his ears as three more blasts filled the cathedral in quick succession. A few moments passed, and when Harding was convinced the impromptu demonstration was concluded he removed his hands from ears that still rang. An odd and strangely beautiful sound echoed into the rafters, causing him to temporarily lose his balance. In that brief moment of dizziness the walls of the cathedral began to dissolve into an eerie transparency. Harding frantically slapped his cheeks, afraid he was going to faint, then covered his ears again. He checked every couple of minutes until the sound had stopped and the cathedral was silent again.

Harding got to his feet and had begun to head in the direction of the altar when the man called Pietro appeared, removing clumps of a waxy substance from his ears as he took up a position, apparently standing guard. Harding dropped immediately behind a pew and took long, slow, controlled breaths to avoid discovery. Ten minutes passed and were well on the way to becoming fifteen when a familiar voice came from a position that Harding assumed must be where the bellows for the great pipe organ resided.

"Matthias, come back, boy, don't do this to me! Oh, God forgive me what I have I done! Matthias! Matthias!!"

Harding slowly stood up, startling Pietro, who sounded the alarm. "Brother Vasquez, someone is here!"

"Keep them away!" Vasquez shouted back as he continued. "Come back, boy! This way, boy, this way! Think of your life with Anna, who waits for you! Look back through your own eyes!"

The priest sounded so distressed that Harding's fear of discovery was instantly displaced by his concern for the boy he loved as his own. Pietro, who on closer inspection turned out to be a young priest in training, attempted to stop the Captain, who pushed him aside like a feather as he marched up the steps, only to be stopped dead in his tracks by the appearance of Vasquez, walking with his arm around a visibly shaken Matthias.

"Matthias, are you all right?" The words had no sooner left Harding's lips than the priest took the offensive.

"Of course he's all right. We came here to see the organ that was dedicated in his mother's name. He was startled by the sound and overcome with a moment of grief for his parents."

Harding looked at Matthias. "Is all as the priest says, Matthias?"

The young man began to mutter, his face a mask of confusion.

"No … it isn't as he says, it isn't as anyone says." Matthias looked up at the vexed expression on Harding's face. "Wh … why did you follow us?"

"I was worried for your safety in a town that burns such honourable men as your father."

"We thank you for your concern, Captain, but I must ask you to pursue the events of this evening no more." Vasquez grabbed Matthias by the elbow and started down the altar steps.

Harding blocked the way with a stern and obstinate stance. "Matthias, my question was to you, not the papist."

"I am fine, just a little dizzy, and Vasquez … is right." Matthias spoke haltingly. "As my friend, I ask you to let this matter drop."

Some hesitation crossed Harding's face, but then he threw his hands in the air. "So be it!" He turned and headed back the way he had come. He was curious, but fear also entered his thoughts. Harding mulled over the words he had heard Matthias say about wanting to see his father one last time, and then the even more curious instruction from what was clearly a frightened Vasquez to "look back though your own eyes." As a devout Protestant, schooled with great prejudice against the Catholic Church, Harding had no problem finding a focus for his fears. There was something sinister and possibly sacrilegious going on, and in his mind it no doubt had papal origins. He began to pray to the God he believed in to save them all.

The priest looked at Matthias with an affectionate expression. "You seem to have recovered from your journey. I was worried when you nearly left my view. Did you see him?"

"No, I saw no one I knew. Why would strangers seek me out?"

"I am afraid I can't answer that question. I believe there are skills that one must acquire on the other side to communicate with those you seek. But we have an agreement, Matthias, do we not? You must not think of these things again. All will be revealed when it is our time."

"Brother Vasquez, we must leave quickly before we are discovered!" Pietro said, trembling with fear. He could not have looked any more anxious had his robe been on fire.

With a nod from Vasquez, the three men walked quickly to the back door and peered out into the empty marketplace. Certain the coast was clear, they closed the door behind them and Vasquez handed the key to the young priest to lock up. Pietro locked the door and scurried up the side street, not seeing a dark, robed figure step out of the shadows behind him.

Under the coarse woollen hood was the dour face of Brother Luke, who repeated curious Latin phrases while he hobbled across the cobblestones. He made sure the rear door of the cathedral was secured then continued on up the street, muttering in a disjointed intercourse with the Almighty, from whom he regularly received instructions. For God had appointed him to be His hands on earth, a responsibility he took very seriously.

10

THE RESCUE PARTY

Toronto, 1989

"Danny needs to try to bring his friend Joel back to his body, Dr. Walters. We have already been out of body once, when Danny played those chords into his friend's synthesizer rig. I stayed longer than him, and here's one curious piece of information—what he says was fifteen minutes here was a blink of an eye for me there … wherever *there* was."

"Mmm." The old man picked up one of his books. "Physics tells us that time becomes quite mischievous at the speed of light, so you see, it isn't the constant we think it is. How will you know when your friend's time is up from the other side?"

"That's a problem. Without the marking of time, somehow Danny must know where he's going so he doesn't fumble around aimlessly."

"Spirit guide, you'll need a spirit guide," the old man said confidently.

"What?" To Danny, Walters's words sounded completely out to lunch.

"I know this all seems a little bizarre to the uninitiated, but Elizabeth Kubler-Ross is the best example I can think of. She began her research into death and dying a complete non-believer in anything like extracorporeal consciousness, existence after death, Heaven, or even God, for that matter. After her research and studying dozens of documented cases, she could no longer argue with the mountains of evidence she had gathered. When her mind began to open up to the notion of possibilities exceeding our crude three-dimensional thinking, she soon began to sense that she was getting guidance from somewhere else. This guidance had love attached to it, she could feel it, and soon she became aware of entities, souls, others who were assisting her. Now she not only professes to have help from these spirit guides, but she also bloody well knows them by name! She believes that most all of us have these guides, and if you ask them for help they will assist you in what you need, though not necessarily in what you want.

"And you must be careful to know the difference between *want* and *need*. *Want* is more tethered to the physical universe, like the frivolity of fashion or the desire for material possessions and affluence. With no body, no cells that require a regular infusion of glucose to burn, no requirement of an acceptable form of clothing to make you fit in with your peers, *want* begins to give way to the more internal resonance of *need*. We might *want* a million dollars to ensure a material future we have no way of knowing we will ever see, when, in fact, we might *need* nothing to carry us to our physical death, which could wait mere seconds away. *Want* can potentially blind us to the inner voice. It is, after all, a building block of greed."

"I'm having a little trouble getting into the sermon, Doc. How do I get to Joel?"

"This is no sermon. Open your mind, boy. *How* you think might very well be the difference between success and failure in finding the entity you know as Joel." Dr. Walters looked at Alison, who was lost in thought, and waited for her to speak.

"So, he can't think like he does here, and he needs a spirit guide … tall order. It seems there is a potential for screwing this up on a monumental scale. How can he get back to his own body in time without any reference to time here?"

The three were once more surrounded by the silence of the puzzle until a light went on in the old man's head.

"Alison." Dr. Walters squinted in thought. "You said the ones on the other side were drawn to the sound of the chord. It obviously is heard on the other side. What if someone here played this musical information at regular intervals?"

"I don't know. How do we know he'd be close enough to hear the damn thing?"

More silence filled the room until Walters spoke again.

"Distance might be irrelevant in a state without physical laws. You may very well just need to keep your mind open to hearing the sound."

"So we might have an alarm bell, okay. That still leaves the spirit guide thing." Alison pondered. "What about these out-of-body experiences you've researched. Are spirit guides always waiting there for you?"

"I don't know, but often a spirit guide will be someone with a vested interest in you that you remain connected to by love and thought, like a recently departed relative or friend."

"I just lost my grandfather," Danny suggested.

"Did you love him? More importantly, did you know him well enough to say there was a relationship?" Dr. Walters asked respectfully.

"Not really. He was pretty much a loner, and the last few years he was right out of it."

"Then there is a chance that connecting with him could be difficult. How about you, Dr. Truman?"

"My mother's sister died of breast cancer three months ago. I loved her to the end. Actually, I was with her when she died. She was more of a mother to me than my mother, who never really liked me that much. My mother can't stand the sight of me. I embarrass her."

There was an awkward silence in the room and Alison began to blush, realizing that she had blurted out more than anyone needed to know. She took a deep breath and gathered herself in order to continue.

"My aunt, on the other hand, I'd have done anything for."

"Were you aware of any unusual feelings or evidences in her passing?" Dr. Walters asked as he walked down to the hall cupboard.

"Just that I still feel loved by her, as crazy as that sounds," Alison said, raising her voice as the old man disappeared behind the cupboard door. A moment later he reappeared wearing a coat and carrying his shoes.

"Well, no sense lollygagging around here. You have a few hours to find your friend, Alison, and you have a prime candidate for a guide on the other side."

"Me? Who said anything about me going?"

"Have you no interest in the answer to the biggest question of all time: Is there life after death? Would you not like to see if your aunt still exists?"

Alison pondered his last question for a moment. "Look, I don't even know where we went earlier. It was out of body, sure, but now you're saying it's the Happy Hunting Grounds?"

"The biggest mystery of all time, and you're not curious?" Dr. Walters countered. "And this young fella might not be able to do it without you."

Alison looked conflicted, then something broke free. "All right, I'll go, but if I don't see Aunt Babs and we don't have a guide, as Dr. Walters puts it, I'm coming back immediately."

"Sounds fair enough. Take me to this synthesizer thing and show me what to do. Someone's got to play that chord sound to keep you in touch with what time it is back here."

"You're not afraid?" Danny asked Dr. Walters, with a look of incredulity.

"Afraid of what? Dying? Hell, I'm almost dead now anyway. I've already passed the average male life span by a good six years. If Maggie is on the other side somewhere, then I'm just sitting in this station waiting for the damn train to stop for me. What the hell do I have to be afraid of?"

Alison smiled at the old man, then turned to Danny. "Well?"

"What if your aunt isn't there?" Danny asked fearfully.

"Then, like I said, we don't have to go anywhere. What have you got to lose?"

"What have I got to lose? I happen to have a pretty good future in the music business, I …" Danny saw his reflection in the glass of the picture window. "Fuck it, let's go. I'm surrounded by lunatics."

Danny headed to the door. The old man followed with Alison in tow.

"You know, young man, you would probably find the world a more pleasant place if your pants weren't so tight. Do your testicles hurt when you sit?" Dr. Walters asked with some sincerity.

"As a matter of fact, they do," Danny shot back.

"And you call *me* a lunatic." Walters followed with a chuckle and a wink at Alison, who was suppressing laughter.

The old man locked the door and carefully placed the key under a potted geranium. He turned for Alison's arm to help him down the stairs, but she stiffened up and pulled way. Danny saw the awkward moment and offered the old guy some assistance. He had no idea what Alison's issues were, but after screaming at him for touching her back in Joel's room and then blurting out how her mother couldn't stand the sight of her, it was looking a little too Freudian for him to solve any time soon.

After getting Dr. Walters belted into the back seat, the unlikely threesome drove away in silence, like a dysfunctional family on their way to church. Each one was lost in thought about what lay ahead.

For the old man it was sheer excitement—a possible key piece of evidence in the puzzle of his life's research, and the kind of proof one would never expect to get before death.

For Alison it was anticipation of seeing her Aunt Babs again. The death had been a hard experience for her—her first brush with the loss of a loved one, and not just any loved one. Babs had been her *only* loved one, as far as she was concerned.

Danny began to worry more about himself than Joel. He was afraid of not being able to get back. But then he kept coming back to why he'd agreed to go anyway—he probably wouldn't be missing much. Sure, the songwriting with Joel showed some promise, but he was nearly forty, a little burned out, and definitely a little too tired to learn new skills. There was his fiancé Karla Rose, she was nice enough, but as he searched himself he knew he didn't really love her. The girl deserved more than being an uninformed participant in an experiment doomed to fail … hell didn't everybody? The closer they got to the Airport Holiday Inn, the more at ease he became with whatever lay in store. He also now felt certain that it was his fault Joel was gone. He wasn't sure he could live with himself if he didn't at least try to get him back.

It was the old man who finally interrupted everyone's thoughts: "If I do this thing for you two and you get back safely, will you allow me a look?"

"And what if you see your wife and you don't want to come back? I'll just have another body in Joel's room, and people are going to think I'm some kind of Dr. Kevorkian angel of death. I don't know, man, how do you explain this out-of-body shit to anyone?" Danny's worries were real, and not without some merit.

"Granted, you don't want to be placed in a position of explaining this, `shit,' as you so poetically put it. We can accommodate that by creating circumstances to place you out of harm's way, Mr. Blum. I simply ask that you consider my request."

***

Joel's room was just as they'd left it. As soon as he entered, Danny felt forever changed by what he had experienced earlier in the day.

He wasn't sure why, but the weight of this new experience was almost depressing. He'd always thought this life was it. So what if this life *wasn't* the end of everything? Maybe it was the worst of it, and maybe that's what suicidal maniacs focused on before they slit their wrists.

He fired up Joel's synthesizer rack. LEDs began flashing, and dim green plasma display windows indicated the last presets Danny had entered. Everything was ready. Dr. Walters looked a little intimidated by it all, and Danny sensed the old man's anxiety.

"You don't have to play a note, Dr. Walters. The chord sequence is loaded into the computer. All you have to do is drag the mouse to the button marked `play' and click on it once. After the sequence has played, wait a few minutes, then move the mouse to 'stop,' click once, then move to the rewind icon, click once, and it will be ready to go again. Hit the 'play' button and repeat."

"Good lord, man, I don't understand a thing you've said."

"I'll show you, and you can write it down."

And so the crash course in music programming began, and it lasted a good five minutes until a few dry runs left the old man comfortable with all that was required of him. They all sat in silence then until Alison handed Danny's his headphones and grabbed a pair for herself. They sat on the edge of the bed while Dr. Walters took up his position in a chair, looking at the computer screen, going over what he was to do. When he was ready, he turned back to Alison.

"Are you thinking of her?" he inquired sweetly.

"Yes," Alison whispered.

"Are they thoughts of love?" he asked, seeking assurance. Alison nodded tearfully that it was so.

"Let's get on with this. Move the mouse to `play' and click once," Danny said impatiently.

The old man looked at them both. "Good luck, you two."

Alison smiled back, an affectionate smile. Danny's face was frozen in concentration.

Dr. Walters looked back to the computer screen, placed the mouse on `play,' as Danny had instructed, and clicked. The program appeared to run. He turned around just in time to catch Danny as he fell backwards onto the bed, eyes fixed.

"Hi," Alison said softly, her eyes full of tears.

"What are you doing, Alison? Didn't it work?" Dr. Walters inquired. But as he looked at Alison, waiting for an answer, he realized she wasn't talking to him, she was talking to someone he couldn't see. He caught her before she fell forward and gently laid her back on the bed. She was gone — eyes fixed, still breathing, but most definitely gone.

Elsewhere, 1989

Alison had let go. Incredulously, she was walking towards her Aunt Babs, who faced her a few yards away. She didn't know why she felt as though she was walking, because she was quite aware that her body lay on the bed behind her. She began to mentally document how she felt as she sought to understand.

The sensation of body was vestigial, a footprint in the moist clay of her spiritual being. Her appearance, she felt, was nothing more than how she thought of herself after so many years of looking in mirrors, combined with the image her Aunt Babs had of her. There was a lightness in her soul that she explored until she hit a wall of low self-esteem built one brick at a time over the years. It had been the plague of a plain girl whose mother viciously competed for every inch of credibility her daughter worked so hard to attain. But that once insurmountable obstacle began to crumble away, displaced by a warm glow of well-being.

Her aunt, who only three months ago had lain in her bed emaciated by cancer, whose skin had absorbed the pallor of faded green hospital walls, now exuded a lively radiance. They walked slowly towards one another. Her aunt's arms were open as she approached Alison, who halted at the thought of being touched. She froze, paralyzed, until she felt the warmth of her aunt's loving embrace.

It didn't upset her in the way she had expected. She responded tentatively, touching her aunt gingerly on the shoulders, and then Alison held her as hard as she could. There was a different feeling in her chest from her memory of hugging someone when she was a child. It had been so long, and yet somehow the doing of it wasn't as satisfying as she'd thought it might be. It seemed to her analytical mind that physical manifestation of human affection—simple human touch—was a power underestimated. But her realization didn't stop there. Maybe all thoughts without a physical manifestation, she surmised, were just that … thoughts, like every unassembled invention, every unrealized dream, or every untested theory.

Aunt Babs went through the motions of stroking Alison's hair while she spoke with a gentle, reassuring sound.

"There, there, dear. What troubles you?"

Alison looked up at her face. Babs was a good fifteen or twenty years younger than she remembered. There was just a strand or two of grey that striped her soft, shoulder-length black hair, framing warm, chocolate eyes. Alison just stared and wept.

"Oh Babs, I've missed you so."

"Mmm, mmm," came a reassuring tone. "I know you have felt my presence since I passed, Alison. There is always an immediate response when I think of you, which is quite often. It's so good to know one is loved. I thank you for enriching my existence so."

"I was pretty sure it was wishful thinking that made me feel good," Alison confessed.

"Wishful thinking works. Why are you here, Alison? It is not your time."

Alison turned around and saw Dr. Walters looking at her body laid out on the bed of the Holiday Inn hotel room, and then she saw Danny's lifeless figure next to hers. As she scanned the room, she saw an odd assortment of others milling around, and off in the distance a bright light silhouetted even more human-looking figures. Her mind snapped back.

"Oh my God … where's Daniel?"

"Who's Daniel, Alison? Ah, Daniel." Babs appeared to find Alison's thoughts.

"He should have entered this place with me."

"There's no *place* to speak of, only what you *think*. So think of the one you call Danny, and if he is thinking of you he will be with us."

Alison thought of him, but to no avail. She called his name a few times, but still nothing.

"Aunt Babs, I am here through artificial means to find someone."

"Artificial means? I see … Verhoevan's Resonance."

"Verhoevan? You know of the priest who wrote the manuscript?"

"I guess."

"What do you mean, you guess? How do you know about Verhoevan's Resonance, as you called it?"

"I just do. I heard the sound for the first time the other day. I think many did, and when I wondered what it was I became aware of Verhoevan. I think many people lost the joy of physical manifestation because of him. Some knew the torture of burning. The pain he caused others is a sadness that exists with him."

"Am I ever glad to see you!" The voice came from behind. Alison spun around to find Danny smiling at them both.

"Where did you get to?" Alison asked.

"I was with a group of smiling people who seemed to be welcoming me. They looked a little strange, and their faces looked sad when you called me. That's about it, and here I am. Is this your aunt?"

Alison turned to her aunt, who was looking off into the distance.

"Aunt Babs, how can we get to Danny's friend?"

"He must want to be found."

"Can you help us?" Danny asked.

"I am not sure. Follow me."

Alison and Danny fell in behind Babs and found themselves in an endless field of wheat. A fragrant breeze rippled across the soft tops of long golden stems. In the distance, a structure of beautiful, glistening stone with high columns, resembling the Acropolis of Athens, slowly came into focus.

"What is that?" Alison inquired.

"It is the imagining of many."

"What the hell does that mean?" Danny cracked.

Babs smiled tolerantly at him and gently answered, "Many thought of beauty in this manner, and so it is."

"So why are we going there?"

"There are Phorians there who may be able to help you."

"Phorians?"

"Structures like the one you see were manifested on earth because of their like. Their passion made things manifest in their time on the physical plane. Most of us think of things we would like, but never make them happen for one reason or another. We all have Phorian within us, but it takes many of us a long time to recognize our own talents, sometimes well beyond physical life. Phorians create for the joy and passion of creating. In this way they create for all, not only for themselves. They are painters, poets, architects, or perhaps simply a loving soul who plants a flower to add beauty to all of our lives. It is all about using whatever creative gifts one possesses and expressing them, but most importantly, sharing them."

"So is this Heaven?"

"It has been called that, and many other names. It is the continuation of the path to enlightenment. This is only one of an infinite number of possibilities."

"So why we are going to see the Phorians?" Alison asked.

"They wish to see you."

Babs's body language became almost meditative as they began to walk up the gentle steps towards the giant white columns near the entrance to the structure. There were people milling around like tourists, taking in the dimensions of the huge and beautiful shape. A woman walked towards Babs, touched her face, and gazed with admiration as she moved on.

"Who was that?" Danny whispered.

"Part of what I am. She was my grandmother. All she wanted from life was a granddaughter. She died before I was born. She had touched my face many times before I knew who she was, and why there was so much love for me in her touch. I am honoured and fortunate to be touched by her."

"Why doesn't she just talk to you?" Danny asked.

"She believes she is not ready. She suffered so much on the earthly plane, and she doesn't want to know me until she has grown beyond that which still troubles her."

"What the heck happened to my mom to have come from such love only to end up … well, you know?" Alison asked.

"You need to ask her in those words when you see her. Because you have asked such a question here, it may have entered your mother's consciousness, so now she will be thinking about it. I can tell you there is a longing in her to love. She needs help to find it."

At the top of the steps Danny stopped and turned to look back over the rippling fields of wheat that stretched out to a distant horizon. He felt as though he was breathing air impregnated with the pleasure of floral blooms. An undeniable feeling of warmth cascaded over him as he heard a voice from behind.

"I am truly sorry about your friend, it causes the both of us pain." The man's voice was soft and knowing. Danny turned to face a handsome, fair-haired couple smiling at him with some familiarity. The woman's wispy blond hair fell on the shoulders of a long white dress. She looked approvingly at Daniel with his mother's expression when she would say, "How's my lovely boy?" The fragrant scent of roses emanated from her as she looked lovingly at Daniel with her beautiful green eyes, and then to the gentleman whose arm she held.

"Uh … thanks," Danny responded sheepishly with a smile before turning to Alison and Babs, who stood waiting for him.

"How did he know about Joel?" Danny wondered.

"He has some connection to you and your journey," Babs answered dryly as she focused on her task.

Danny turned and looked at the couple and smiled again. They bowed politely and moved on.

The Great Hall before him was almost as endless as the wheat fields. Statuary punctuated breathtakingly beautiful canvasses of all shapes and sizes, depicting everything from pastoral landscapes and human portraiture to flights of architectural fantasy. The structure hummed with passionate inquiry, debate, and laughter from every corner. Danny attempted to catch up with Alison and her aunt, but he stopped dead in his tracks, slack-jawed, as a startlingly beautiful nude woman paraded across his path and on through the crowd. She was aware of those who stopped to look at her and responded with a slight bow of gratitude for their appreciation.

"Danny!" Alison called with a tone of impatience.

Danny's eyes remained on the woman's exposed backside as he headed sideways towards the sound of Alison's voice. When the nude woman was out of sight, he finally turned to catch a glare of disapproval in Alison's expression.

"Did you see that gorgeous woman?" he said, with more breath than voice.

"That is a brilliant Phorian artist," Babs responded.

"Do they all look as pretty as she does?"

"Actually, that was a male Phorian of great skill who presents himself in various female configurations to see which one gathers the most appreciation. He has been engaged in this study as long as I have been aware of him. It is rumoured that he is about to paint again—there's much excitement about the possibility."

Babs headed towards a tall archway that led into another chamber, with Danny and Alison in tow. When they passed through the arch, she held up her hand, signalling them to stop. They were in a massive amphitheatre that circled one hundred and eighty degrees around them. It was almost empty except for a woman standing, facing a box seat at the far end in front of them. An elderly couple and a young boy sat in what looked like a royal box. The woman fell to her knees, weeping uncontrollably.

"Why?" she wept.

"Because he is not yours to have," the elderly woman said lovingly. "His spirit no longer appears in the image you conjure, and as you continually summon this image you disturb him from his passion. He must be allowed to create … he is on the brink of a realization that will move his spirit forward."

The boy sitting next to the elderly couple began to blur to the eye until his image became transparent and then was gone. The woman wept uncontrollably and turned to leave the room. As she passed, Danny detected a foul odour and caught a glimpse of her face. It was distorted with such anguish and unrest that it rattled him to the core. She walked out into the Great Hall and was given a wide berth by those in her path. In a few strides she vanished into thin air.

"What was that all about?" Alison inquired sympathetically.

"She held the boy back from his potential in the physical realm through her possessiveness. I believe she was his biological mother and thinks the giving of physical life entitles her to have some claim to his soul in perpetuity."

"Sounds like a bad recording contract," Danny quipped.

"Where did that little boy go?" Alison asked.

"He was never here. His mother is now only able to conjure up the image she holds of him, which interferes with his existence wherever he is. She was summoned here to be informed of the damage she is doing. But I fear her concerns for herself remain greater. We'd better be quiet," Babs whispered. "The sitting Phorians look at us."

"Sitting?" Danny asked.

"The ones whose turn it is to sit on council," Babs replied, without any appearance of speech.

Danny and Alison turned their eyes to the elderly couple. The woman signalled them to approach with a blink of her gentle eyes. As they went farther into the amphitheatre, Danny looked up to see there were many Phorians in the higher seats around them. There was an intricate relief of human figures sculpted into the bleached white marble wall that separated the floor from the seating. Ornately carved high-backed seats, richly upholstered in deep-green velvet, circled the floor.

Each seat was carved differently, which Alison presumed somehow identified those who would sit in them, like a coat of arms. The seats reached up in rows towards the upper walls, which were festooned with tapestries in brilliant colours. The ceiling was a complex grid of gold-framed paintings of sky, but on closer inspection he realized that the clouds were moving and the images constantly changed, like giant computer screen savers.

Some of the Phorians were engaged in discussion that stopped as Danny, Alison, and Babs walked across the floor. Even more were entering the hall from side chambers. They moved quietly towards their respective seats, slowly filling the amphitheatre, and all looked inquisitively at Danny and Alison as though they were expected. When they reached the foot of what looked like a royal box, the elderly-looking gentleman spoke first.

"We have been looking forward to your visit. Welcome." The tone of his voice was surprisingly spirited, and the words were followed by a thundering noise that was unnerving until Danny and Alison realized it was the sound of the others banging the arms of their seats, like sitting members of an English-style parliament.

"So, you have entered here through Verhoevan's Resonance and seek the other who preceded you. Who brings these two before us?" The elderly woman stated her question affectionately. She appeared to know Babs, but she was engaged in some kind of formality.

"One who belongs, and responded in love," Babs offered.

"Then we thank you and welcome your presence," the elderly man replied.

The room fell to silence as all eyes focused on an empty seat twenty feet to the left of the royal box. Soon a figure in a crudely woven brown robe began to materialize. His face was wizened and displayed an uncomfortable expression.

"It is good to see you again, Verhoevan. We have missed your counsel and thank you for agreeing to join us," the elderly woman greeted him.

"He's been hiding with his guilt," someone called from higher up.

"As does many an honest soul for a time, and as you will, as you come to understand the pain of your remark, my friend," the old man replied to the silent acknowledgment of many. "We have asked a kindred spirit to join us here by common request, to which he has graciously consented."

"Thank you, old friend." Verhoevan smiled, then turned to Alison and Danny and stared at them sternly. "You who have crossed and seek the one who has crossed before you, do you wish to return to physical form?"

"Yes, we do," Alison answered in no uncertain terms.

Verhoevan looked at Danny and waited.

"Uh … I do as well, sir," Danny choked. He sensed that all who appeared in that forum had to make their intentions clear, and that no one had the right to speak for another. In that thought, Verhoevan nodded as if to say, "You are correct."

"Then you are in a precarious position. Do you know of the time from where you come and how little it relates to where you are now?"

"We have a friend who will sound the Resonance, as it is called, at four-hour intervals," Alison offered.

There was a hum of thought in the room, and Verhoevan looked surprised but also somewhat unnerved.

"Clever, but dangerous. What will stop him from crossing?"

"He has promised not to place the devices we use to hear the Resonance over his ears."

Verhoevan nodded in approval of Danny's words. He seemed pleased with the assurance that more who didn't belong wouldn't be crossing over for the moment.

Danny continued, "How do we find our friend?"

"He will have to want to be found," Verhoevan replied.

"We were told that Phorians here could assist us in this manner. Can't you summon him here, as you did Mr. Verhoevan?" Danny asked.

There was complete silence as he scanned the room waiting for an answer. Verhoevan spoke softly.

"We don't know your friend or where he may be. My associates in this chamber all know me, and so could make a request of me, to which I chose to respond. Such is possible if and only if one knows whom they seek.

Alison entered the fray. "We have been told that the Phorians here are an illustrious group of evolved creative thinkers. Am I to believe that in such a group there are no other options to discuss?"

"You will show respect!" Verhoevan stated firmly.

Alison's feisty streak kicked in. "I trust that respect is earned in this place, not given blindly. How can I respect that which I do not know? How can I respect one who has created the predicament in which one of us now finds himself? Are you expecting a posture of gratitude?"

There was a hum of words in the room, sprinkled with a light dusting of laughter. Babs looked a little shaken at her niece's rudeness, but Alison stood her ground.

The old woman spoke first, and with great kindness in her voice. "You can respect the one who has caused you danger by feeling his remorse, and understanding the extraordinary creativity inherent in that which no one else has created before or since. You can also respect him by not being so simplistic as to affix all blame where only a portion of it lies, for you are here of your own accord."

Alison liked her rationale. "I couldn't respect remorse of which I was not aware. I am sorry if my ignorance has been hurtful. I can, however, respect the monumental achievement of ingenuity that discovered the Resonance, and I certainly wouldn't wish to blame another for any choice I have made. My question however stands. Are there no other options?"

The room began to hum with discussion. One man stood looking at the royal box until the elderly gentleman acknowledged him. Then he bowed and sat down. A woman on the opposite side stood and did the same. A handful more followed suit, all focused on the royal box for a brief moment, until the elderly gentleman smiled and spoke.

"There are many amongst us who delight in your spirit. We look forward to your entrance into these chambers when your passage is clear and your own passionate inquiry has born more fruit. Verhoevan now has our thoughts and has agreed to be with you until such time as you feel his remorse and find a way to the one you seek." The elderly gentleman looked at Babs and nodded in the direction of the entrance. The message was clear.

"We are to leave," Babs said softly to Alison and Danny.

As they turned to go, Verhoevan stood waiting for them at the entrance to the chamber in the archway. Danny turned around to see Verhoevan's image slowly dissipating in the seat he had occupied moments before. A man with a serious expression stopped on his way in and looked at Alison and Danny. He bowed slightly and smiled.

"Welcome, Daniel and Alison, I look forward to our next encounter." His face cracked a knowing smile, then he brushed by them across the floor into the chamber to a loud rumble of approval. It was clear all in the chamber were excited to see the petitioner, whoever he was.

Verhoevan led Alison and Danny to a grouping of marble benches that surrounded an architectural blueprint of a modern office tower. He looked at the blueprint, then huffed in disapproval as he sat down.

"It has height and that is all it informs us of. Its creator has gone back to think of something that answers to more than the memory of economic want."

"Wow, that's something of a value judgment, isn't it? I would have thought a higher plane would have evolved past the ignorance of subjectivity," Alison observed.

Verhoevan looked at her curiously, then chuckled. It was a playful laugh of acceptance that demonstrated a love of debate.

"The subjective can be both informed and uninformed. If we possess no values, we have nothing. For what are our values if not that which defines us, and what defines us if not our own honest subjective view, the way light refracts through our individual prisms? The knack of it might be how much light we allow to enter our prisms. However, young lady, to create merely to answer to cost and potential profit simply has no value to those without physical need. There is enough evidence in the physical world to support an understanding that profit alone has limited value there, as well."

As Verhoevan spoke, Alison became aware that Babs was gone, and she looked around the Great Hall to no avail. Verhoevan stopped until her attention returned, then continued.

"Your suggestion that this is a higher plane is an uninformed supposition. This is merely a continuation. The adjective 'higher' is appropriate only in as much as there are those achieving greater enlightenment in this state of being. There are others working at levels lower than some achieve on the physical plane. Our earthly religions have imagined many fantastic visions of perfection to which the faithful are promised entrance."

"So Heaven is a lie?" Danny interjected.

"Not at all, the very idea of Heaven stems from an inward knowing of some kind of continuation beyond an earthly existence. How it continues has been the subject of conjecture for poets and scribes, and that question has been exploited by religions to their own ends."

"So where is Joel?" Danny asked impatiently.

"You are so like another I know of your line, Daniel. Your friend is around, but you must be cautious."

"What do you mean?" Danny was taken aback.

"There are those whose lives were wrapped in the summoning of religious rapture who sold metaphor as absolute truth on earth." Verhoevan sensed an incoming thought from Alison and stopped. He nodded in the affirmative as she asked her question.

"Fundamentalism?" Alison inquired, dumbfounded. "It exists here, in the face of all the knowledge that surrounds them?"

"Why not? It is a consciousness well trained in the physical realm to seek no more than a singular answer to all that is, which makes every thought outside of that answer of no interest, invisible or wrong, a threat … heretical, blasphemous, et cetera. This germ of human frailty was brought back like a virus from the physical world by priests, rabbis, ministers, mullahs, gurus, politicians, the wealthy, right down to the most common of poor souls who simply learned to feed on the insecurities of others to empower themselves."

"So how can they hurt us?"

"When one submits to dogma, one is often led to fear that which is outside of that body of thought. There are those who are ready to find and capitalize on well-imbedded fear. We call them Soms."

"Who was the distinguished-looking individual who entered the chamber to loud approval as we were leaving?" Alison asked.

"Ah, interesting connection of thought. Bernard is a wonderful and very old Phorian emissary. His passion takes him to other places, to free those who remain controlled by the chains of dogma and abused by the Soms."

"So, if we try to go after Joel, these Soms will try to stop us?" Danny asked, trying to understand.

"Oh yes, most certainly. They will mislead and do everything in their power to stop you and your friend from returning to an earthly existence with the knowledge you now possess. Such thought might plant seeds that could eventually be the downfall of their power. They want your energy, it is as a drug to them." Verhoevan looked at Alison, who shook her head in disgust.

"So we are just as stupid and dangerous to ourselves here as we were on what was supposed to be the more crude existence on earth."

"Ah, the higher plane supposition again. Well, yes … and no. There is an infinite potential for enlightenment here, and a very limited version in the physical realm, but …" Verhoevan smiled.

"So how do we deal with them?" Alison asked.

"Soms can project all kinds of suffering on you, and it will feel real. They will invite you in the guise of friendship, smile as a friend, while seeking to damn your soul to pain and suffering."

"Follow me or burn in Hell?" Alison quipped.

A darkness came over Verhoevan's face, and his eyes seemed to pierce the inner reaches of Alison and Danny simultaneously.

"Do not take the Soms lightly. All you know as *self* can be lost. The old metaphor of Hell is applicable. There are places in your consciousness where one can be trapped until the very energy that is soul is bled dry. They, in essence, will feed on your energy until all that is you is spent."

"So how can we defend ourselves?" Alison went with the flow.

"Remember who you are and fear not. Reality in this place is, after all, of your own construction."

"Yeah, so what is this place, then? I sure didn't construct it," Danny argued, weary of the chase.

"You are here. How did you get here if not by your will? In this manner you have created the circumstances that define where you are. Others of like mind who wish to be here give further body to the thought of this place. This place is merely one idea. As more invested in this particular idea, its appearance acquired greater substance. Listen to your inner voice with a good measure of the well-pronounced skepticism in your lineage, Daniel."

"So what now?" Alison asked.

"Go back the way you came and think of Joel. But think also of who you are and where you crossed. This memory must remain present at all times."

"That's it. That's the sum total of the thoughts your associates in the chamber gave you to help us?" Danny said, with obvious disappointment.

"It is all I am allowed to give you. Your reality is yours to conceive. It will not be conceived for you; there is no growth on that path. I have armed you with the seeds of what you need. They will grow if you care for them."

Verhoevan walked Alison and Danny to the top of the steps and wished them well before his image dissipated into thin air.

"Man oh man, thanks for nothing." Danny started down the stairs at a fair pace. Alison stood concentrating and in an instant appeared in front of him.

"How the hell did you do that?"

"I watered one of Verhoevan's seeds. *Reality is of your own construction,* remember? I visualized myself in front of you and here I am. Amazing!" As soon as Alison spoke Danny observed her image begin to slowly dissipate.

"Alison, what is happening, what…?" Danny was talking to nothing. She was gone.

11

TEMPTATION'S WAY

Hamburg
March, 1848

A few weeks had passed, and Harding's word was indeed his bond: there had not been one word uttered about of the occurrence in the cathedral.

As for Matthias, his curiosity since crossing over with Vasquez ate away at him until it dwarfed any fears he had of the unknown. He had been outside of his own body briefly, and his curiosity was piqued.

He felt like an idiot for having expected to meet Saint Peter or the Virgin Mary in clouds surrounded by angels, and so his religious upbringing began slowly to unravel. His own foolish acceptance of tall tales posing as absolute truth began to crack as he searched within. On the other side, he had felt an incredible peace that he could only identify as similar to his love for Anna. But he needed more answers. There had been no time to see his father or mother … if they were indeed there at all. These were things of which he could not speak without being presumed mad. But one thing was emerging as a certainty: he wanted to cross over again to get more answers.

Vasquez noticed immediately that there was something different in Matthias. There was an introspection in the boy that he had never seen, and it worried him.

***

Matthias managed to put his spiritual turmoil aside in order to find the necessary nerve one day to go to an address that he, quite frankly, had hoped never to see again. He stood outside, afraid to enter, until he thought of the poor wretches who worked within. He took a deep breath and walked into Frau Hoffman's lair.

"Well, well, if it isn't Matthias Dopp," her voice snarled from a table in a dark corner, where she sat grinding an herb with a wooden mortar and pestle.

"Making a little something to slip into some unsuspecting soul's ale, Frau Hoffman?" Matthias smiled.

"You stole my new girl, and now you would mock how I attempt to make a living?" she snapped as she stood, pulling a knife from her apron.

"No need for your knife, Frau Hoffman, unless you wish to kill any chance of the repayment of her family's debt."

"You have the money on your person?" The woman's voice was more demure now as she slowly sat back down. "Perhaps you have time for an ale . . . or one of my girls? We do have some new lovelies since your last visit here, Herr Dopp." She pulled the neck of her dress down, exposing an inordinate amount of cleavage, and smiled, causing Matthias to feel slightly nauseated.

"That wouldn't be wise for one who has lost his purse to you once before."

"If it is wisdom you profess, Herr Dopp, why would you pay a whore's debt?"

"Because she asked me to, and because one should obey one's wife, shouldn't one?"

Frau Hoffman put the mortar and pestle down and slowly looked up at Matthias in disbelief.

"Why would a man of your position marry a common…?" She halted her thought and moved on to what really interested her. "So how is it you'll repay what is owed me if you carry no purse?"

"I need to know where her family is. I have been to their old address only to find it burned to the ground. You wouldn't know anything about that, would you?" Matthias's voice sounded as suspicious as, indeed, were the circumstances of the fire at the Grubers' home.

"Do you want to know the whereabouts of Anna's family, or do you want to find out who started a fire in a shit-hole?"

"The family… if you'd be so kind." Matthias insisted.

"After the debt is paid in full. Come back when you have money, if *you* would be so kind, Herr Dopp … good day to you." Frau Hoffman's tone was one of smug superiority.

"And to you, Frau Hoffman. I am sorry we could not do business on the only terms acceptable to me." Matthias turned and headed out the door. He could always come back, but he'd played Hoffman well. She jumped to her feet and ran after him.

"They have fled to the south, I am told … to Munchen."

Matthias was already heading down the street, but he stopped and turned. "And this is all you know?" he asked

"I swear," Frau Hoffman said, with the most sincere face she could muster.

"I will send a man tomorrow to repay the debt."

Matthias turned and picked up his pace. He would never see the woman again, but she would be repaid to end all claim and threat of vengeance.

***

Matthias sent correspondence to some business associates, and also sent a man from his mill that Jorge Hacker knew to be very familiar with the town of Munchen, all to begin the search for Franz Gruber, his wife, and their two children, Anna's siblings, Wilhelm and Greta. Vasquez, for his part, sent a letter to his Franciscan brothers in Munchen who might prove more successful if the Gruber family had maintained their allegiance to the Catholic Church. They would be found, of this Matthias was certain.

There had been one letter from Anna that arrived on a merchant ship via England. The reading of it made his longing for her unbearable at times, and he would often hole up and read it over and over, smelling the paper she had trickled her perfume over before putting pen to ink. Her writing and command of English was much improved, revealing what a quick study she was and the nurturing that surely came from Mrs. Harding, of whom she spoke with some affection.

It was a sunny afternoon when Matthias asked Vasquez to enter the office and close the door behind him.

"I have received an exceptional offer for Dopp Textiles, our warehouses, factory, and even my father's house," he announced.

"And what of those whose families you feed?"

"I believe they will be in good hands. The buyer, as it turns out, is a wealthy relative of Jorge Hacker's. He is a godly man, and one who believes part of the reason we prosper so is because of the loyalty our employees hold in response to their fair treatment."

"Sounds promising."

"I would relinquish power gradually, over five years, and only when satisfied my people were being treated fairly. There is also more profit to be made in financing the buyer."

Vasquez started to laugh in approval of the young Dopp, but then other thoughts occurred to him. Matthias sensed them immediately.

"If I were to sell, what would you do, Vasquez? Would you go back to the priesthood?"

Vasquez had been dreading this piece of the future he had known would intersect his path sooner or later.

"Matthias, I am afraid I no longer believe what the Church requires of me. Verhoevan's work has, of course, placed more than honest doubt in my mind. Although I see value in some areas of the Christian metaphor, I can no longer espouse it as the one and only truth. The flock looks to the shepherd for a certainty I can no longer profess."

"I know the doubt of which you speak, my friend. So what will you do? Will you marry?"

"I don't know. I don't think so. I confess … I have no desire for women."

"You don't mean…?" Matthias's face betrayed his prejudice.

"Would you think less of me if I was what you think I am?"

"I … well … I'm not sure, my friend. My religious upbringing would have me think less, but I …" Matthias stumbled.

"Let me say only this, and it is something I have told no one. I have loved another man as you love Anna, though not physically. I have loved him nonetheless, and now he is …" Vasquez broke down, and Matthias was taken completely off guard. This was a strong man, a man who had saved his life, who had helped him get back on his feet. How could such a man be reduced to tears?

"Your love is dead?"

"No, merely gone from here. He has passed from this life." Vasquez sniffed, wiping his nose on the sleeve of his robe.

"The same way as my father?" Matthias asked.

Vasquez responded to Matthias's question with a nod in the affirmative.

"Did he leave of his own choice?" Matthias continued.

Vasquez's face grew pained. "Yes and no," he muttered.

"What does that mean?"

"He loved his work and was seeking more knowledge on the other side. He meant to return. I was tending to a sick friend in Köln and returned too late. They said Verhoevan had an illness …" There was a hard sarcasm in his voice.

"What illness?"

"That's what the Brothers called it, but I knew better. It was as you have witnessed … breathing … eyes wide open, but no presence of soul. With fear of disease as an excuse, a fearful old soul hid Verhoevan's body in the tomb of a nobleman in the cathedral. I managed to locate and open the crypt, but what I found gave me a heavy pain I will carry in my shattered heart until my own demise. Verhoevan had returned into his body only to discover he was entombed. His back had bled through the shredded cloth of his robe from attempting to push the lid off of his stone prison. I found him face down on the dead body beneath him, his body still warm. I was but moments too late.

"Then I heard people gathering, upstairs in the sanctuary, for the dedication ceremony in memory of your mother. When I heard the Resonance, I realized to my horror that the Brothers had delivered the wrong manuscript to the organist for the dedication ceremony. By the time I made my way up to the sanctuary, it was too late, all were gone from body. The work of Verhoevan that was to be performed in memory of your mother will never be heard. It was such a beautiful inspiration of love."

The priest's face was lost in the reliving of his greatest sorrow and he began to weep in short bursts. It was an odd, painful sound, one that stirred familiar and haunting feelings in Matthias that slowly came into focus. He had never heard Vasquez cry … but he had.

"That night in the cathedral, the only sound I heard was weeping. It is a sound that comes to me in the dreams of my father's death. I thought that it was coming from the paintings and statues of the holy ones. It was a weeping I had never heard before … it was you!"

The priest acknowledged the charge with a tearful sigh. "Yes. I wept and prayed for his well-being at the tomb that held his mortal remains."

Matthias mind was absorbing all Vasquez had said. In the loss of his father, in his deep love of Anna … in these private places, he felt the priest's pain.

"I am so sorry, my friend." Matthias walked over and put his hand on Vasquez's shoulder. "I will do all I can to make sure you have enough to live in comfort. Will you go to your sister in Magdeburg?"

The priest entertained the question for a brief moment. "I am not so sure she'd welcome me if I returned as an ordinary man who has shed so much of her God and the God of my fraternal oaths."

"I understand – and I'll stand you passage to the Americas."

"You would travel with *an abomination in the eyes of God*?"

"Well … I wouldn't travel with … any abomination … certainly not a great big abomination, but I could find room for a stubby little abomination who has saved my life in ways beyond generosity or fair play."

Vasquez looked up at Matthias as a grin spread across his face. "So I'm a stubby little abomination, am I?" he chuckled.

Matthias grinned back, and the two started a laugh that soon turned to uncontrollable hysterics. It was the laugh of undeniable friendship.

"I have much to do before the day is gone, my friend," Matthias reminded himself.

"True words. I will see to the last run for the day." The priest thumped off into mill with the audible squeak of his complaining sandals. "Stubby little abomination … ha!" he cackled over his shoulder.

Matthias waited long enough for Vasquez to reach the second floor looms before closing the door and opening the false panel in the office wall. There he found the priest's leather satchel, containing Verhoevan's manuscript. The need to satisfy his curiosity had eaten away at him to the point of obsession. Would he feel his father's presence and say the proper goodbye of which he had been robbed? Would he see his mother? He had returned safely once before, why could he not again? His promise to Vasquez was that he would never ask him to cross again, and he would keep it.

***

At the cathedral, Pietro waited nervously in the shadows. He was a budding young musician who had been under the tutelage of one of Hamburg's finest pianists, and of course, Verhoevan. He stepped out from behind a pillar as Matthias passed.

"Where is Brother Vasquez?" he said firmly, scaring the daylights out of Matthias.

"Must you sneak up on a man so? He will join me later. Now come, we must move quickly."

"This is not right. He should be here. What if something should go wrong?"

"Please, Pietro, spare me your fear. There is enough fear in the world without yours. Did your learned Brother Vasquez not bring me here before?" The monk nodded yes. "Well, the business we had together I need to complete, while he tends to another matter. Hurry, time is of the greatest importance."

The young monk reached into a leather pouch around his waist and pulled out clumps of wax and cotton that he began to force into his ears as he followed Matthias. At the organ, Matthias handed him the manuscript.

"You are quite a musician I am told, Pietro."

"Enough of one for what is required. I study and am allowed to play the great organ for a couple of simple masses each week."

"Does the wax and cotton stop the sound?"

"No, but my own breathing becomes loud enough to serve as a distraction so I am not drawn away. Are you familiar with the bellows?"

"I remember what to do."

"Well, good luck to us both."

The young man of the cloth disappeared up the three spiral steps from the bellows chamber to the organ. Matthias began to pump the bellows as instructed. Pietro, for his part, finished packing his ears with the wax and cotton compound, then sat behind the three manual keyboards and opened the manuscript to the central page, where the musical notation was located. He perused the fingering of each one of the four chords, all of which required both hands. Matthias heard the soft thump of ivory hitting felt gaskets as Pietro pull out the selected stops that sat in two rows above the top keyboard. Matthias braced his back against the wall of the narrow corridor as he pumped the bellows with all of his might.

The first massive chord hit, followed immediately by the remaining three. Matthias stopped pumping as the notes began to bleed together in the magnificent reverberation of the great Hamburg Cathedral. As they rang off instead of decaying, once more the harmonic structure of the combined, massive chord began its metamorphosis. Beginning with the most obvious harmonic structures and partials, it moved into the more exquisite, complex combinations that appeared to create melody as they were exposed and exponentially increased in speed to an almost unbearable climax.

Matthias didn't feel his body fall. As the sound dissipated, Pietro flew off the bench of the organ and ran down the steps to the bellows. Matthias lay crumpled on the floor, eyes wide open and fixed. The monk called to him but Matthias was unable to respond. He simply wasn't there.

***

Some two hours later, back at the Dopp house, Vasquez began to worry. Matthias was late for a dinner that sat drying out in the kitchen. Harding saw the look on his face and, as usual, addressed the problem head on.

"Where is Matthias?"

"I don't know."

"Then why do you look so worried, my friend?"

"I am not sure."

"Does it have anything to do with that of which I am sworn not to speak?"

"I don't think so."

Vasquez's tone worried Harding. It was as if the subject that was not to be discussed was a possible option Vasquez was indeed mulling over. The two men sat in silence for a good ten minutes more until a knock at the door sent Harding flying out of his seat. The door was opened by the time Vasquez caught up with him. Pietro stood there, shaking nervously.

"It has been too long, Brother Vasquez. I wish you had not sent him alone."

"What?" Vasquez shot back. "Sent who alone?"

"The fact that he is not here is the answer to that question!" Harding stated loudly. "Where is he, boy?"

Pietro looked at Vasquez and tears streamed down his face.

"Oh God, no!"

Vasquez flew out the door. Harding grabbed his long coat and followed. Young Pietro, for his part, tried to offer an explanation as he gasped for air, stumbling to keep up with Harding and Vasquez.

"He said, he, he was to finish what he started the last time we used Verhoevan's manuscript. He said you had another matter to—"

"What is done is done. He has taken advantage of your trusting nature."

"What has happened, Vasquez?" Harding demanded.

"I will tell you once I have assessed the situation myself."

The two men hurried down the cobblestone street with young Pietro in tow until they were at the back door of the cathedral. The door remained ajar, as Pietro had left it in his haste to find Vasquez. As they walked down the corridor, they could see candlelight ahead, then the sound of voices echoing in the sanctuary.

"Anyone with you and Matthias, Pietro?" Harding asked.

"No, sir."

"Then who is in the sanctuary?"

"Indeed," Vasquez worried.

"Halt!" a voice shouted from the altar. Vasquez looked up to see a groundskeeper with one of the parish priests, Brother Nicolas.

"Gentlemen, is everything all right? We discovered the rear door open and entered to make sure no one was defiling the house of God." Vasquez spoke authoritatively, then turned to Pietro and whispered, "You will say nothing." Pietro nodded sheepishly.

"Brother Vasquez, someone has been at the organ. I found this manuscript. It is the work of Verhoevan," Nicolas said, somewhat uncomfortably.

"That was stolen from my possession earlier today, Brother Nicolas. Let me inspect it to see if it has been damaged."

Nicolas responded reluctantly to the authority of his senior but seemed conflicted. As Vasquez pretended to be inspecting the manuscript, he prodded for more information.

"Is there anything else out of order here? Has anything been stolen or any damage done?"

"We have only just arrived. Herr Wentland came to get me after he was startled by someone playing the great organ at this hour and found the rear door open."

"Mmm, well, you two go to the front of the cathedral, inspect the shrines, and work your way back. I will take these men with me to inspect the lower levels and work our way back up. Be thorough, someone might still be here."

Nicolas deferred to the authority of Vasquez and set off with the groundskeeper, but he kept looking back at the priest with a worried expression.

Vasquez prodded Harding and Pietro to continue the charade.

"Come with me. We will split up on the lower levels."

Vasquez grabbed some large utility candles and lit one from the flame of a burning candle on the altar step. Once out of earshot, he turned to Pietro and stared, awaiting instruction. It finally struck Pietro what Vasquez wanted, and he led the way.

"He's down below by the bellows."

Moments later candlelight flickered in the bellows chamber where Pietro had last seen Matthias. He was gone.

"But … but he was here. Perhaps he has gone home."

"Were his eyes open wide with no consciousness, as those who were burned?" Harding shot back.

"Why yes. He—" Pietro began.

"Silence, Pietro!" Vasquez cut him off. "I see you have been inquiring into unspoken subjects, Captain Harding. If what I think has happened, we should move off from here and return at another time."

"And what of Matthias?"

"If he is not at the mill or at home within the hour, he is in danger. Pietro, have you ever seen Brother Nicolas conversing regularly with anyone at the monastery."

"No, sir."

"Hmm …what about in the dining hall?" Vasquez continued

"He always sups with Brother Luke," Pietro answered dutifully.

An expression of slow realization came across Vasquez's face. "This is not good. We must finish a search charade for the benefit of Brother Nicolas then leave quickly. Pietro, you must not say a thing or we may never see Matthias again. Captain Harding, please play along and I will explain everything back at the Dopp house."

"Is he dead?"

"Not if we are successful this night. No more chatter, we may be heard by those who could very well be in league against us," Vasquez whispered.

Harding's face held the frustrated anger of ignorance imposed through oath. What he was sworn not to discuss may have taken the life of Matthias, whom he viewed as a son. It was the helplessness of the situation that angered him. He had no choice but to go along with Vasquez.

The three men pretended to call loudly to one another as though they were conducting a search, then headed back up towards the altar, where Nicolas and Herr Wentland waited. Once it was agreed that the intruders must have fled, the men walked towards the back door, where it was closed and locked. Nicolas instructed Herr Wentland to have all entrances watched during the night.

Once out of the square, Harding confronted Vasquez, with no room for negotiation.

"I swore an oath on what I believe is a matter related to the condition of Matthias. Now I am owed an explanation, and it had better be as detailed as all the information you possess."

Vasquez looked at Harding and nodded in agreement. It was decided to let Pietro return to the monastery. Vasquez would say nothing to Harding until they were in the privacy of the Dopp home. It was there, over a brandy as he warmed himself by the fire, that the sturdy priest spoke.

"What I am about to tell you will sound fantastic, like the musings of a madman, but I must assure you it is truth."

Harding sat, unwilling to believe what he was being told. It destroyed all that he held dear as to the way of things. He kept insisting to Vasquez that there was another explanation. His mind would admit that, indeed, the sound of the great organ might be able to render one unconscious, but anything one returned with was but the stuff of dreams. He was infuriated that Vasquez had led the boy to believe he could communicate with his dead father by means of this fantastic tale. To Harding's way of thinking, this was simply exploitive of a young man's grief.

With his efforts to convince Harding stopped at every turn, Vasquez took another tack.

"Captain Harding, I will try to convince you no more. It is clearly a waste of our time. I will say only this. We are imperfect mortals and therefore cannot possess the knowledge of all things. You have no proof to refute my claims, so might we agree that I, and the knowledge I possess, might be the most informed way of trying to get Matthias back, whether or not you believe what I am saying?"

Harding thought long on the words of Vasquez. To agree to them would hold a modicum of defeat in all that he held as terra firma. He didn't know where to go with his thoughts and could only look to his heart.

"I will do anything to assist you. Not because I believe your tall tale, but because I believe you love Matthias and have shown him nothing but generosity. These are not the actions of a sinister purpose. As an honest man, I think you believe what you have told me, so I am yours to command to get Matthias back."

"Good."

"So where is he?"

"I fear his body is buried in a crypt below the cathedral."

"Which one?"

"I don't know."

"You don't know! So what do we do?

"We make a few educated guesses by looking at the lids of the sarcophagi. There will be signs of recent disturbance—melted candle wax, ground stone dust, footprints. It's how I found a dear friend, and I fear the same lunatic may be responsible for the disappearance of Matthias."

"Brother Luke, the one Nicolas sups with?"

"You are an observant man, Captain Harding." Vasquez nodded in approval.

"I am in charge of a fair-sized crew. I simply watch and listen. So, Vasquez, how are we to get in an out of a guarded cathedral?"

"The same way I got Matthias out the night they would have burned him."

"And if we are successful in locating Matthias's body?"

"We take his body to a safe place, and then I must try to find his consciousness."

"And how will you do that?"

"Why, through the Resonance, of course."

"Oh, of course," Harding said, mockingly.

"You will need your oldest boots and clothes, and we'd best have the assistance of a few of your most trusted crewmen."

***

An hour later, Harding and three armed men stood at the mouth of the sewer that emptied into the harbour. At Vasquez's instruction the men tied off rags he had brought with him to cover their mouths and noses in order to ward off the stench of their own kind. Rats scurried off in every direction as lit torches led the search party along the narrow ledge of the sewer tunnel into the bowels of the city. None too soon, Vasquez hauled on the iron grate that punctured the bricks-and-mortar sewer wall. As they made their way up the stone passageway that led to the cathedral, the putrid fumes of the sewer began to dissipate. The men overcame their nausea just in time to concentrate on the desecration of the dead, gingerly walking upwards over scattered bones until they hit the iron door that gave entrance to the cathedral with a blood-curdling screech.

Harding looked ahead into the stone passageway that appeared to dead-end at a wall some twenty feet away. Vasquez moved to one corner and pushed. The wall swung ajar with a well-balanced ease.

"Wait here and I will see if we are expected." With that, Vasquez disappeared, and a few minutes later his head turned around the corner of the wall to face four guns and four very serious faces.

"Nice to see you wide awake, gentlemen. It appears all the guards are on the exits outside the building. Follow me."

The men continued on down the hall until they hit the spiral staircase and followed Vasquez down to the lower level. The Franciscan stopped at the sarcophagus of a reclining nobleman and appeared lost in thought for a moment. Harding noticed many burned out candles lying around and assumed the place held some kind of religious significance.

"Is this the one?" Harding looked at Vasquez and his torchlight caught the glistening trail of silver tears that streamed down the man's face.

"No, there is another here who was more than friend."

"Are you all right?" Harding ventured.

There was no response, only a signal to continue as they began inspecting stone coffin after stone coffin. Some were ornately carved, others were simple stone boxes, while yet others were sealed, rectangular vaults. Ferguson, Harding's first mate, stopped at a crypt with the unfinished carved figure of a woman on the lid. The others had passed it by but something on the opposite wall caught the man's attention.

"Captain, this one has been disturbed."

Harding and Vasquez turned around and inspected the coffin.

"But nothing looks disturbed to me," Vasquez offered.

"I have been looking under the rims of the lids to see if iron bars have been used, even though they clearly had not on the one that held your friend. This one is chipped in four places, and look over here." He held his torch up to the wall. "Look at the stonework on the wall. Someone has stuffed freshly chipped pieces of a different coloured stone into the cracks in the wall. The chips appear to be the same stone as the lid of the coffin. They must have been trying to tidy up their sacrilege."

"Ferguson was a stonemason," Harding explained to a curious Vasquez.

"Hmm, they're getting more clever at their work," Vasquez said to himself.

The men shoved on the lid but it wouldn't budge.

"It has an interior ridge. That's why they used the bars. We will have to lift all four corners, then slide." The men surrounded the lid and heaved unsuccessfully until Vasquez joined in. The lid slowly gave up, and once it was moved to one side Harding peered into the void.

"Ugh." He pulled his head back and heaved with the foul stench of rotting flesh. "I see only a woman who can't have been dead for very long. He's not in there." They began to put the lid back on when Ferguson stopped.

"I think her body is high," Ferguson said, holding his nose

"You're telling me it's high," Harding responded.

"No, sir. I mean, her position is high given the size of the box. She is either on a pedestal or … there might be something, or someone, underneath her." Ferguson looked at Vasquez and Harding, who looked sick to their stomachs.

"Remove the lid again," Harding ordered.

Once the lid was off Ferguson shoved his hand down the side of the corpse and felt around blindly while straining his neck to keep his head as far away from the stench as possible.

"There is warm flesh underneath the dead woman, sir," Ferguson said sheepishly.

"Good God … surely not. Remove the corpse, men."

The crewmen looked at one another with an expression that said they were seriously considering disobeying an order. Harding read their faces.

"You all know Matthias. Would you have him die this way?"

With some grumbling, the dead woman was carefully pulled out, and two crewmen vomited with the rotting flesh that pulled away in their hands. Vasquez reached in with Harding and they pulled Matthias out.

"Does he breath, Vasquez?" the Captain asked fearfully.

Vasquez held his ear to the young man's nostrils. "He breathes! He breathes. We're not too late!"

"Oh, but you are!" said a thin voice from behind them. The men swung around to see an old priest with three ragged toughs in tow.

"Brother Luke, I presume?" Harding looked at Vasquez, who nodded in the affirmative.

"So, Luke, I see you are now at the business of killing people God tells you to!" Vasquez stated sadly.

"It is the gift that I and only I possess," Luke said, reverently.

"Really, and has God told you to kill us all tonight?"

"You must all pay for your sins," Luke responded.

"And the men behind you, do they speak to God, or are they just ordinary murderers?" Vasquez looked at the frightened expression on the faces of the men with Brother Luke.

Harding gave Ferguson a nod and they all produced pistols and pointed them at Luke's men. Vasquez took his cue.

"Well, Luke, do you wish your men to die for your madness tonight, or shall we call this one a standoff?"

The men behind Brother Luke turned and ran.

"Quickly, men, return that woman to her foul business."

Harding's men picked the corpse up and placed it in the sarcophagus. Vasquez and Harding joined in, and the lid was dropped into place. Brother Luke invoked Latin curses at them all as the rescue party passed by carrying the body of Matthias. Vasquez grabbed Luke's torch on the way past.

"Maybe the dark will slow down your plans for the night … oh, and while you're speaking to God, perhaps you might ask Him for forgiveness."

Vasquez caught up with the others, leaving Luke screaming in Latin. As they entered the tunnel, Luke's voice echoed through the subterranean passages. The false wall moved into place, covering their exit.

"What was that madman screaming on about?" Harding shuddered.

"Oh, he was saying that God speaks to him and only him, and we are all damned. He has been going odd of mind for a few years now. He used to be one of the most devout of us all, but his devotion to his faith has curdled in the acid of his fears. The surety of his faith has been replaced by the voices he hears in his head. The problem is, he still wears the vestments of the brotherhood, so some poor souls think him holy instead of plain mad."

As the men approached the end of the sewer, Harding instructed all to put out their torches so that they might not be conspicuous. Matthias was lowered into the boat, and Ferguson stood awaiting instruction.

"What about your crew? What will they think of a man in such a state as this?" Vasquez fretted to Harding in hushed tones.

"They will do as their captain orders. Can you offer the protection of like authority anywhere else in the city of Hamburg?"

"No argument from me on that score. Might I accompany you to the *Southern Belle* so that I can observe Matthias?"

"Of course."

Harding gave the order and the oars hit the water. The tide was strong that night and not in their favour, forcing the oarsmen to dig in. With an overcast sky they pulled into the headwind in the cover of night, and soon the gunwales of the rowboat bumped against the motherly belly of the *Southern Belle*.

Once in the Captain's quarters, Matthias was stripped of his foul-smelling clothes, washed down, and put to bed in one of Harding's own nightshirts.

"Ferguson, make sure you and your men bathe in salty brine, and be sure to throw your clothing away. Heaven knows what that poor woman died of, or what vermin her flesh carries in her present state."

"Aye-aye, Captain." Ferguson opened the door to exit.

"Oh, and Ferguson. Tell the lads each of you will find a bonus in your wages for this evening's festivities." Harding smiled at his man. “I am deeply grateful, Ferguson. Without you, we may not have found Matthias.”

Ferguson smiled back at his captain. “Glad to be of service, sir. May the young man have a speedy recovery.” With that, the first mate closed the door, leaving Vasquez and Harding both staring at the wide-open eyes of Matthias.

“What now, Vasquez?”

“We observe him for one more day. If there is no change, I must attempt to find his soul and bring him back.”

“I can’t allow you to engage in such madness.”

“You have no choice, my friend. The only option you have, unfortunately, is the hope that my madness has some merit. I trust this is not too much for you to endure. I do understand the need you have to keep the world in the order you have assembled it in your mind.”

“You would mock me?”

“No at all, Captain. You forget, you are talking to a priest. The information I am now privy to also holds my own life in turmoil. I had such focus and singularity of purpose when I believed I possessed the answers. It is unsettling, to say the least, to realize what few answers I actually had. I am beginning to understand the bliss of ignorance.”

“I don’t like the sound of your words, but I believe you to be of honourable intent. If you attempt to find him and bring him back, as you say, what assurances are there that I won’t have your body on my hands as well?”

“Let’s cross that bridge when we come to it. I will tell you this. Do not let anyone destroy Matthias’s body or mine should I appear to fail. If we don’t return, our bodies will die without assistance. I must return to town, for the business of the mill must continue tomorrow. I will make my play at nightfall.”

Harding stood on deck and stared at the harbour, dumbfounded, as Vasquez was rowed back to the wharf. He would stay on watch for the dregs of the night. That the sun would eventually make its way into the sky was about the only thing he felt sure of at that moment

12

OF THEIR OWN CONSTRUCTION

Elsewhere, 1989

Danny waded waist-deep in golden fields of wheat, dragging his hands along the feathery tops of the long stalks. He felt undeniable peace for the first time in his life. A restlessness he had always known was slowly sifting out of him. Behind him, the massive Phorian Acropolis glowed in the warm orange-yellow of what amounted to a glorious sunset, except for the conspicuous absence of a sun. If all in this plane of consciousness was of Phorian design, it appeared they dabbled in a rendering of day and night. Apparently even the spirit needed rest.

His momentary state of peace began to spring leaks. *Life* — the word had most certainly expanded beyond an earth-bound definition in the last twenty-four hours. In that thought came a brief dalliance with uncertainty over just what the hell he thought he was doing alone in a field … if you could call a Phorian simulation a field.

An unsettling fear began to seep into his being. He turned to face the direction it seemed to be coming from, and that was when he noticed a group of blurry figures moving towards him, becoming more and more defined with proximity.

"I think we'd better move away from them." Alison's voice came from behind.

"Where the hell did you go?" Danny was clearly startled.

"I went straight ahead, and I was going to wait for you to catch up to me. But … there are some in that direction who I think don't mean you well."

"You mean Soms … the ones Verhoevan warned us about?"

"Think so. You were feeling loneliness that turned into fear just now, weren't you?" Alison asked the question with as little judgment as possible.

"Well, uh … yeah, I guess so." Danny was embarrassed.

"That's when I felt them behind me. They moved past me and headed in your direction, or maybe, more accurately, in the direction of your fear. It was as if they couldn't see me, except one of them stopped and looked around, sensing my presence for that brief moment when I felt what you were feeling."

"You felt my fear?"

"When I looked at you it was like I could smell it. Then one of the dark figures stopped as though he could sense me. So I took my mind to more pleasant thoughts, and whatever it was, it appeared to lose its awareness of me and headed back towards you." Alison looked at the dark figures approaching in the distance. "We'd better head in the opposite direction. And think about something pleasant, will you?"

They headed off across the field, but the figures still followed until one appeared ahead of them. A kindly-looking middle-aged man stood to one side of their path.

"Welcome, friend," he said, looking at Danny with an overly sincere smile.

"What am I, chopped liver?" Alison snapped. But the man didn't even raise an eyebrow in acknowledgment.

"Do you not also welcome my friend?" Danny asked innocently.

"Of course, as a friend of yours, he too is welcome."

"Well now that's funny, because *he* is a *she*. You can't see her, can you?" Danny asked.

The man's smile drooped a little and he focused on Danny's eyes. A cold shiver ran through Danny as he felt his fear uncontrollably increase. In seconds there were seven or eight more individuals around him, all smiling the same phony smile.

"Don't let them creep you out. That's how these idiots get control of you, Danny!" Alison warned.

"Easy for you to say. They can't see you!"

Some of the others began to look around, sensing Alison's presence. She disappeared completely, leaving Danny alone again.

"We are your friends. We only seek to help others in the name of the Lord God. As his only son, Jesus, said, `I am the way.' You will only find the Kingdom of God through Him. Do you accept Jesus as your personal saviour, young man?"

"Well, I … uh … I'm Jewish, actually," Danny offered.

"So was our Saviour," the man replied, with an even greater smile.

"That's very nice. I am happy you are all saved. I really must be going." As Danny turned to move away, he was quickly surrounded by people whose smiles all began to look a little more sinister than happy. He felt claustrophobic as the circle closed in on him.

"You take the Holy Scriptures too lightly, young man." The words had no sooner left smiling lips than Danny felt a searing pain in his head and crumpled to the ground. He looked up as the circle closed around him.

"Do ye of no faith feel the displeasure of the Lord your God?"

"That's *you* inflicting … stop this pain in my head!" Danny squeaked in agony.

"Do you accept the Lord as your saviour? Will you open your heart to Him and follow Him?"

"Will that stop the pain?" Danny whispered.

The man knelt beside Danny and put a cold arm around him as if to comfort. "Ours is to help others see the way, friend. Believe, and know no pain. Join us … open your heart to our Jesus."

Danny looked into the man's face and was startled by Alison, who stood behind him making faces. Then she stuck her tongue out. It was so completely juvenile and out of character for Alison that it caught Danny off guard and he laughed out loud. In his laughter, the pain diminished considerably.

The man's smile tightened into a pursed grimace that held back anger like vomit. "Those who do not seek the way of the Lord God will burn in eternal Hell!" he spat, and he pointed at Danny as if to inflict more pain. That's when Danny sensed a foul odour that he recognized as the same putrid smell that had emanated from the woman who had left the Phorian council chambers in tears. It was then that Danny began to find his own sense of things. Alison winked, and Danny pulled farther out of his fear until the pain began to dissipate.

"If your Lord seeks to burn people in Hell, he might not be a generous enough spirit for me." Danny walked past the man, whose anger intensified.

"Blasphemer! You will surely burn in …" He stopped mid-sentence and looked around. Danny was nowhere in sight.

"Well done, Danny boy," she whispered proudly.

Danny grinned back. "Thanks to you, Alison. Man, that is some crazy, whacked-out group of ugly souls." As he spoke, he noticed that the angry man was now a poorly defined shadow that began to dissipate into nothingness, as did the shadows of his minions.

"Let's head this way, and tell me about Joel." Alison looked at Danny and tentatively held out her hand. Danny sensed that this was a big step for her, given how timid she appeared in the doing of it.

"Are you sure you want me to touch you, Alison?"

"Well, it isn't really touching here, but yes, I am interested in seeing what it feels like to touch your hand."

Danny reached out and gently took hold of her hand. As the two began to walk, he was moved by the sweetness of Alison's gesture. In an instant, the most affection he had ever felt from someone tingled up his arm. It felt good … no … it felt new. New? He had held plenty of hands in his time, so what was new? He searched for an answer, and then he realized it was a new feeling for Alison to hold someone's hand, and he shared in her excitement. As he examined his own feelings, he became aware of a growing affection for her, which fascinated him, because she still looked like … well … such a nerd!

"So how would you have me look, Daniel?" Alison pulled her hand away. She was getting the hang of wherever they were, too quickly. Danny was now aware Alison was receiving his thoughts.

"Wha … what do you mean?"

"You were thinking you liked the feeling we shared, and then you struck it down by dismissing me as a nerd, and therefore somehow unworthy."

"I am so sorry, old habits die hard," Danny apologized. "Forgive me?"

"Sure. You can think whatever you want. I've been told worse. I don't know why, but here I'm not so insecure about how I look for some reason. I guess I could conjure up something a little more acceptable to you with some practice, if you wanted."

"Alison, please don't. Right now you're the only familiar face around here. I don't want to have to guess who the hell you are, And besides …"

"Besides?"

"Well, I liked what I felt when I touched you. And part of what I know as *you* is the way you look. That you would wish to change yourself to suit me makes me feel ashamed."

"I liked what I felt when you touched me, too." Alison drifted in thought for a brief moment, then pulled back to the task at hand. "Joel, we have to stay focused on Joel."

"How?"

"We might start focusing on his nature in order to find him. You know who he is, his likes and dislikes."

At that moment an odd sound rang in their ears. It grew until it morphed into a low, singular note that vibrated like the distant rumble of thunder. As it grew in intensity, the field around them began to change. The warm colours bled out, bleaching everything around them. The tall grasses bent away from them, as if at the mercy of a strong wind. It took a second for Alison to realize that the reason the colours were less vibrant was because an intense light source behind them was washing them out. She spun around to look.

"It's the bright light I saw the first time we crossed over, Danny. And look at all of those people in it."

Danny turned, and it was just as she'd described it.

"What's going on? Who are they?"

"I don't know … unless . . ." Alison turned forward again, and an image began to appear in front of her. It was Dr. Walters, sitting at Joel's keyboard in the hotel room.

"Are we back?" Danny asked, looking at the same image.

"Not quite. But now we know what Verhoevan's Resonance sounds like from this side. It also seems to summon that light. Maybe when someone crosses over there is a temporary link between the physical plane and whatever they call this one."

"So Walters just gave us the first four-hour interval?" Danny asked.

"I believe so."

"Man, this is crazy, it feels like we've only been here for fifteen minutes or so, and we've already blown about a third of our time."

Danny looked at Dr. Walters, who got up from the seat in front of Joel's synthesizer. He looked curiously in Danny's direction as a figure moved past Danny towards the old man.

"Who is that?" Danny asked Alison

"She looks like the woman in the pictures he has scattered around his house … I think it's his wife, Maggie."

"What is she doing?"

"Maybe she sensed his spirit near a point of departure, even though it was artificially induced by the Resonance. He must have been thinking of her as well. I think the Resonance somehow amplifies the thoughts of the person still in the body."

The woman moved close to her husband and touched his face. He sat on the edge of the bed where Alison's body lay, and his eyes filled.

"Do you think he knows she's right there?" Danny asked.

"Don't know, but he sure loves her. Can you feel it?"

"Yes."

Alison and Danny observed the old couple for a moment until Maggie Walters turned to Danny. Her face held a gentle expression of genuine empathy for her husband's sadness and longing.

"He is such a good man. It won't be long now," she said in a soft tone. "Your friend is … confused. He believes he is dreaming." Her words took a moment to register.

"My … you know where Joel is?" Danny asked.

"Yes and no. I don't know where he is, but I can take you to where there is much thought about him."

"How is it you know where he is?" Alison asked.

Mrs. Walters turned to her and studied Alison's face briefly. "You know my husband. He feels affection for you."

"I don't know him well, Mrs. Walters, but I believe him to be a good and interesting man," Alison said, finding her way to her own feelings.

"You are like-minded, and you remind him of our daughter."

"I didn't know you had a daughter, Mrs. Walters."

"She died in her second year at university."

"I'm so sorry."

"No need. I no longer feel my pain for her, only his. He doesn't know that her spirit is joyous."

"So what do you know about Joel?" Danny interrupted.

The old woman turned once more to her husband and smiled, then looked back at Danny. "Where you last saw him is the door. He is on the other side of it." The words were no sooner out of her mouth than Mrs. Walters was gone.

Alison looked at Danny, whose expression had changed to one of disbelief.

"Wow," he exclaimed.

"Interesting, huh?" Alison said pensively.

Danny didn't answer, he just pointed to something behind Alison. She slowly turned around, and Mrs. Walters stood facing the body of Joel in the ICU. His parents were sitting stoically at his side.

The ICU was filled with a heavy sadness. A black woman sat praying for her son, the sturdy-looking high school athlete Danny had seen wheeled in on a gurney when he'd visited Joel and his parents. The young athlete's body was on a respirator, forcing his chest up and down in a crude, mechanized facsimile of life.

His mother's prayers gave way to convulsive interludes of suppressed weeping that subsided back into the tranquility of her faith, only to be overcome by another wave of maternal horror.

Her anguish tunnelled into dark depths only a mother could feel. What she didn't know was that her son stood beside her, looking down on his body. Her pain was now his as he stood glued to the life force that had created him. It was as though the love he had always taken for granted was now completely known and understood. The love that a mother felt for her child held him in awe. He looked up at Danny and Alison with a curious expression, smiled in acknowledgment of their presence, then returned to his mother's pain. He touched her gently on her cheek and a peaceful look of faith returned to her tortured soul. Somehow she sensed him and that his love for her existed … somewhere.

All hell broke loose as the machines hooked up to a patient started beeping. One of the nurses called "Code Blue" and staff rushed to the bed of a young girl. It was the beautiful girl who had been injured in the same accident as the black athlete in the next bed. Her father stood staring with a look of horror on his face and pulled his wife out of the way of the medical staff. The sadness in the room was without a doubt the most pain Danny had ever felt. This new ability to feel the pain of others was almost unbearable. Being without body, his emotional empathy, like the hearing of a blind man, had taken on a heightened level of acuity. The girl stood briefly with her parents, looking at her body. Then, as though she could no longer stand the pain, she turned and walked past Danny and Alison towards shadows that had assembled in the light behind them.

"Paddles!" The nurse wheeled the voltage unit over and handed the doctor the paddles. The girl's body heaved as the electrical current shot through her. Her heart monitor began to show blips on the screen.

"We have a heartbeat!" There was a collective sigh of relief. The parents hung on to each other for dear life. "Nurse, fifty milligrams of coumadin in the IV line, just to play it safe." The machine was rolled away and the nurse followed through.

"But she's gone," Danny said

"Still breathing, though. I suppose when she stops breathing they'll put her on a respirator, and then someone's going to have to give the order to pull the plug. What a mess."

Danny went to Joel's body and stood behind his parents, looking over their shoulders. Joel looked straight up, eyes fixed but breathing on his own. A young Asian doctor strolled in and went to the other side of the bed, facing Joel's parents and Danny.

"The blood work came back from toxicology and shows nothing out of the ordinary. Your son wasn't on anything we can find. I'm sorry, but I have no answers to give you at this point as to why your son is in this unconscious … I, uh … well, I've never seen anything like this before. We are wondering if it's viral in nature."

Joel's parents just stood paralyzed, looking stoically at their son. Joel's mother kept glancing over at the parents of the young girl, who were attempting to subdue uncontrollable anguish.

"So where is Joel now?" Danny asked Mrs. Walters.

"He is on the other side of here. He is drawn by his parents' pain but he is being held by someone … or his own curiosity."

"Oh, not the smiling bastards again!" Danny quipped.

Mrs. Walters looked oddly at Danny until she understood his statement. "You have met them twice already. How is it you have not been drawn to them like many of us are for a time? … Oh, my." It was clear something else had entered her consciousness, and she turned to Alison.

"It's you. You are the reason he let go of his fear. You have much together." She smiled at them, and her image slowly dissipated until it was gone.

Danny was drawn for a moment to the young black teenager standing with his mother, staring at his own body.

"Are you okay?" Danny asked him.

"I don't know. Am I dead?" The teenager looked a little confused.

"I can't say, but you sure appear to be having an out-of-body experience."

"My mom's pretty amazing, huh?"

"I can feel some of what you are feeling." As he focused his attention, Danny was deeply moved by a flood of incoming information. "Her love for you is powerful."

"Am I supposed to go with you?" the teen asked innocently.

"I don't think so. We are looking for someone else," Alison said softly as she came up behind Danny and the young man.

"Someone is coming for me … I think." He then looked back at his mother and attempted to console her.

"Danny, we should go." Alison headed back to Joel's bed.

Danny put his hand on the young man's shoulder as he passed by. "Good luck to you."

The kid smiled a puzzled smile, then returned to another wave of his mother's pain.

Back at Joel's body, Danny and Alison attempted to get a sense of him. He was nearby, as Mrs. Walters had said. They could both feel him, but something wasn't right. Danny thought as hard as he could until a vague image of Joel began to appear before him.

"Joel, is that you?" he asked, but there was no answer. "That's Joel, Alison. Can you feel his presence?"

"No, I only feel his confusion," Alison answered. "This isn't him."

"What do you mean, it isn't him?" Danny asked.

"Maybe it's like the woman who summoned images of her son when we were with the Phorians. You made a piece of him appear, but he is not coming to you."

"Why not?"

"Either because he doesn't want to … or, he can't. Maybe he doesn't know it's you calling. Actually, I think he's … afraid of us."

"What? I'm his best friend. Why would he be afraid of his best freakin' friend?"

"I don't know."

"So what do I do with this image of Joel now that I have it here?"

"I feel something … uh, kind of weird."

Alison began to move strangely. Danny looked at her and started feeling a little sensually aroused, and it was then that he began to see what looked like Joel. The ICU dissolved into the background as a huge garden opened in front of them. There were people bathing in an elegant pool of crystal-clear water cascading from marble statuary of graceful male and female nudes. Others reclined on elegant furniture, laughing, talking, and making love. It all felt so wonderfully decadent, and right smack dab in the middle of it all was Joel, with two scantily clad women on either side of him, completely engaged.

A man and woman in flowing satin robes approached Danny and Alison. It was their smiles that set the alarms ringing in Danny's head.

"Welcome," they said. The man, strikingly good looking with an exceptional physique, went right to Alison and kissed her. She was taken aback at first, and then a curious look swept across her face and she responded passionately, surprising the hell out of Danny, who was being welcomed himself. The woman in the satin robe ran her hands over him, and it felt as though his body was responding—quite a trick, he thought, to get a body that wasn't there to respond.

"Hey, what do you think you're doing?" Danny said half-heartedly.

"Only what you were thinking," she said, taking him by the hand towards a pool of water. She slowly removed the image of his clothing while managing to drop her own robe and urging Danny into the pool with her.

"What is this place?" Danny gulped.

"It is a place where one only seeks to offer others memories of physical assurance and pleasure. There are those here in need of giving and those in need of receiving." She led Danny into the soothing waters of the pool. Danny looked over at Joel, who was grinning back at him.

"Well, do you want to know how to give me great pleasure?" Danny asked in a mock-sensual tone.

"Name your greatest desire," the woman whispered back invitingly.

"Take me over to my friend Joel."

"I didn't sense in you a preference for a male image." She looked at Danny as though trying to read his thoughts, then pulled away and turned to another couple in the water, who welcomed her.

Danny watched her kiss the other woman and then the man as they took an oddly clinical approach to passion. It appeared as though there was an immense amount of concentration and energy being expended to simulate physical expression. It was virtual sex, an acquired mental skill. It was work, not the easy get that he was used to.

He looked to Alison, who was completely lost in a passionate embrace with the handsome-looking image who had greeted her. Why was she doing this? Maybe her fantasy was so strong that her mind was doing it all. unaware of the energy she was expending. She certainly had a powerful enough mind … more powerful than his, at any rate, he thought. He had seen her power with the holy-rollers who preyed on fear. She obviously had a knack for this place, whatever it was.

He realized in that moment that he was more than a little attracted to her image, and taken aback by how wonderful she looked in her nakedness. It wasn't the best body he had ever seen; in fact, it was the idea of the spirit that inhabited the image that made her so attractive to him.

This was new stuff to Danny, and that's when he felt a twinge of jealousy. As soon as he was aware of the feeling, he noticed that many had stopped what they were doing and looked towards him with odd expressions. Alison had the most curious look on her face as she stared at Danny, who quickly took his mind to another task to get rid of the thoughts that so disturbed the atmosphere. Everyone again returned to passion. Feelings of jealousy were clearly not allowed.

He got out of the pool and, looking at the image of his nakedness, made a few attempts to create the image of clothing. Pants and a shirt, that's all he wanted, but every time he finished the pants and started on the shirt, the pants began to slowly disintegrate. How had he managed thus far? There was some knack to maintaining this appearance thing in an autonomic manner that was eluding him in that moment of self-consciousness. He solved the immediate problem with a robe, a single garment that required only one image. Enough time on wardrobe, he thought … he was there for Joel, and moved towards him.

"Joel, you've worried the hell out of us all!" Danny said as he sauntered over to his best friend.

"Danny?"

"One and the same. I'm here to help you get back, being as I'm responsible for this whole mess, and in particular what this is doing to your mom and dad." As Danny thought about Joel's mother and father, he noticed his friend's face become sombre. "Do you have any idea how much pain your parents are in over this?" Instantly they were in the ICU, over Joel's body. Joel's mother was weeping again, while his father stroked her hair in a fruitless attempt to console her.

"What's this?" Joel looked at his body and the blank stare on his face. "How the hell did this happen? Is this real?"

"Actually, that depends on what you mean by the word 'this.' Are we out of our bodies? The short answer is … yup. Are your parents in ICU worried sick over their son lying unconscious in a hospital bed? Well, this picture's gotta be worth a thousand words."

"How the hell can that be … I was just dreaming about … okay, it was a pretty creative erotic dream, but no way that was real! I mean, a place where there's a non-stop orgy going on … is real? And this? My God."

Joel looked at the pathetic scene. His mother agonized over her only child. Joel went to her and gently stroked her face with the back of his hand. She immediately stopped crying and looked around the room, then screamed.

"Don't you do this to me, Joel. How dare you do this to me!"

Joel jumped back and looked at Danny. "She can *see* me!"

"Maybe *sense* you might be a more accurate description. She wasn't looking at you, she was looking all around her, sensing … maybe hoping for your presence."

"The last thing I remember, I was playing those chords on that pipe organ sample, and all of a sudden my synths started playing themselves. Then I saw these people in the light and one was this beautiful chick who somehow knew me, and the next thing

I know I'm surrounded by beautiful half-naked women who want me! How long have I … I mean, has my body been here?"

"Since you left it and walked into the light two days ago."

"No way, man. I've just been here a little while."

"Time is a little funky here compared to the physical world, Joel. In the physical world, you're seriously running out of time."

"You sound like I'm going to die or something."

"You are down to a matter of hours before your body will die. If we …" Danny was interrupted by the sound of the Resonance. It was Dr. Walters checking in.

"Hey, isn't that like the sound I heard from your grandfather's manuscript?" Joel's face was a little confused.

"We knew it could be heard from this side. A friend is marking off four-hour intervals."

"So how do I go back … if I want to?" Joel said, looking at his body.

"You just look through your own eyes."

"I what?"

"You literally get in your own body and look out of the eyes, then somehow body and spirit are reunited."

"What do you think I should do?" Joel asked.

"Look at your parents' pain … there has to be an answer there. Would you want to do that to anyone?"

"I guess you're right. But I do feel really amazing at the moment, like I don't have a problem in the world."

"Yeah, I know, I feel it too," Danny confessed.

"You coming back, Danny?"

"Yeah. I love the idea of the two of us writing some good music together."

"Funny, huh, that's the one thing I can think of that makes me want to go back. Actually, I've had some pretty cool ideas I've been kicking around. I hope it isn't like one of those dreams that when you wake up it's either gone or the brilliant idea sounds really dumb when you try it."

"I've done this back-and-forth thing once briefly, and I think you will remember everything you're thinking or feeling now. In dreams, your consciousness is still tied to your body, so I think things can get pretty muddled up." Danny was fascinated by the thoughts.

"So I climb into my body and look outta my eyes, huh?"

"Yes," Danny answered."

"You gotta admit, this is some creepy shit," Joel said, with some trepidation.

"Oh yeah," Danny deadpanned.

Joel went to his body and began to recline in it. "Hey, where's your body?"

"The Holiday Inn," Danny replied.

"That's gotta be a little less depressing than this place, I imagine," Joel cracked as he looked around the ICU at people with long faces hanging around loved ones hooked up to machines. "You promise you're coming back?"

"Yes, I promise. Oh, and Joel … it might be best if you don't tell anyone about this. They'll only think you're nuts anyway."

"I *am* nuts, I'm about to climb back into my own body, for Pete's sake. Doesn't get nuttier than this." Joel looked back at his worried friend. "Don't worry, Danny, I'll plead ignorance, all right. So tell me, am I in Heaven right now?"

"Heaven, Valhalla, the Happy Hunting Grounds … I think all of those fables are the shallow end of the data stream."

"So where the hell is God?" Joel asked snidely.

"Apparently, traces of the answer to that question reside somewhere inside of you."

"So, been to Heaven … no sign of God, bummer."

"Not really. Remember how good you feel at this moment. I think some of God might be in that feeling and … maybe God is the sum of all of us."

"Hmm." Joel seemed to be perusing the possibilities. "Somehow that doesn't feel disappointing once I wrap my head around it. It's just … you know, so ethereal compared to the Grizzly Adams living in the clouds image we've all been brought up with." Joel was lost in the thought when his mother fell into another round of heaving sobs. "Looks like I'd better help Mom out of her misery. See you on the other side, Danny."

"You bet, my friend."

Joel took a look around, then back to Danny for reassurance.

"Just look out of my eyes, huh? Man, this is some creepy shit. I'm hoping this is just one big, bad, fucked-up dream."

Joel lay back completely into his body. He looked out of his eyes and in an instant Danny was gone. He suddenly became aware of how sore his eyes were as he looked around the room and blinked. His mother gasped as she watched his eye movement, and Joel looked into her worried face. It wasn't a dream, and Joel was shocked at how harsh the reality of it all was.

"Hi, Mom. Hey, Dad," Joel said softly.

His mother grabbed his arm with both hands and burst into tears. "Oh Joel, oh my God, Joel!" She wept as she looked at the reanimated face of her boy.

"You sure had us worried, son." His father's voice cracked as he hung on to his male bravado by a thin thread. "We, uh, we thought you were going to … well, you wouldn't believe where our minds have been."

13

TRAVELLER IN A FOREIGN LAND

Elsewhere, 1848

Matthias had stepped out of his body as it slumped on the floor of the bellows chamber. In the light ahead of him, he sensed the presence of his mother. Her silhouette moved closer and her voice was warm.

"Why are you here, Matthias?"

"Is it true? Are you Miriam?"

"I am Miriam, and I am also Maria, your mother. You know me and my love for you. Does one name mean more than the other to you?"

"I guess not, I …"

"What troubles you?" Miriam immediately felt his need. "You have come to see your father."

"Now that I know you are here, I think I want to know more about him. I tried once before but there was nobody here that I knew, and now I see you, I ..." Matthias was overcome by the image of her. She was so young and elegant-looking and gazed on him with obvious approval.

"You will see me again, Matthias, if you so desire."

"I have to return to someone I love. I can't stay with you, Mother."

"I feel your love for her, Matthias. It is a good love."

"But before I go … where is Father?"

'I don't know. I am sure he's with those he loves."

"Well … wouldn't that mean he would be with you?"

"He never returned my love for him, Matthias. It was my father's wealth he needed."

"This cannot be true! He grieved for months after you died … for months!"

"I feel that was more guilt than grief, as you might think of it. He knew I loved him, yet he used my love to benefit himself materially."

Matthias was shattered. He had invested so much in the thought that he was born from love. He felt a warm embrace from his mother.

"Why are you troubled, Matthias? You are loved, and I know I am loved. This is all there is, and it is good." She spoke very gently.

Matthias looked into the image of her face. "You said he is with those he loves. Then why isn't he here with me?"

"I can't answer that. I only know that he is with love, and that love is not possessive. He will be with you if it is where he wishes to be. Perhaps he wishes this moment for us."

"You're here … so how did you…?" Matthias merely began the question when his mother nodded, understanding his thought.

"When I heard the Resonance that sent your father here, I sensed your need. I saw you briefly the last time you entered, but you went back before I could communicate with you. You must go back, Matthias. It is there that your greatest love awaits you." She spoke with such finality that Matthias sensed his audience was over. He looked up as her image began to dissipate.

Others began to move towards him. Some he thought were merely curious, but there were those whose smiles held something more that unsettled him. Matthias turned to re-enter his body, but it was gone. How could that be? He had only just crossed over. He saw the bellows chamber, but it was empty. Where was his body? Who would have taken it? Fear gripped him with the possibility that his body had somehow been destroyed and he would never have the chance to love Anna for the lifetime he had envisioned.

"Hello, friend." The voice came from behind, and Matthias spun around to face a smiling man in front of a group of people who all looked his way expectantly.

"Do I know you?" Matthias asked.

"If you know the Lord Jesus Christ you know us all, young Matthias. Do you know Jesus as the one and only true path to God? For it was Christ who said, `Follow me, I am the way.'"

Matthias sensed a foul odour that increased with his fear.
"What are you talking about? I am not here to find Jesus. I . . ." The group crowded around him. He looked at the smiling man, who gripped his arm like a vise until the sensation of an exquisite pain

began to erode his consciousness. How could this be? Consciousness was all he was!

***

Matthias didn't know how long he had been nothing, only that he was in some black void and was slowly becoming aware of singing in the distance. As he emerged from complete darkness, so did a familiar foul odour. His vision gradually cleared, revealing row upon row of crude wooden pews facing a shiny black pulpit that rose well above the faithful. From that perch the smiling man scanned his flock intensely as he led a few hundred sorry-looking souls in repetitive hymns of praise. Matthias was now aware enough to realize that he, too, was standing and singing in the drone that slowly drew to a close with the chant of "Amen." How was it that he knew the words to these hymns? How long had he been in this place? It wasn't a Catholic church, by the look of it.

The congregation all seated themselves in unison with the wave of a hand from the smiling man, who was apparently acting as priest or minister. Matthias noticed that he had no control over his visible form. He was caught in the trance-like synchronicity that surrounded him. The smiling minister then began to bear witness.

"I began life, like many of you here, a Godless man, and near the point of damnation finally found God though our Lord and Saviour Jesus Christ. I blasphemed. I was an adulterer, and worse, a doubter. But I found the light, and now I seek only to save souls for the Lord. We must punish the idolaters of the papacy, the Jew, and the pagan, those misled by the false prophet Mohammed, and all others misled by the Devil. We must free them and lead them here to Jesus or eradicate them from our midst, for this is the Kingdom of God."

"Hallelujah!" Matthias responded automatically with the rest of the congregation. He was horrified by the sound of his own voice speaking words that had no origin in his own thoughts. He tried to look around the room but couldn't move his head. Once again, with no warning, his body stood as the congregation began to sing another hymn of praise that had an anaesthetic effect on thought. Matthias felt the control of the minister increasing and began to lose his grip on consciousness again.

Hamburg, 1848

Darkness draped the city, only mildly disturbed by the feeble flicker of gaslights in the distance. Vasquez climbed the stairs to the wharf as Harding's men turned the boat around and began to row back to the *Southern Belle*. While most of Hamburg slept, Vasquez walked a straight line between a few desperate nocturnal scavengers in rotting rags and the occasional drunken tough looking for a face to accommodate the aching in his fists. All gave a wide berth to the priest with the stern expression who strode like a man determined to walk through any obstacle in his path.

Vasquez had no idea how he would find Matthias. Crossing over was not the problem. It was his ignorance of the other side, and more importantly getting back to his body, that unnerved him. The night he'd tried to help Matthias see his father had been only his second, brief crossing. His first dalliance into the unknown had been a cursory glance with Verhoevan the day the power of his work was discovered. He'd been amazed at Verhoevan's sense of all that was happening on that momentous occasion. It was almost as if Verhoevan had travelled across before, as there were those on the other side who had not only known him but also seemed to have been congratulating him on his accomplishment.

That night when he'd helped Matthias cross over, he had made no effort to engage any of the figures he'd seen in the light, or satisfy his own raging curiosity. Instead he'd kept his own body in sight, and called after Matthias in order to keep his presence and location known to the boy. When he'd been overcome with the uneasiness of some of those approaching them, he had called on the boy's love for Anna to entice him back to his body before it was too late. This, he found out later, was indeed what had snapped Matthias out of his state of wonder and helped him regain focus.

The potential of distraction once one crossed over was powerful. Verhoevan, despite his brilliance and knowledge, had died a hideous death, trapped with a corpse in decaying finery. Though Vasquez had planned to tend to the day's run at the mill, he now thought it more prudent that the rescue mission wait only until daylight. By then, the guards Brother Nicolas had posted at the cathedral would likely be gone. More importantly, the conspicuousness of another organ recital in the middle of the night would simply invite far too much attention. In the morning, Pietro would be playing for early mass.

That was as far as Vasquez's plan went, for as he wearily scuffed the thin souls of his sandals up the familiar stone steps of the Dopp house, sleep became his most immediate objective. He had to at least be rested and with his wits about him for what lay ahead. He fell face down onto his bed and managed to find what felt like only a couple of minutes of peace before his eyes opened wide to the realization that morning was already upon him. The smell of fresh baking was in the air, and as he passed the dining room Vasquez grabbed a chunk of bread and cheese that had been laid out on the table by the housekeeper and headed out at his usual quick pace.

He was brushing the last few crumbs from his robe by the time he reached the cathedral. The great doors were spitting the faithful back into the suffering of their daily lives with the hope that their tithes and obedience would earn them all a place in the promise of Heaven. Pietro was humming the refrain of an organ postlude while he put his music away. His joyful mood deflated instantly when he heard the familiar squeak of complaining sandals. He looked up at the leather-bound manuscript under the arm of Vasquez. Every time Pietro had been in proximity to that manuscript, he had found himself embroiled in trouble.

"Has the boy recovered?" Pietro asked sheepishly.

"No, and I am afraid I must impose on you once more, my friend, to correct what has occurred."

"But I cannot endanger another, Brother, there has already been too much harm brought about by Verhoevan's work. It is surely cursed!"

"Don't speak nonsense. His work is brilliant. It will be us who are cursed if we don't help bring the boy back, Pietro. Don't forget that you helped dispatch him to where he now lingers!"

"But Brother Vasquez, I …" Pietro stopped mid-sentence. Vasquez had hit the nail of guilt squarely on the head. "All right! But this is the last time I will ever assist you in such things! Am I clear?"

"Bless you, Pietro. I know this is difficult for you … and yes, you are quite clear."

The two men made sure all had left the sanctuary as they prepared. For his part, Pietro began to stuff one of his ears with candle wax and cotton. Vasquez grabbed his hand.

"After I am gone, come to the bellows chamber, close my

eyes, and keep watch. If I am discovered, say I have fallen and hit my head. Then take my body to my room at the monastery."

Vasquez turned to a stone pillar, took a deep breath and smashed his forehead into it. When he turned back to Pietro, a trickle of blood ran down his face from a nasty-looking abrasion.

"There, now we have evidence of a fall. I am off to the bellows chamber."

Pietro's heart pounded as he finished packing his remaining ear and opened Verhoevan's manuscript. He glanced at the manuscript, then hit the first massive chord, which filled the sanctuary, then followed immediately with the remaining three. The young monk waited a good couple of minutes, then gingerly removed the earplug from one side and listened for a few seconds. Nothing, all sound had left the building on its journey. As he pulled the rest of the waxy cotton stuffing from his ears he headed down to the bellows chamber, and there was Vasquez, sitting on the floor, eyes wide open … gone. Dutifully following instruction, Pietro closed the monk's eyes and stood, sensing the presence of someone near.

Elsewhere, 1848

Vasquez watched Pietro close the eyes of his corporeal shell from behind the young priest. He knew the boy was afraid and sought to comfort him. Vasquez placed his hands on Pietro's shoulders until a look of peace came over him. Pietro somehow understood, but didn't want to know.

"Amazing," Vasquez muttered. He turned to face the bright light resplendent with the shadowy figures heading his way.

"Well, let's see who you lot are, and what use you can be to the task at hand." There was one figure well ahead of the pack striding towards him.

"Vasquez, I am glad to feel your presence but unhappy with the circumstances."

Vasquez was overcome. He stood staring incredulously at Verhoevan and began to weep. Verhoevan embraced his friend.

"You dear soul, I know why you are here and I know where he is."

"Matthias?' Vasquez inquired.

"Yes, of course … the boy," Verhoevan answered. "He is

being held by a Som, a powerful fear monger. The boy is so young and subservient in matters of faith that he is unsure of his own power. When one is schooled to believe priests are closer to God, it is sometimes difficult to find your own way. Oh Vasquez, we were engaged in such folly in our search for God, for it was not God many of us found in our earthly search, only power over others as we meted out the laws of the Church."

Vasquez's curiosity was too much for him. "Ha-have you met … Jesus of the Holy Virgin?"

"I have discovered the beauty of the idea we called Jesus, or farther back Yeshua, or farther back even still the Egyptian myth of Iusa. Is the man more important than the idea? Surely you, my friend, know the importance of allegory? As for the holiness of the Virgin, ask yourself this: what could be more holy than a child conceived out of wedlock in the pure innocence of love?"

Vasquez stood shaking his head. "This is not as I thought … I …" Vasquez halted. His worry for Matthias overshadowed his burning questions. "You said Matthias was being held by a Som?"

"They are Somatic … of the body, ones whose spirit is trapped in a singular body of truth impervious to growth. Many can believe in love only if Jesus *was* a divinity on earth, a man-God, who physically rose from the dead, defying the rules of the physical universe. Many of the faithful deify the messenger, like Jesus, Mohammad, or even the Buddha, in some cases, remaining static in a mantra of worship rather than absorbing the philosophy and moving on in their spiritual growth. These ideas should be stepping stones in one's growth not dead-ends. Where personal expression of spirit is surrendered to another, there is the possibility of death for the individual soul. Oh Vasquez, I look forward to our great talks soon, my friend, but now let us deal with your anxiety. We must get the boy before it is too late.'

"Too late? Is he in danger?"

"Soms feed from the spirit of others until there is nothing left. That is why they constantly seek new recruits of an impressionable sort steeped in religious dogma … the younger, the better. Soms have replaced love with power, and yet the thing that still propels them forward is an aberrant need to be loved, which they can never know until they relinquish power. I could pity the Soms if I didn't feel a greater pain for the souls they devour. Come, hold my arm. You may need to sense a physical connection to me in order to follow at first, but try to find me in thought, for thought is all we are here."

Hymns of praise rang out from within a simple-looking white clapboard church.

"What is this place?" Vasquez inquired.

"It is a place of great suffering. A powerful Som controls many here who believe in the fear of Hell. There are many churches, mosques, and meeting places here, though they are usually something of an optical illusion … deceivingly humble and welcoming on the exterior. The Som in this place is an old spirit with much power and holds hundreds of souls. I must warn you now to focus only on thoughts of love. Fear to a Som is like a perfume. He is drawn to it, and he will find the tiniest discomfort, magnify it, and use it against you. As he magnifies your fear, he feeds from it, and it intoxicates him. All those who sing within this place are trapped by their own fear."

"Matthias is trapped here?"

"Yes. Now remember, only love … feel only love, and you will be fine. I will engage the Som while you find Matthias. Try to get him to recognize your love for him and lead him out. The boy may not know you, but he will recognize your love, so it is love for him you must feel, and the love of one he holds dear, of whom he must be reminded."

"I do love the boy as though he were my own son."

"I know, my old friend, now use it. Use the most powerful thoughts of love you hold within your breast. We may not have much time, so when you see the Som engaged in thought with me, find the boy immediately and move him to the door."

The two priests held one another briefly. Verhoevan smiled, then swung around and entered the church. Vasquez took a deep breath and followed. Verhoevan was more than he remembered, somewhat invigorated and almost youthful in his stride.

Once inside, Vasquez gasped at the endless number of pews that stretched as far as he could see, row upon row of souls with blank faces droning a hymn in unison. The two men stood inside the door facing an altar that appeared close when viewed head on, but when Vasquez turned to the side to look at the congregation, his peripheral vision told another story of an altar that appeared a great distance away. All singing stopped abruptly. The minister smiled at them until he recognized Verhoevan. Vasquez waited a moment until Verhoevan engaged the Som.

"So, Verhoevan, isn't it? The Phorian elitists sent you to do the Devil's work!" He turned to his congregation, face red with anger. "Beware, my children, they come to take some of you to eternal damnation!" he screamed, provoking fear on the faces of his captives as he strode down the aisle towards his two uninvited guests. Verhoevan was completely unaffected by the bluster, moving calmly and gracefully forward. Vasquez made his move to a side aisle and began searching for Matthias.

The Som walked slowly until he stopped, face to face with Verhoevan.

"So, what is it that troubles you, my friend?" Verhoevan began. "Why is it that you do not seek your rightful place at council?"

"My what?" The Som was taken off guard. "My rightful place at council?"

"Why yes, we speak often of your great power."

"You have spoken of me at council?"

Vasquez had passed a good thirty pews before he saw Matthias, expressionless, staring forward in the middle of a row. He shoved his way through a dozen dazed souls until he held Matthias by the shoulders and spoke quietly face to face. Verhoevan continued to stroke the Som's vanity with the news of the Phorian council's interest in him. Vasquez attempted to engage Matthias.

"Matthias, you are being held by a malevolent soul called a Som." Vasquez opened. "Use your mind boy. Anna and I are quite worried about you and wonder if you would like to live and love again?"

The young man blinked and struggled to speak. "Aaa … Anna? Whaa, what is this place? A Som? Where a-a-am I?"

"From what I am told, you are here because your fear is greater than your love and this is food to the Som. Is your love for Anna not the most important thing to you? Is it now so weak that you cannot keep your mind on it long enough to return to it?"

"But my love for her is … did you say re … return? Yes, I must return to Anna." Matthias's speech was slurred and drunken-sounding. "Vas …Vas… quez?"

Vasquez was so distracted by his concern for Matthias that he did not see the two shadows moving towards him. They had the appearance of a happy middle-aged married couple.

"Yes, my friend, now you must think only of your love for Anna. Concentrate and we will leave. Hold my robe, think only of Anna, Anna, Anna. She waits for you on the other side." Vasquez moved towards the outer aisle with the boy in tow, where he was met by the smiling couple.

"There is an idolater amongst us. A papist who seeks to twist the mind of one of our flock!" The Som sneered at Verhoevan and vanished, only to materialize inches from Vasquez.

"You and the Phorian will need more weapons than flattery to steal one of my flock!"

"Go in peace, my son," Vasquez purred back in a tone of rapture.

"Your son? Why … don't you know your own father?"

Vasquez recognized the voice, and as he looked closer at the Som he was shaken to his core as the Som slowly transformed into the likeness of his father. The Som probed Vasquez's fear for more ammunition.

'So, you would sleep with men and see fit to wear the robes of a priest? Are you not ashamed by your lowly life of buggery? You are an abomination in the eyes of the Lord and a great disappointment to your mother and me!"

"You, this can't be…" Vasquez fell back and felt as though he was suffocating. Before the Som could continue, Verhoevan spoke calmly but forcefully as he appeared at the altar.

"And so, my children, observe how it is that an idea known to some of you as the Devil works. It will appear as those you once loved and trusted. That love and trust will be twisted and used against you for a darker purpose. In a place of God, should you not find forgiveness for your transgressions? How many are aware of your minister's ability to transform into the body's of those you love?" There was a murmur growing in the congregation, and the Som moved quickly back to the altar to shore up the cracks appearing in the dam.

"Beware of these imposters! They would turn you against your own! We are one in the body of Christ!" the Som screamed.

Vasquez got back on his feet and pulled Matthias up. Matthias looked curiously at him.

"Wh-who is it you lo-love, Vasquez? Should you be thinking only of love, like me?"

Vasquez came to his senses, grabbed Matthias's hand, and

Matthias followed him towards the door. Verhoevan smiled at the Som, then turned to the congregation, sensing an opportunity.

"How many here have someone they love who they long to see again? If you love them dearly enough, they are probably waiting for you to come to your senses. If not, you can remain here and sing endless songs of praise, or you can take the Christian metaphor of love to your hearts and find the infinite love that lives beyond this place of fear. Find the love of that which you call God that dwells deep within each of you. One can never know Jesus or Muhammad or Buddha or whoever you fancy as your messenger of truth as long as you don't find some way to love all of them, or at least the metaphor of what those ideas stand for. For each one of them holds but a sliver of the notion of the idea that you call God. The truth you seek lies in trying to understand the common inspiration that was their motivation, the embrace of that which is bigger than us all. Think of love and you will not know the fear that holds you in this God forsaken place. Bless you all, and good luck. Oh, and by the way, if anyone wants to join me I'm going to a place of love. If you wish to join me and seek infinite possibilities simply let go of your fear and make it so."

The Som raged towards Verhoevan and swung at him in anger, but his hand passed through Verhoevan's body like a blind man's staff through mist. Verhoevan smiled at him.

"Oh, we really have rattled your cage today, haven't we, you poor soul? Remember, you are free to join us at anytime." Verhoevan moved off the altar, and as he walked slowly down the aisle a handful of souls followed.

The Som shrieked from the altar, "Beware of wolves disguised as sheep, for this is truly Satan leading you to the fires of Hell." He began singing frantically until he had the attention of the congregation, who began to lose themselves in the familiar drone.

Once outside, Verhoevan turned to see he had more than a dozen souls in tow, looking to him for some kind of guidance.

"Think of one you love that has gone before. Feel that love, think of the image that goes with that love," Verhoevan softly instructed.

One by one, shadows appeared on the horizon heading towards the church. One by one they were recognized with tears of overwhelming joy. The reclaimed souls from the church could hardly move; they were disoriented, as though waking from a long sleep. Those who came for them understood and spoke soft words of comfort. One old man stood at the door of the church squinting at a handsome man whom he thought he recognized.

"Hello, Father," the handsome young man said softly.

The old man heaved in convulsions of emotion. "I am so sorry for what I did. I … love …" The old man wept.

"I know. I've felt it for a long time. You've suffered for too long, Father. Come, there are more of us who love you, waiting."

"Ha … Harding, your name is … Harding," Matthias said with a look of confusion.

The young man and his father turned and stared at Matthias.

"Yes, we are both named Harding," the young man answered.

"I b-b-beg your pardon … you look f-f-familiar. I thought you were a m-m-man I know named Harding, but now that I see you c-c-closer ..." Matthias became unsure.

"I know who you are," the handsome man murmured. "Give my brother John my love, and thank him. Tell him his prayers played a part in all of this." The young man touched his father's shoulder and their images slowly faded until they were gone.

One by one all the souls met with loved ones or guides and left, until only Verhoevan, Matthias, and Vasquez remained. Inside the church, the congregation continued droning another hymn. Verhoevan turned to Matthias.

"Well, young man, you have caused more than your share of trouble."

"I am sorry, sir. I … I only wished …"

"You only wished for answers and privileges not afforded to those of an earthly domain. You have a good life ahead of you there, don't squander it with any more foolishness." Verhoevan turned to Vasquez. "My friend, you must go back and try to destroy the manuscript. Close the gateway to that which will be known to all in their own time."

"I am sorry your body was moved. When I finally found out where you were, it was too late." Vasquez was overcome.

"Oh, my dear Vasquez, I do thank you for your tears, but my time was not cut that short, for as it turned out I had a weak heart that was looking for the right moment. It won't be long until we see each other again, but now you must return."

"Very well." Vasquez looked sadly into the eyes of his

friend and felt immense love.

"I will see you sooner than you think." Verhoevan smiled and was gone.

"Well?" Matthias looked at Vasquez.

"Well what?" Vasquez answered with some distraction.

"Let's get back to the cathedral."

"Your body is not at the cathedral. You lie in Captain Harding's cabin."

"How did I get…?" Matthias didn't finish his sentence. They were in the Captain's cabin, where Harding knelt by the bed, deep in prayer.

"Look through my eyes?" Matthias asked.

"Just like before, Matthias."

As Matthias lay in his body, he could sense Harding's prayer. When he looked through his own eyes, he felt the awareness of Harding's thoughts evaporate into the shallower stream of only Harding's words as he finished. The words in the earthly plane conveyed so little of the thoughts behind them. In the other place, the thoughts were far more deeply complete. In Harding's thoughts, Matthias had become aware of how much the Captain cared for him and the pain he had caused him. Harding's voice summoned the end of his prayer.

"In the name of Christ Our Lord, Amen." Harding looked down at Matthias and was startled to see him looking back. "Matthias?"

"Your brother … sends his … love and thanks you," Matthias said haltingly as he sought control of a dry throat.

Harding jumped to his feet and backed away from Matthias as though he had seen a ghost.

"You . . . you … you're back, you live. Thank God."

"Actually, thank Vasquez," Matthias said as he slowly sat up. He felt a little strange with the weight and sluggishness of his body. "I never knew you had a brother."

Harding was visibly shaken at the mention of his brother and looked at Matthias with a measure of fear. .

"How do you … we have not spoken of my brother since his death. He died in a drunken brawl, a Godless man."

"And yet, you prayed to him."

"I did no such thing. I was praying to my father."

"Mmm … but it was your brother who saved your father's

soul from the evil one."

"The evil one?"

"I guess this all sounds crazy to you, but I have just met your brother and he said that somehow your prayers played a role in him finding your father, who was trapped in the same Hell I was."

"My father surely was not in Hell! What you speak of is witchcraft and Satan's domain, Matthias."

"Forgive my insensitivity, but I swear I did witness your father find love, apparently for the first time since his passing, and it was because of your brother's presence. Let's find Vasquez before you burn me at the stake!"

Matthias attempted to walk to the door but collapsed. His strength had been totally sapped.

"Matthias!" Harding's concern for the boy was a reflex. He helped Matthias back to bed, then sat on the edge of the mattress staring out of the stern window. His lip began to quiver but his expression remained hard.

"I think of my brother often and wonder if I could have prevented his death."

"He's fine, and more important, he's with your father, giving your father ... forgiveness, yes, that's it ... forgiveness. What did your father do to your brother?"

Harding stood and looked angrily at Matthias. "This is madness!"

"Yes, it is. And there is madness on the other side as well. I have seen it. Wherever we go, we take our madness with us. I think we create it, for reasons that escape me. In both places, though, love appears to be the goal and where the answers lie. Please don't be angry with me for telling you what I have seen because it might not fit your religious beliefs. I have no idea what God is any more, but perhaps we can hazard a guess that if you believe God is omniscient there is a good chance He is not vindictive."

"How dare you talk of God with such irreverence! You blaspheme!" Harding fumed.

"Look at me, Captain Harding." The Captain looked into the boy's eyes as Matthias spoke. "It is not curious that the only anger I have ever seen from you is now in the defence of your religious beliefs. And you are directing that anger at me, one who loves you. Think on that. Would you end a friendship in defence of a belief rather than the truths found in the poetry of the belief? You have been taught, like I was, that if you were not good you would go to Hell and burn for eternity. Think about it. That's fear that you have been sold. Now think about love. Is there any fear there? On which side of these two ideas would you rather err? Was love not what Christ preached? What about 'cast not the first stone' or 'judge not lest ye be judged'?"

Harding studied Matthias for moment.

"I don't know what to think, only that you have changed, Matthias. You seem to be in possession of a wisdom well beyond your years, and I'm not sure if your newfound wisdom isn't destructive."

"I've been called many things, but wise? Now there's a word that has never been thrown in my direction. I have changed, though. I can feel it. I have been trapped by my own fear and seen how others exploit it. I will …" Matthias fell back on the bed. "…I will never be trapped by my fear again. We need to find Vasquez, I … must not sleep I ..."

With that, Matthias dropped into a deep sleep. Harding took up his post at his young friend's side, shaking his head at all he'd been told and for the first time in his life … unsure.

14

THE WAY BACK

Elsewhere, 1989

Danny stood watching Joel's family reunion, which ended abruptly when curious medical staff rushed over. They didn't know what to do. His consciousness was as much a puzzle as his unconsciousness had been. The physician in charge was paged and appeared in a matter of minutes to join in the chorus of "What the…?"

Mission accomplished, Danny now had to find Alison and return. He had left her at the Roman baths and wasn't sure how to get back there other than to visualize, and so that's what he did. And sure enough, there he was, and the lovely woman he had earlier rejected came to greet him again. A side of him liked the idea of learning the skills of unbridled sensuality, but as he pondered the idea, he realized that those words more or less described his life, to that point. Being the rock star — okay, the rock "wannabe" star — and bedding pretty much everything that moved, for years, had burned him out. He sensed that his life in physical form had been a waste in most ways, apart from his love of singing. He did have some musical talent that had got sidetracked by the humdrum of the road.

"I thought you might be back," the naked girl said, planting a seriously wet kiss on his lips.

"Have you seen Alison, the one I came here with the first time?" Danny asked, ignoring her sensual invitation.

"The one responsible for your jealousy?"

"That would be the one."

"Why no, she left this place some time ago."

"Where to?"

"I can't say, but she left to see someone whose need for her was strong. I believe they knew each other. Will you not join us for a time, then?"

"Uh … no, I really need to find Alison," Danny muttered, wondering what his next move might be.

"Then you will, if she wishes to be found," the woman said as she turned to welcome another newcomer, who looked very glad to see her, indeed.

Danny was at a loss. He was now worried about Alison and also curious about who had spirited her away. He pictured himself in the fields at the foot of the Phorian Acropolis and materialized standing in the tall grass. A group of overly friendly people sensed his discomfort and headed his way. These ones looked a little different, but he sensed their objective was the same.

"Hello, friend," the spokesman began.

"Oh piss off, you idiots." Danny flung it out as he walked towards the stairs. They followed briefly, but as Danny approached the Phorian structure, one by one they began to drop back, until only one remained, and he halted just short of the first step.

Danny turned to face him. "You're curious about this place, aren't you? I feel it."

"May Allah forgive you your ignorance, infidel."

"You didn't answer my question. What stops you from coming with me?"

"It is a place of infidels, and you will burn in the fires of Hell if you do not accept Islam and find Allah through his one true voice, Mohammed."

"Man, the song is the same, just different saviours. All right, are you Sunni or Shiite?"

"How dare you insult me so? The Shiites have corrupted the wisdom of the Koran with the poison of the Talmud. I am Sunni, we are the true believers of the uncorrupted word of Allah as it is written."

"Yeah … well I'm a Jew, and you know what? This was written way before your guy was a twinkle in his father's eye: *we* are the chosen people of God, pal. You don't even register on God's A-list. And you know what else? If you bug me, God might make your rivers run red with blood and send down a sky full of locusts upon you, and all of your firstborn sons will die, but *our people* will be safe and sound, because we'll splash goat's blood over our doors. Does that sound a little wacky to ya, pal? Good, because now we've established that we both know what wacky sounds like, and therefore you've got to know how fucking wacky you sound to the rest of God's creations!"

"You are a mad infidel!"

"Oh, so now you're a psychiatrist assessing my mental state! Not only do you know what God thinks, minute to minute, but you can also look into the minds of others? If you had half an intuitive brain you'd know I'm not mad, I'm probably in love for the first time in my life, and you know what else? I think I'm into fidelity for the first time in my life! So you're wrong on both counts, Brainiac. Now I'm going to tell you something that is in your own thoughts. You really want to come up these stairs yourself, don't ya? You sense something more out there than what you've been sold. You're curious, aren't ya? But you don't have the balls to follow your own mind because all you have are fears and threats. The fear of what your own damn kind will do to you — not your God … but your pals! Mmm, nice belief system, buddy! Stops you dead, doesn't it? You know what that makes you? A pissant! A spineless pissant with no real friends, just an insane, vindictive General for a God and military police posing as your friends! Now there's a lofty, enlightened spiritual ideal for ya!"

Danny ran up the stairs two at a time, and when he reached the top he spun around to see the man staring at his feet, his face a mask of confusion. He was shaking visibly as he slowly lifted one foot up and placed it on the first step. Danny couldn't believe his eyes, and he called down to him.

"Hey, be careful now, this could be the stairway to Hell! Don't forget your fear!"

The man quickly removed his foot but continued to stare at the steps. "That's quite an interesting technique."

Danny turned around to see the man who had come into the Phorian chamber when he and Alison were leaving. He was the one Verhoevan had said brought back many souls from the clutches of the Soms. Danny was embarrassed and didn't know what to say.

"I've never tried 'spineless pissant' before, but it seems to have been highly effective on this one. You seek to shame one into the direction of reform. Where did you study?"

"I'm sorry for the language. I'm not supposed to be here," Danny offered with embarrassment.

"Oh, to the contrary, I think we could use your like around here. The name I use is Bernard, Daniel, and you made me laugh for the first time in quite awhile."

"Nice to meet you, Bernard. So, you're the one who rescues souls?"

"In a manner of speaking. Some unfortunately lose all life over a period of time and dissipate into nothingness. It is a great sadness that there are those amongst us who are so predatory. They robbed people of so much, even life itself on the physical plane, and here, over a period of time, they seek to rob their prey of existence itself. I would have thought after all this time that we would have evolved past such behaviours, but over and over the cycle repeats itself. In seeking religious renewal, our species keeps reverting to ancient words written by fearful men from ignorant, fearful times. I am beginning to think that the dominant religious texts persist merely to try us. They could well be obstacles we must learn to overcome. They are a constant reminder of who we were when we sought a singular answer to all that is plural by design. Sorry for the sermon, I get carried away."

"Don't be sorry, I like what you say. My people's faith has always felt dark to me. Most faiths unfortunately seem to come to a similar point of exclusion: be one of us or be cast out. What's that all about? Is that just insecurity talking?"

"It arises from the dichotomy of our need to know set against our inability to know everything. It's a formula for madness, until we grow to understand that the joy is in the struggle, the pursuit of small pieces of the puzzle, some of which we don't find and will never know. If all were known, existence would lack the stimulus to seek, which is the joy of it."

"I guess I've … uh … pretty much wasted my life so far," Danny said with shame.

"That could be a simplistic view. It might be better framed that such a realization shows thought, remorse, and a desire to grow … an understanding that you can be better than you are. So you are on your own path and timetable. This is good. You think you love the one called Alison now, and this is a new road for you," Bernard suggested in a friendly tone.

Danny looked at Bernard and thought seriously. "I don't know why. I hardly know the woman … but yes, I think I love her. She isn't a woman I would have gone after if all this Resonance stuff hadn't happened. In fact, I wouldn't have given her the time of day if we had been introduced under ordinary circumstances. There is a little girl in her, an unspoiled spirit that I saw when we first crossed."

"Interesting. And now we have a real problem, don't we? And I'm not sure, but you might be the first."

"What? What problem?" Danny asked.

"Something has been revealed to you here that might not have been revealed in the physical world. If you are successful in going back, what will the world do to that love? Will it remain, or will the pull of the material world corrupt it or hide it like an embarrassment? Over and over I have seen love flourish here where it couldn't on earth. It's a fascinating dilemma."

"Bloody tragic, I'd say," Danny added.

"That all depends on how you look at it. As a point of realization, as an obstacle course that love must traverse to find its way, all is as it should be. Without the struggle, that which cannot be lost cannot be gained. The love that survives is stronger for the journey. You have seen a soul here that you love; that soul will always be. Think on that, Daniel. I must be off, but I have enjoyed engaging your spirit. Your frustration with the Soms reminded me of a younger version of myself, and I confess I am invigorated by your love for Alison. That's what drew me to you. Thank you, Daniel. I look forward to the time our paths will cross again, my friend."

"Careful, the Soms call everyone `friend.' You don't want to be mistaken for a Som, now do you?" Danny smirked.

"Ah, but it's all in how it is said, my *friend*."

Bernard smiled, and Danny felt an unbelievable sense of well-being wash over him. In it was a realization that he had just met someone far more powerful than he had ever met before in his life. It was as if he had received a jolt of unconditional love. He watched Bernard head down the stairs then stop at the indecisive Som, and heard his thoughts.

"Look into your own heart and you will find your longing. In your longing you will find your reason, and then your courage, for the first step will slowly appear. Good luck to you, Mustafa, my brother." Bernard placed his hand on Mustafa's shoulder, then turned to leave. Mustafa wept as Bernard's image dissipated into the tall grasses, and he was gone.

Danny was deeply moved and, for some reason, totally exhausted. He entered the Phorian structure and went to a bench to sit for a minute, only to recline and drift off. It was as though the energy he'd expended in the last few hours was greater than he had ever experienced. Grieving with those parents in the ICU, seeing

Joel reunited, the realization that he might love someone for the first time in his life … this was all way too much for anyone to absorb in such a small window of time. His mind surrendered to a state of rest.

Someone called from a distance. He recognized the voice but couldn't quite place it. It was an old voice. It sounded very content, and it continued to call his name. He looked into the eyes of a kindly woman. It was Maggie Walters. But he had heard a man's voice, and then he heard it again, very clearly.

"Hello, Daniel." Next to Maggie stood … Dr. Walters.

"Dr. Walters? Wh-why are you here? You promised you wouldn't use the Resonance. Where is…?" Danny sat up, dazed.

"I didn't use the Resonance, Daniel. I'm afraid I have crossed over from natural causes. It wasn't long after the second interval I sent you that I felt it come over me like warm water. I believe I had a massive stroke and fell. By the look of me when I left, I think the fall did the rest of the job. I'm sorry I've failed you. I've been looking for you for some time but you've been unreachable. I'm told that when one rests here one cannot be found."

"So how did you find me?"

"You must have been coming around when both Maggie and I looked for you, because we ended up here in front of this bench, and then your image started to appear."

"Oh no! How much time has passed on the other side?" Danny's face was animated with worry.

"I have no idea. Maggie and I were having a wonderful reunion and I must confess we have had a period of rest ourselves. It came over me so quickly that I just drifted. Maggie joined me."

"Alison. Have you seen Alison?" Danny asked, worried.

"Well … no. I tried to find her first but was unsuccessful. I am so sorry, Daniel, I didn't think about the possibility of dying. I …" The sound of Dr. Walters's voice faded as Danny's thoughts took him somewhere else. Maggie watched as Danny slowly dissolved in front of them.

"Something's wrong," she said, and her husband drew her closer to him.

***

The hotel room at the Airport Holiday Inn materialized in front of Danny. There was no sign of his body or Alison's or Dr. Walters's. There were, however, a couple of policemen standing holding coffees, while a plainclothes officer appeared to be dusting for intruder prints on the balcony and sliding glass doors. Joel's keyboard and synth rack were gone, as was Verhoevan's manuscript. So where was his body, and was it still breathing somewhere? He tried to sense his body, then he just pictured himself looking out of his own eyes, and *bingo*.

Danny remembered Maggie Walters's words. Something was wrong, all right … very wrong. His body felt horrid, as if it no longer fit, and he couldn't feel or move his hands. Then he became aware that he wasn't breathing. It was very dark and voices approached from somewhere behind him. He couldn't feel or see until he heard the click of a metallic latch. Then he seemed to float out into dull light. A shadow reached across his face and slowly pulled a thin sheet down, revealing a fluorescent light overhead. Where were the voices he had heard? There was sniffling, the sound of shoes on concrete, and then … his mother's face looking down at him. She heaved with convulsions, and her pain was so excruciating that it ripped through Danny like a saw. Danny leapt from his body with a shudder and looked down on the morgue drawer that held it. His mother stared down at the lifeless corpse of her son, flanked by a guy in a lab coat and another person in a drab brown suit.

Please let this be a dream, he thought. *I'm still asleep in the Phorian Acropolis. I can force myself awake. Wake up, Danny, you idiot, before you scare yourself to death!* But nothing happened. He looked down on his body. The colour of his skin was something from a horror movie. His cheeks had sunk and his mouth was agape, pushed open from the last long breath of air that his lungs had taken.

The man in the brown suit approached his mother, speaking softly, sympathetically. "Is this the body of your son, Mrs. Blum?"

She couldn't answer verbally, she only nodded, reluctantly, then ran to a stainless-steel sink a few feet away and vomited. Being the habitually tidy person she was, she washed it away with the faucet wand and launched into loud, rhythmic sobs. Danny couldn't bear it. The man in the lab coat began to cover up the body but she stopped him.

"Don't you dare cover up my lovely boy yet!" she sobbed. Danny's mother went back to the body and stroked his hair. "You have left me with no one. I have no grandchildren. I am alone. Why did you do to this to me. Daniel? Why? Why? *Why?*" She screamed and sobbed some more. The depth of her anguish was unbearable to her son. Danny felt an exquisite pain he had never known.

"When can I bury my lovely boy?" she asked the man in the suit.

"Once cause of death is determined the body will be released. I'm sorry, I can't be any more precise than that. The only person who we have answers for at the moment is the old gentleman found with your son and the young lady. His death was from natural causes. At this point, we don't suspect foul play." The man put his hand on her shoulder. "I am very sorry about your son, Mrs. Blum, very sorry. I can't imagine how you must feel."

Danny's mother stared down at the dead body of her boy. "You said he was with a young lady?"

"Yes, a woman by the name of …" The man searched his memory then spat it out. "… Alison Truman. Her ID indicates that she was a professor of ancient languages in the Department of Religious Studies at the University of Toronto, and we have just received confirmation of that."

"How did they die?" Mrs. Blum blurted out between sobs.

"At the moment, all we know is that the two of them appear to have been lying on their backs on separate beds wearing headphones, no signs of a struggle, and toxicology says no sign of drugs of any sort. They appeared to have died in their sleep approximately a day or so after the elderly gentleman."

"You say there was an elderly gentleman. Who was he?" Mrs. Blum needed information.

"He was a former cardiologist by the name of Walters. Did you know him?"

"No," Mrs. Blum said, covering Danny's face gently with the sheet. "May I see the girl he was with?" she asked.

"I'm, uh, sorry, Mrs. Blum, they're performing an autopsy as we speak."

With those words Danny reeled. "No!" He thought of Alison, and in that same moment he stood looking at her body. Her chest was splayed open but her face, even in death, somehow managed a quirky smirk of defiance. The coroner looked to be going for brain samples, and Danny knew he had to get out of there when the saw hit her cranium with a screech.

This nightmare had to stop! He needed Alison. He needed her like he had never needed another soul.

15

RETURNS OF THE DAY

Hamburg, 1848

Vasquez was looking at the body of Pietro and noticed the chest cavity moving with shallow but steady respirations. There was some blood and a fair-sized lump on the back of the young priest's head where someone had obviously delivered a severe blow. He was so worried for Pietro that it took a moment or two for Vasquez to realize his own body was not where he'd left it. So . . . where was it?

Luke. Luke's was not a keen mind, and old habits would be hard to break. Sure enough, in the passages beneath the cathedral he saw the flickering of torchlight ahead. He came upon Luke standing as three men grunted, lifting the weight of Vasquez's body over the lip of a sarcophagus. Vasquez grabbed Luke by the shoulder, causing the old man to spin around and recite a vivid damnation in Latin. Vasquez moved quickly and with mischievous intent. In an instant he came alive in his body, screaming like a devil from Hell.

"*Haaaaaa*, you are all damned! You are marked by Satan!!! *Haaaa!!!*"

The men screamed and dropped Vasquez into the coffin. He rose again, and in the flickering of Luke's torch he must have looked like Beelzebub himself because all three men ran for their lives.

Luke's dour expression turned to one of highly focused hatred, and as Vasquez was climbing out of the sarcophagus he felt a sharp pain in his back. He looked up at Brother Luke, who held a dripping dagger in his hand.

"Brother Luke, what have you done?" Vasquez was in pain. "Have you lost even the basic commandments of your faith?"

"Don't talk to me about faith! Your faith is with the Devil himself, and with Verhoevan, the Devil's messenger! I know what you do. I will dispose of you and I will destroy Verhoevan's book."

Vasquez flung himself out onto the floor and reached back to assess the damage, and in that moment of distraction he felt another sharp pain in his chest. Luke had lodged the dagger deeply. Vasquez was speechless. He sensed that the jab to his chest was a mortal wound, and a rage consumed him.

"I will put an end to you and your vile work, you poor, demented old fool." Vasquez grabbed the old man, who weighed nothing to him, and threw him into the sarcophagus. He reached in to pull Verhoevan's manuscript from the old man's grasp, but Luke held tight and tried to sit. Vasquez punched him squarely on the bridge of his nose with his hard fist, stunning the old man, who fell back with a groan. Vasquez grabbed the manuscript, placed it on the floor, and pushed his ox-like strength to the maximum. He heaved, and slowly the lid of the sarcophagus began to slide shut. With an inch to go, the old man screamed from within as he realized what was happening.

"It is time for you to meet the God you think speaks to you, old man, for you have killed for the last time. May He be more merciful to you than you deserve." With one last grunt Vasquez shoved, and the lid clunked into place. Luke's screams were barely audible to Vasquez, who was now spilling blood from his chest wound at an alarming rate. He stumbled down the passageway to the bottom of the stairs, where he fell to the floor, clutching Verhoevan's manuscript.

His head grew light with the blood loss. It wasn't such a bad death, as deaths go, he thought … and he had seen some nasty ones. The pain began diminishing to a warm glow. He had saved a young friend who could now return to his lovely wife. He wondered what life might be like for them in America. He fancifully considered it as an option himself for a moment, but then again, an old priest would just be in the way of youngsters starting a family and a new life together. Maybe all was as it should be. It was their time.

A light appeared ahead of him, and at first he thought he might be rescued from his mortal fate, but then he saw the shadows moving in the light and recognized the one in the robe heading in his direction with a familiar lanky gait … Verhoevan. Ah, he understood, with a sweet sadness.

***

At that moment, Matthias's eyes opened to Harding, who was sitting by the bed like a doting father.

"How long?" Matthias croaked.

"Let me get you some water." Harding reached for a pitcher, then poured a glass and handed it to the lad. "You've been asleep for a good hour or so."

"Something is wrong. We must find Vasquez." Matthias stood and pulled himself together. Harding called for Ferguson, who appeared in the doorway moments later.

By the time Harding and Matthias walked onto the deck, a boat had been readied. They climbed down the rope ladder and the oarsmen put their backs into the short haul to the wharf.

They walked up the cobblestone street and passed Frau Hoffman's brothel. Hoffman stood in her door, burgeoning cleavage on display, and glared at Matthias, remembering how close she had come to a sum of money she could never attain from a thousand years on her back.

The world was cruel to some, Matthias thought, as he walked by the vile woman. Maybe there was a reason for cruelty … maybe not. Maybe it was all as it should be. There would always be people so disgusting of soul that they served as a beacon for others to find more loving, more admirable responses to the adversities all were bound to face in one way or another. Harding tipped his hat to the woman. She snarled in their direction until a potential customer stopped and flipped her a coin. She laughed a well-practised laugh, exposing a few missing teeth, and grabbed the man by his privates. The spider led her prey, crotch first, into the inner reaches of her nest. He would be made as drunk as possible, depending on his purse, robbed of the balance while he fornicated, and his carcass would be spat out onto the street as soon as he regained some of his senses.

As they approached the back door of the cathedral, Brother Nicolas was hurriedly directing two men who carried Pietro on a board. The young Pietro was unconscious, and there was an obvious wound to the back of his head. When Nicolas saw Harding and Matthias, the blood fled from his face. "What has happened here?" Matthias asked with concern.

"Uh, no cause for alarm, Herr Dopp. Pietro has fallen and given himself a rather severe bump to his head. He will be taken to the monastery, where his wounds will be tended. Now, if you'll excuse me, gentlemen." Nicolas pushed his way forward and was followed by the men carrying Pietro. Harding and Matthias headed into the cathedral, and Harding spoke quietly under his breath.

"That fellow is up to no good and his face cannot conceal it. The bump on Pietro's head wasn't from any kind of fall. I'd wager he's been hit, and from behind."

Outside, Nicolas stopped in his tracks as a thought moved across his face like the shadow of a cloud, bringing about a change of plans: "You men take Pietro to the monastery. I have another matter to tend to." With that, he ran off in the opposite direction.

Matthias and Harding went to the bellows chamber, where they saw a trace of blood Harding assumed to be from Pietro's head. There was no sign of Vasquez.

"Pietro was watching over Vasquez's body when he was struck from behind. Who would do such a thing?" Matthias looked at Harding, and they both said the name at the same time: "Luke." Harding grabbed candelabra with three lit candles and the two men headed down to the burial chambers. At the bottom of the spiral stairs they saw a heap of dark cloth. As they neared, the light from the candelabra revealed the crumpled body of Vasquez.

"No!" Matthias screamed as he rushed to his friend and looked for signs of life that were not forthcoming. He held the priest in his arms and shuddered in tears. Harding looked around for any signs of a struggle and followed a trail of blood that stopped a good twenty feet away. It was when he returned moments later that the candlelight revealed the blood on Vasquez's back.

"Matthias, we must leave."

Matthias looked up and Harding could see he was glistening in what had to be blood from another wound to Vasquez's chest. "This is not going to look good, we have to get out of here now!" Harding grabbed Matthias, who was reaching for Verhoevan's manuscript. The two men climbed to the top of the stairs, where Brother Nicolas waited with two policemen.

"There they are, they have stolen a holy book and, oh no, they have killed Brother Vasquez, the keeper of that book! Look at the blood. Oh, may God forgive them!"

"Is your entire brotherhood evil?" Harding asked angrily. "Constable, we were looking for our friend and found him at the bottom of the stairs, dead from mortal wounds to his back and his chest."

"Mortal wounds *you* inflicted, for he was alive when I left him but moments ago!" Nicolas lied through his teeth. "Would you believe a man of God or murderers covered in blood?"

The constables responded to the moral authority of the priest and took Matthias and Harding away, under Harding's loud protest. Matthias was lost in guilt for the death of his friend. It was more than he could bear. As Nicolas watched them leave, he casually walked to the front pew and picked up a folded piece of altar linen, revealing a leather-bound book. He quickly wrapped Verhoevan's manuscript in the cloth and spirited the sacrilege away.

Matthias and Captain Harding were escorted to the cellars of the Rathaus and placed in a crude cell with thick oak doors clad in iron sheeting. The room reeked with the smell of human excrement from a thief who had relieved his fretting bowels the entire night before they'd dragged him out, screaming, to the gallows. The door was slammed and locked behind them. The two new prisoners stood, afraid to move or sit anywhere for fear of stepping or sitting in something they sensed was pretty much everywhere.

A good couple of hours later familiar voices approached. News of murder travelled fast in Hamburg. It usually meant there was entertainment to be had in the near future at the gallows. When Jorge Hacker had heard of the arrest of Matthias Dopp and an American ship's captain for murder, he had immediately sought the assistance of Herr Becker, from the bank. He knew that a man well positioned in the wealth of the city would be given audience and respect.

When the door opened, Becker's face turned pale at the foul odour.

"Guards, place these men in a clean cell that I might speak with them!" The guards responded immediately to the tone of authority. Harding and Matthias squinted in the light as they emerged. Jorge gasped at the sight of the blood that covered Matthias's clothing.

"All is not as it might seem," Harding assured them as they were pushed into the next cell.

"We will have light and some seating, guards!" The door to the new cell was briefly locked until the guards returned with two crude wooden benches. Becker and Jorge were locked in the cell, where they sat facing Harding and Matthias.

"Vasquez is dead." Matthias sniffed. "It's all my fault."

Harding put his arm around his friend and addressed Jorge and Becker. "We were worried about Vasquez, who had put himself at risk in a personal matter for Matthias. We found him dead in the bowels of the cathedral. Matthias held the body of his friend tenderly and was bloodied in the doing of it. There is treachery afoot, and it involves the priest they call Brother Nicolas."

"Please. Lower your voices and tell me everything you can that might be of some use."

After everything Harding could think of had been shared, and some strategy discussed, the guards were called to open the door. Becker demanded to be escorted to the office of the Chief Inspector of the Hamburg police, whose office was on the second floor of the Rathaus. They were escorted by one of the constables and waited in the hallway while the Inspector was informed of their presence. The constable emerged and signalled Becker and Jorge to go in. Inspector Berndt Johansen was an overfed man. He sat stuffed behind a large desk that he managed to make look quite small. Johansen ignored them for a moment while he finished polishing an ornamental pistol.

"Beautiful, isn't it?" He held the weapon up for their perusal. "Elegant curves that please the eye like a beautiful woman. Although a beautiful woman would not be as easy to hold, she could be just as deadly, I dare say!" He laughed heartily at his own joke while he rose to an imposing height and carefully placed the gun in an ornate, inlaid wooden box that sat inside a narrow cabinet with open, etched-glass doors. Becker knew Inspector Johansen to be a shrewd man who played the buffoon well. It was part of his success. He benefited from those who underestimated his intellect. Johansen went back to his desk and grunted back down into his seat. When he had managed to find a comfortable position for his bulk he looked back up with a stern expression.

"So, you are here about the young Dopp boy and a Captain Harding, who currently reside in one of my cells accused of murdering a priest by the name of Vasquez. I have not had an opportunity to interview them yet but I understand you have done so, and quite extensively. Perhaps you can fill me in on your investigation. But let me say, I have viewed the body of the priest who lies in the morgue, and he was surely and deliberately murdered by knife wounds to the back and through his heart."

"The deceased," Becker began, "is one of the dearest friends of Herr Dopp. When he found his friend bereft of life he held him and wept, oblivious to the fact that his friend's blood was soaking into his own clothing. Herr Dopp and Captain Harding were looking for their friend, who was late for an appointment. As you may know by now, Herr Dopp, the priest Vasquez, and Captain Harding are all business associates."

"And why would they be looking in the cathedral for a business associate?" Johansen interjected.

"Because the priest had gone there to retrieve a leather-bound work of music that Gert Dopp, the deceased father of Matthias, had commissioned in memory of his wife. I must also add that a priest known as Verhoevan is also missing and presumed dead."

"I see. And where is the piece of music now?"

"It was ripped from the hands of Matthias by Brother Nicolas, a priest of the same order, who fetched your constables and escorted them to the cathedral."

"So you say Brother Nicolas, to whom I have already spoken, is in possession of the property of Herr Dopp. I must tell you that Brother Nicolas made no mention of a musical manuscript, and so it remains the accused's word against his, as does the ownership of this manuscript, if it indeed exists … most troublesome. The word of a sailor and a blood-spattered boy against the word of a man of God."

"There may be another witness," Becker continued.

"And who might this be?" Johansen's eyebrows rose.

"A young priest by the name of Pietro. His body was being removed from the sanctuary when the accused, as you call them, arrived. He, according to Captain Harding, appeared to have been hit on the head and rendered unconscious."

"Well, I think it's time we all paid a little visit to the monastery. Let's see what Brother Nicolas has to say about the work of music you claim belongs to Herr Dopp, and the whereabouts of the one called Pietro. You know, there are many people of wealth and power in this city who receive the sacraments and view the Church and its servants as infallible tools of God."

"I also know you to be a Lutheran like myself, Herr Johansen," Becker said, with a whiff of piety.

"A Lutheran? Yes, indeed I am, Herr Becker, but whether I am like or unlike yourself remains to be seen." Johansen stood and headed out the door. "You may accompany me," he called over his shoulder.

Inspector Johansen, once downstairs, summoned the two constables who had arrested Harding and Matthias and ordered a carriage. The five men arrived at the large oak door that filled the stone archway to the quarters assigned to the Brothers of Saint Francis. Johansen was first to the door and rapped the door with the silver handle of his cane. A young novice answered and ran to fetch Brother Nicolas, who appeared looking surprised and uncomfortable.

"I trust I haven't interrupted you from your holy work, Brother Nicolas, but I need to speak with Brother Pietro."

"I am afraid, Inspector, that he is unable to speak and is being attended to by one of our order who is a healer. When he is able to speak, perhaps I can send someone for you?"

"That would be most kind, Brother Nicolas. I would also like to know when you found my constables how you knew that the priest they call Vasquez had been murdered, as you told them, and why you did nothing to stop it."

"Oh but I did. I ran for the police."

"I see. And what of the manuscript of music belonging to Herr Dopp?" The Inspector's glare was searing, and Nicolas stumbled.

"I, uh … know of no such manuscript," he blundered.

"How unfortunate, for that statement puts you at odds now with four other people, two of whom are my constables. You have now lost my confidence, and you may very well have lost your game, sir. Please hold this man here," Johansen barked at one of his men.

The Inspector stormed into the monastery with Hacker, Becker, and the remaining constable and stopped another young novice.

"Boy, take me to Brother Pietro. I fear his life may be in danger!" The novice, clearly intimidated by the towering bulk of the Inspector, did as he was told, and at the end of a long hallway he showed them into a room where an older priest held a pewter cup to the mouth of an unconscious Pietro.

"Stop what you are doing or be prepared to hang for it!" Johansen screamed. The priest was so startled he dropped the cup. Johansen grabbed it from the floor and shoved his nose into it to get a whiff of the remaining contents.

"What is this brew?" he demanded.

"It is a b-b-blend of herbs to give our f-f-fallen brother strength," he stammered.

"And how does an unconscious man drink? Or does he just … drown?" Johansen sneered. "Hold the priest!" he barked at his constable, then he turned to the novice. "You, boy, get me something to carry this man out of here." The boy disappeared and Johansen gently tilted the head of Pietro to one side and saw a small trickle of blood on his pillow from a nasty-looking bump on the back of his head.

"This one has indeed been struck from behind, Herr Becker. I would concur with Captain Harding's assessment. Your story is beginning to look like it might carry the day."

The young novice returned, carrying a board that was gently slid under Pietro's body.

"Herr Hacker, is it?" Jorge nodded in the affirmative. "Perhaps you might help this young man carry Pietro to the carriage."

Jorge took one end of the plank and the novice the other. The constable pulled the attending priest along by the elbow, while Johansen grabbed the pewter cup with his free hand and held it carefully to keep the rest of its contents from spilling. Brother Nicolas was visibly shaken at the sight of his man being escorted by the constable, a look that intensified as Pietro was carried out.

Inspector Johansen went to Nicolas and held the cup to his lips. "Care for a libation?" he said coolly.

Nicolas pulled his head away rather abruptly.

"I didn't think so," the Inspector sneered. "Constables, if you would be so kind as to escort these two `holy' men back to the town hall and place them in a cell for safekeeping. Should they offer resistance, don't hesitate to use your weapons."

Pietro was laid out across the seats of the carriage. Herr Becker and Jorge secured his body so it would not fall. Johansen, for his part, after much huffing and puffing, made it up to the seat with the driver.

Once back at the Rathaus, the Inspector told his carriage driver to wait and a physician was summoned to Johansen's office. He administered smelling salts to Pietro, who opened his eyes and winced with the pain from his head wound. He was lying on a settee surrounded by the Inspector, Becker, and Jorge Hacker, and he looked back at them all for the strangers they were.

"Allow me, young man, to explain your current circumstances. Someone has hit you on the back of the head. Can you tell me what you last remember?" Johansen inquired.

"I was waiting on Brother Vasquez to return in the bellows chamber …" Pietro looked worried with his words and regrouped. "… I mean, regain his consciousness, and then ... I guess that's all I remember."

"And why was Vasquez unconscious?" Johansen asked softly.

"He had fallen while he was working the bellows for me to perform a piece of music," Pietro offered, feeling grateful he had managed to tell the truth—just not all of it.

"It would seem the church is becoming a dangerous place, Pietro. So, you have no idea then how Vasquez ended up in the catacombs beneath the sanctuary?" Johansen continued.

"Is he all right?" Pietro worried.

"I will answer your question, but only after you answer mine," Johansen said firmly.

"I have an idea, but I am afraid an idea is all I have, because I last saw him in the bellows chamber."

"And he was unconscious. So, someone moved this unconscious man, of a fair weight I might add. Now, what is your idea of how that was accomplished?"

"There are these men I have seen with Brother Luke. I know one of them works at the stables nearby. I have seen them emerge from the burial chambers on at least one occasion. I believe Vasquez knows of them as well. You might be better to talk to Brother Vasquez."

"That will be difficult, Pietro. Brother Vasquez has expired from stab wounds to the heart and back. We are holding two other members of your order, who, let's say, have been less than forthcoming, and I believe may very well have been trying to poison you. Do you know who might want to do such a thing and why?"

Pietro was about to respond, then his lip started to quiver. Tears soon followed, but he sputtered on. "Oh, Brother Vasquez. Who could do such a thing?" he cried.

"Do you know any reason why your life would pose some type of threat to Brother Nicolas?"

"Nicolas!" Pietro put a little of the puzzle together and offered it up. "Nicolas assists Brother Luke in his work."

"And where is Brother Luke?"

"Maybe at the monastery, I don't know," Pietro answered.

"Do you feel well enough to travel, Pietro?" Johansen asked sympathetically.

"I, I think so."

"I will be back in a moment."

Johansen left the room and went directly down to the holding cells. He had the guard open the cell holding Harding and Matthias. The two men came out and looked at the Inspector with some trepidation.

"Don't look so worried, you two, I'm not going to bite." Seeing the state of Matthias, Johansen regrouped and decided that a more sympathetic stance was called for. "Herr Dopp, I am sorry for the loss of your friend, and I believe you could use a change of clothing. Captain Harding, if you would be so kind as to escort Herr Dopp to his house and wait there until you hear from me. Your freedom is a courtesy at this moment. I have arranged for a carriage that waits in front of the Rathaus." Johansen turned and headed back up the stairs to his office, where Becker and Hacker waited with Pietro.

"Herr Hacker, you and Herr Becker may join your friends, who will be leaving for Herr Dopp's house in a few moments. Pietro, you are with me." Johansen helped Pietro to his feet.

Out front, Matthias and Harding squinted in the light as Jorge Hacker and Becker ran out to welcome their friends back from the squalor of the Rathaus cells. Johansen watched their carriage pull away and was confident. Never had two murder suspects looked more innocent than those two, he thought. Foot on the step plate, he gripped the handle on the side of his carriage, which groaned under his weight. He reached out to assist Pietro, who seemed a little dazed, and practically lifted him in.

"Take us to the town stables, driver!" Johansen barked as he got in. The horse's hooves slipped on the cobblestones until they found some purchase. The carriage jerked forward, then rolled away, tilting somewhat obviously to one side.

16

ALISON

Elsewhere, 1989

Danny faced a long white wall covered in ivy. The wall was made of huge, elegant marble blocks with a gated central archway. Ivy draped down over the passage, suggesting that entrance was welcome. The beauty of it all suggested Phorian design, but, oddly, Danny sensed a few Soms skulking about, as though drawn to the playful sound of children that emanated from within. Danny recognized the foul odour that matched their foulness of spirit.

One female Som approached and attempted to enter, but an elegant female Phorian in a plain white dress appeared in an instant to question her. The Som hissed something vile at the Phorian, who smiled sadly with the words, "I hope that one day your heart will hold the love that the young spirit within deserves. On that day you may enter."

The Som grew angrier, until her image slowly disintegrated and she was gone.

Danny walked up to the Phorian, expecting to be questioned, but she just looked at him with curiosity and spoke sweetly. "You will find her inside, Daniel, but please tell her your news outside the confines of the sanctuary. There are many inside these walls whose needs are far greater than yours. Some hang onto the slenderest threads of hope."

"So what is this place, if you can call anything around here a *place*?"

"This is a place of refuge and repair. There are many souls here in need of healing and greater self-esteem in order to move on. Some are impeded in their own spiritual growth by the pain and selfishness of others. Any sadness you hold must remain at this threshold, Daniel. You may enter if it is only your love you take within."

"I guess I will need a minute to prepare myself."

The Phorian nodded and her image dissipated into a mist that washed over his face. Danny felt he had the Phorian's trust, and in that trust his resolve to respect her wishes was amplified. The horrors he felt in the images of autopsy tables and his grieving mother had to be filed somewhere. If he felt them surfacing, he would leave instantly and regroup, but at all costs he would not betray the Phorian's request. He barricaded himself inside thoughts of love, then entered.

As he passed though the archway he felt the pain of many within. There were children of all ages and sizes. Some resembled adults but spoke as children and played childlike games alone, as though trying to find a childhood they'd never had. Those souls, Danny felt, had never learned trust or the security of parental approval. His dug down deep and thought of everyone in the place as a tender soul in need of some of the unconditional love he had experienced from his mother. He found the knack of it, stopping momentarily as a child ran up to him and asked him to watch her do a somersault in the soft grass. He watched her, then praised her efforts. Smiling in his approval, she ran on to another person seeking the same. How anyone could not approve of the unbridled joy in a child's heart was beyond Danny's powers of comprehension.

There were many children in the presence of adult Phorians. Some sat holding the little ones while others told magical stories that conveyed metaphors of greater magnitude, seeds planted in the fertile soil of needy imaginations. An older child sat on a bench weeping while a Phorian held him. Danny sensed that some of these children were old souls so badly damaged that they might never have the security to leave … and yet Phorians returned regularly to sit with them for long periods of time, listening, holding them, never giving up on a single soul. Danny was humbled deeply by such love for others and moved around in awe of it. An understanding came to him that some of these Phorians were seeking to love these souls in a way that they had denied their own children. Parenting in the material world was fraught with so much human frailty, and this garden, he now knew, was equally healing to many of the healers.

Under a large willow tree he saw Alison with a girl around nine or ten years old, laughing and holding one another. Danny immediately saw in Alison a soul who had been denied a childhood. Her thoughts were confused and her self-esteem almost negligible. It appeared as though the little girl was there as much for Alison's well-being as her own. Alison soon felt Danny's presence, and when she turned to face him, her face glowed. She grabbed the little girl by the hand and the two of them ran to him. Alison held him and kissed his lips. His heart was overcome, but he held the dam and kissed her back.

The little girl started to giggle. "Shame, shame, now I know your boyfriend's name," she chanted.

Alison started to laugh and made an introduction that Danny felt before he heard her words.

"Daniel, this is my big sister, Avril."

"I never knew you had a big sister."

"Neither did I, until she was introduced to me by a kindly Phorian who found me," Alison responded joyfully, then she continued the introduction. "Avril, this is Daniel, the boy I was telling you about."

"I know, I'm not stupid," Avril said in the way only a ten-year-old could.

Danny remembered his instructions and knelt down.

"Hello, Avril. You know, I think you're just as beautiful as your sister."

Avril kissed him on the cheek and giggled.

A Phorian appeared and looked sweetly at Avril. "Avril, it's story time at the fountain. Would you keep me company?"

Avril looked at Alison and Daniel and gave them a look beyond her years. "You two probably want to smooch. Come and see me at the fountain when you're done."

With that, the Phorian held Avril's hand, whispered in her ear, and the two walked away laughing.

Danny looked at Alison and the dam began to burst. In the blink of an eye they were outside the wall.

"What a generous soul that Rebecca is. She is the Phorian who took me to Avril. Daniel, I never knew Avril existed. She died when I was two. My mother hid or destroyed all the pictures of her and never spoke of her. She drowned in a pool that used to be in our backyard but was filled in after her death. My mother ran into the house to tend to me, and when she returned Avril was gone. She looked around the backyard, then ran out front, then went to the neighbours to see if anyone had seen her. By the time it dawned on her to look into the still waters of the pool, Avril had been lying on the bottom too long … she was gone. Don't you see, Daniel? That's why my mother never loved me, she blamed me for my sister's death … my sister …this is so unbelievable. We've laughed and played, we've even had a sleepover, all the stuff girls do. I'm glad I got to know her as a kid. She's almost ready to move on but was waiting to see me, like she knew I was coming. I've done so much, and yet so little time has passed. There have been only two soundings of the Resonance. We've got time to …" Alison's face changed in an instant. "Daniel? What's wrong?"

"Dr. Walters is here."

"What do you mean *here*?"

"He had a stroke, Ali, and he passed. We didn't hear the Resonance because he couldn't perform his duties. You spoke of a sleepover with your sister. From what I gather, when the spirit enters a rest state it's a serious rest state. I also slept … and too long!"

"Too long, oh God!"

She grabbed Danny's hand, and it was she who led.

They both appeared at the empty hotel room, then Danny followed Alison as a cemetery appeared before them. There was a small gathering of people and a minister. Danny held Alison's hand as they approached. Alison's mother's body shook as she clutched a small brass urn so tightly that the blood left her hands. The minister spoke with a smile on his face and an attitude that suggested funerals were graduation ceremonies for the righteous.

"And so this is a day of celebration as Alison joins her sister in this beautiful place of rest with God and Jesus Christ our Saviour. Mrs. Truman, you may place the urn on the pedestal."

With some reluctance, Alison's mother put the urn on an oak pedestal that stood next to a small hole in the ground next to a flat, engraved stone. Alison glanced down on the stone and read the inscription: "*Our dear daughter, the brightest light of our lives, Avril Barbara Truman, 1947–1956.*"

"Jesus, I'm dead. I'm being buried next to Avril." Alison put her head on Danny's chest, watching and listening as the rest of the service flew by. The gathering moved off a few minutes later, leaving Danny and Alison at the burial plot. "My mother didn't even cry, Daniel," Alison said sadly. "God, she's so messed up … didn't even cry at her own daughter's funeral. You can bet she cried her eyes out for Avril." Then it started. Alison broke, and her soul was overcome with such a monumental sadness that it swept over Danny as well. She cried for herself. then she cried for her mother, then she looked at Daniel and wept some more.

"Great, I finally meet a guy I think is sweet on me and we both die … dead as doornails. This is some kind of Shakespearean tragedy."

Danny held on to her, but somehow the doing of it was not as satisfying as he knew it would have been in physical form. He thought of what it would have been like to make physical love to her and felt sad … no, it was a little angrier than sad … he felt ripped off.

Alison looked at him. "I know …" she said. "I feel ripped off too. Let's make love. I know how to approximate the act here."

"I noticed. I watched you at the baths," Danny said, trying not to sound judgmental.

"I hope you're not angry with me," Alison said by way of an apology. "No one had ever wanted me like that fellow, and he was so handsome and loving. I was curious, and he filled me with a confidence I had never felt before. I felt no shame in sharing a sensual discovery with him. I have since dreamed of you and me in that way, and I am breathless in the imagining of it, Daniel."

Within moments they were in the baths.

"Why here?" Danny asked.

"It is more possible here. This place is imbued by Phorian investment with a power to assist the simulation of things physical in nature. I think eventually you can create such things on your own, but I believe it takes time to acquire the skill. Love me, Daniel. Let's lose some of our sadness in the doing of it. I have never made love to one I was so … in love with. Oh Daniel, I do think I love you, please love me."

Danny looked at her with the sensation of tears rolling down his cheeks. "I don't know how this has happened and frankly I don't care, but … I do love you, Ali. I love you dearly."

Slowly they removed the images of clothing from one another and the tenderness of what they felt was amplified. There was a climax of a sort and Alison whispered to a slightly disappointed Danny, "Now again. It will only get better, my love." And so it went, until the two of them lay in one another's arms saying nothing, but feeling everything the other felt. There was conversation without words, a joining of two souls in such depth that for a time they were oblivious to everything but each other, as though they were floating in a void. Other imagery would only consume the energy they needed to love with such intensity.

It was Daniel who felt it first. “Someone is trying to summon us. Our images are being formed somewhere. Do you feel it, Ali?”

“Yes. Ignore it,” she said as she snuggled into his chest. A moment passed and she looked into his eyes. “You can’t ignore it, can you?”

“I sense it’s one I have met who is an extraordinary soul,” Danny responded, deep in thought.

“Who’s Bernard?” Alison asked, and before Danny could answer she spoke again. “Oh … the one Verhoevan said recovered souls.”

“Yes. He’s a powerful and loving presence. He can only want us for good reason. I think we should let ourselves be drawn to his presence.”

“Sure,” Ali responded, making Danny smile.

“That was quick.”

“Well, it’s important to you. I love you … therefore it is important to me.”

“I so love you, I ...” Danny began, only to realize that they were already standing with Bernard.

“Why thank you, Daniel,” Bernard said with a smirk, knowing full well the words were not intended for him. “ I love you, too.”

“I was talking to …” Danny stopped and laughed at his own stupidity. “Like you didn’t know the thought was for Ali … Nice to see you, Bernard. What can we do for you?”

Ali looked at Bernard and understood immediately that she was in the presence of someone of great spiritual power. She tried to get a sense of him and found there was something she could not penetrate. Bernard smiled at her efforts and then opened his arms.

“You wish to know me and so I will allow you to,” he said politely.

“I am sorry, Bernard,” Alison responded. “I didn’t realize I was presumptuously intruding.”

“No need to apologize. You cannot intrude where you are not allowed. It is a skill you may master over time. In my pursuits in darker places I have learned how to keep areas of myself a mystery to others.”

Even though Alison withdrew her efforts, she felt a powerful source of love and goodwill washing over her first.

"Daniel and Alison, I know you two have just discovered your love for one another in a way few ever do. It is only because of the strength of that love that I feel a measure of hope for a successful outcome in what I am about to ask of you. It is a request that cannot be given a flippant answer. It must be given serious thought by both of you. I will be comfortable with any decision you make."

Danny and Alison looked at one another, then to Bernard.

"Well, you certainly have baited our curiosity," Danny said with a smile.

Bernard looked at the two of them. "Sit with me."

In an instant they were in the Phorian Great Hall, and Bernard motioned to them from a bench under a picture of light fanning downward through massive clouds. Beams of light flickered in variations of intensity while clouds moved through them. Ali sat leaning into Danny's embrace so their energy mingled while Bernard spoke.

"I think there is a way back for you that can accomplish some good, while at the same time giving you the opportunity to know the gift of physical love."

"But our bodies are dead. I've been cremated," Alison interrupted.

Bernard nodded and then signalled a group of people talking excitedly to join them. There was an older couple, a few young people, and a beautiful young blond girl. She looked at Alison and Danny curiously.

"I know you, don't I? I saw you when I passed," she said, with a sweet voice.

Bernard smiled lovingly at her and said, "They only wished to welcome you. We are glad you are with those who love you. Good luck in all that you discover."

The group, sensing the moment was over, moved on, but the girl looked back and smiled oddly at Alison before turning to investigate some excited chatter going on amongst the others.

Alison looked at Bernard. "The young girl in the ICU?"

"Yes …" Bernard answered, "and there is another. Look who comes to greet her."

Danny and Alison watched as the sturdy black athlete walked over and embraced the young girl.

"He left his mother? He stood with her for some time," Danny remarked.

"He is a good soul who endured her pain in order to remove some of it by informing her soul that his love for her was not dead," Bernard said with admiration.

"So she got the message?" Ali asked.

"Fortunately for him, she was open to the idea of it and found his love in amongst her own thoughts," Bernard replied.

"So what did you want to say to...?" Danny began, but the answer appeared. "It's them, isn't it? It's something to do with those two teenagers."

"They are potential vessels for the powerful love you have found, if you act quickly. But that is the gift … not the task."

Ali looked at Bernard curiously. "But their bodies are dead and could no longer support life. Isn't that how it works?"

"More often than not. But in the case of the young girl, she chose to leave the pain and move on. Her body lives, for the moment."

"And what about the guy?" Danny asked.

"His body is strong, but there was head trauma. I think an empowered energy like yours, Daniel, could re-establish neural paths to life where he no longer could."

"Empowered?"

"Your love is strong, Daniel. Your desire to love Alison presents a powerful will to live. You could reanimate the brain in a different configuration. The problem for the boy is that many of his neural paths, the ones familiar to him, will not reconnect. This is why he deserted the body. Consciousness, as he had come to know it, was not possible. Will, such as yours, can be everything in such situations."

"You said I *could* re-establish life. What happens if I fail?"

"Then you fail and you can return to Ali."

"And the task?" Alison's tone was full of worry.

"It involves preventing one life being taken out of anguish, and another from becoming so dark as to be lost from all hope of ever recovering from the monumental guilt she feels. The two souls of which I speak will slip easily and forever into the darkness of the Soms when they cross over. This will not be an easy task, but I believe it to be truly worth the effort. The only reason I'm even suggesting such an action is that I feel your love might be strong enough to bear the journey and to make a good contribution to that world."

"You say that our love *might* survive," Danny said with a measure of discomfort. "What could happen to it?"

"Think on that, Daniel. You would be a black man in a time that has not yet moved entirely from racial insecurities, that is certainly not without its trials. The world is still a sad place in some regards, and you will be facing the ignorance of prejudice. Alison, you would be a young, cosmetically desirable female in a world that markets the same. Your academic aspirations, your intellect, will be given very little consideration. It's your appearance that will be admired and objectified. Now put the two together—a black man and a white woman in a world foreign to you and intolerant or even hostile towards you as a couple."

"The two souls you mentioned, who are they? . . . Oh, no." The answer to Danny's own question drifted into his consciousness with a wave of sadness.

Bernard looked at him and felt his anguish. "Danny, Myra is approaching the point where she will take her own life. Her own existence has been rendered meaningless to her. She has never invested in herself, only others. For years it was her son, then, when you left, she had her father to care for. She is now at an age where the idea of any investment in life feels like an insurmountable task. Because she has never watered the seeds of her own creativity, she has no idea where her interests even lie. How can she follow her passion if she doesn't know what it is? And so, taking her life is the option she is arriving at over and over again."

Bernard turned to Alison now. "Alison, your mother is riddled heavily with the pain of losing both daughters, compounded by a shameful guilt for blaming you in the death of your sister. You didn't live long enough for her to beg your forgiveness. She is sliding into a trench so dark she will carry it with her after her own physical death. Though she remains self-centred enough not to take her own life, she will focus the anger she feels for herself on others. Her spirit will become so self-loathing that when she passes, the Soms will pick her like a ripe apple. Anything left of her spirit will wither and be lost."

"But you must know I hold no affection for my mother," Alison stated flatly.

"I know what you say is a partial truth. I ask you this. Who might be more successful at helping one such as your mother? A stranger, or one who knows the pain she has inflicted through her own guilt? It was always herself she hated, but you were the whipping post. There is a remorse so crippling in this woman that, believe it or not, it far exceeds any pain you have felt. It is only your forgiveness that can do battle with her guilt. As you experienced in the garden with Avril, love from one's bloodline can be the most powerful medicine. There is a monumental weight you bear that will be lifted in the forgiveness of the one who causes you such emotional pain."

"I don't know if I can face the woman." Alison shuddered.

"You now have Daniel's love, and Avril's. You have never faced your mother with these new strengths."

"You said we must act quickly," Danny said.

"How much time do we have?"

"Not much. The young man's mother has asked to have him removed from the respirator, and the process is beginning as we speak."

Danny looked at Alison, who turned to face him. They held one another tenderly.

"Do you think we can do this? God, why couldn't I have more time to think about this?" Alison asked.

"I know. A part of what I love is the image of you, Ali. I've been down the blond bimbo route. You are so unique to me."

"It would still be me, wouldn't it, Bernard?" Ali asked with hope.

"To a point. The soul would be you, but some talents would be physically genetic. Over time you stand a reasonable chance of getting the genetics more in line with your spirit."

"Well, " Danny injected, "I don't think I could do any worse than I did the first time around. Do I take who I am with me, or is this like some reincarnation deal where my knowledge gets checked at the door?"

"This is unusual ground. You entered here by extraordinary means. If you act quickly, I believe you may return with memory intact, which will implant into the organic cells of the host body. Daniel, I know you are evolving into much more than you may believe is possible. There is so much potential in both you and Alison. I say this that you might understand your worth, as you will be up against obstacles the like of which you have never known. This task requires a strong will, which you both have demonstrated in your innate abilities against the Soms. And you possess the power of your love for one another."

"So … you want to see if you love me for real, Danny?" Ali asked with a serious expression.

"Do you have doubts that I love you for real?" Danny countered, but knowing she did before she answered.

"Not here. But here I can find your thoughts. There I will worry about what they may or may not be. How can I know back there?"

"You can't," Bernard answered. "You can never know what others are thinking. That is the joy of discovery. You can, however, slowly learn to trust through the repeated physical manifestation of it. You can learn someone loves you by how they treat you over a period of time … how it is demonstrated. This is the true beauty and power of the physical realm."

"Well then?" Danny asked. "Might I be allowed the chance to demonstrate my love for you?"

They looked at one another and began to appear in the ICU. Danny looked at Alison, and they held onto each other for dear life. Bernard had clearly helped them to the place where, in a moment, a young man would be removed from the respirator. What lay ahead was daunting, to say the least: to see if their love could survive in the physical world in different bodies, and the task that Bernard had thrown across their paths regarding their mothers.

A nurse and doctor had joined Vera Bishop, the mother of the young black athlete, at her son's body. The nurse began to remove the respirator tube.

Alison took one last desperate look at Danny. "I'll always love you, Daniel, no matter what happens."

"I'll always love you, Ali."

"Tell me that on the other side," she said.

Danny sensed that any time they had was up. The respirator tube was removed and breathing ceased in the patient as his horrified mother listened to the air leave her son's lungs for what she expected would be the last time. Danny climbed into the body of the young man. He lovingly looked back at the image of Ali and committed it to memory before lying back into a strange universe … someone else's body.

17

CORROBERATION

Hamburg
Spring 1848

Inspector Johansen gingerly lowered himself from the carriage.

"Wait for us here, driver."

He and Pietro headed towards the stone stable with the thatched roof. Manure was piled high in the courtyard next to a wagon in need of repair, and the air was rife with fermenting dung. A burly-looking smith of some years banged a piece of red-hot iron into submission on his well-worn anvil. The Inspector stopped and looked the man over before making his request.

"I am Police Inspector Johansen, and I wonder, sir, if you would be so kind as to prohibit anyone from running though this doorway in a moment or two. We mean the man no harm and do not seek to press any charges. We only seek his assistance in gathering information. Are you up to the task?"

The smith eyed the man sternly. "There is but one person in there at the moment and he is my son. How do I know all is as you say and that you mean my son no harm?" he responded curtly.

The Inspector looked at him and grinned. "I do love a suspicious mind, sir. In answer to your question, you can't know I am a man of honour until such time as any honour I might possess is put to the test, so at this time all I ask is the opportunity to prove myself. You have only my word on this matter."

The Inspector put his hand out and the smith eyed it. Reluctantly he put a huge, calloused hand out and gripped hard, causing Johansen to wince slightly before responding in kind, so as not to be bested. The smith felt considerable power coming back his way and concluded men of such strength and position usually didn't ask – they just took. The smith nodded and the grip contest ended.

Johansen and Pietro entered the stable and, on seeing the young priest, the smith's son bolted. As he flew out the door his father held out an arm, catching him square across his brow and dropping him to the ground.

"They would only have words with you, idiot! Stand your ground like a man and answer for yourself! I would not mind knowing what in the name of Mary Mother of God you've gotten yourself into this time."

The young man was shaking his stun off when the Inspector came out behind Pietro.

"He is one of them, and there were two others," the young priest asserted.

Johansen looked at the man, whom he estimated to be in his early thirties, average build, and very possibly not too quick of mind.

"Sir, I am interested in the goings on in the chambers below the cathedral. I seek only to find some answers to a few riddles and not to punish you in any way, as I suspect you have merely been used by those with a darker purpose." The Inspector waited for the man to assimilate what he had been told.

Prompted by a kick in the backside from his father he spat it out. "I have only been carrying out the orders of the Holy Brother who works for God against the Devil himself."

"I see. Well that sounds an honourable enough task," the Inspector offered. "And might you divulge what that holy work entailed?"

The boy looked at him, not quite getting the question, until his father kicked him in his hindquarters again and translated, "He wants to know what the hell you were doing beneath the cathedral."

"We carried the bodies of Satan's messengers and buried them. The last time, one came to life and spoke like the Devil himself. We fled for our lives. I am not sure if Brother Luke survived his wrath."

"How many of these devils have you buried?"

"Three … but one got away. Like I said, he rose from the dead and …"

"And what, young man? Please speak freely," Johansen encouraged.

"I saw one breathe as we lowered him down, but Brother Luke said we had to close the lid or we would all be damned to the fires of Hell. Brother Luke knows of such things."

"Can you show me? Don't worry, we will take some constables and this priest so that you may be well protected." Johansen looked at the smith. "I know I said I would only question your son, but he can save us much trouble by taking us to the tombs involved. You have my word I will allow no harm to come to the young man. I fear he has been taken advantage of in this matter. You may join us, if you wish."

"I have no time for such things. Bring him back to me in one piece. There is more to do here today than I can manage on my own before I sleep. And tell your driver his horse will be lame if he does not tend to it soon … he is shy of one front hoof that is badly shod. I heard it in the animal's step as you approached." With that, the smith put his head back down to the work at hand.

Johansen smiled. He loved an observant mind and a man who was not afraid of hard work. *I could use someone like that*, he thought as he followed Pietro and his witness to the carriage.

They stopped at the Rathaus, where Johansen requested three constables meet them at the cathedral. Before hopping back into the carriage Johansen admonished the driver with his newfound powers of deduction.

"See to it that you get that horse to the smith. He is shy of one badly shod foot and will become lame if not tended to soon!"

The driver watched Johansen get into the carriage and then shook his head in amazement at how little escaped the observational genius of the great Inspector.

Moments later they arrived at the cathedral, and Johansen spoke to Pietro as they headed in.

"Perhaps while we wait for my constables you could show me where you last saw the one they call Vasquez and how his body was positioned."

The smith's son looked frightened.

"What's the matter, son?" Johansen asked.

"Vasquez. This is the name of the heavy one who came to life," he said timidly.

In the bellows chamber, Pietro described how Vasquez had been positioned and where he had been when someone struck him from behind.

"It was not me or my friends who struck your priest."

The smith's son was now starting to open up as a rather helpful individual. He continued to describe how hard it had been to carry Vasquez, and when the constables arrived Johansen asked to be taken to the spot where the smith's son said they had laid the first "Devil" to rest. Torches were lit and the party headed down the spiral stone staircase to the burial chambers. They stopped at a sarcophagus surrounded by melted candle wax. The constables, aided by the smith's son, pushed the lid back, releasing a foul odour of decay. Pietro looked in and gasped. He recognized the ring and hair, but most importantly the sandals he had made for his mentor.

"Verhoevan!" he choked.

The Inspector looked at the bloodstains on the corpse's back and his body position. "This man was alive when he was placed in here," he deduced.

"Yes, this is the one Brother Luke said would damn us all if we did not close the lid, even though he breathed," the smith's son blurted. Then he recoiled with a feeling of remorse. "Have we done wrong, sir?" he asked Johansen, who looked at him with a measure of pity.

"Not knowingly, son. Your only crime is that you trusted a man who one would expect should be worthy of such trust. Leave this one open, men. Let's see where the others are."

They moved slowly in the dark to another coffin in a small alcove. The lid was pushed back and there were a few groans, the smell was so foul. The smith's son looked in.

"The young Devil we placed under the dead woman, but ... he has gone! Has he gone back to Hell, priest?" he asked Pietro.

Pietro looked sympathetically at the man, but it was Johansen who spoke.

"So, the one you placed here is gone … interesting. Men, put the lid back in place. This one is in the middle of a vicious rot and some privacy should be afforded the poor woman to finish her task."

His constables quickly had the lid in place and the party moved off in the opposite direction, stopping at another stone tomb. Johansen noticed there was blood on the floor and under the lip of the lid.

"And what happened here, young man?" he asked the smith's son

"This is where the Devil came to life and we fled," he answered, with fear in the recollection.

The lid was pushed back and a groan was heard from within. "He lives! We will all burn in Hell!"

The smith's son ran off into the dark. He hit a wall a few feet away and cursed. Farther away, another stumble was heard, followed by yet another curse, and finally he must have hit the staircase as a painful yelp echoed from the abyss. Johansen assumed the lad was going to run clear across town and not stop until he reached his father.

"Let him go. We know where he lives if we need anything more from him," Johansen ordered. "He's told us about all he can for today."

Pietro's curiosity caused him to look into the coffin, and a hand lashed out at him, slicing him across the cheek with a knife.

"Die, spawn of Satan!" a voice coughed from within.

Pietro was completely startled and jumped back, the side of his face bleeding profusely. Johansen held a torch up to look at him and yelled to one of his constables, "One of you men get this young priest above to have that wound tended to!" A constable, looking more than a little spooked, stepped forward quickly and led Pietro away.

Johansen carefully leaned over the coffin, keeping his head as high as possible, and again a knife swung up, blindly slashing, and a thin voice called out. "You will burn alive in the fires of Hell for your sins! God has told me so," Luke raged.

Johansen, at first startled, regained his composure. "Ah, the venerable Brother Luke, I presume. I must ask you to surrender your knife." The Inspector waited for a reply.

"You can't fool me, Vasquez. Let me finish dispatching you to your Maker in the Kingdom of Hell!"

Johansen turned to his constable. "And there we have the confession. He's as mad as a rabid dog, but his words reveal his complicity. Remember them, constable, we may need your corroborative testimony. I do love a good day's work. We have a murderer, and we have his accomplices in a cell back at the Rathaus."

Johansen held the torch towards the feet of Luke, and when he slashed the air with his knife in the direction of the torch, Johansen grabbed his wrist and smashed it into the side of the tomb. Luke screamed in agony and the weapon dropped to the floor.

Johansen looked at the knife. "Ah, and now I believe we have the murder weapon."

The Inspector and his man lifted the writhing old priest out and carried him to the bottom of the stairs. Johansen went on ahead for assistance, leaving a worried-looking constable listening to curses that spewed from the old priest like vomit.

Fortunately, the Inspector returned with more men minutes later and the madman was escorted out, after having his arms tied behind his back and a gag stuffed in his mouth. Johansen then saw to the removal of the murder weapon and Verhoevan's body, which was placed in a wooden coffin awaiting transport to the morgue.

***

A carriage pulled up to the Dopp house about an hour later, and Johansen heaved his bulk onto the street and looked up at the nicely appointed stone home. He climbed the stairs and was still out of breath when Harding opened the door.

Matthias sat sipping on a brandy in the parlour, and he stood when Inspector Johansen entered the room. Harding offered the policeman a drink, which was readily accepted. It was obvious to the Inspector that Matthias grieved the loss of his friend Vasquez, but Johansen's curiosity could not be kept at bay.

"Herr Dopp, how was it that you came to know the priest, Vasquez?"

"He saved my life," Matthias answered, offering as little information as possible.

"An interesting choice of words. Your life … not your soul … so it was not in a professional capacity that you came to know him. And your life was saved when…?" Johansen paused for an answer that he knew, so he just continued, "… when the local folk had a little fire in the square behind the cathedral … the fire that took the life of your father and a few other good citizens of our fair town, I might add."

"Yes." Matthias's voice still held incredulity at the insanity of the night forever burned into his memory. "They would have thrown me on the flames as well, if Vasquez hadn't hauled me away."

"A tragic night, indeed. And Vasquez, I am told, was an assistant to a man named Verhoevan, who was commissioned by your father to write a piece of music?"

"Yes."

'And you were carrying that piece of music when you were arrested?"

"Yes."

"Interesting piece of music. I don't know how, and I don't think you are about to tell me, but somehow this piece of music is behind the death of Vasquez and Verhoevan, who was buried alive in a crypt below the cathedral. It is my understanding that you have spent a little time in the coffin of a rather foul-smelling woman? Was it Vasquez who saved you again?"

Before Matthias could answer Harding jumped in. "It was Vasquez and me, Inspector. I believe Luke thinks Matthias should have died the night of the fire and was somehow cursed. Fortunately we found Matthias in time."

"Well, that's certainly a neat and tidy story, Captain Harding. But my experience tells me that this is not such a neat and tidy sequence of events, And the musical manuscript is still missing. I have asked Pietro to ascertain if it is at the monastery. Well, by the looks on your faces, I believe I have learned all I am going to learn here." Johansen stood. "Thank you for the refreshment, gentlemen." he headed towards the door.

"Inspector?" Matthias got up and followed. "What is to become of the bodies of Vasquez and Verhoevan?"

"They will be returned to their brotherhood for interment, I presume."

"Would it be possible for their bodies to be released to me? I would like to see to it that my friend is properly buried next to the body of his colleague and friend. I don't trust the brotherhood's history with the disposal of bodies."

"I won't argue that last point. I will think on the matter and have an answer for you tomorrow. And Matthias …" Johansen looked quite sternly at him. "I don't know what it is that you hide from me, but I will get to the bottom of it, as I most always do. For the time, I am convinced that you loved your friend and associate Vasquez and am therefore deeply sorry for your loss."

Johansen opened the door and found the trip down the stairs much more to his liking than the climbing of them, and he was even able to project the guise of being light of foot as he entered his carriage.

Back upstairs in the parlour, Harding sat with Matthias. "A formidable individual to pit your wits against. It might be advisable to conclude our business and bid farewell to this God-forsaken town as soon as possible," he suggested as he poured them each a generous glass of whisky.

18

SHAUN BISHOP and JENNIFER GLESSING

Toronto, 1989

Danny looked out of someone else's eyes for the first time. In an instant he realized how bad his own eyesight must have been, because the world seemed to have way more detail than he remembered. A tearful black woman, Mrs. Bishop, stroked his hair, while the attending physician warned her gently that her son's heart would stop now that the respirator had been removed. She sat there with her hand on his chest, feeling his heart beat, wanting to share the last moments of her son's existence so he would know he was not alone. It was a sad and generous last moment of caring. Danny felt her sadness, and then blinked.

"Doctor, he blinked!"

"It happens," the doctor reassured her. "Sometimes when a body is shutting down nerves can misfire and cause random mechanical movement."

"I r-r-r-read about that s-s-s-somewhere," Danny said, with a scratchy voice he had never heard.

The mother gasped and fell off her chair to the floor. The medical staff was so stunned at words being spoken by someone who had been pronounced brain-dead that it took a moment for a nurse to help Mrs. Bishop, who was slowly coming to her senses. As the nurse helped her to her feet, Mrs. Bishop wept tears of joy, dumbfounded, for the spark of life dancing once more in her son's eyes.

"Praise the Lord! Thank you, merciful Jesus! Praise God! Shaun, oh Shaun, you're alive!" She smothered him in kisses, until the doctor moved in.

"Please, Mrs. Bishop, we've got to make sure all vital signs are stable." He pushed the mother out of the way and looked the boy over while dishing out orders. "Hook up the heart monitors again. I want oxygen sensors, saline IV, come on, let's move, people!"

Danny looked back as his … mother? Well, she certainly was the mother of the body he was in, so yeah … he looked at *his* mother while she stood aside and tearfully stared back. Danny began to feel messages from his new body. He felt a toned musculature that he had never felt in his life, and strangely there were volumes of memories that weren't his. His thoughts felt fractured—the energy was his, but it was struggling down neural paths that had been created by someone else's life. As he sought to find more of himself, he slowly became aware of an increasingly intense pain in his chest, accompanied by a colossal headache. There obviously had been some significant head trauma and internal injuries. This body had not been vacated without reason, and Danny was rudely awakened to the idea that it would be an uphill climb back to good health. Bernard had apparently glossed over that particular piece of information.

In pain the likes of which he had never experienced, an awareness of feelings for the woman who looked down at him seeped in. Though he had never met her, his body had. There was an organic conversation occurring. His cells were recognizing like stuff, the lineage of their origin. He also recognized that he now had the weight of expectation from two mothers … this wasn't going to be easy.

He watched as the young blond girl's parents came over to share in Mrs. Bishop's joy. They all looked excitedly at Danny.

"Speak to me again, Shaun," Mrs. Bishop asked, seeking reassurance that this wasn't one of those random nerve things the doctor spoke about. Danny grimaced in agony but searched for words to comfort her.

"Hey, M-M-M-Mom … it's a … you know … real g-g-g-good to see you again." Danny's throat was raw from the respirator tube.

Mrs. Bishop looked at a nurse on her way by. "Could you get my son something to drink? He can hardly speak, his throat is so irritated from that horrible machine of yours." The nurse nodded and reappeared in a flash with water in a Styrofoam cup.

It felt good to Danny, who sipped at it, then looked over at the body of the blond girl he had met with Bernard. She was indeed a beautiful girl, despite the stitches in her head. When was Alison coming? Maybe she was waiting to make sure he was going to be all right before committing to the journey. Maybe she had returned to say goodbye to Avril, as she had promised. It didn't matter—it was the thought of not being with her that flattened him out.

Danny's new mother followed his eyes to the girl. Then she looked back at him with a look only a mother could concoct.

"Why don't you keep your mind on getting yourself better, son."

A wave of fatigue came over Danny and began to suck him under like a whirlpool.

"I th-th-think I need to r-r-r-rest," he croaked.

"Oh, you've been resting for days, could you talk to me just a little longer? I need to hear your voice and not just think I do." Mrs. Bishop held her son's hand and looked at him lovingly.

"What sh-sh-should I say?" Speech was difficult. Danny was forming sentences in a manner that was strange to the normal patterns of the brain that now held his energy. It was as though he was requesting the brain and vocal cords to speak in a foreign language. The word choices were not what Shaun Bishop would have used; the inflection and expression of the words was uncoordinated. This was going to take time.

"Maybe you should thank the Lord for saving your life. Jordan has been here by your side praying with me."

Danny searched Shaun's brain cells for some recollection. The name was familiar, but beyond that he couldn't seem to find any point of access.

"Who's Jordan?" As soon as the words were out, Danny realized he shouldn't have asked the question, but it was so hard to think clearly.

Mrs. Bishop looked at her son with worry. "I'm certainly glad she didn't hear you say that. She would have been heartbroken. You've been dating her for six months; you said you thought she was forever. Don't worry, I'm sure it'll all come back to you."

***

It was well into the night when Mrs. Bishop finally left her post by her son's side and went to the waiting room to sleep on one of the vinyl couches. Danny was worn out after trying to deal with her needs. Sleep had already swept over him in waves of utter exhaustion.

He awakened from a deep sleep in the middle of the night and looked over at the blond girl. She was a good fifteen feet away and directly across from him. As he stared at her, he thought of Ali, what she used to look like, and then worry moved in. There had obviously been some head trauma so there was no way of knowing what she was going to be dealing with either. It had also been a few hours since Danny had been back, and still no sign of Ali, so what was going on?

He looked around the ICU. Joel was gone, probably removed to a regular room for a day or two of observation. There was a nursing station at the far end of the room with two nurses engaged in modern professional practices--paperwork. A couple of beds over from the blond girl lay an old man, who, although on a respirator, feebly held up a hand to wave. Danny waved back, and the man nodded rather pathetically as he looked around the room, clearly not wanting to be there. Before Danny had crossed back into Shaun Bishop's body he had sensed the man's pain. The old fellow was wide awake in a hell of Hippocratic oaths that had overridden both common sense and his DNR bracelet. He just wanted to … no, he *needed* to die, and the look on his face conveyed the message loud and clear. The machine forced air into his chest, hissing in regular intervals. Every time his chest expanded his face grimaced slightly, then relaxed, only to grimace a moment later with another undesired breath forcing its way into him.

Danny knew the feeling well, or at least his body did. It remembered the physical sensation of having air forced into the lungs, which also explained some of the discomfort he felt in his chest and trachea. He understood the old guy's grimace and the longing for an end to it. It was, in part, what had chased Shaun away.

His eyes moved back to the blond girl and his love for Ali. He remembered her embrace and her touch … wait a minute … something had touched his hand. He looked around but, of course, saw nothing. Still, there was undeniably some kind of presence.

"I love you, Ali," he whispered. He waited for another touch but nothing came.

A few moments later he became aware of movement across the room. He looked over to see the blond girl's feet stirring. Then she opened her eyes and blinked repeatedly. A few seconds later her hands were up in front of her face. She was looking at them and then … she looked at Danny, and her face crumpled into tears. Danny wanted to go to her but he was still rigged to heart monitors and oxygen sensors and an IV. A nurse buzzed by and the blond girl closed her eyes, trying to avoid attention. The nurse checked the old guy then patted his head before moving on to the blond girl for a cursory glance, then across to Shaun Bishop.

"You really should try to get some sleep, Shaun," she said, inspecting the heart monitor and oxygen levels. She took his blood pressure and changed the IV bag before going back to more paperwork and a beckoning coffee that the other nurse had just brought in.

Danny looked over at the blond girl. She looked at Danny, then around the room, then back at Danny, and she whispered something he couldn't hear. His face obviously had an expression of incomprehension because she whispered it again only louder.

"I … l … l … love you, D-D-Danny."

He'd heard it. Ali had arrived. His heart raced, and he took a deep breath.

"I love you, A-A-Ali," he whispered back to her, frustrated with the stutter.

Ali began to weep again. Danny could feel his heart pounding in his need to go to her. He heard a beep down at the nursing station and a nurse jumped up and headed towards him.

"What's going on with you?" she said, inspecting his heart monitor.

She got the armband out and pumped it up again to check his blood pressure.

"Hmmm, your pressure's up a little as well. Were you having a nightmare or something?"

Danny looked at her and smiled. "A r-r-r-romantic dream," he said, staring straight ahead at Ali, who smiled and closed her eyes as the nurse turned, following his sightline. "We know each other and we have a … well, we have a th-th-th-thing, you know."

"Were you in the same class at school?"

"Kinda."

The nurse looked up at the monitor, which now showed readings in the normal range, and looked at Danny with an odd smirk. "Kinda? That's an odd answer. Try to get some sleep, and steer clear of romance if you can, or I'll have to come back and my coffee will get cold."

"S-s-s-sorry."

"Don't be silly. It's real good to have you back in this world." The nurse smiled kindly before the rubber soles of her white Wallabies squeaked all the way back to her station.

Danny smiled at the truth of her statement, then looked back at Ali, who carefully opened her eyes, making sure no one else was aware that the comatose blonde in the bed was actually conscious. She had successfully avoided the nurses' gaze, but the old man on the respirator saw her and raised his eyebrows. She held her finger to her lips, and the old guy smiled and nodded a curious understanding.

Danny and Ali just stared at each other and continued to mouth "*I love you*" to one another while the old man's eyes darted back and forth, observing with warm reminiscence. For the first time in weeks he was able to observe something good in life, albeit not his own.

In the morning, Danny found the button on the rail of his bed and slowly elevated his head until he was sitting up. The nurse ran over immediately with some concern, but her patient looked very alert.

"What does a guy have to do to get some br-br-breakfast around h-here?" Danny asked

"I'll see what I can rustle up once I get permission." The nurse checked his blood pressure once more. "It won't be long. The doctor will be on rounds in about fifteen minutes."

"I'd l-l-like steak and eggs, t-t-toast, and home fries," Danny continued, knowing full well the ridiculousness of his request.

"No problem. This hospital is well known for its menu. You'll be amazed what our kitchen can do with food," she replied, deadpan, and as she turned she caught Ali smiling.

"Oh my God, what is going on around here?" She yelled down to the other nurse, "Get Dr. Woods … the Glessing girl is conscious!" The nurse went to Ali and looked at all her monitors.

"Well, young lady, can you hear me? Are you with me?"

"D-d-depends on wh-wh-where you're g-going," Ali said, with difficulty. Danny chuckled. Her voice was airy and higher pitched, but it was Ali all right.

The nurse looked at her. "You don't feel woozy or disoriented, oh, never mind answering questions, why don't you tell me how you feel, and no jokes!"

"I have a fair amount of p-p-pain where the stitches are and … do I have a broken foot or something?"

The nurse pulled the sheet up from the bottom of the bed and looked. "Which one hurts, Jennifer?"

"The left one h-hurts Jennifer a fair bit," Ali replied.

After some prodding the nurse located a sore spot. "Gee, you know, there is some bruising there … could be a small fracture in one of the bones, don't know how we missed that. I'll have the doc take a peek when he gets here, which shouldn't be long. Oh, honey, are your folks going to be glad to see you. They've been here pretty much around the clock. I think last night was the first night they both decided to go home for a good night's sleep."

Dr. Woods walked in at a brisk pace. "Well, well, look who's awake." He was man of around five and a half feet in height, with slicked-back reddish hair and the hint of an Irish accent. " Looks like the surgery saved the day." He scanned the monitors, took her blood pressure, and gave her a good look-over.

"All vitals are presenting normal, as you can see, Dr. Woods, but she's complaining about a pain in her left foot, which shows some discoloration. We may have missed a small fracture."

"Let's have a peek." Dr. Woods examined the foot, causing Ali to wince. "Well, I think we should get an X-ray once we're confident about the brain injury. Welcome back, Jennifer. Just to bring you up to speed, you had some swelling from the head injury and we had to drill small burrs to alleviate the pressure. Given where the stitches sit on your hairline, once your hair grows back there will be no visible scarring. Any questions?"

"No, I don't think so, except for h-h-how long am I going to be here?"

"I would say, best case, if all your vitals stay normal, another couple of days of observation here in ICU, in which time we'll have that foot X-rayed. If there is indeed a fracture, we'll immobilize the foot with either a plaster or bandage, depending on the damage, and then you can leave." Dr. Woods turned to the nurse. "Have the Glessings been called yet?"

"Not yet, Dr. Woods."

"I'll make the call. I'd love to give Jim and Carol the news myself. Nice to have you back, Jennifer. You've had us all pretty worried." Woods patted her good foot, turned, and left.

It was a half hour later that Jennifer's parents arrived, and Shaun's mother entered the ICU ten minutes after that. Ali and Danny kept looking at one another patiently as the parents discussed the miracle of their children's recoveries. Ali listened with sympathy to the stories about the pain of the last few days, which her parents replayed in great detail. Their comments about Jennifer's dance classes and music lessons and, and, and ... called for very little comment, so Ali learned as much as she could about Jennifer while feigning some memory loss. Danny noticed she was having the same kind of trouble with speech that he was.

Mid-afternoon, Ali was shipped down to X-ray to have the foot looked at and returned with a small cast on her leg. The rest of the day was exhausting, as both Ali and Danny tried to deal with parents so excited they couldn't shut up. Ali was allowed to stand and take a few tentative steps with crutches, and all were pleased when the exercise went off without a hitch. It was nine at night when everyone agreed on a good night's sleep, and the Glessings and Mrs. Bishop were reminded to observe proper visiting hours . . . for a change.

As soon as the parents left, Ali gave it another half hour and swung her legs over the side of the bed, causing the nurse to run over to her immediately.

"What do you think you're doing?"

"I really need to stretch. Shaun and I have been dying to speak to one another all day long but couldn't with our parents all over us. Do you mind?"

The nurse looked over at Shaun, who was wide awake and waved back. Then she turned to Jennifer and smiled. "I don't see why you couldn't have a short visit. Take my arm." The nurse helped Jennifer to her feet and walked her slowly over to the chair next to Shaun's bed.

"I'll be back in about fifteen minutes. This is an ICU, after all, and not a social club." With that the nurse headed back to her station.

Ali looked Danny over, then focused on his face. "Is that really you in there, Danny?"

"Yup, h-how do you like the n-new me?" Danny asked in return

"I don't know," Ali said frankly. "This is all so weird. I'm in love with a guy I've only known for a few days and now he looks like a guy I've never met before. Is that screwed up enough for you?"

"How, c-come you don't stutter any m-more?"

"You have to think the sentence first, then speak, otherwise the body's established neural paths in vocabulary and sentence structure get in the way."

Ali caught Danny off guard just as he was about to speak and kissed him passionately on the lips. He kissed her back. It was a long, investigative kiss and passions ran quite high.

"There you are, Daniel," she said, smiling tearfully.

"How is this g-going to work?" Danny asked.

"Focus on the sentence, then speak to me, Shaun," Ali said in a mock-motherly tone.

Danny followed her instructions. "How is this going to work?" he said, amazed there was no hesitation.

"Like that. One step, one sentence at a time, Daniel. But we're going to have to start using the names these bodies were given or we're in for a trip to the psych ward. I don't know how much time we have to do what Bernard asked of us."

"My mom, shit, I almost forgot." Danny's thoughts went to his mother's pain.

"Don't tell me you thought about using the word `shit' in a sentence before you said it," Ali said, with a look of incredulity.

"Actually … no, I think that must have been a word Shaun used all the time." They laughed and held on to one another until the nurse put an end to visiting hours.

Jennifer Glessing was moved from the ICU the following morning and spent two more days in a private room before being released. It took Shaun Bishop four more days in the ICU for the concerns of internal bleeding to be put to rest. The day he was to leave the ICU he stopped in on the old man he had waved at every day.

"How you doing, sir?" Danny asked sympathetically.

The man motioned to a paper, pad, and pencil on the table beside the bed. Danny handed it to him, and he started to write.

"*Want to die—no one will let me*," the scrawl read.

"I understand," Danny said softly. "I have died and seen what we're not supposed to know."

The old man's eyes widened and he looked at Danny, then nodded his head as if to say he understood. His hand started scribbling again and he handed the pad back to Danny.

"*Me too … saw bunch of people in the light before I got paddled back … who are they?*" Danny read, and he smiled at how bizarre the discussion would have felt to him a couple of weeks ago. He thought for a moment then responded, "Don't know who all of them are, sir, but some of them you'll know. The trick of it is, if you love someone dearly who has passed … and they love you, if you picture them and think of them, chances are they will be there."

The old man went back to the pad. "*Do you think my dad would come?*" he scribbled.

"Did you love one another?" Danny asked.

Tears welled in the old man's eyes and he nodded.

"Then there's a real good chance he'll be there," Danny replied.

The old man grabbed Danny's hand and squeezed, then he wrote on his pad. "*See you on the other side.*"

Danny smiled at the words and responded just as the orderly approached with a wheelchair to take him to his new room.

"You bet, sir, it would be real nice to have a real chat. I'll stop in on you tomorrow. If you should pass before I return, remember one thing: fear nothing, take only your love with you. That will help you on the other side," Danny said with a smile.

The old guy nodded, then winced as the respirator shoved more air down his throat. Danny was rolled away in his chair and couldn't help but find it odd that an old man's father was still the most important loved one in his life. Danny searched Shaun's memory for any sign of dear old dad and found nothing other than the feeling that Shaun had never known a father. Danny Blum had known his but just plain didn't like the man. This was both due to his father's lack of interest in anyone but himself and what a complete shit the man had been to Myra, his mother. Looked like there would be no new information on father-son relations coming his way in this new family he had been dropped into. Danny's thoughts also went to how complex accomplishing Bernard's mission might be. Sure, they were back to help Myra and Mrs. Truman, but there was the potential to screw something up big time in the lives of Mrs. Bishop and the Glessings.

The next morning Shaun conned an orderly into taking him up to the ICU to see the old guy again, but when he got there, the bed was empty. The ICU nurse saw Shaun Bishop staring at the empty bed and came over.

"He's gone, Shaun. Unfortunately, he had a massive heart attack and didn't respond to any attempts to revive him."

Danny dropped his head and closed his eyes as he listened to the words, and he thought how the term "unfortunately" rubbed him the wrong way. Never was there anyone who longed to leave this world more than that old fellow, and still they had tried to revive him. What would Hippocrates have thought of paddling old, dead souls back to life with a zillion volts? Welcome back to the real world — Danny shuddered — where someone's passing from a physical life dependant on machines was viewed as "unfortunate."

"Good for you, buddy," Danny muttered under his breath, causing the nurse to give him an odd look.

"Oh, and by the way …" The nurse went back to her station and returned with the old gentleman's scribble pad. "Do you know what the heck this is all about? It had to be from his conversation with you because you were his last visitor and I saw him writing on his pad. What does this mean?" The nurse looked at the pad and read aloud. "*Me too … saw bunch of people in the light before I got paddled back … who are they?*'" And then the next line asks, '*Do you think my dad would come?*'"

"We were just talking and I just, uh, you know … said what I think he wanted to hear." Apparently the neural paths of Danny Blum were much more fluid with lies than those of Shaun Bishop. The nurse looked at him as though she wasn't buying a thing. "I'd better get back to my room. I'm a little tired," he said, avoiding her eyes.

The orderly began to turn the chair around but the nurse stopped him, leaned over, and whispered in Danny's ear.

"You know. I see it in your face. When someone comes back from the other side they have a look about them. It's happened too many times around here to ignore. Have a good rest, Shaun, and welcome back." She patted him on the shoulder affectionately and headed back to her desk.

Danny was quiet on the ride back to his room. If anyone might know about such things it might very well be an ICU nurse, he thought. Then his mind turned to a list of wishes that were invading his thoughts. A wish that an old man who wanted to see his dad might be granted that gift, wishes for Myra, wishes for Mrs. Truman, and a wish not to complicate the lives of these new parents who believed their children were back. Danny did know there was something about him, as the nurse had said. He knew he had been forever changed by his journey. He had never felt so deeply for the well-being of others. The feeling grew in his chest, and with it a measure of remorse for what a self-centred fool he had been as Danny Blum.

***

A week later, Shaun Bishop was put in a wheelchair for the farewell procession to the front doors. Mrs. Bishop pulled up in an old Toyota Corolla and opened the door with a huge grin on her face. Her boy was coming home. Shaun stood holding on to the roof of the car, then winced as he lowered himself into the passenger seat. There was still some serious healing to do.

It had been a few days since Shaun Bishop had seen Jennifer Glessing. She had returned home to her parents' beautiful house in the suburbs. James Glessing was a wealthy lawyer and his wife Carol worked part time as a family therapist. The ride home was one of excitement for parents who days before had thought they were going to lose their only child. When they pulled into the driveway and stopped the car, Jim and Carol Glessing looked at one another and shared a smile of satisfaction, followed by a sigh that signalled the end of an exhausting emotional journey. Alison looked out of Jennifer's eyes at them affectionately with an understanding that these people loved one another and … her. It was overwhelming, and she found herself unable to control the tears that streamed down her face. This was a good family, and she was now part of it. It was something she had never known.

The Glessings helped her into their home and fawned over her for the rest of the day. Anything she needed appeared almost before the words were out of her mouth. Fortunately for Jennifer it was her left foot that was incapacitated so she would have no problem getting around in the brand-new automatic 3 series BMW her daddy had bought for her seventeenth birthday.

Ali was a little taken aback when Jennifer's boyfriend arrived and couldn't keep his hands off her. Brendon was a really good-looking young man from a very wealthy family and they had been dating steadily for about a year, so needless to say he knew something was wrong right out of the gates when Jennifer initially didn't respond favourably to his kiss, even though she clearly kissed him back on instinct.

"Oh Jen, I thought I had lost you." Brendon held her and gently stroked her hair. There was a familiarity to his touch that unnerved her as her body responded. It was even more unnerving that her mind was responding as well. She was in deep water that she could sense went way over her head.

Shaun Bishop lived in a huge apartment complex that his single-parent mom was barely able to afford on wages from her job at the local branch of the Bank of Montreal. Ali and Danny were on the phone as soon as he arrived home, and on his first day alone, moments after his mother left for work, Ali arrived. Danny met her at the door and she looked up, startled at his height. Danny looked into her eyes and she turned away. He chalked it up to nerves and pulled her into his arms as he closed the door.

Once their eyes were closed they found one another again. Unlike their experience on the other side, there was no need to conjure up physical passion; their bodies led the way in the natural outcome of the love they shared. Clothes were gently removed from the aches and pains of injuries, and when Ali glanced downward, a smirk came across her face.

"I think Shaun has a little more to offer than Daniel did," Danny said with some embarrassment.

"We'll just have to make do," Ali replied, ending all conversation abruptly.

The morning was lost to love and exploration that would have continued well into the afternoon if Shaun's mother hadn't arrived unannounced ... with Shaun's girlfriend, Jordan.

19

JUSTICE

Hamburg
April, 1848

An armada of dark clouds sailed in ceremoniously from the North Sea until the morning was shrouded in a persistent wash of rain. Puddles turned to pools that fed currents down the cracks of the cobblestone streets towards the harbour.

The driver of a glistening black carriage waited stoically in front of the Dopp house with his collar pulled up against the wet cold. He was greatly relieved when he saw Harding and Matthias running down the steps towards him, and he managed to hop down just in time to open the door for his fares.

The two men shook what water they could from their cloaks and sat silently all the way to the Rathaus, where the trial was to take place. Their testimony would help tie the hangman's noose around the necks of Brothers Luke and Nicolas. Matthias wanted no part of it, having seen quite enough of the suffering humans inflicted on one another to last him a lifetime. Yes, Luke and Nicolas had made many suffer, but making them suffer in turn simply meant perpetuating the madness.

The Inspector met them at the door and thanked them for taking time out of their busy schedules, which of course was a complete waste of air given their lack of choice in the matter. They were led to an oak bench in the courtroom, where wet cloaks were removed and an attempt was made to rub some warmth into cold hands. A moment later, the blacksmith appeared, shoving his son ahead of him onto a bench on the opposite side of the central aisle. Two rough-looking men followed them in and sat behind them, after giving a dutiful nod to the smith.

The Inspector took his seat next to the chief prosecutor in the front row. Moments later spectators were allowed in, and they quickly took seats as close to the front as possible. Closest to the front soon meant the back row as the courtroom filled to the brim.

There was a spattering of anticipatory conversation until the prisoners were brought up from their cell. An audible gasp at the stench and filth of the two Franciscan Brothers rippled through the room. Luke was muttering in Latin, as usual, seemingly oblivious to the real world, but the look of fear on Nicolas's dirty face suggested that he already knew the outcome of the trial. The shackled prisoners were escorted to two chairs in a metal cage off to one side of the Magistrate's desk by a surly guard who carried a persuasive-looking leather-covered club in his belt. As soon as the Magistrate entered, the room quieted, and Matthias understood why Nicolas looked so frightened.

The Chief Magistrate, Herman Koller, was a man whose reputation preceded him among those of the Catholic faith. Matthias had heard about the dogmatic Lutheran judge from Vasquez, who had attended his court for a trial involving a thief who was the son of a Catholic friend. Upon entering the court, Koller had looked at Vasquez, in his priestly robes, with obvious disdain. A religious zealot, Koller held a strong distaste for Catholics, who were all idolaters in his view. Idolatry was a pagan practice that had become synonymous with the Devil himself to devout Protestants, despite the fact that the very idea of worshipping a man-God who rose from the dead was itself an old and obviously pagan idea.

Therein, Vasquez had said, lay the template for the mind of Herman Koller. When such a mind was made up, evidence might serve very little purpose. The innocent son of Vasquez's friends was thrown into a prison, where he died of dysentery in the second month. People were often damned in Koller's court if he simply didn't like the look of them. His stride was ceremonial and full of self-importance. He walked up a few steps to his elevated bench and sat down, glaring under thick, greying eyebrows at all who sat in his courtroom. It was a look meant to intimidate, and it conveyed with certainty the Magistrate's power to send anyone to the gallows with a wave of his hand. He briefly looked at the documents in front of him, then looked through wire spectacles at the prosecutor.

"Who have we before us today?" Koller began.

The prosecutor stood and bowed respectfully. "Your grace, today we present Luke and Nicolas, two monks of the Franciscan brotherhood, who are charged with the murder of Peter Verhoevan, also a Franciscan monk. With the help of three men devoted to the papacy and on threat of excommunication from the Holy Roman

Catholic Church, they entombed the living body of Herr Peter Verhoevan in an occupied coffin, after which the lid and his fate were sealed. Further to this —"

"Occupied coffin?" the Magistrate inquired, with a look of distaste at the accused.

"Yes, your grace, indeed it was the stone sarcophagus that contained the mortal remains of a baron by the name of —"

The Magistrate shook his head in disgust and cut the prosecutor off with a wave of his hand. "What have you to say for yourselves on this charge?" he asked, flipping through the documentation in front of him.

Luke and Nicolas said nothing, and an uncomfortable silence filled the room. The magistrate signalled to the constable, who reached for his club and struck Nicolas across the shoulders.

"You will stand when the Magistrate addresses you," the constable barked.

Nicolas stood and pulled the muttering Luke to his feet.

"We will offer you one more opportunity to answer my question," the Magistrate said softly, still feigning interest in the paperwork in front of him.

"It was Brother Luke who commanded that we remove Verhoevan from our midst, for he did the Devil's work. Brother Luke is my senior, so I obeyed."

"So if any old man were to ask you to kill someone, this would give you an adequate cause to do so?" the Magistrate asked coldly, not awaiting a reply. "Sit down."

"But sir, I was —" Nicolas's words were cut short by another blow to his body from the constable's club.

Luke looked around the courtroom as though he suddenly realized where he was, then he scowled at the Magistrate. "You are surely damned for interfering in our holy duties. For I am the hand of God!"

"Blasphemy! Constable, see to it that that man is silenced. He has forfeited his right to speak with his un-Godly madness!" Koller roared, red in the face with anger. Luke was gagged and forced to sit screaming his muffled indignation at the idea that anyone would interfere with the very hand of God on earth.

"And the next charge?" The Magistrate's voice was soft and warm as he signalled to the prosecutor to continue, with an artificial smile.

"Thank you, your grace." The prosecutor bowed. "The one called Luke is also charged with stabbing another monk of his order by the name of Vasquez. He has confessed the crime to Inspector Johanson in the presence of a constable and there is a witness."

"Is that man here today?"

"Yes, your grace. Would Herr Mader please stand?"

One of the rough-looking men who sat behind the smith and his son stood, trying to contain his trembling hands. The Magistrate saw the man's obvious fear and smiled smugly.

"Herr Mader?" The Magistrate's stare caused the man's trembling to increase significantly.

"Yes … Herr Magistrate," Mader's croaked, his voice barely audible.

"If you might inform us of what you saw?"

"The fat one called Vasquez came to life in the coffin. He screamed at us like the Devil himself and we fled for our lives. I saw Brother Luke stab him before we ran for our lives."

"Thank you, Herr Mader. Before you sit back down, can you give me any reason why you should not be hung by the neck as an accomplice?"

"But … we thought the men were dead … we were told … we …" Mader began to weep uncontrollably.

"Herr Mader, you said `men' in the plural. I was referring to Vasquez. Who else have you killed?"

"I … I killed? No, no, I killed no one … I ..."

"Very well, Herr Mader, who else did you think was already dead before you killed them?" The Magistrate was pulling the wings from a fly.

"We didn't know they were alive, I—"

"Who?" The Magistrate's tone grew short.

"The one they call Ver … Verhoevan, and Herr Dopp." Mader's voice grew breathless as his fear increased.

The Magistrate's eyebrows rose as he perused the papers before him, looking for something that wasn't there. "The Herr Dopp you speak of, is he here today?" he inquired with greater interest.

Mader turned and pointed with a trembling hand at Matthias, who stared straight ahead. The Magistrate looked at Matthias with a curious expression, as did Inspector Johansen.

"Sit down, Mader." The Magistrate's eyes then fixed on Matthias. "Herr Dopp, I see here in the papers before me that you are a living victim of the deeds perpetrated by the accused. I am quite interested in how a strong young man such as yourself is mistaken for dead, buried, and yet survives to sit in this courtroom today."

Matthias slowly rose while gathering his thoughts. He didn't wish to lie, if such a lie would help put the noose around the necks of men.

"Your grace …" Matthias began, in a respectful tone he fortunately found at the last second, despite the fact that he felt no respect for a man he had decided was undeniably cruel. "I was rendered unconscious at the time my body was spirited away, and had it not been for my friend Captain Harding, led by the suspicions of Brother Vasquez, I fear I would have met the same fate as Verhoevan."

"I see. And how were you rendered unconscious, young man? Were you struck on the head or the like?"

Matthias thought it through and decided the truth, though not the entire truth, was the safest approach.

"Well, your grace, what I remember was listening to music in the cathedral and then waking up on board Captain Harding's ship, and nearly two days had passed."

"His spirit left his body. It was the work of Verhoevan, a messenger of Satan!" Nicolas accused, eyes on fire.

"If you would be so kind as to gag that man, constable. We will have no unsolicited testimony in my court." Under protest, Nicolas was gagged, and the magistrate again turned to Matthias.

"Did you know the one called Verhoevan?"

"No, your grace, I did not," Matthias answered truthfully.

"That will be all, young man … for the moment."

Matthias sat down, relieved. The Magistrate rifled though the documents in front of him, then looked to the prosecutor.

"Does the prosecution have any information regarding the attempt on Herr Dopp's life?"

The prosecutor whispered to Inspector Johansen, who whispered something back quickly, then he responded.

"No, your grace."

"It would seem only my own thorough inquiry is unearthing the breadth of this case," the Magistrate huffed.

"If I might continue my opening statement, your grace, I —"

"I shall disregard the prosecution's impertinence in the name of expediency. Proceed."

"I thank you for such consideration, your grace. There is indeed another charge of attempted murder, a murder that was foiled by our own Inspector Johansen. Another Franciscan brother by the name of Pietro was rendered unconscious from a blow to the head and was about to be poisoned when Inspector Johansen arrived on the scene at the monastery. It was Pietro who later led the Inspector to the men who had assisted Brother Luke. So now with what we have heard from Herr Dopp, which your grace has so skillfully solicited, our charges include two murders and two attempted murders. The prosecution, on behalf of the City of Hamburg, is requesting the maximum penalty of death by hanging. This is the least we can do to protect the citizens of our fair city for whose safety we find ourselves responsible." The prosecutor sat down.

"I have a few more questions, if the prosecution doesn't mind?" The magistrate didn't wait for a response. "Sometimes it might behoove the prosecution to look into why a crime has been committed in order to better protect the future of these citizens *you* find yourself responsible for. Now we have just learned about Herr Dopp, who woke up on board a ship having no idea of how he got there. I, for one, am curious. Perhaps the one called Captain Harding can enlighten us. Is Captain Harding in the courtroom?"

Harding stood and spoke firmly. "I am, your grace, and I would be pleased to answer any questions you might have of me."

The Magistrate looked Harding over, finding his stern tone a challenge.

"*Pleased* is not a word I would use in the course of hanging men charged with the horrid crimes we speak of today," the Magistrate lectured with a parental tone.

"Indeed, sir, I was not aware the trial was over and such a decision had already been made." Harding's words caused a look of anger to flash across the Magistrate's face that he brought under control as Harding continued. "I would certainly take no pleasure in hanging anyone, but I would be greatly pleased to divulge any information I might possess that might lead to some type of justice for those whose lives have been taken unnecessarily. Any hanging that is to be done is clearly a great weight of conscience that rests with you, your grace." Harding's words were succinct, and the

Magistrate's face indicated that he felt he had been bested in his own court, despite Harding's almost comical English-accented German. Harding's accent, however, gave his words a disarming innocence.

"I thank you for your willingness to assist us here today, Captain Harding. How is it you came to find Herr Dopp on your ship when he regained consciousness?"

Harding described the events of Matthias's rescue, and how they were confronted by Luke and his men.

"Did Herr Dopp display any evidence of a blow to the head or the like?" the Magistrate asked.

"That he did not, your grace, and when he awoke, apart from being fatigued, he appeared totally normal in my estimation."

"So, we are left with the mystery of how this boy might have been rendered unconscious. Do we have any theories in this regard, Inspector?"

Inspector Johansen stood and bowed. The Magistrate looked his way in anticipation.

"You may speak, Inspector."

"Your grace, when I found the one they know as Brother Pietro, he was about to have a brew, ordered by brother Nicolas, administered to his lips. It would appear the brotherhood is well versed in herbal medicines and may very well have used such means to render Herr Dopp unconscious."

Brother Nicolas wriggled in his seat and babbled excitedly into the gag. The Magistrate looked at him and thought he might be worth another try.

"We will remove the gag if you will promise to speak to us like an intelligent man. Otherwise, you will once again forfeit your right to speak. Do you agree to my terms, sir?"

Nicolas nodded in approval and the constable was ordered to remove the gag.

"Herr Dopp was rendered unconscious by the devilish work of Verhoevan. It was the call of Satan that pulled his soul from his body, he —"

With a wave of his hand the Magistrate signalled the constable and Nicolas was gagged again.

"It would seem we are getting nowhere with the Papists today. I find Inspector Johansen's intuitions of more scientific benefit to a court of sane men. This court is satisfied with the testimony it has heard and rules in favour of the prosecutor's request. Constable, please help the prisoners to their feet. At the first light of day, Brothers Luke and Nicolas, you shall be escorted to a public place where your crimes will be read aloud and you shall be hung by the neck until dead. We can only pray God will find something redeemable in your souls. Perhaps in the time you have left on this earth you might pray for forgiveness. This court is adjourned."

Nicolas and Luke were dragged out, protesting through gags, as the Magistrate retired to his chambers. Matthias stood with a sad expression. Harding looked at his friend and gently put his hand on his back.

"It will be quick, Matthias, and they are indeed murderous scoundrels."

"They were just afraid of what they couldn't understand," Matthias returned. "Let's get out of this horrid place where so many have been condemned to death by that dark, ugly soul."

"Luke is all of that," the Captain commented.

"I meant the magistrate," Matthias corrected him.

They turned to leave, but Johansen blocked the way.

"The puzzle of your loss of consciousness, Herr Dopp, I believe is the key to the deaths of Verhoevan and Vasquez. Two men of the cloth have had their cages rattled by something they could only blame on the Devil, and I think I heard you say they were just afraid of something they couldn't understand. I don't suppose you would be willing to share this information? You would find me a reasonable man."

"What is it you would have me say, Inspector? Would you believe me if I told you I went on a fantastic journey into what some call Heaven or the netherworld and visited my dead mother? Would you believe me if I told you I was held captive in that place by fear mongers and would have perished there if not for the spirits of Verhoevan and Vasquez, who came to rescue me? And even if I told you this, would an explanation, from a reasonable man, not be that I was the victim of some kind of induced hallucination? So tell me then, how would any of this information be of use to you?"

The Inspector looked down and scratched his head in thought. He stood to one side and held his arm out towards the door, signalling to Harding and Matthias to leave. As they were brushing by, Johansen grabbed Matthias by the arm and looked him in the eye.

"Your friend is right, Herr Dopp. Justice was served here today, and two murderous scoundrels go to the gallows for the deaths of Vasquez and Verhoevan. The deceased, whether they were touring the netherworld at the time or simply hallucinating, were indeed murdered. My curiosity is not so easily satisfied as that of the Magistrate."

The Inspector turned and went back to speak with the prosecutor.

Harding and Matthias stood on the front steps of the Rathaus for only a moment before their dutiful driver pulled underneath the portico out of the rain. Matthias took one look at the drenched state of their driver and pulled his dry cloak off and handed it to the man.

"You might remove your sopping cloak and try this for the ride home, with my apologies, sir. I will pay you for the rest of your day so that you and your horse might seek some warmth."

"*Danke*, Herr Dopp."

The door was closed and Matthias sat solemnly. Harding looked at his friend curiously.

"You have changed, Matthias. I don't know what you have been through, but I have never seen you so aware of the suffering in others. You didn't even want justice for the madman, Luke."

"Since I awoke in your cabin I feel so much pain and suffering around me it is almost unbearable." Matthias looked out the window. "I am ready to see Hamburg disappear on the horizon forever. Maybe in America, in the presence of Anna's love, I can be myself again."

***

The next morning Pietro was admitted into the fetid prison cell to minister to the needs of Luke and Nicolas. Nicolas shook with fear, while Luke muttered to himself as usual. Pietro felt sick to his stomach as he looked at his colleagues, brothers of the same order about to be killed.

"Nicolas, I am so saddened at what has happened to you." Pietro wept in a halting fashion.

"Don't offer me your sympathy, for you are in league with those invested in the sinister forces of Hell," Nicolas snapped.

"I bring a message from Matthias, who did not wish to play any role in your deaths. He truly takes no pleasure, only sorrow in your fate."

"He is a messenger of Satan himself!"

"Think on this, Nicolas. A man who is saddened by your suffering, does this sound like a devil? Think, man! Think! Don't be confused by the madness of Luke."

"Oh, now the pupil would lecture his teacher?" Nicolas shot back.

"You are about to die, Nicolas. You go to your Maker crazy with anger and snarl at one who seeks only to offer you comfort. Is this how you have grown as a Christian? Did our Lord snarl at His executioners even as He bled on the cross?"

Nicolas looked at Pietro and for a moment considered the young man's words.

"Get out!" Nicolas turned to face the wall.

Pietro felt a powerful frustration that any man could drift so far from his own sense of reason.

"Before I go, Nicolas, there is something I have been asked to tell you. It is simply this. When you see the light, take only your love with you. Try to rid yourself of fear. Search for the strongest feelings of love you can … for it is fear that …"

Nicolas turned around slowly and stared at Pietro. Pietro was expecting more spew, but Nicolas looked different.

"It is fear that *what*?" Nicolas asked.

Pietro repeated the last words of the message from Mathias. "It is fear that can condemn one's soul to nothingness. Think of those you love who have passed before and they will meet you. That is all I was told."

"No doubt by Vasquez," Nicolas pondered out loud.

"No, it was Matthias, who pains for you and your journey this day."

"Now I am to seek spiritual guidance from a veritable boy? You're all mad. Get out!"

Pietro was about to call for the guard when the door opened. It was time, and Pietro swung around to see a shiver of fear course through Nicolas's body.

"Love, Nicolas, love. No fear! Think of someone who loved you who has passed!" Pietro was brushed out of the way and two guards grabbed Luke and Nicolas by the elbows and ushered them out. Pietro followed with eyes blurred by curtains of tears.

Out in the street a bloodthirsty mob had been increasing in size, and now it began to hum in anticipation of the morning's entertainment. Nicolas climbed the steps of the gallows behind Luke, who was virtually carried up by guards on either side. When Nicolas faced the crowd, he saw jeering faces, waiting to be titillated by witnessing his misfortune, and then he looked on the face of Pietro, and something profound occurred.

In Pietro's crumpled face he saw only love and sadness for what was about to occur. The crowd was there to be frightened and thrilled by the dancing of the damned at the end of a rope. In Pietro, Nicolas found one who grieved for him. Seeing that grief, his own feelings of love emerged for the boy he had tutored. His love then moved on to those he had loved who were "no more," as Pietro had advised, and there he found another source of something good. In his last moment Pietro had given him a gift that began to well in his chest. As the noose was tightened around his neck, he looked to Pietro, nodded, and smiled a grateful smile.

Pietro's eyes widened and more tears flooded in.

Luke dropped first, and with such force that his head was ripped clear from his body to excited squeals of disgust, ugly humour, and applause. When Nicolas dropped, Pietro closed his eyes and walked away. The crowd cheered death on, as its darkness slowly devoured the flickers of life in Nicolas's eyes. He didn't give his audience the dance they had hoped for but simply gagged as air sought a way in that no longer existed. The crowd in front of him began to spin in a waft of the surreal. He felt something warm and realized his bowels had given way, then his eyes began to bulge with his own weight pushing flesh and blood upwards from the noose. It was time to command the rest of his muscles to give up in order to put an end to the spectacle. He was surprised, in that moment of letting go, that he felt no fear, only the gift Pietro had reminded him of. It was a gift he had bestowed on others in his younger days, one that he now felt again. There it was, in the light ahead … emanating from a familiar shadow heading his way … unguarded, unconditional … undeniable … love.

20

THE MISSION

Mississauga, Ontario, 1989

The door to Shaun Bishop's bedroom was open and gave his mother quite an eyeful as she rounded the corner. Her naked son's bare backside was quite obviously between two legs, and one of those legs was nearly as white as the cast on the other. Shaun's girlfriend, Jordan, looked over Mrs. Bishop's shoulder and let out a gasp. Mrs. Bishop exploded.

"Shaun Bishop, I have never been so ashamed in all my life as I am at this moment! We will be in the living room once you two make yourselves presentable!"

Shaun's mother slammed the door and escorted Jordan to the living room. Jordan burst into tears with the mantra of the scorned: "How could he do this to me? How could he do this to me?"

Moments later, a sheepish Shaun and Jennifer appeared fully clothed in the living room. Shaun went to Jordan and attempted to comfort her, only to be struck hard across the face. *The girl packs quite a punch*, Danny thought as he reeled from the blow. It hurt like the dickens, but he knew Jordan's hurt was greater. Danny held his pulsing face and joined Alison on the loveseat by the window. They both sat stoically until Mrs. Bishop spoke again.

"What do you two think you're up to?"

"We know this is sudden, Mrs. Bishop but Da …" Alison stopped herself from saying the name Daniel. She picked up a similar phonetic and continued, "… death and hospitals have created some deep bonds for us."

"What are you saying, girl? Nobody died."

"We feel we connected somehow while we were both unconscious, Mrs. Bishop, as weird as that sounds."

Mrs. Bishop was seriously contemplating the words when Jordan flew off the handle.

"Oh, this is just sick! I know what you're doing, Jennifer Glessing. You're just selfishly fooling around. Everyone at school knows you and Brendon are in love and will probably get married. How can you do this to me and Shaun?" Jordan looked at Shaun then. "I thought we were forever, Shaun. Isn't that what you said?"

Danny didn't know how to respond. There were some strong feelings for Jordan, and they felt like his own, but they couldn't be. To add to the confusion, the smell of her perfume excited something in him, as did the way she looked. Then he looked at Alison, all dolled up in her American princess blond bombshell body, and that image wasn't exactly working. Only when they spoke and when they kissed did he know it was the Alison he loved. There was far too much to deal with, and he knew whatever he said was going to sound pretty lame.

"Jordan, Mom, I'm not going to say anything today. I'm sure this is all pretty weird for everyone, Jennifer and me included. I think we all need some time to process the events of the last few days."

"Process? I'll give you something to process!" Jordan pulled off a ring, threw it at Shaun, and stormed out.

Mrs. Bishop sat shaking her head with an obvious look of disapproval. Alison went to her.

"I'm so sorry, Mrs. Bishop. I know how this must look. I don't know what to say to you other than —"

"Miss Glessing, please. The way this *looks* is the way it *is*. You have caused my son to betray his commitment to a very lovely young woman who I'm quite sure he *was* in love with. Then you come into my house and lure him into bed. This isn't *appearance*, young lady, this is what has *happened*. I would like you to leave my house now!"

Alison went to the door and Daniel followed

"This isn't going to be easy, Daniel," she said quietly. Then she kissed him on the cheek and left.

Danny turned and faced Mrs. Bishop. "This isn't the end of the world, Mom."

"No, the end of the world was when they told me you were brain-dead and there was no hope. But I don't know how much of this behaviour I can take. This is not how any son of mine acts. Why, I felt closer to you when you were lying in that hospital bed unconscious than I do now."

Danny was curious. "Did you feel your son standing behind you with his hands on your shoulders when you wept?" The words were out, and Mrs. Bishop's eyes opened about as wide as was physically possible.

"In the name of Jesus, don't you speak of such things." She went to her room and closed the door.

Danny gave Alison enough time to return to the Glessing home and then called. Her mother answered and called out for Jennifer to come to the phone.

"Ali?"

"I'm so sorry, Daniel."

"Listen, Ali, before things get any more complex around here, I think I need to get to my … uh … Danny's mother. I don't know how much time she has."

"Do you think you're going to need me?"

"Yeah, I uh, I don't know … moral support? Comfort in numbers? A ride to Montreal? Maybe if I'm striking out with her, you might think of another approach. If you help me, I'll back you up when it comes to your mother."

"God, I'm not looking forward to that one. All right, Montreal is a long drive, and remember, I am a seventeen-year-old girl so I'm going to need one hell of an alibi. I'll call you back."

Twenty minutes later it was decided that they would leave early the next morning. An overnight was out of the question. If they left at five they would arrive in Montreal by ten, and if Danny needed to stay he would have to take the train back.

Mrs. Bishop heard Shaun showering before sunrise but drifted back to sleep until the front door clicked shut. She lay half awake for a few minutes, then got out of bed and went to the window to see her son, crutches and all, getting into Jennifer's car.

***

Ali and Danny were driving east on Highway 401, watching the sunrise with groggy eyes. Danny reached over and quite innocently put his hand on Jennifer's thigh. It was only a matter of seconds before he began to feel aroused, and Ali looked over at him.

"Perhaps you'd better take your hand off my leg or we're never going to make it to your mother's today."

"You too, huh? Man, this young love stuff is powerful. I mean, sure, I've wanted to get laid before, but my love for you is so strong I can't think of anything else. I wonder how long it's going to take for me to see *you* in that body."

"I hear your voice more and more, Daniel. It's changing. The words are sounding more like your own every day. I must confess, I want to feel you, Danny, with my eyes shut. Oh brother, I'm ready to pull off the highway and screw your brains out!"

"You know, when I first met you I never would have had you pegged for a horn-dog."

"A horn-dog?" Ali burst out laughing, and Danny lost it too. It was as though a dam had burst. Two hours later, after gassing up, they pulled into a rest area with picnic tables, and in a matter of seconds clothes were being unbuttoned and unzipped and lips were locked. When the deed was done, they just stared at each other's eyes, looking in as far in as they could. Ali smirked.

"That ought to hold me for a few miles, Daniel Blum."

"We're going to get arrested at this rate for lewd acts in a public place."

The car pulled out onto the road, and for the rest of the journey strategies for talking to Myra Blum were discussed and discarded. Ali felt that their story was just too fantastic for anyone invested in the physical world to comprehend, least of all a grieving mother

Danny sensed Bernard's presence, and it directed him to his mother's pain, for motivation. It was there, her pain was his. The crumpled face he saw hanging over her son's body at the morgue had made him cry. His sadness now turned to resolve. Somehow, Myra Blum had to know that her lovely boy was still in her otherwise empty world.

Danny directed Ali to Point Claire on the outskirts of Montreal and they pulled into the driveway of the late Sid Feldman's house. Myra looked up from the kitchen table, where she had been sitting, staring at her coffee. Moments later the front door opened and she stared curiously at two youngsters awkwardly getting out of a shiny BMW, one with a cast and the other on crutches.

"Can I help you?" she asked with a look of confusion.

"We're here to help you," Alison opened. "We need to talk to you about Daniel and Alison."

"Alison? The woman my son was found with?"

"One and the same, and if it's of any interest to you, he's still with her," Alison answered.

"Might we have a coffee and talk about your lovely boy, Myra?" Danny asked.

Myra gasped and held her hand up to her mouth. The voice and the choice of words sounded so like Danny, but who was this young black man standing in her driveway? She pulled away from the front door and drifted back into the house, with teary eyes. Danny led Alison into the kitchen, where Myra leaned against the sink, just staring at two total strangers who had walked right into her home.

Danny saw the coffee was hot in the percolator and he absent-mindedly went to the cupboard where the mugs were kept. He pulled out one for Alison and his old favourite, a pottery mug with the words "cup o' jo" lettered in a folksy, deep-blue script. Myra watched this stranger move around her kitchen with such familiarity that it frightened her.

"What do you think you're doing? If you're here to rob me or kill me, just get it over with. I could care less. Just tell me what you want."

"I'm sorry, Myra. I should have asked you if we could have some coffee," Danny said in a familiar tone.

"That was Danny's favourite mug," Myra said as she collapsed onto her chair at the table and began to weep.

"I know. Okay to have a coffee?" Danny asked. Myra motioned with her hand that it really didn't matter, nothing did.

"Geeze, Ali, I don't even know what you take in your coffee."

"One sugar and a little milk."

After giving Alison her coffee, Danny noticed that Myra's mug was empty and he filled it. Myra studied the young man as he put two spoons of sugar and no milk in her mug then placed it in front of Myra.

"How did you know I take my coffee with two sugars and no milk?"

"You quit putting milk in your coffee after your husband left and you didn't have much money. You said it was so you would never run out of milk for your lovely boy, and then you just got used to it."

Myra's jaw dropped and wheels turned.

"You called her Ali. The one they found next to my son was called Alison."

"Yup. Remember the book we found with your father's things? And you asked me to look into what it was, or what it might be worth?"

"How … I asked Daniel that, not you. Who…?"

"Well, I found out what it was, and I went looking at the university for someone to translate it, and that's where I bumped into Alison."

"Wearing the tightest pants I'd ever seen in my life, I might add." Alison chuckled into her mug before taking a sip of her coffee.

"You said I asked *you* to see what my father's book was worth? I asked my *son* to do that, not you!" Myra was getting angry.

"I don't know how to say this, so here it is straight up. I *am* your son, Mom. It's me, Daniel. I may not look like your lovely boy any more but, man oh man, have I got a story to tell you! Now, ask me any questions only Daniel could answer, anything at all."

There it was, boldly out in the open. Myra started to weep again.

"You're certifiable, young man. I don't know who you are or how you know what you do, but you are *not* my son. Leave, before I call the police!" Her face was red with mounting anger. "What on earth is the matter with two young people like you, playing sick games on someone who's just lost her son? Read it in the papers, did you? Thought you'd have some fun?" Myra stood shaking.

"We were allowed to come back to try to stop you from taking your own life, Mom." Danny went to her and tried to hold her, but she pushed him away.

"Don't you dare!"

"You might get a sense of me if you close your eyes and touch me, Mom," Danny said softly.

"Oh, you're sick. I'm not touching you, fella … get out! The both of you get out! GET OUT!"

Myra began to cry hysterically. Danny went to the refrigerator and pulled a piece of paper from a magnetic "Grocery List" pad that was stuck to the door. He found a pen on a small table by the phone and scribbled some information down.

"Here's the phone number for where I'm staying near Toronto. I ask that rather than take your own life, you simply consider that something fantastic has happened. Your Danny is not dead, and there is something good ahead of you in this life that you haven't experienced yet. That's why I came back, Mom."

"Get out!" Myra screamed.

Ali and Danny let themselves out and walked sadly to the BMW.

"Well, Daniel, that strategy really worked like a charm," Alison said sarcastically.

"Yeah, psychology and the paranormal are two of my specialties. God, she's always been stubborn like her dad. I wonder if that's part of the reason my father left her. Nah, never mind, my dad's just a selfish prick."

Myra watched the two youngsters get back in their car and pull away, then she cranked the kitchen casement window shut. She had heard every word. She looked down at the number written on the piece of paper and thought there was something familiar in the hand. Myra started to tremble, then crumpled the note up and threw it in the trash.

***

It was close to five o'clock when Ali finally pulled up in front of Mrs. Bishop's apartment building.

"I'd better get back to the Glessings. I have some explaining to do."

Danny reached over and kissed her. The kiss didn't last long enough for an ever-present need, but it was a little too long for Mrs. Bishop, who sat shaking her head at her living-room window, where she had waited all day.

Danny, having taken no keys, looked for Bishop on the tenant display board, dialled the number, and was buzzed in. His fingers hit the fifth-floor button on the elevator automatically, causing him to smile. Some of Shaun's neural paths were alive and well. He thought of Shaun and what life might have been for such an athletic young man. Would he have become a professional athlete? Would he and Jordan eventually have married? Jordan was certainly a beautiful young woman, whose heart was badly wounded at the moment. A strong waft of guilt came over Danny in that territory. Thoughts began to flood in that made him wonder why he hadn't already considered them. He had been so distracted with his love for Ali that all of the other lives affected hadn't been given a shrug of thought.

I am a selfish asshole, he thought. *I have always been selfish and here I am on a second chance at life, being selfish yet again. These are human beings with human hearts who are feeling pain I have never been subjected to. I have never known the death of someone I love dearly. I have never been jilted by someone I love.* The list was long enough for an elevator journey of a thousand floors, but the doors opened on the fifth. Danny stepped out and walked down the hall that smelled so familiar. He stopped at the number on the door that Shaun's eyes had known as home for years.

The door was open and Danny went in. Mrs. Bishop stood in front of him and was about to speak when Danny just put his arms around her and held her. She had lost her son. Did she need to know the truth or could it slide? Danny swayed gently with her as he had done with his own mother at his grandfather's funeral. Mrs. Bishop seemed to absorb the affection for a moment and then pulled back. Her voice was soft but her expression confused.

"I don't know what's happened to you, Shaun, but you haven't allowed me to hold you like that since you were a boy. What is going on with you and that Glessing girl?"

Danny sensed such kindness in Mrs. Bishop that he wanted to tell her everything and to let her know her boy was all right, but the truth had already failed miserably once that day.

"You are such a kind soul," he began. "I would never ever wish to hurt you. I'm caught in such a duplicitous situation, no matter where I turn I'm going to hurt somebody."

Mrs. Bishop sat down, and her look of confusion was now one of worry as she fought back tears.

"I don't know who you are, but you surely don't sound like Shaun Bishop. Duplicitous? Now there's a word I've never heard outta my boy's mouth. But … it's not just your words, your voice is changing … the way you speak is not my Shaun. I don't believe Shaun would have done what you did to Jordan yesterday … nosiree, I must say, I don't know who you are."

"I'm so sorry for the pain I'm causing you and Jordan. I need some time to get it together before I open my mouth again."

Danny went to Shaun's bedroom. Mrs. Bishop sat back down and stared into space. Danny had an idea and grabbed the phone on Shaun's desk, dialling a number that fortunately he knew, and a familiar voice answered.

"Joel, it's Danny."

"Danny? Fuck off, Danny's gone. My best friend is dead, you sick bastard."

"Well, how about the little trip we took outside of our bodies?" Danny tried again.

"You don't sound at all like Danny, whoever you are. Impressions aren't our thing, pal … don't give up your day job."

"Yeah, well you ought to get a load of how I look. Do you have any memory of the other side?"

"Who is this?" Joel was immovable.

"We need to get together to talk in private."

"Maybe. So who is it they're burying tomorrow if you're who you say you are?"

"Burying tomorrow? What do you mean?"

"Well, my mom just got off of the phone with the Police Department and they said Danny Blum's body was released this afternoon and the funeral is tomorrow in Pointe Claire. Next time you want to freak someone out, you might read the obituaries first, asshole."

"Everything's happening too fast. Can you call and find out what time the funeral is?"

"Sure. So who are they burying tomorrow?"

"Me."

"What?" The phone was silent on both ends for a good five seconds before Joel broke the stalemate.

"Jesus, if you're Danny, are you going to die or something?"

"No, no Joel, my body is dead. I'm, well … I'm in another body now, which is why I sound different … these aren't my vocal cords."

"You know you sound fuckin' crazy, man, crazier than me."

'I know, I know this whole thing is crazy. Find out from my mom when the funeral is tomorrow and call me back, will ya? And don't say a thing about this stuff to anyone, just offer her your condolences or whatever and call me back."

"Oh yeah, I might slip up and tell a grieving mother her son isn't really dead, he just called me from another man's body. Look, give me your number and I'll do it and call back in a couple of minutes."

Danny put the receiver back in the cradle and started pacing the floor. He wasn't sure if Joel believed anything he had said. What if he had just promised to call in order to get rid of him? It was a good ten agonizing minutes before his phone rang. Danny jumped and grabbed it before Mrs. Bishop could pick up.

"Joel?"

"Yeah, man, it's me. Look, they're going to bury Danny's body tomorrow at eleven next to your grandfather. I've got directions if you want."

"No, that won't be necessary, I know where it is. I was just at his funeral. Are you going, Joel?"

"Yeah, and so are my mom and dad. Danny's fiancée Karla Rose and her folks are coming up from Nashville. The band members are coming, they're real shook up. I guess cause it's one of us … you know, peer group, close to home, that kinda thing. So?"

"So … what?" Danny countered

"Well, how will I know who the fuck you are, mystery-man?"

"Remember the black kid who was in one of the beds next to you in the ICU?"

"Yeah, the Bishop kid. We spoke with his mom the day I left. My folks and Mrs. Bishop did a little bonding in the waiting room."

"Well, that's me now."

"What? Get the fuck outta Dodge!"

"I'm serious."

"Whoa, this is getting too strange, man. Strange enough to be true."

"No more strange than going to my own funeral. See you there, pal. I have to call Ali."

"The nerd from the university? You two still happening? Jesus, Danny, is that really you?"

"Tell you all about it tomorrow, Joel." Danny saw Vera Bishop standing in his door. "Gotta run." Danny slammed the phone down and looked at Mrs. Bishop. Her eyes were wide open and she spoke first.

"Joel? Is that the Joel from the ICU?"

"Uh, yes. We sort of know each other."

"Oh, is that so? Do you know what he asked me when he left the ICU? `What's your son's name, Mrs. Bishop?' Does that sound like someone you sort of know?"

"Do you think I'm sane, Mrs. Bishop?" Danny began earnestly.

Mrs. Bishop clutched her chest and slid down the doorjamb to the floor as it slowly dawned on Danny that he had used her surname. What son would be that formal with his mother? He could not have done any more damage if he had tried, but now the door was open, and Mrs. Bishop gingerly pulled on the string that hung next to her darkest thought.

"Where is my son?" Mrs. Bishop's voice was dry and she appeared to be gasping for air.

Danny sat down next to her and held her. She sobbed in arms she knew. Danny threw caution to the wind and slowly started the story from the beginning, hoping for a better result than he'd achieved with Myra. Mrs. Bishop listened silently until he was through the incredible tale. Then, without moving from his embrace or looking at him, she spoke with a deliberate calm.

"I felt my son leave. I also felt the presence of others in the ICU that I couldn't see. I remember someone named Daniel from the day my son was admitted. He visited Joel and was very kind to his parents. So you say it was your fault Joel crossed over?"

"Yes," Danny confessed with remorse. "I am responsible for this whole mess. Shaun's passing would have been a normal one, and you would not be suffering this way now."

"Yesterday you asked me if I had felt my son's hands on my shoulders while I wept over his body in the ICU."

"He loved you deeply," Danny muttered sadly, causing Mrs. Bishop's façade to crack.

"My boy is gone." The words stuck in her throat like sand.

"Well, in spirit, yes, his energy has moved on, but I still have some of his memory, and it seems much of his great love and admiration for you is firmly imprinted in these brain cells. I can say with honesty that even though I have just really met you, I love you … pretty deeply . . . and —"

"And things couldn't be a bigger mess, could they?" she sputtered. "This is what happens when you start fooling around with the natural order of things."

Danny and Mrs. Bishop sat in silence. A tremor would occasionally shudder through her body, but it was a good hour or so before she spoke.

"So, they're burying Daniel's, or as you would have me [illegible] body tomorrow?" The words came out calmly.

[illegible]." Danny sighed.

"Daniel's mother is as low as a human being can be. She has seen the dead body of her boy and she is alone." Mrs. Bishop's words hung in the air while Danny grappled with the selflessness of them. "I have not had the pain of seeing my son dead. In a way, if what you say is true, he still lives, and some of his love for me lives in his body. Right now, that woman has nothing. Do you have any idea what nothing must feel like?"

"I've never thought of it like that." Danny fell into an even deeper worry for Myra.

Mrs. Bishop got up and went to her laundry room. A few minutes later she reappeared, flipping through the pages of a newspaper she had rescued from the trash. She stopped when she found the page and presented the paper to Danny. "This is Alison?"

Danny looked at the paper. There was an article on the mysterious deaths of three people at the Airport Holiday Inn. There was a rather youthful picture of Dr. Walters, a cheesy rock 'n' roll picture of Danny from a promotional eight by ten, and there was Alison from a university yearbook. He looked at her and his heart sank realizing how much he missed his nerd. Her look of innocence charmed him. It was the honesty of her appearance that played so heavily in what he loved and now missed.

Mrs. Bishop studied Danny as he stared at the picture.

"You loved her, didn't you?"

"Well, now, that's an interesting question. I love her, and part of what I love is in that picture. The first real love I've ever known, but I never knew it here. It was on the other side that I fell in love with her. Part of the reason we came back was to know physical love here."

"Well you certainly didn't waste any time."

"I'm sorry, that must have been so upsetting for you and Jordan. It's so odd when you have to close your eyes and kiss someone to know it's them because they look so different."

"Do the Glessings know their Jennifer is gone?"

"I don't think so. Ali can play her cards closer to the chest than me, besides I think she's enjoying being a teenager of beauty and privilege, and …" Danny realized something he didn't want to know.

"And what?"

"I sure hope we make it through all this."

"We get no guarantees when we sign on for this life. You might as well get used to it." Vera Bishop's tone was unsympathetic.

"Oh, I'm used to failure, Mrs. Bishop. I don't know why I figured anything would be different this time around. Maybe because I'm in love."

"Well, I loved my Shaun, so love is no free pass either."

Mrs. Bishop stood and brushed her clothes off while attempting to gather her senses. She turned, walked down the hall to her own room, closed the door, and wept. Danny listened sadly to her for a moment and then called Ali, but Mrs. Glessing answered the phone. He asked to speak with Jennifer but was told she had gone out with her boyfriend. After some friendly small talk, Danny asked her to pass on the message that Danny Blum's funeral was at eleven the next morning in Montreal and that he was going. If she wanted to talk at all he would be home for the evening.

Mrs. Glessing started to ask who Danny Blum was when Danny cut the conversation off with a curt, "Gotta run, the other line is ringing." When he hung up he couldn't believe the jealousy he was feeling. Ali was out with her boyfriend.

There was no return call, and it was after midnight when Danny knocked on Mrs. Bishop's bedroom door.

"Come in," a weary voice instructed from within.

Danny went in and saw that Vera Bishop was still fully clothed, and there was a pile of used Kleenex on her night-table.

"I have to go to the funeral tomorrow, Mrs. … uh … Mom. I thought I could take a train if I can't mooch a ride with anyone else."

"What about Alison and her fancy new car?"

"She's out with her … with Jennifer's boyfriend, and she hasn't called back. I, uh …" Danny felt a stream of tears roll down his face.

Vera Bishop squinted at him, then put on her glasses and shook her head slowly back and forth. "Well, my lord, I haven't seen tears on that face since it was the face of a little boy."

***

Mrs. Bishop's rusting Toyota Corolla had seen better days. The look and sound of it didn't inspire confidence that they would actually make it to Montreal. In the five hours on Highway 401 they spoke non-stop. Vera Bishop turned out to be one of those people who claimed to see auras and have spiritual powers, but Danny wasn't convinced. She spoke more about how she had sensed the presence of other spirits in the ICU, then looked at Danny and asked a shocker.

"Who's Bernard?"

"Why do you ask?" Danny was taken aback by the mention of a name she had no way of knowing.

"Not sure. The name seems to be in the air around you."

Danny's skepticism about her began to fall away. He explained who Bernard was, and she just nodded, as though it made some kind of sense to her. It was Mrs. Bishop who redirected the conversation to the subject of Myra Blum, which once more made Danny realize how unfocused he was. He had been more or less sulking and worrying about Ali on a date with some other guy ever since he had hung up the phone. But now, thanks to Vera Bishop, he had been reminded of the one whose needs were the greatest at the moment.

Mrs. Bishop wanted to know everything about the mother who was about to bury her only son. She felt a powerful empathy for a woman who had raised a boy on her own. Mrs. Bishop's husband had left her soon after she'd become pregnant. Actually, she'd kicked him out for screwing around. He'd come back once to see his baby son, and Mrs. Bishop thought she might have taken him back but for the fact that he'd disappeared off the face of the earth the next day, never to be heard from again.

It was around ten o'clock at night when Danny directed her off the highway to a Holiday Inn he told her he had played on many occasions. Vera took that piece of information oddly. With little in the way of financial resources they had to share a room with two beds, and they chatted for a good hour about what lay ahead the next day before giving in to exhaustion. As he drifted off, Danny heard Vera Bishop sniffling into her pillow. He realized in that moment that she might not have been entirely convinced by the story of Danny and Alison and might have come along out of parental worry for a son with possible deep-seated mental issues.

***

Danny awoke to see Mrs. Bishop watching the sun the rise. She sat in a barrel chair in her housecoat with her hands held fingertip to fingertip, as though in meditation.

"There's another chair here, Shaun."

Danny got up and hobbled over to the chair next to her, turned it towards the window, and sat. It was a magnificent sight that, as a rock 'n' roll singer, he had never really taken in. Like vampires, late-night entertainers usually found early-morning sunlight a painful reminder of a world they didn't know. They were night creatures, sleeping with drapes drawn and "Do Not Disturb" signs hung on doorknobs without fail. Yeah, he had been missing the beauty of the real world for his entire life. Pretty hard to catch much of anything resembling light with your head up your ass. Come to think of it, most people he knew in show business had their heads up their own asses … it came with the territory of needing to be seen, heard, and recognized on a well-lit, elevated platform in order to feel you existed.

Every night as a performer he would get on the stage like some little kid who wanted others to watch while he tried some lame trick. Sure, there were some performers and musicians who gave much to the world, but he'd never been one of them. So what could he do with this second chance? Danny watched Mrs. Bishop, a woman just a little older than he was, first time around. She had raised a child on her own, established a career for herself, and now here she was putting herself out for someone else.

Mrs. Bishop reached out to hold his hand as they watched the sun come up. It was a gesture that endeared her to him. That hand had been in Shaun's many times. He held it willingly and lovingly, and he knew he had much to learn from her.

They took turns with the bathroom and headed down for breakfast after showering. Danny felt odd freeloading with no cash. Contributing financially was something that needed his full attention once his body healed.

They hopped in the Corolla and it sputtered out of the parking lot. Mrs. Bishop, even though she understood that "Danny" was from this area, was nonetheless intrigued that the soul claiming to inhabit her son's body had an uncanny ability to direct her to the place where his Grandfather Feldman was buried. It was a small cemetery off the beaten track and nearly four hundred miles from where Shaun Bishop had grown up. This surely was not Shaun. The more proof she gathered, the deeper sadness grew within her. Saying goodbye to anyone needs time, but these circumstances were like being stabbed over and over.

As the car turned into the cemetery they saw the freshly dug grave. Mrs. Bishop pulled over and they waited. A few minutes later Joel and his folks arrived in a car with a Hertz sticker on the bumper. Moments later a hearse appeared with a black sedan in tow. Both cars pulled up to the gravesite, and one of the funeral home employees opened the door for Myra.

Danny's heart sank. She looked awful … pale, sleep-deprived, cheeks wet with the dues of grief. He wanted to run to her and hold her but knew he couldn't in his present form. God, somebody should comfort the woman. One of the men in black from the funeral home led her to the hole in the ground and she shook his arm off, saying something to the effect of "Thanks but no thanks." Danny understood. Paying someone for sympathy was just too pathetic … even though her need was great.

Her face did perk up to see Joel, and she had come to know his parents over the years as they had trucked around to one bar or another in support of their boys. She was holding onto Joel when the band van pulled up. Brian and Ron got out wearing their best stage clothes, looking totally ridiculous in open shirts and bulging satin pants. Ron opened the side door and an unfamiliar woman got out—his latest, no doubt. They went over to Myra, who was of course glad to see anyone who'd known her lovely boy.

A late-model Audi pulled to a stop carrying the rabbi from Myra's synagogue and a couple of members of the congregation who were popular at funerals because they could cry at the drop of a hat. Ringers, she thought to herself, like some of the paid professional singers who infiltrated the ranks of the choir to encourage the pathetic singing of the congregation.

Everyone watched as the casket, covered in a shawl emblazoned with the Star of David, was unceremoniously rolled to the grave. Mrs. Bishop and Danny got out, and when Myra saw the young black man who had terrorized her in her own home, her angry eyes cut through him like lasers.

Joel walked over and stood in front of Shaun Bishop.

"Danny?" he whispered.

Mrs. Bishop gasped then regrouped. It was another pin in another balloon that had held her sinking hopes aloft.

Danny saw her anguish and put his arm around her.

"Hey, Joel, it's so good to see you. Have you finished the new tune yet?"

"Jesus Christ it *is* you … un-freaking-believable, man." Joel hugged his friend, causing Myra's eyes to widen.

"Joel, you remember Mrs. Bishop?"

"Mrs. Bishop, so you … uh, you know what's going on?"

"If I am to believe what I am told, you boys have been on quite a journey," she said rather sternly.

"I'm, uh, sorry about your son, ma'am, I don't mean to be insensitive," Joel responded sheepishly.

Danny cut in, sensing Mrs. Bishop's distress. "Can you give Myra some kind of story so we can go back to the house after?"

"Like what?"

"Like I'm a dear friend, or we're driving you back to Toronto," Danny replied.

Mrs. Bishop interrupted. "Boys, maybe we'd best get over to that poor woman standing next to the coffin who doesn't know she has anyone at the moment. Let's keep focused, there's a soul amongst us whose needs far exceed our own." Danny reached for her hand. Mrs. Bishop readily accepted the comfort that it offered and they headed to the grave.

"Joel, would you stand with my mom and sort of, you know, comfort her? She won't take it from me, looking like I do," Danny said quietly, looking at the face of Myra Blum staring at her son's coffin.

"Yeah, sure … of course. Man, this is a freaking 'Twilight Zone' episode. We have to talk. I gotta talk to someone before I have a breakdown or something," Joel muttered back as he went to the grave.

21

REUNIONS

Hamburg
April, 1848

It was midday when Matthias and Captain Harding went to the livery to commandeer a wagon and two old, reliable horses. Inspector Johansen had agreed to release the bodies of the murder victims to Matthias, since there seemed to be no one else willing to give the job of burial its proper respect and care. Tending to the dignity of the mortal remains of Vasquez and Verhoevan was the task of dutiful friends, and so they were taking the carriage to collect the bodies from the town morgue. Matthias had decided that Vasquez should be buried in his old hometown of Magdeburg, and that Verhoevan should be buried next to him. It was the most meaningful act he could conjure up in the matter of a final resting place for one he loved.

Such sweet thoughts were rudely grounded by the decomposition that filled the air. Even though the bodies had been sprinkled with cloves and a variety of spices, the smell of death prevailed. They took the corpses to a local specialist in the field of prolonging the solidness of the flesh, where they were left overnight to be bound tightly in layers of hopsacking soaked in scented oils and placed in pine coffins for the journey. Pietro arrived before dawn to provide appropriate prayers over his two brothers as their coffins were nailed down, and he waited for Matthias and Harding, who arrived soon after. The coffins were loaded into the wagon once again and they set out on the road to Magdeburg.

Matthias and Harding dressed in the shabbiest old clothes they could find so as not to attract too much attention in a countryside where the peasants were in a state of revolt and anarchy reigned. Many of the wealthy had to flee for their lives as their homes were ransacked and burned. The dirt road was thick with a confusion of people heading to Hamburg, seeking food for their families, or leaving the cold stone city looking for open land where they could at least plant or forage. Fortunately, a wagon carrying two coffins, two scruffy-looking individuals, and a monk was given a wide berth out of a combination of respect for the dead and fear of disease.

By mid-afternoon on the first day they pulled off the road and cut across a field to a slow-moving river in order to water the horses. The housekeeper had packed a large hopsack with cheese, smoked meats, and bread for the journey, and jugs of water and wine had been stowed out of sight. Now they sat in the shade of an ancient oak that had somehow managed to survive the ever-increasing need for lumber and began to savour a little cheese and wine.

It was Matthias who sensed their presence. Some hundred feet away, under low-hanging trees, hungry eyes stared in their direction. A family had taken shelter under a hastily constructed lean-to hidden beneath the camouflage of foliage. Four poles and sparse thatching were their only defence against the elements, and judging by their emaciated bodies, they hadn't been eating much for some time.

Harding, munching away on a piece of bread, became aware that Matthias had stopped eating. He watched his young friend, who began removing small portions of smoked meat, cheese, and bread for their own survival, then stood with the nearly full bag, eyes focused on the family under the tree. Harding gave Matthias a knowing nod as the young man removed a jug of wine and headed down the riverbank. Pietro followed, while Harding stayed with the wagon.

The woman, who was breastfeeding her infant, gazed out of sunken eyes and kissed Matthias's hand as he laid the bag of food down beside her. The father, a proud man, offered to repay them in some way, and to that end insisted on tending to their horses with some grasses that he was bundling for thatch. A small, skinny boy tore into a chunk of cheese like a vulture ripping at carrion.

Matthias reached into his pocket and handed two gold coins to the man. "The food will give you strength for the journey. Go to Hamburg. One coin will help you find lodging and feed you for a time. Then go to the Dopp textile mills. Ask for Jorge Hacker. Show him the other coin and tell him Matthias Dopp gave it to you, and the promise of a job to feed your family." Matthias patted the man's shoulder, and he began to weep.

"How can I ever repay you?"

"By raising your children to be good citizens, and by working for a fair wage, that they might have hope of doing the same." Matthias turned and headed back to the wagon.

The woman seemed to need to offer prayers of thanks, and even though she professed she was not a Catholic, she asked if Pietro would lead them in a prayer, a task he readily accepted, delighting in the privilege.

Within the hour they were back on the road. Nothing was said, but Pietro was quite taken with what had just occurred. Harding was lost in thought about his own beliefs, humbled by the demonstration of a powerful compassion the likes of which he had rarely seen.

Vasquez and Verhoevan were to be buried in the cemetery adjacent to the humble chapel where Vasquez had not only first found his faith but also his dear friend, Peter Verhoevan. Matthias had requested that Pietro preside over the burial, and it would be the young monk's first such ceremony.

Pietro appeared to love the role of priest, and the love that the novice brought to his practice of Christianity showed Matthias a glimmer of hope, maybe even some use, for a religion he could no longer subscribe to.

It was a longer journey than anticipated, and in some respects it felt like a pilgrimage in honour of a good and true friend. The first night was spent under the stars, talking, until the rigours of the road produced increasingly frequent yawns and drooping eyelids. Everyone bade a good night in order to get moving at daybreak for the second leg of what would be a, fortunately, uneventful journey.

The hour was late when the wagon stopped at an inn on the outskirts of Magdeburg on the third night. After a tankard of ale, Harding and Matthias were joined by Pietro, who had seen to the horses. Another round was ordered to toast the memory of their friend and his cohort. There was much praise for the departed, and Pietro lamented that Verhoevan's brilliant work would die with him. They had one more round and retired to beds that, as crude as they were, felt wonderful after the hard ground the night before.

Matthias slept restlessly for a good hour while a seed that Pietro had inadvertently planted in his consciousness picked at him until he awakened. He got up and put on his trousers and boots. The innkeeper was still up with a couple of drunken friends and was surprised to see that his guest had arisen. Matthias informed him that he just wanted to look in on his horses, two special old members of the family.

"My wife eats like a horse," one of the drunks slurred.

"She whinnies like one, as well, when you mount her," the other drunk added. All three men burst into hysterical laughter and Matthias continued on his way, confident he wouldn't be followed

Once in the stables at the back of the inn, Matthias looked around until he found what he needed. He took a flat-ended iron bar from the smith's block and went to the wagon. Looking around to ensure that there was no one watching, he pried open the lid of Verhoevan's coffin. Foul-smelling gasses nearly made him ill, but he persevered until he was looking at the leather-bound manuscript lying on the still chest of its writer. Pietro must have found the work at the monastery and sought to put an end to an era.

Something about burying such an important discovery didn't feel right to Matthias. Would the answer to the greatest mystery of life not have some use in the future of mankind? Was it not in some respects an antidote to the stupidity of Brother Luke and his like … men who presumed to know the wishes of God? With the knowledge provided by Verhoevan's work, might men stop killing other men defending the insecurities of what they didn't know? Would this eventually lead to the end of the dark predatory Soms like the one that had held him captive? He grabbed the manuscript and placed it under the bench seat of the wagon in a hidden compartment designed to keep bills of sale and on occasion small sums of money safe from the elements or thieves. He had rented that wagon before for business and requested it so he could safely stash a small amount of emergency money.

He couldn't very well start banging the coffin lid back down with a hammer in the middle of the night without waking the entire inn, so he stood on the nails with the heel of his boot and pushed them all back into their holes. A few stuck out a little, which was rectified by placing the flat iron bar on them and then thumping them the rest of the way in with a wooden hammer.

The following morning the meagre gathering assembled at the monastery in Magdeburg. In its modesty, the small stone chapel seemed appropriate to Matthias. It held no visible wealth and was devoid of gold leaf and statuary, with the exception of the wooden Christ with brightly painted red, dripping blood hanging above the altar. The church was under the charge of the resident Franciscan brotherhood, and so Pietro was welcomed and allowed to preside over the ceremony, at Matthias's repeated insistence.

Vasquez's sister had been informed by messenger and she arrived with her children and husband, Herr Muller, the local miller. She was a compact woman with warm eyes and hands well accustomed to hard work, not unlike her brother. Her husband had clearly learned that it was easier to obey her many orders than to argue, but he also freely offered comfort to the mother of his children in the loss of her brother. She wept gently, clutching the little boys who held on to her tattered dress as Matthias and Harding offered condolences.

At the end of the funeral mass Verhoevan's casket was removed from the altar first. Matthias watched over Vasquez's coffin with his sister and the boys until the pallbearers returned. Matthias dutifully offered his arm to Vasquez's sister and they followed the box carried by Harding, Herr Muller, Pietro, a priest, and a novice. A few more words and prayers were offered while the coffins were lowered into the ground.

A rather odd-looking man in shabby clothing who had stood in the background came forward to speak with Vasquez's sister as she turned to leave. She signalled Matthias and introduced the man as a local stone carver. Pietro had conveyed the message that Matthias wished a monument to be erected that the good names of Vasquez and Verhoevan might linger on in the Magdeburg cemetery. He had requested that the text be etched extra deeply into hard rock to stave off the unstoppable erosion of time. Vasquez and Verhoevan had left this world far too soon, but their names might at least be read every so often by a passerby or the curious. It was the last thing Matthias could do for the memory of his friend and, indeed, the men who had saved his life. He also gave the carver a small piece of parchment that held some words he wanted printed over their names. The carver lifted an eyebrow after reading the request, then assured Matthias that all would be done as he asked.

Matthias, Harding, and Pietro stopped in at the miller's thatched cottage in the early afternoon. The boys were playing in the tall grass next to the towering stone structure of the adjacent mill. The giant stones within rumbled out a small amount of flour for the insatiable hunger of the local population.

Matthias produced a bag of gold coins for Vasquez's sister, much to Harding's surprise. She refused it until Matthias explained that it represented her brother's wages, and Vasquez would have delighted in his sister having something he had earned to ease her life. On those terms she and her proud husband accepted, and as the wagon pulled away, Matthias saw the excited expressions on their faces when they looked inside the small leather bag. It was the fortune of a lifetime to hard-working folk of such humble means.

Harding looked at Matthias, further impressed by the caring the young man demonstrated for others. Something has indeed happened to his friend as a result of his curious journey.

"You're a generous soul, Matthias," Harding said, looking straight ahead, hands on the reins.

"You are mistaken, my friend. The money belonged to Vasquez."

After a moment of thinking about his friend, Matthias smirked and told the story of how Vasquez had knocked Herr Schmidt off his feet in the bank for trying to swindle the son of a good friend. Harding roared with laughter, and everyone fell to pieces when Pietro imitated his mentor's donkey-like laugh. Good memories of a good friend and a presence that would be sorely missed.

***

It was early evening when they finally rolled into Hamburg. Jorge Hacker was in the office of the mill talking with the new owner, who was to take over as soon as the *Southern Belle* sailed for America. Matthias liked the man, though he felt a measure of guilt for selling his father's business. Nonetheless, he did have some control in the mortgage he held, and he would be involved in the business of the mill as a privileged customer, with wholesale prices on weaves that would bring a tidy profit across the sea.

As he was leaving, Jorge Hacker mentioned a ragged-looking individual who had presented a gold coin and told him he was given the promise of a job by a generous young man on the road to Magdeburg.

"Does he possess any skills?" Matthias asked.

"None to speak of, but he seems an honest man, not afraid to work hard and eager to learn. I have started him in cleanup and we'll see where we go from there."

"What of his family?"

"My wife has found them a place to live. Nothing fancy, but it has a good hearth and the roof doesn't leak."

"Thank you, Jorge."

"No father should see his children starve. They'll be on their feet soon enough. You've seen to that."

Harding had left to tend to the provisioning of the *Belle*. Her refit had gone much more quickly than he had anticipated, and it was beginning to look as though both the *Southern Belle* and the leased *Branden* would set sail for America around the same time. The *Belle* was a much lighter vessel and would make better time.

It was later in the evening that Harding joined Matthias at the Dopp house for dinner. Matthias had invited the new owner and his wife, as well as Jorge Hacker and his wife.

Jorge's cousins, Herr and Frau Fogel, were people of reasonable wealth, but their devout Protestant faith pointed them towards a humble life, and made them averse to displays of garish wealth. That they had bought the Dopp house to be nearer the business was pushing the limits of the humility they deemed proper. The outside of the house, however, was quite conservative, and Mrs. Fogel would no doubt make the interior much more austere should any Church elders drop in.

Jorge's wife was very withdrawn until Matthias managed to get her laughing on the subject of her children. He was doing his best to charm all who dined under his roof, and appeared to be succeeding.

In the dining room, the chef Vasquez had hired presented Vasquez's favourite meal: venison, boiled cabbage and sausage, fresh bread, and a full-bodied red wine. The wine came from a case that the sturdy monk had procured from his favorite vintner, a priest in the Rhine Valley. The evening was formal but friendly and had been put together in order that Matthias might observe the treatment of Hacker and his wife by his wealthy cousin. There appeared to be a solid level of mutual respect, which pleased Matthias and left him with a positive feeling about his choice of successor for the family business. As small talk continued around the table over sweet cakes and sherry, Matthias looked around the dining room as if to say goodbye. It was his first formal dinner as head of the table, but it would not be his last. The table, like the other heirlooms in the house, had belonged to his mother and would go to America with him. There was room on the *Branden* for it and a few other keepsakes from the Dopp household so that he and Anna might set up a good house of their own in reasonable style.

One more week passed before all business was finalized and the furniture was loaded onto the *Branden*. There was still no word of Anna's family, who had apparently disappeared off the face of the earth. Matthias's man had scoured Munchen and the nearby countryside only to come up empty-handed. Matthias paid the man a good sum of money to continue looking virtually anywhere.

Matthias felt he had failed Anna somehow as he stood on the ship's deck waving farewell to Herr Fogel and Jorge. He felt conflicting emotions when the *Southern Belle* hauled anchor and the wind filled her sails, causing her to keel gently. On the aft deck, he watched as the land of his birth grew smaller and smaller. He somehow knew he would never set foot on those shores again. It was now time to look completely to the future, and so Matthias slowly released the tethers to the past, until he felt as though he had dropped the ends of them into the swells beneath him, and turned to face the North Sea. His thoughts were now fully focused on Anna and the New World. His love for her had only been magnified by the distance and distress of the last month. He remembered her scent, the softness of her hair, and every night as he retired to his cabin he lay on his back, eyes closed, trying to remember her kiss, longing to wake up next to her with the smell of her on his skin.

The winds and seas appeared to be as invested in a speedy Atlantic crossing as those held in the bosom of the *Southern Belle*. The *Branden* was left well behind them, and this crossing would be one of the fastest Harding had ever logged. South Carolina traced the curve of the horizon, and with good breezes the *Belle* soon moored off shore. Ferguson, the first mate, was left in charge to see to it that the ship was towed to the wharf as soon as a berth for her became available. Harding and Matthias, meanwhile, were rowed to shore, and with every stroke, the two female figures standing on a small pier to the south of the main wharf slowly came into focus.

Anna's hair blew gently in the breeze, and the look of her made Matthias weak. His heart was in his throat as he climbed up the ladder from the rowboat and stood ten feet from his love, staring at her, slowly sipping her image as though savouring a fine wine.

Anna appeared frozen where she stood. The man before her was the one she had indeed been dreaming of, and yet he looked as though he had aged a little. Somehow his boyishness had changed into the strength of a man. He looked as though he had been through much that she wasn't sure she wanted to know, but the way he looked at her filled her up, nonetheless. It was a look of unfettered adoration. It was a look of desire. It was a look that she wanted to live out her days with. It was the look of her Matthias's eyes.

They walked somewhat tentatively towards one another, hearts pounding, and when they finally touched, even though they thought they had reached the limits, their hearts pounded even louder as their lips locked in a kiss about as passionate as ever had been rendered on that spot. Harding and his wife were a little embarrassed at the public display the youngsters were obliviously engaged in as they politely and barely kissed each other on the cheek. There would be no such public displays of affection from the Captain and his wife, who had more invested in appearance as it pertained to their faith. However, a healthy need resided just beneath the surface, and both knew it would be allowed its moment, and fairly soon, as Mrs. Harding sensed in the tightness of her husband's grip.

Back at the Harding house there was some regretful discussion about the loss of Vasquez, and Anna learned, with great sadness, that her family had vanished, even though the search continued. Mrs. Harding, in an effort to avoid any awkwardness from Anna's emotional state, very politely suggested the men folk retire, as they must be quite spent from the long journey. She and Anna were to remain and tidy up. Harding took his cue and bade all a good night, and Matthias followed suit, looking somewhat longingly at Anna before heading up the stairs.

The dishes were removed to the kitchen, where Anna seemed so distracted she dropped one of Mrs. Harding's good teacups, which shattered on the floor.

"Perhaps you had best get a good night's rest, my dear, before you drop anything else. We have much to do tomorrow."

Anna nodded in agreement and went up the stairs, her silk petticoats rustling like the sound of children playing in leaves. She closed the door quietly behind her and went to the open arms of Matthias and the abandon of passion.

For her part, Mrs. Harding took a goodly amount of time to tidy up thoroughly. She crept up the stairs to her bedroom rather shyly and quietly clicked the door shut behind her. The Captain sat on the edge of the bed, having just removed his boots, and looked at her in a manner she had seen before. She turned her back to him and began to remove her dress, only to feel him behind her. He wrapped his arms around her middle and kissed her neck. After accepting another kiss, she blew out the lamps in order to maintain some proper Quaker modesty in the dark.

22

ADRIFT

Pointe-Claire, Quebec, 1989

Joel had his arm around Myra, who willingly accepted the comfort that her son's friend offered. He was, after all, about the best, if not only friend Danny had ever had. The boys had been buddies since public school. They had giggled together over smuggled *Playboy* magazines and kept the forbidden fruit hidden between the box spring and mattress of Danny's bed. Mrs. Blum was always careful to put them back after changing the sheets and turning the mattress, not wishing to embarrass them. The two boys had managed to laugh their way through an awkward, pimpled adolescence by dreaming of being cool rock stars, and early on in grade nine, loud rock music had begun to blare up from the basement. It was an awful noise at first, but Myra was as tolerant of their musical exploration as she had been with the magazines.

Their passion for music had made them inseparable, and, finally, desirable in the eyes of an increasing number of girls after they played their first high school dance near the end of grade eleven. Their dreams had been answered—they loved playing music, and they loved girls … perfect! Over the years, Joel had all but become a member of the family, and in this horrid moment before her, he was the closest thing to family remaining in Myra Blum's life. His arm around her held real comfort, although she found his cheery disposition incongruous in the shadow of death. Something wasn't right, but she couldn't put her finger on it.

Danny's father, Leonard Blum, sporting bronzed skin from serious boat time in the Caribbean, had been waiting at the cemetery in a late-model Jaguar with a late-model, equally bronzed girlfriend. Joel's dad stood behind Mr. Blum, as though he didn't want to get too close to Danny's casket. The image of standing over his son's wooden box was one he had imagined with horror while Joel was unconscious in the ICU. He silently thanked God over and over for

Joel's miraculous recovery as he watched Myra Blum, who would from time to time shake uncontrollably. Hers was the pain he had feared and narrowly escaped.

Myra's eyes burned on Shaun Bishop and Mrs. Bishop, who stood on the other side of the grave. She still resented his visit with that little blond hottie and their ridiculous story. She wasn't sure if it was a drug-induced or a natural insanity. It didn't matter. Either way, she wasn't interested.

The rabbi began, and Myra stared at the coffin, looking up every so often when she heard Hebrew responses coming from Shaun Bishop. Unless he was a member of the lost tribe or related to Sammy Davis Jr., Hebrew coming from a black man was not a usual occurrence. Danny, of course, had gone to Hebrew school and knew the responses, having uttered them, and in the same tone, at his grandfather's recent funeral. Myra took particular interest in the startled look on the mother's face when her son started speaking Hebrew. Myra was certain the woman had never heard her son utter such strange words in her life. The only thing this young black kid had going for him in her mind was that Joel knew him and had embraced him. Maybe her son had somehow known the nut as well. Maybe it was an inability to cope with grief that had made the kid go nuts.

Myra's gaze moved to Karla Rose, Danny's fiancée, and her mother, who were weeping openly. Mr. Rose stood between them, offering what comfort he could. Danny looked at Karla and felt badly for having led her down a matrimonial path, out of which he probably would have bailed. She was better off without him he thought and given her stunning good looks would have no trouble finding someone to love her. He moved on to band members Brian and Ron, who looked down sadly at the coffin. Ron's girlfriend's expression was oblivious, as if she were just having a nice day in the park. In fact, she had a look that said every day was probably a nice day in the park. Ron held her hand the way he usually did the first day of a romance; by day two or three the hand-holding would end in order to begin the severance process before the entanglements of relationship had been given a chance to take root. Danny had never seen her before, so he could only conclude that she was recent.

There was a sad Hebrew song the rabbi led that got everyone's attention. Its dirge-like melancholy served only as a reminder of the inevitable sadness in life. The grief ringers from the synagogue drowned out the weeping of Myra and the Roses. Ron and Brian looked uncomfortable; the strange tune with even stranger lyrics created a hard feeling of exclusion in the burial of one of their peers.

When Myra's face crumpled in grief, it was like someone stabbing Danny in the chest. He looked around for Ali, who was a no-show. How could she not be there for his own damn funeral? Dumb thought … he threw it away. She must have had a good excuse; she was, after all, just a seventeen-year-old girl with protective parents. Joel was right, this was the freaking "Twilight Zone," or some invention of Poe or Stoker.

At the end of the singing, the rabbi went to Myra, who had expressed no interest in seeing any dirt thrown on her lovely boy or his shiny box. With Joel on one side and the rabbi on the other, she was led to one of the funeral home's cars, where she asked Joel if he would accompany her home. Joel of course agreed. Everyone else followed in their cars at a ceremonial speed, until the only vehicle left at the cemetery was the Jaguar. Leonard Blum remained at the grave, weeping as his young gold-digger attempted to console him. He appeared annoyed at the touch of her hand and he flipped it off with a flick of his fingers. Her words must have been even more annoying because Danny, watching through the window of Vera's Toyota, overheard him telling her to "Just shut up!" Danny felt no pity. He knew his father would soon shrug it all off and surrender again to the dictates of his selfish nature. It was a well-worn pattern that had become the man.

"I don't know what you're feeling right now, Daniel," Mrs. Bishop began. "If all is as you say, I surely would not like to have attended my own funeral and viewed that kind of pain on my mother's face."

"Worst I've known." Danny's head was down; he was locked into feelings of guilt and responsibility. It was his family's manuscript that had brought about the tide of events. Had others in the family felt the sting of Verhoevan's discovery? If so, what had they done? Verhoevan seemed like such a well-meaning man, and yet his genius and curiosity had conspired to find something so powerful that it could destroy lives. How could he ever convince Myra that her son was still alive, simply changed by an incredible journey? Bernard had obviously thought Daniel possessed the means to divert Myra from a dark path of self-destruction. He could think of only one way, and he wondered if this was the source of Bernard's confidence. It would be dangerous, and he would need Joel's help.

***

Back at the Blum house, Myra had uncovered two plates of smoked-meat sandwiches from the local deli and started the large silver coffee urn, unused since the days of entertaining her husband's business associates. The rabbi and the professional mourners mercilessly attacked the sandwiches, ensuring they had a good share before anyone else made it to the buffet. Joel had asked on the way home if the black woman, Mrs. Bishop, and her son Shaun might be allowed to join them, as they were his ride back to Toronto. Myra had explained that she thought Shaun was certifiable and that he and some young blonde had already been out to see her with an extremely disturbing story. But Joel had persisted, and Myra, not wishing to be obstinate, had agreed to go along with it all, for Joel's sake.

When Joel saw Mrs. Bishop's rusting Toyota pull into the driveway, he ran out to meet them. Myra watched as Joel approached the car. The tall black kid got out, and she could see he had been weeping. The thing that caught her off guard was how the expression on his face was oddly familiar. Joel embraced the fellow and the two slapped each other on the back, just the way Danny and Joel always had. When Myra glanced at Mrs. Bishop, she was shaken by the look of incredulity on the woman's face. She kept shaking her head repeatedly with each sentence that came out of the mouths of her son and Joel. Myra wondered how this young kid could have a relationship with Joel, or Danny, for that matter. Had one of them had a relationship with the mother? Was this young man who claimed to be Daniel Blum an illegitimate child? Was that the connection? She was looking for resemblances when Shaun looked up and stared into her eyes.

"Oh Myra, I know *you* understand how I feel!" Karla Rose said, and Myra Blum had to turn away to accept the tears and condolences of her son's fiancée and her parents.

***

Back outside in the driveway, the conversation continued. "So where did the manuscript end up?" Danny asked.

"I picked it up with the rest of my stuff from a storage room at the hotel when I got out of the hospital. Nobody seemed to think it had anything to do with what happened to you guys."

"Yeah, yeah, but where is it now?"

"Back at Brian's folks' basement in Toronto. I left it there when I went to my folks' place in Pittsburgh. There was just too much shit to take."

"So Joel," Danny said with some hesitation, "without listening and therefore making yourself susceptible, could you run the program with reverb and make a DAT copy?"

"No probs," Joel answered.

Mrs. Bishop looked at the two of them as if they were crazy. "You would get into this foolishness again after what you've put everyone through?" she asked.

"How else can I convince Myra? Did you see the way she looked at me? I know that look. I saw her look at my father that way after she found out he was screwing around. I am tried, convicted, and sentenced in her mind—persona non grata. There is nothing I can say to her in this physical form that will affect her judgment. How soon can you run that dub and return here, Joel?"

"Well, I would have to take the van back to Toronto, set the stuff up in Brian's basement, run the dub, and get back on the road. So …" Joel shrugged, "… a day and a bit?"

"Mrs. Bishop, can you afford another night at the Holiday Inn?" Danny felt bad even asking, knowing it would stretch the hard-working woman's resources.

"My card has a couple more nights in it, if need be, and I …" Mrs. Bishop stopped mid-sentence. Danny looked at her curiously in the long pause before she spoke again.

"I need to see this for myself." she said firmly. There, it was out in the open.

"Oh God." Danny rubbed his head with his hands. "Why does this thing have to keep spinning out of control?"

***

Myra turned when she heard a door slam and the engine of the Toyota start. She saw Shaun Bishop hug Joel, then get in the passenger side of the car and leave. They weren't coming in? Were they still driving back with Joel? Her curiosity was piqued.

When Joel came back in, Myra gave him a sandwich she had rescued from the platter just before one of the annoying women from the synagogue could spear it with her long, glossy, red talons. Joel looked as though he had something to tell her, but didn't say a thing.

***

At the Holiday Inn, Danny waited until Mrs. Bishop disappeared to take a bath and then he called the Glessing residence again. This time Ali answered the phone.

"Ali? Didn't you get my message?" Danny said, sounding somewhat annoyed.

"Please don't scold me like some little kid. Things are pretty confusing around here." Ali sounded distressed.

"I'm sorry, Ali, it's just I … oh, shit, sorry." Danny realized his frustration was misplaced. "So, what's happening with you? What's so confusing?"

"Well, this guy Brendon, for one. He's seriously in love with Jennifer and it's powerful. I'll be damned if I don't … feel attracted … actually, more than attracted to him?" Her statement curled up into a question. She was confused all right. "But Danny, its okay, I know I love you," she said, recovering.

"Did you make love?" Danny asked, not really wanting to hear the answer. There was silence on the other end of the phone. "Never mind. I don't think I want … or need to know. Look, it just dawned on my selfish self you've already been through this even though we weren't physically there."

"Oh Daniel I …" Alison choked up.

"Are you alright?" Danny waited patiently for her reply.

"It's my mother … I called her. I told her I was a student of Alison's from the university and wanted to offer my condolences. She was so cold hearted. There was no remorse in her. Not one teardrop shed over the death of her daughter. I asked how she was coping with the loss, and do you know what she said to me? She said, not to worry about her, she's just fine. She said that life has a way of working out, and that Alison is probably better off now than as an aging spinster whose students probably ridiculed her for having such laughable taste in clothes. I think my death saved my mother embarrassment, that selfish bitch! My dying saved her from any more embarrassment because of me! Jesus, am I so …" Ali choked again.

She'd thought she was done caring whether her mother loved her or not, but to think that her death was viewed by her mother as a good thing pushed buttons that she hadn't even known existed.

Danny sat silent on the end of the phone, powerless as Ali wept. How did anyone deal with that? His pain was for a mother who loved him … the way things should be. There was security in his mother's pain, because it was proof that he was loved. It was the ultimate physical manifestation of love. Ali's pain was an aberration in the way of things. Without a mother's love, the baseline, the first building block of security, how could one muster up anything resembling self-esteem? Ali was an emotional house of cards that had just been blown over. She had come back to help a woman she had successfully removed from her thoughts for years as a way of coping. Now the woman, and everything she represented, was back in her face, full force.

"Ali, you knew coming back for this wasn't going to be easy, you —"

"I have to go. I'm going shopping with my mom, uh, Mrs. Glessing, and Brendon is coming over for dinner. I'll call you later." Ali hung up. She wanted to escape into her new life. The pain of her old one ate at her insides like acid. Unfortunately for Danny, he was a part of that life.

Danny stared at the receiver dumbfounded. Mrs. Bishop had reappeared a minute or two earlier, cocooned in a Holiday Inn bathrobe, and her eyebrows were raised as she looked at him. She just walked over and put her arm around him with a concerned expression. Danny reached for her and pulled the good soul close and didn't let go for some time as he blurted out everything Ali had said.

"My Lord." Mrs. Bishop drew in a deep breath and let it out slowly in a long, deep sigh. "That poor girl is trying to find love where she can at the moment. She feels Mrs. Glessing's love and she's drawn to it."

Danny looked at Mrs. Bishop. She was kind, she was wise, and it seemed as though nothing could faze her. She looked at him as though she had something even more profound to say, then grabbed her purse.

"Let's eat. I'm starving, and if you know what's good for, you'll drag your hungry, mixed-up self along." Danny fell in behind her as she headed out the door.

The restaurant was decked out in wallpaper depicting picket fences and green gardens filled with colourful vegetables and wildflowers. Below that, dark-green wainscotting dropped to the floor to give it that homey, country feel. Homely was more like it, but each to his own. There wasn't much a chef could do to ruin a grilled cheese sandwich, coleslaw, and fries, but this one had managed to pull it off. The bread didn't taste like bread. How did they do that? And the cheese, well, it left an aftertaste reminiscent of licking a basketball, but he was so hungry he ate the second one anyway. Mrs. Bishop was finishing her droopy fries smothered in ketchup when she looked at Shaun and deliberated on a question.

"If you feel something for me, do you also still feel something for Jordan?" Her look was earnest and required a reply in kind. Danny nodded a reluctant affirmative. "Then you know the territory Alison is in," Mrs. Bishop said sympathetically, finishing the thought.

Danny spent the rest of the day in and out of the swimming pool, trying to stretch muscles that had begun to lose tone. His new body, he sensed, was quite powerful. The cells in his muscles screamed for exertion like a well-tuned thoroughbred ready to explode out of starting gate. After dinner he worked out some more then went for a very tentative walk for the first time since the bus accident. His cracked ribs complained, as did some internal bruising, but it seemed his stamina was endless. Even ten minutes of the pace he was keeping and Danny Blum would have been on the side of the road wheezing his guts out.

Joel returned the following evening in the van. Ron had complained about losing the wheels, but the lease was in Danny's and Joel's names so he had no choice. Joel had set his gear up in Brian's basement. A five-inch floppy disc still contained the program he had stored, unbeknownst to Danny. Whenever he programmed he always hit "save." He had lost far too much work since learning to program music into a sequencer not to have acquired the "save" reflex. He didn't bother hooking up any speakers. He had no interest in tripping the light fandango across the abyss to the other side again; in fact, he now feared it. All presets were automatically sent via midi to his synthesizer rack and his

Lexicon PCM 70 reverberation unit. He loaded a fresh DAT tape into his Casio portable digital audio tape recorder, hit "record," then hit "play" on his sequencer. He watched the screen on the computer run the chord. The VU meters on his eight-channel mixer danced as the chord went through its harmonic chain reaction, and a few minutes later the signal died out and the VU needles fell flat. Joel waited a minute for good measure, then he packed his gear back into the road cases. He left with the Casio DAT recorder, the manuscript, a road case that held a few pairs of headphones and a headphone splitter box, and another hard-shell case that held his small mixer, in case he needed more power to boost the signal from his DAT machine.

When he arrived at the Holiday Inn on the outskirts of Montreal, Danny was in the foyer waiting, pacing the floor with muscles that needed to move. They went to the room, where Mrs. Bishop, who had been watching a *Star Trek* rerun to kill time, shut the TV off immediately.

"*The Trouble with Tribbles* … bad comedy, bad science fiction, worst episode ever," she said as she joined Shaun and Joel to sit in on the plan that was being laid out.

***

Myra heard the Toyota pull into her driveway and looked up from her kitchen table, where she had sat crying for the best part of the day. She watched with some curiosity as Joel and the Bishops got out and headed to the house. Joel let himself in, as he had done for years, and gave Myra a well-received hug and kiss.

"What are *they* doing here?" Myra asked curtly.

"We need to have a chat, Myra. Can they come in?"

"Is this the fruitcake thing about my Daniel being in that young man's body again?' Myra shot back, clearly nervous about being subjected to a repeat performance.

"Not totally … but in part. We only need fifteen minutes. May they come in?" Joel stayed on script.

Myra sat back down. She didn't want to hear Shaun Bishop's tale again, but she was interested as to where Joel fit in and what his relationship was to Mrs. Bishop and her son.

"Let's get this over with," she said, like a wounded soldier about to have a leg removed.

Joel went to the door and signalled to the Bishops, who got out of the car. Joel and Danny took out the road cases from the trunk and headed into the house. The cases were left in the front hall as they all gathered in the kitchen, where Myra sat staring at nothing. The images of her son's dead face at the morgue, and the shocking deterioration of his flesh at the funeral home before they'd closed the coffin, ate at her soul. Those gruesome pictures replayed over and over in a slide show from hell, irrefutable evidence that her life was over and now meaningless in the loss of her greatest creation. Her future was to live her worst nightmare — a world without her son.

"Myra, this is Mrs. Bishop," Joel said.

Mrs. Bishop held her hand out. "Please call me Vera, Mrs. Blum." Her tone was sweet and unthreatening. Myra mustered a half-baked smile in an attempt to be civil.

They all sat down at the table and Myra stared at them, moving from face to face as they looked back at her. The silence was deafening, but Myra felt no need to speak, no discomfort, she didn't give a damn. *There is nothing you can say to me that can rock this boat. The boat has bloody well sunk to the bottom of a black sea. You can't even dredge it up because the timbers are rotting with my boy. The hell with all of you and your sympathetic faces.*

"Myra, this is where it all started. This is the work of a Franciscan monk by the name of Peter Verhoevan." And with that, Danny placed her father's leather-bound manuscript on the table.

23

SAVANNAH

Savannah, Georgia
June, 1848

Two weeks had passed since the return of the *Southern Belle*. It was a beautiful Sunday morning, and Matthias insisted that Anna come with him for a walk. There was something unusual about his insistence, and Anna began to worry.

She wondered if it had anything to do with the fact that the leased Dutch vessel, the *Branden*, had not yet arrived. Both Harding and her husband stood to lose money if the square-rigger had indeed gone down in rough seas.

They walked towards the gardens in the middle of town, then down a side street, until Matthias stopped at the gate of an empty white, Dutch Georgian house. It had two storeys, with squared pillars, and gardens in need of attention. There was a cracked fountain on the pathway to the front doors, and down one side shallow wagon ruts led to a coach house of the same architectural design.

"What is it, Matthias? Why did you bring me here?" Anna held his hand tightly.

"I wanted to show you our new home." Matthias looked into her eyes as they widened and turned to look at the house. She began to weep, and dropped her head to her husband's chest.

"What is it, my love?" Matthias asked. "I brought you here to see joy on your face, maybe even a little excitement, and you're sad?" Matthias was completely baffled.

Anna gathered herself and spoke haltingly. "It feels like only days ago I was dropped at Frau Hoffmann's door to pay my parents' debts, and now my husband shows me a palace I am to live in, while my parents, brother, and sister still suffer, God knows where … if they still live. Matthias, to have so much when others have so little

… it doesn't seem … Christian. It doesn't feel right." Anna looked at her husband and saw his eyes fill.

"I feel ashamed of myself in the presence of your heart, Anna. The search goes on. We will find them and bring them here. It is, as you have said, the right, the loving thing to do. But I …"

"What is it?" Anna looked concerned.

"I have something to tell you, the one person in my life from whom I should hide no secrets. I can no longer profess certain things that I was sure of in my life."

"Oh Mary Mother of God. You no longer love me." Anna took a deep breath and her eyes opened wide.

"Of course I love you, that is the one thing of which I am sure … maybe the only thing of which I am sure."

"You have changed, Matthias. Since you returned, there is something different about you. It's as though you carry some horrible secret. What has happened to you, my love?"

Matthias took Anna by the hand to the front step of the house, where they both sat down.

"What I am about to tell you will sound like the musings of a madman, but I assure you, it is all true." Matthias told her of the events in Hamburg …of crossing over and seeing his mother. He told her about the powerful Som and how Vasquez had saved his life. He told her of meeting Harding's brother and father and how he had stood over his own body before re-entering it. He shared every last detail with the woman he loved and felt such relief in the doing of it.

Anna sat, stunned. It was too much information to grasp. She felt as though her faith was being unravelled, and with it a piece of her sanity.

When Matthias finished the tale, he looked at Anna, who trembled as tears streamed down her face. In that moment, he realized that his fantastic story should probably have been kept to himself. It simply was not for this world.

"The world has gone mad." She wept. "I want to live as a Christian, but I cannot speak to Mrs. Harding of my religious beliefs. The Quaker's don't have a favourabe opinion about Catholics, so I have to be careful what I say. Do I now have to be careful what I say to you, my husband? Many Protestants here, while claiming to be good, righteous people, are hideously cruel to their slaves, and even use the Bible to justify their actions. They say

God condoned slavery in the book of Ephesians Chapter 6 verse 5 where he instructs " servants be obedient to them that are your masters according to the flesh." They interpret the scripture to suit their selfish needs ... as though God would condone man's cruelty to his own kind. And now my Catholic husband informs me that he is no longer a Catholic, and that the Holy Mother and Jesus may have never existed, and I am denied even the idea of Heaven as it is promised."

"Promised by whom, Anna? By mortal men who have never been there, and on terms invented by their kind." Matthias reined himself in and took a deep breath. "Anna, my love, at some point we all come to our own common sense. I simply ask you to look for it in all that you've been taught. One thing remains an undeniable truth: love itself is all we need to live by. In this thought you are not at odds with your faith, for was this not the message of the New Testament?"

"I need some time with all of this. Matthias, does this have something to do with what that rabbi said? Is it because now you know for certain that your mother was Jewish? Do you wish to follow their traditions, according to the book they worship on their altars?"

"No my love, I am beginning to learn that my faith is internal. I will answer to the traces of God that I feel within, not the dictates of an institution drunk with its own power. Worshiping a book on an altar makes no sense at all to me, whether it's a Bible or a Torah. Actually, I am not so sure the vanity of requiring worship would be worthy of an almighty God. I know it is your heart that motivates you, Anna, not fear of damnation or excommunication. You already embody that of which I speak. I came to feel such things through extraordinary means, and here you sit, living what I seek to be. Do you believe any of what I have told you?"

"Why would you lie to me, Matthias? But I have believed something for a long time, and now I am told it is all a fairy tale. So now am I a fool?"

"No, Anna. You are being given new information. A fool might be one who believes he knows all there is to know. The core of your belief is the same, the lessons of the fairy tale are valid. They were the reason for the fairy tale."

"Do you mind if I remain faithful to the Church?" Anna asked, as though hanging on to a lifeline.

"Oh course not, my love, and … do you mind if I don't?"

Anna looked at her husband and shook her head with a look of confusion.

"Please, no more of this right now. Let's just … oh, let's just look at this God forsaken house."

Anna got up and Matthias followed, pulling a key from his coat pocket.

The great hall had a stunning chandelier where light from an unshuttered window stopped to play, but no one looked up. There was no celebration, no joy as the two went through the building, not really looking at anything. Anna thought only of her upside-down world and entertained dark thoughts of her family, who for all she knew might have perished in abject poverty across the Atlantic. Matthias was feeling selfish—he had done the wrong thing in confiding in Anna, even though her mind was evidently opening to manifestations of religious hypocrisy that went against her own sense of right and wrong.

***

Over an unusually quiet dinner with the Hardings, Matthias broke the strained silence with the announcement of a financial transaction to acquire the house they had seen earlier in the day. They would be moving into their new home once it was repaired and painted and ready to impress.

The Captain and his wife had known this would have to come sooner or later and so appeared happy and enthusiastic that the young couple would be starting their new lives. Elizabeth was somewhat miffed, however, that such worldly things were being discussed on the Sabbath, and she conspicuously bit her lip as Matthias and Captain Harding retired to the parlour, as they always did, for even more business discussion.

Matthias stood at the window and watched through the curtain as Anna and Mrs. Harding headed down the path for a brisk evening walk. They had scurried off like that every evening like clockwork since he had returned, and Matthias was wondering what they got up to with such regularity. It seemed that no matter what was going on the two women had to take that evening walk, and the men were not welcome. He confronted the Captain about the peculiar sense of responsibility this walk appeared to embrace. The Captain sloughed off Matthias's suspicions but agreed that the next night they might follow their wives at a discreet distance, if only to ensure their safety.

***

The two women left the house at their usual time the next night and walked at a fast pace, saying nothing to one another. They stopped at a house about a block away, where another woman looked around and ushered them in. Moments later they emerged carrying two canvas bags that appeared to be quite heavy. Harding and Matthias waited behind a large magnolia tree and took up the hunt when the women disappeared around a corner and down a side street. They hurried along, but by the time they got to the street there was no sign of them.

"This is all rather strange," Harding said. "It would seem your suspicions were warranted, Matthias."

"What do you think was in those bags?"

"I've no idea, but I know the home where they stopped to get them. That woman at the door is the Pastor's wife. I've a mind to go to that home and speak to Pastor McLean to see what these women are up to," Harding huffed with a serious tone.

Matthias held the Captain's arm. "Let's watch and see what house they come out of, first. Then we'll have two pieces of the puzzle."

The two men waited at the end of the street, where an alleyway provided a servants' entrance for a large home. A good thirty-five minutes later, Elizabeth Harding and Anna Dopp emerged from a house halfway down the street. The two men ducked into the alley, only to reappear behind them as they headed home. Once again they stopped at the first house and dropped off the canvas bags, and then they continued to the Harding household.

Once the women were out of sight, Harding knocked on the Pastor's door and Mrs. McLean answered. When she saw Harding and Matthias, she looked concerned.

"What can I do for you, gentlemen?" she asked politely.

"I would speak with the Pastor, if I may, Mrs. McLean," Harding said firmly.

"I'm afraid that he's ..." she began, only to be cut off by a man's voice from inside.

"No need to make excuses that could become wee lies, Ellen. Show them in."

Ellen McLean opened the door, and as soon as the two men were inside she poked her head back out to see if anyone was watching, then closed the door quickly behind her. She showed Harding and Matthias into the Pastor's study, where Alexander McLean, a man who appeared older than his years, looked up through bushy salt-and-pepper eyebrows from his desk, where he was preparing a sermon for Sunday morning.

"What brings you two souls out for a visit this evening?" McLean stared at the men through wire-rimmed glasses that hung off the end of his nose.

"It would seem we might be owed the courtesy of an explanation as to the errands our wives are doing that involve both of our households," Matthias responded instantly.

"Hmmm. I'm afraid you have me at a disadvantage, for I am sworn to secrecy. I can only tell you that it is an errand of mercy, and indeed in the spirit of Christ our Lord and that wonderful instruction, 'Do unto others as you would have them do unto you.'" The Pastor smiled, unaffected by the stern looks on the faces of his visitors.

"So you would not tell us, then?" Harding tried to reopen a conversation that had just been ended politely.

"I think the answer to your questions should come from the mouths of your wives, and perhaps you might owe them an explanation as to why you were following them. Are they not honest, faithful women?" The Pastor was quite deft at doling out guilt as a way of steering discussion. Harding knew they would get nowhere and was about to thank him and leave, but Matthias was more than a little miffed at the man's evasiveness.

"How dare you suggest that our wives are anything but faithful as a way of avoiding a simple question for which you obviously have an answer. Are all men of your faith so conniving?" Everyone stared in silence at Matthias, who had dared to say such a thing to the Pastor. The Pastor looked at him quite seriously.

"Just the smart ones, young man, just the smart ones. Now, I suggest that you ask your questions of your loved ones. I have a sermon to finish. Good night to you, gentlemen. Please show these two sleuths out, Ellen." The Pastor returned to his work, and moments later Harding and Matthias were out on the street.

"I think that went very well, don't you?" Harding started to chuckle.

"How can you laugh at a time like this?" Matthias snapped angrily.

"Get that wind out of your sails, Matthias. The Pastor is a good man. My wife Elizabeth is as good a woman as exists, and I have never seen any wife more smitten with her husband than your Anna. There should be no room for anger in our hearts, only a light and loving curiosity. Let's go and apologize for following them and inquire as to what duties they attend to on their walks." With that, Harding started towards his house. He stopped to turn and look at Matthias, who had not moved. "Well?"

Matthias started walking and did as he was told, heeding Harding's words and doing his best to "get the wind" out of his sails. When they walked through the door of the Harding house, the women, having just returned, stood facing them with curious expressions.

"Where have you two been?" Elizabeth Harding asked.

"We followed you on your walk and stopped in on the Pastor on the way home. What he had to say was quite interesting." Captain Harding played his hand well—no lies, but the illusion of knowing more than they did was a way of flushing out confessions, like grouse from a bush.

Mrs. Harding blushed, and Anna sat down on the one chair in the hallway with the look of a condemned criminal.

"So, how long have you two been up to this?" Harding continued.

Elizabeth Harding looked at her husband, and her demeanour changed from fear to resolve.

"I'll make some tea and we will talk of this properly in the parlour."

Ten minutes later, tea and biscuits were laid out. The Captain maintained a stern face in order to play his hand through, and after pouring tea for everyone, Elizabeth Harding began.

"It started out quite innocently the day the two of you left for Hamburg. Workers from the Smitherim plantation were down at the wharf picking up supplies when one fell, breaking some china he was carrying. Jacob Smitherim laid into that poor black man and whipped him over and over until he bled. It was Anna who stopped him. She walked right up to Smitherim, yanked the whip out of his hand, and struck him across the face with it."

Matthias was about to speak but Captain Harding gripped his knee to silence him, not wanting anything to pull the confession off its course.

"So how did this event lead you to doing what you've been doing with your evenings?"

"The black man who was beaten was given no care, his wounds were never cleaned, and we learned that he died some two weeks later, leaving a wife and two children. The poor man's widow was a strong woman who, as it turned out, had caught the eye of Mr. Smitherim. He apparently had his way with her against her will and she became pregnant. We found out that he has had his way with many of his female slaves, and when they become pregnant they would conveniently disappear, never to be seen again. It is believed that Smitherim has killed them all rather than allowing his bastard children to be born with claim to his property or embarrassment to his person. This young black woman feared for her life, so a good soul from our church took her in and hid her from Smitherim. The woman from the church knew that Anna had stood up to Smitherim and came to speak with us to see if we could help. This is where we heard the whole story."

"So you are hiding this black woman so that she might give birth," the Captain deduced, prematurely.

"Oh no, she lost the baby. She left Savannah weeks ago with another man and her two children. Through a series of safe houses, they are most surely across the border to Montreal by now."

"Safe houses? Montreal?" Matthias asked.

Anna looked at him and stopped Elizabeth Harding from continuing. "Elizabeth, they don't know anything. Pastor McLean has told them nothing."

"Oh dear!" Elizabeth Harding gasped.

"You are very perceptive, Anna," the Captain observed. "But I'm afraid the damage is done. So, you two are involved in helping slaves escape their bondage and move north. Did you know many of them are captured, returned, and severely punished for attempting to flee? Some are even hanged as an example to others who might be entertaining the possibility."

"Would you risk the chance of escaping from slavery, or stay and be victim to the whims of a man who would beat you for enjoyment then pleasure himself with your wife?" Anna spat her words out with angry disgust. Matthias was taken aback by how passionately she spoke, but he also liked an element of what he had heard.

"So you hit this Smitherim with his own whip?" Matthias asked in disbelief.

"The man is inhuman!" Anna snapped.

Matthias held back a grin of approval, while Harding looked back and forth between the two women, seeing they were obviously comrades in arms.

"He is a powerful man, Elizabeth. You and Anna should be more cautious. So, what is it you two get up to in the evenings?"

"We take food that members of our congregation donate. They leave it with the Pastor and we take it on to a safe house, cook for the blacks, and pack provisions for the first part of their journey," Elizabeth said. She looked to her husband for some sign of approval, but he just shook his head.

"You're helping remove labour that has been bought and paid for from an industry that counts on it for its survival. You must realize there is a down side to the good you think you're doing."

"You would side with the slave owners? Don't tell me, Captain Harding, that you are in favour of slavery!" Anna's anger again overwhelmed her.

Captain Harding thought for a moment, and the silence aroused Matthias curiosity as he, too, now waited for Harding's answer.

"No to both questions, my dear Anna. But in order to prepare a proper defence against the opposition you must try to understand their view. To understand it is not to agree with it. Now, I worry for you and Elizabeth. If you have been engaged in this clandestine activity for some months, I must think the people you are up against might be trying to put a stop to your work. Just recently a man received quite a beating and nearly died for his part in helping a negro slave flee to the north through Maine. There are forces in Congress seeking to pass a bill that would make it legal for bounty hunters to seek out runaway slaves and return them to their owners. There will be laws soon, if that legislation passes, to make it illegal to help slaves flee their owners. How many slaves have you helped escape Savannah?"

"Twenty or so," Elizabeth admitted quietly. "Oh John, have we placed anyone in harm's way?"

Captain Harding was moved by the fact that his wife was more concerned about others than herself.

"I'm afraid you have, my love, even though your motivations are honourable. I will need to do some poking around, put some feelers out to see what is being said about the incident with Anna and Jacob Smitherim down at the docks. If you have shown yourselves to be sympathetic to the slaves' plight, you might be a person of interest to those seeking answers to the whereabouts of missing servants."

Matthias saw fear on Harding's face for the first time. The fear was not for himself but for his precious Elizabeth. Tears crossed Elizabeth's face and she ran upstairs, not wishing to be seen in such an emotional state. The good Captain bade Matthias and Anna good night and went upstairs to comfort her.

"I have brought this on us all." Anna was devastated. "If only I had not pulled the whip from Smitherim's hand."

"Everything we do has a consequence that directs our lives. That's just the way of things. If it hadn't been for Frau Hoffmann, we might never have met," Matthias said, off the cuff.

"You will never speak of Frau Hoffmann again!" And with that, Anna stormed upstairs.

Matthias had known it was the wrong thing to say as soon as the words had left his lips. The old world and what Anna had been forced to do in it was a shame that she felt in her spine. Matthias followed her and apologized.

When Anna had drifted off to sleep, exhausted by her anguished tears, he slipped her head from the cradle of his arms and crept out of the room. It was still just evening, and time to do something that had been needling away at him for months.

A good fifteen minutes later, Matthias approached a synagogue and went right to a couple of gentlemen standing outside, laughing at the punch-line of a joke that had been told in German. One took a defensive posture at the quick approach of a stranger.

"Excuse me, gentlemen, would you know if the rabbi is in? I would like to speak with him," Matthias asked politely. The defensive one of the two was silent and looked suspiciously at Matthias while the other one spoke.

"He instructs our sons in Hebrew at the moment and won't be done for another half hour. You are welcome to wait with us, Mr. . . . ?"

"Please pardon my rudeness. I am Matthias Dopp of Hamburg, and I couldn't help but notice you were speaking German."

"Well, that would be because we are from Hamburg as well, Herr Dopp. Are you by chance the son of Gert Dopp?"

"I am."

"Have you come looking for Esther, your aunt?" the suspicious one asked. Matthias was beginning to think he was the only one in Savannah who didn't know his lineage.

"Actually I have come to offer an apology to your rabbi, but as a matter of fact, I am also looking for my aunt. How is it you know of her?"

"She is my mother," the man offered carefully.

"Then you are my . . . cousin?" Matthias asked, incredulous.

"Well, the last time I heard of sisters having children they were called cousins. I don't think the rules have changed, Herr Dopp," the man said with a smirk.

"I'm sorry, I must appear a fool to you," Matthias began. "I was only recently told I indeed have an aunt, and now I discover I also have a cousin. This is more than a little overwhelming."

"I was sorry to hear of your father's death, Herr Dopp," the man said rather coldly.

"You have me at a disadvantage, sir. Might I know my cousin's name?"

"I am Frederich Heinyl, son of Esther and Schmul Heinyl."

"Well, I am pleased to meet you, Frederich," Matthias said in a genuine tone.

"I would prefer you call me Mr. Heinyl, Mr. Dopp. Your father was cruel to my mother. He took much of our family's fortune through your mother's blind trust and love, then he had her disown the lot of us because our Jewishness was an affront to him. I am afraid I don't wish to have anything to do with you."

"I see, Herr Heinyl. So, the son is to be damned for the sins of the father? Sound thinking. Would it be my lack of Jewishness that offends you, sir, or just my lack of any knowledge of my Jewishness until recently?"

"You would mock me, sir?" Heinyl said with anger.

"I suppose it sounds that way … I don't think I was mocking you any more than myself. When I was told my mother was Jewish I was initially offended, and yet, as I have thought about it for some time, I have realized the feelings of offence were not mine but my father's. I can honestly say now that I am no more offended by Jew than Catholic or Protestant, or however one grapples with the ideas of God or tribe. If you choose to have nothing to do with me, that is indeed your prerogative. I am sorry for the ignorance and apparently the less than ethical dealings of my father. I will look into somehow righting those wrongs and …" Matthias stopped in fatigue. "Actually, I think I do owe you more honesty, so in answer to your question … I'm afraid I do mock your logic and blind transfer of intolerance and what has the appearance of hatred. I am attempting to correct such behaviour in myself and so should not readily condone it in others. My apologies for my father's sins still stand, but whether or not you choose to speak to me might depend on your own understanding of justice."

Heinyl came at Matthias, fists flying, but Matthias moved to one side and managed to trip him and pin him to the ground. His friend, who moments before had been so kind and friendly, jumped on Matthias and began to pummel him from behind. It was at that moment that two toughs appeared out of nowhere and pulled the man off Matthias and began kicking both Heinyl and his friend. When Matthias came to his senses and realized the two Jews were getting the hell kicked out of them, he sprang to his feet and slugged one of the toughs, who looked at him and sneered.

"What the hell are you doing? We're takin' care of your problems for ya. They're just a couple of stinkin' Jews!"

"Really?" Matthias slugged him and swung at the other tough until Heinyl was on his feet. Now with three against two the toughs backed off. One looked at Matthias, confused.

"Yer crazy, mister! Two Jews are kickin' the shit outta ya and you come to their rescue? Yer just plain crazy!"

"Actually, I'm only half crazy, and the other half, I believe, is Jewish," Matthias replied.

The toughs moved off. Heinyl and his friend brushed the dirt from their clothes, and Matthias offered a handkerchief to his cousin, who was sporting a bloody nose. Heinyl took it grudgingly, and as he wiped the blood from his face he glared at Matthias.

"You're not ashamed of your mother's blood?" he asked.

"I don't think I could ever be ashamed of anything to do with her. She brought me into this world and she loved me dearly," Matthias answered.

"Well … then … call me Fred," Heinyl muttered with a slow smile.

"Fred, if we might start over, I am Matthias, your cousin, and it is indeed a pleasure to meet family I never knew existed." Matthias put his hand out and Fred shook it firmly.

"Nice to meet you, Cousin Matthias. So, what brings you to see the rabbi?"

"I owe him an apology, and I also thought he might know where my aunt lives."

"Well, it just so happens I do, funnily enough." Fred turned to his friend. "Ben, would you take my boy home for me? I think we have a family reunion coming up."

"Of course. I'm sure you two have much to discuss."

"Shall we, Cousin?" Fred said, smiling at Matthias.

"Absolutely, Cousin." The two newfound relatives headed off.

"Did you know my mother?" Matthias inquired, wishing to speak of her.

"I saw her a few times when she stole away to visit us. By that time she was already forbidden to let you know we existed, or indeed of her being a Jew. Your father had said it was for business reasons and threatened her with something she feared. We never did find out what it was. She and my mother were the best of friends and managed to maintain contact like a couple of spies. She was always nice to me and brought me sweets."

"Oh, she loved her sweets," Matthias remembered fondly. He was just about to ask another question when Fred turned up a pathway

"We're here," he said over his shoulder.

Matthias was suddenly nervous. What would his aunt look like? Would she resent him, as Fred had done?

When the door opened, a middle-aged woman with long blond hair down to her shoulders stood with a stunned look on her face. She was a fit-looking woman with a gentle face that slowly dissolved into tears.

"Matthias, Matthias, oh my God … Miriam's Matthias." She repeated this until her husband came up behind her, just in time for her to faint. Matthias and Fred ran to help carry her into the parlour.

"Is it true? Are you Miriam's boy?" Schmul Heinyl puffed from the exertion of carrying his wife.

"Apparently so, Mr. Heinyl, although until your rabbi informed me I knew her only as Maria," Matthias replied, while helping him lay his wife down on the settee. Mr. Heinyl ran for a cold cloth and returned to place it on his wife's forehead. She came around and stared at Matthias.

"Oh Matthias, let me look at you. You are so like our father. I sat in the back of the church for your mother's funeral." She began to cry. "I had to wear a veil so your father wouldn't recognize me. Oh Matthias, it's you!" She stood up and hugged him until her husband and son started looking uncomfortable. She even smelled like his mother, Matthias thought, immediately taken with his aunt. In her embrace, he felt as though he were holding a piece of himself.

"We heard you had dealings with Captain Harding, with whom we have also done business in the past. We further heard that you have moved here with your wife?" Schmul Heinyl, asked as though seeking confirmation of the gossip.

"That is correct, sir. We currently live under the kind hospitality of the Hardings. They have become family to me in the loss of my own."

"You *have* family," Esther Heinyl corrected him. "You have always had family that your father refused to allow into your life, may God forgive him. And now that that horrible man has moved on to the next world, perhaps things may be as they should."

"Esther!" Schmul huffed at his wife's insensitivity.

Matthias looked at her and sensed the pain his father must have inflicted.

"Aunt Esther, my father was always fair to me. I don't know what to say to any of you about the man you knew. All I know is that at this moment I am thrilled you all exist. I would love you to meet my wife."

"You must come for dinner on the Sabbath. We can offer prayers of thanks to God. Will you come to temple with us, that we might introduce you to your people?"

Matthias felt a bit odd at the reference to Jews at temple as "your people." He realized he had years of training to undo and looked to the love and esteem he held for his mother in order to find the necessary resolve. "I'm sure that would be fine, and I would like an opportunity to apologize to your rabbi. I was rude to him some months ago when he informed me that my mother was a Jew," Matthias confessed.

"You are ashamed of your Jewish blood?" Mr. Heinyl sounded offended.

"Maybe more ashamed that I knew nothing of my own heritage, and ready to do battle for who I thought I was, as convoluted as that may sound."

Matthias seemed pensive for a moment, and Esther asked him to sit while she brought out some tea. Matthias had many questions about the family he never knew. He heard about the clandestine meetings between Miriam and her younger sister, Esther. There had been humorous disguises, and the sisters had actually managed to make a game of it for a time … until Gert Dopp had had his wife followed and put a stop to all contact with her family. There was much emotional pain in Esther's loss of her sister, to say nothing of the cruelty and financial drubbing that Gert Dopp had inflicted on his wife's family.

It was quite late when Matthias bade them all a good night, and as he walked home there was some sadness in his step. His mother's death felt even more tragic to him, given the pain of what her life must have been like. Gert Dopp was turning out to have been quite a complex and conflicted man — revered in the business world, fair to those who worked for him, and cruel to the woman who loved him. His financial good fortune had come from Miriam's family, and once he had used their connections and Miriam's money, he had distanced himself from all of them.

As Matthias thought back, this new information began to make sense. He loved his father, but he had always felt inadequate in his presence. He had never been able to please the man, no matter how hard he tried.

When he'd used Verhoevan's Resonance to try to find him, his father had not come. It had seemed such a cold rejection at first, but the more he thought of it, the more he realized this was in the nature of their relationship.

It became clear to Matthias that an expectation of love was all he had ever had with his father, for there had never been any real demonstration of it. With his father's death had come the death of that unanswered expectation, and that was what he grieved for.

Somehow the weight of that expectation had been lifted from his shoulders now. There was a brief measure of freedom in letting go, but a sadness soon filled the vacuum. The sadness was for a man who couldn't even love his only son. What kind of troubled soul was that?

In the distance Matthias saw the lights of the Harding household and was warmed by the thought that people who cared for him were waiting up for his return. When he came through the door, the Captain and Mrs. Harding stood in the hallway, obviously agitated with worry.

"Where have you been?" The Captain's tone was stern.

"I have met relatives I didn't know I had until today. Why do you ask … what is wrong?"

"Anna went out to look for you. I told her to wait for me, that I was going to get my coat and go with her. She was waiting on the front walk, and when I came back she was gone. It was no more than thirty seconds and she was gone! I looked up and down the street and there was no sign of her, only a carriage that was moving away — a little too quickly, in my estimation. I have done trips in every direction looking for her and have just now returned."

"What about the carriage? Did you know it?"

"It's a very common make. There must be dozens of them in this town."

"Do you think it was some disgruntled slave owner?" Matthias worried.

Harding was about to answer when a carriage pulled up outside. Matthias looked out the parlour window to the street and saw Harding's first mate, Ferguson, step into the road with another member of the crew, while a third waited with the carriage.

Ferguson strode up the walk to the front door with the crewman and met Harding.

He handed Harding a pistol, which the Captain quickly placed into his coat pocket, but not quickly enough to escape the wide eyes of Elizabeth, who gasped at the sight of the gun.

Harding looked at her and smiled sweetly. "Don't worry, my love. It's just a precaution. We'll be leaving Atkins here with you while we are out, should there be any unwanted visitors. Atkins, are you armed?"

Atkins was a short, wiry man who grinned back at his Captain and lifted his jacket, revealing two huge knives. "Aye, sir. Don't worry. I will set myself up to be well prepared with a few utensils from your kitchen as well, sir, if you don't mind. Guns can be a bit noisy at night."

Harding patted his man on the shoulder then turned to Matthias. "The plantation owners are a good place to start, and one in particular — Jacob Smitherim. If it is he who has spirited Anna away, we'd best move quickly, the man is mad!"

24

BEHIND THE CURTAIN

Pointe-Claire, Quebec, 1989

Myra sat staring at the leather-bound manuscript, the one that had been found in her father's suitcase and now sat on her kitchen table.

"I have already heard your fairy tale about this magical manuscript and I don't buy it." Myra's tone was terse as she faced Shaun Bishop.

Joel jumped in. "Myra, this is no fairy tale. I wasn't in a coma when you called my parents at the hospital, I wasn't in my freakin' body."

"Oh, not you too, Joel! Is everyone crazy here except for me?"

Mrs. Bishop looked at her, then just reached out and grabbed her hand. "My son may no longer be here, Mrs. Blum. If it's all as they say, his body lives but he has left it, and there is a stranger in it. There is behaviour I can't make sense of. Out of the blue, he now knows how to speak Hebrew, of all things. What if it really is your boy, Daniel, who is in my son's body?"

"That's it. You're all nuts. If you won't leave, then I will!" Myra stood up and was about to storm out when Danny stood and blocked her way.

"Please, Myra. Give us ten minutes more. I promise that if you don't see Danny the way you remember him within the next ten minutes, we will all leave."

"What do you mean, see Danny?" Myra started to shake. Mrs. Bishop attempted to comfort her but she pulled away.

Danny gave Joel the nod and he brought in the cases and set up his DAT player. Then he unloaded his mixer and the headphone junction box and plugged in three sets of headphones.

"What do you think you're doing, Joel?' Myra was beginning to hit overload with the mess adding to an already crowded kitchen.

"Like Danny said, *ten minutes*. If you don't see your son then we're all the hell out of here! Don't you have at least ten minutes left in your life to entertain the possibility that Danny still exists and we're all telling the truth? Have I ever lied to you, Myra?" Joel waited for an answer.

"Yes. You lied to me when you told me you didn't know where Danny was when he was at your house stoned out of his mind."

"Myra, I was sixteen, covering for my best friend! That doesn't count." Joel handed her the headphones. "Put these on. Ten minutes won't kill ya. You know I wouldn't hurt a flea!" Myra grudgingly put the headphones on. "Please, sit down, I don't want you to hurt yourself," Joel insisted as he led her back to her chair.

"I can't say for sure if Shaun will be there, Mrs. Bishop," Danny said sympathetically as he handed Mrs. Bishop her headphones.

"Oh, if all of what you have told me is true, I know my boy will be there for me. Don't you worry about my Shaun. No sir, don't you worry about my Shaun." Mrs. Bishop spoke with such surety that Danny felt reasonably confident the strength of her beliefs would make it happen. He also saw the desperation on her face.

They all sat at the table and Joel loaded the DAT tape into the machine and hit "play." The first chord hit, then the other chords followed in quick succession. Joel watched their faces as the chords began to ring off into the digital reverberation. Mrs. Bishop was the first to glaze over, and Joel rushed to her to make sure her head didn't smash onto the table. He folded her arms and positioned her so that she was well balanced, then stayed put and waited for Danny … and finally Myra. He laid all of their heads gently on the kitchen table. They were gone.

Elsewhere

Myra looked at her body sitting in the kitchen chair. Then she turned and saw Danny.

"What are you doing to me? I have been drugged or something. I want to go back! This is not right!"

"Myra . . . Mom . . . it's me … no drugs, what do I have to do to convince you?" Myra was fighting for her sanity and admitting she could see her dead son was a major hurdle. Danny tried to reach for her but she rejected his touch. That was when she heard Mrs. Bishop weeping uncontrollably. Myra turned to see the woman holding her son, Shaun. Myra's head swivelled back and forth from the image of Shaun, head down on the kitchen table, to Shaun holding his mother.

"I knew you would be here for me, Shaun. Oh my baby, why did you leave me?"

Myra was so overcome by the reality of Mrs. Bishop's pain that it pulled her away from her own. There were shadows in the light heading towards her.

"Who are they? What do they want?"

"I'm not sure, Mom. Some of them could be those who loved you who are gone. Some might just be curious, I can't say. Mom, do you know it's me? Do you know this is no joke? Do you know how much I have always loved you and will always love you? Do you know your pain is the reason I came back? Look for those answers—they are all around you and accessible here, if you open your mind. I didn't mean for my body to die, but I was given a chance to come back to help you through this." Danny reached for her, and this time she touched him. The truth of his words became obvious, but so did something else.

"Danny … it's you … and you're thinking about … Alison?"

"I came back with her. I …"

"You love her?"

"Yes."

"She loves you?"

"I think so. Well she did … in here."

"You came back to love her in the physical world."

"Yes."

"Oh Danny, I feel you … I feel … you. Oh, my lovely boy, my lovely boy, it's really you." Myra's joy was overwhelming, and once again she felt Mrs. Bishop's sadness. She looked at Shaun, who held his mother and smiled back at Myra.

"So what now?" Myra asked.

"Now we go back," Danny said firmly.

"I'm not going back there, Danny. You're dead and buried back there. It's much too painful back there."

"Well I'm going back. The love I have for you will be there, not here. If you don't go back with me, we will truly be separated."

"Stay here with me, Danny."

"I have to go back for Ali, Mom. I know this is all a bit weird. Living with what we now know will be weird." Danny looked over at Mrs. Bishop and began to worry that everything was coming undone. "Mrs. Bishop, our time here is up, we must return now!"

Shaun watched a thought ripple across his mother's face. She didn't want to leave her son. "I know this is hard," he told her, "but the world needs good souls like yours, Vera Bishop. This is not your time. I'll see you in the blink of an eye. You know I still exist, and you will see me again." Shaun's words were lovingly soft and unspoken.

Mrs. Bishop looked up at him and understood, then turned to face Danny with a stoic expression on her face.

"How do I get back, Daniel?"

"Look out of your own eyes. Sit into your own body, then look out of your own eyes. You must look through your own eyes to be one with your body."

Mrs. Bishop took one last look at her boy. "You are the best thing in my life, and now I have to wait until I die to see you again." She wept.

"Just like you always told me, Mom. If it ain't worth waiting for, it ain't worth having."

"How dare you feed my own words back to me at a time like this? Don't you be so impertinent, Shaun Bishop!"

Shaun looked his mother and a big grin took over his face. "Thanks for everything, Mom. I'll be here when the time comes." Shaun held his arms open and Mrs. Bishop went to them for the warmth of spirit they held.

"Ladies." Danny stood holding his hands out. Myra stared at her lovely boy and took his hand. Danny led her to her body, where she stood, reluctant.

"Myra, I'm coming too, but I need you to understand something. I now love two mothers, because this body holds the memory of Shaun's love for Vera Bishop. We all need each other on this thing. We'll sure have a bigger family than we started out with, and then there's Ali … well, life will be full and complicated. From what I gather, life is supposed to be one big beautiful mess, and the way this is going, I'd say it fits the bill."

Shaun approached with Mrs. Bishop. "Take good care of this woman, Daniel," he said lovingly.

"Shaun, if there's one thing I know about our mother, she takes care of everyone else, but I can tell you this. I'll do my best, and I will always love her. Ladies ..." Danny pointed to their bodies, heads down on the kitchen table.

"You said just look through our own eyes, Daniel?" Myra asked with a good measure of skepticism. Danny nodded. She leaned forward into her head and instantly sat up in the chair, scaring the heck out of Joel.

Mrs. Bishop took one last look at her son, who smiled back with a relaxed confidence. The look told her everything was as it should be. She nodded confirmation then leaned forward and looked through her own eyes.

Danny was about to follow suit when something stopped him. He looked at Shaun, who clearly had something he wished to communicate. Then it filtered into Danny's mind.

"If she ever buys this story, Shaun, I will indeed tell Jordan how much you love her. I'm sorry about the way this has all turned out."

"Oh, you don't need to apologize. Bernard has told me why you went back. Good luck with Alison. I think my road might be easier than yours."

"See you later, Shaun."

"Later," Shaun replied as he turned and headed away.

Danny leaned into his face and looked out of his eyes. When he looked up, Myra was cooking and Mrs. Bishop was setting the table around him, while Joel finished packing his gear into the road cases.

"Well, it's about time you got back. We waited for a good ten minutes before your mother suggested we all needed something to eat," Mrs. Bishop said, signalling Danny to lift his arms off the table so she could slide a place mat into position. Danny looked at his mother, who was staring at him from her position at the stove.

"Is that really you in there, Daniel?"

"I'm afraid so," Danny replied.

"Afraid so? Now just a minute, you two! Daniel, you should be honoured to be in such a beautiful body as my Shaun's, and Myra, you should be grateful your son is here!"

Myra reached for Vera Bishop and the two women held each other tightly in silence. Danny sensed the importance of what the two women were communicating and went to Joel.

"Hey, man," Danny said with a look of exhaustion.

"Danny, I wasn't sure what I would have done if something had gone wrong. We should have talked about that before you went. It's just way too fucked up to see people breathing when nobody's home. I started to freak out when you were gone so long. This has been a heavy trip from the get-go."

"It was only a minute or two on the other side. Sorry, man, I don't think we could have been any quicker."

"So what now?" Joel asked with a serious expression. "Do we still write songs together? I gotta tell you, writing has been my only escape from all of this shit. Do we try to get some tunes to publishers?"

"Joel, you're really the writer. Every good idea was always yours. I just came in and polished them and made you think I was doing more than I actually was. You should go see Mr. Rose, Karla's dad. He's the one with the contacts in Nashville who like your stuff."

"You never told me that."

"I know. I guess having the contact gave me some kind of control. I wanted a career in music so bad that I was willing to hang onto your coattails. You're the real McCoy, though, Joel. You're a good writer. I've always been just a half-assed guitar player and a poser."

"Hey, lighten up, will ya? You're my best friend, Danny, and a pretty damn good guitar player."

"So … you're going to be okay?" Danny asked, almost miffed by the way Joel had absorbed all the information with no real surprise.

"Yeah, man. I think I'll be fine. I've got some real good ones up my sleeve that I can hardly wait to record. What are you going to do?"

"I've been given a second chance to do something in this life. When I was at the university, the day I met Ali, I saw kids there eager to learn. I want to learn, Joel. I'm not sure *what* I want to learn, but I want to learn."

"We'll still be friends, though, huh?" Joel's question said it all.

"Have been all our lives, Joel, no reason to stop now."

"Cool. Mind if I call you to talk about this stuff from time to time if I start to freak out?"

"Anything, anytime. Like always." Danny and Joel were interrupted by requests for how they wanted their eggs. Fresh Montreal bagels were in a basket on the table with Montreal smoked meat. Montreal could never have survived through the years, Danny thought, without those seriously good contributions from the Jewish community.

It looked to Danny as though Myra was going to be fine, too. A dark veil had been lifted from her spirit. Her state of "nothing" had been washed away by a new and powerful reality that contained love. Danny's love for her was alive, and therefore there was a reason to live. And she and Mrs. Bishop were now family, through this bizarre new connection. There was a strange bond created by the knowledge that they were both mothers of the same boy, who loved them both. There was no jealousy because each had experienced the other's pain, and each of them had what the other didn't. Mrs. Bishop could see the physical image of her son but not talk to him, while Myra could speak with her son but not see him. Fortunately, the bridge between those two realities was the knowledge that they both possessed because of Verhoevan's Resonance. Danny thought that, for once, Verhoevan might be pleased that his creation had been responsible for some good.

Danny longed to get back to Toronto, to Ali, but they all agreed to stay the night with Myra. She made up beds for everyone and was delighted to have a full house. Danny sensed that Myra needed to feel more of her new reality in her own home before it was empty again. She needed time for this new reality to create enough of an imprint to offset the finality created by the images of her son's physical demise. Those were snapshots of an experience that certainly didn't belong in any mother's family album.

There was some discussion of Myra selling the house and moving to Toronto, as there was nothing for her in Montreal any more. She needed a new beginning. Myra confessed that she had already put the house on the market out of necessity and had serious interest from a man who had been transferred to Montreal and wanted to get his family moved and settled quickly. The man had showed her pictures of his two boys and wife, and Myra found comfort in the idea the house would be a noisy, family place again.

***

The following morning the Bishops headed back to Mississauga. Myra was to come up by train the following weekend to visit. Vera Bishop felt a new need, and that was to be with Myra. They were "joined at the heart," as she put it.

Joel left in the van with a plan to head down to Nashville to set up camp and visit all of Mr. Rose's contacts with his material. He was going to stay in touch to let Danny know how he and his music were doing.

For most of the return drive to Toronto, Danny was, of course, consumed with thoughts of Ali and as soon as they got home he was on the phone. Her voice was oddly cold and distant.

"What is it, Ali?"

"Daniel, I think things are more complex than I ever imagined. Look, I guess what I'm trying to say is …"

"Can we at least do this in person, Ali? I would like to see you and hear what it is you have to say in person."

"Okay." Ali's tone was reluctant.

Twenty minutes later they met at a Harvey's restaurant that was the hangout for a lot of the kids from the high school. Danny saw her car pull up, and his heart sank when he saw that she wasn't driving. Brendon was at the wheel. He waited in the car and watched her walk over to the table where Shaun Bishop sat. She sat down, and Danny looked into her eyes.

"Jesus, I can't believe what you're going to do. You're going to dust me off, aren't you?"

"It isn't like that, Daniel."

"Okay. Please explain it to me, and I'll try to understand."

"My mother, Alison's mother. I can't escape what she does to me, and what she's always done to me. At least in this body she has no claim to me. I feel I've been given a second chance to live a life I've never lived. My new parents love me and I love them dearly. I actually get to be a teenager again, and one who is loved. It's a life I used to dream about, Daniel. I need a chance to experience it."

"And the guy in the car?" Danny knew what was coming.

"Yes, and I have feelings for him, too."

"I understand, Ali. I really do. Joel asked me what I was going to do now and I said I felt like I'd been given another chance to do something with life rather than fritter it away playing someone else's songs to drunks in bars. I think I'm going to finish high school and maybe go to university."

"That's great, Daniel. Look, I don't know how much time I'll need, but I want you to know I love you and I always will."

'What about your mom, I mean, Alison Truman's mom."

"I honestly can't face her right now. Part of me thinks that she's made her own bed and she should lie in it."

"Wow, that sounds a little cold. What if something happens to her before you get around to doing what we came back here to do?"

"I don't know. I really don't know. How's Myra?"

"Joel recorded the resonance on a DAT. We set up a playback system and Myra, Mrs. Bishop, and I crossed over and back. Myra is going to be fine."

"You crossed over again? Did Mrs. Bishop need to see her son to believe you?"

"She is amazingly intuitive. I'm pretty sure she believed me before, but ultimately, yes, seeing is believing. Myra was a much harder sell. This world is so disengaged from even the thought of any other kind of reality. But Ali, if it worked for us, it could work for your mom."

"Yeah, or someone could end up dying again … I don't know, Daniel. What if I were to fail? Or what if on the other side my mother confesses she never loved me and still doesn't? I don't know if I can live with that one."

"I can't answer any of those questions. Ali, you see what you are investing in don't you? It's fear, the very thing you taught me how to dispel with the Soms. Why there and not here?"

"I guess free of my mother I'm stronger. I don't know. I need time, Daniel, I need time!" Alison was ready to implode.

Danny saw her distress and backed off. He knew his only choice was to retreat and let Ali find her way, which would hopefully be back to him.

"Okay, Ali … whatever time you need, no strings attached. Have the life of your dreams."

'For a while, Daniel, just for a while."

"You know where to reach me."

"Thanks." Ali reached over and kissed Danny on the cheek while glancing self-consciously out the window to see if Brendon was watching.

"Does lover boy know anything?" Danny asked.

"No. Nobody does. And nobody ever will," Alison answered firmly.

"I love you, Ali."

"You too, Daniel."

That was it. Ali walked out the door. Danny finished his Coke and stared out the window. His heart was pretty much broken, but then again, what wasn't? Everything was upside down and surreal.

Man's curiosity regarding the big question was best left a question, to his way of thinking. Actually having the answers that Verhoevan's Resonance had revealed was its own kind of hell. With the great mystery of life removed, so too was an element of motivation to seek answers. The whole thing seemed to be boiling down to motivation and struggle. The commonly accepted philosophy he had heard a million times — the joy was actually in the struggle, in seeking. Too much food, you just lie around and get fat. With barely enough food, you keep looking and hunting, staying fit in the process, and there's some purpose in your life.

Danny left Harvey's and started to jog as fast as his injured body would move. An hour later ran up the circular drive to Mrs. Bishop's apartment.

As he felt the powerful muscles in his legs he reflected on the power of the physical world. He thought Ali was about the strongest person he had ever met, and she had been pulled right off of her perch in the blink of an eye. Of course she was attracted to Brandon, he was a handsome young man who loved her. Danny reflected on an undeniable attraction to Jordan. Their bodies had been in the process of selecting mates before the bus crash. Even new spirits had only briefly interrupted the laws of physical attraction, all part of a pretty elaborate human mating ritual. These bodies they inhabited appeared to have paths of their own. It was like they said, there's someone out there for everyone, and often you can't pick who that is, you just get drawn in like a bug to a Venus flytrap. Bernard had said the love Danny shared with Alison was an exceptional one … hmm, maybe in time. Yeah, that was it, maybe in time. Now, back to the struggle.

Danny opened the door and got in the elevator to resume a life in progress. When he came though the door, Mrs. Bishop looked at him and sensed all was not well. She didn't say anything, just made a pot of tea and pulled some fresh scones out of the oven. They sat there together quietly for a while looking out the window at cars full of people driving to places they needed to get to. Some in a huge hurry … others taking their time. Families, couples, singles returning home to empty apartments and microwave dinners.

"Ali needed some time with her new life?" Mrs. Bishop asked, hitting a bull's eye.

"Ali may need a completely new life with the time she's been given," Danny answered.

'Worse than you thought, huh?"

"In some ways, I guess. She wants what Shaun has, what you as a mother gave him in spades. She wants to know all about unconditional love from a parent. I've known it and taken it for granted. I guess it's kind of a building block for the soul."

"Never crossed my mind to do anything other than love my boy."

"Your mother love you?" Danny asked through a mouthful of scone.

"Oh, she was a bottomless pit of love, that woman, yes sir, a bottomless pit of love." Mrs. Bishop poured the tea that had been steeping.

"There you go, a great soul from a foundation of solid building blocks of love. For you, loving others was easy with all that strength under you."

"What about Myra?"

"Well, there goes my theory. Her mom was a beauty queen and loved herself more than anyone else. I think Myra wanted me to have what she never had."

"Takes all types, Daniel. All types. There are a million paths to salvation."

***

At the end of the school year, Danny was at the top of his class. His teachers couldn't understand how Shaun Bishop's marks could have improved so dramatically while he continued to excel in track field and basketball at the same time. Danny would see Ali in the hallway from time to time and they would chat briefly, but it seemed better to avoid than confront with an expectation of a progress report.

Myra moved into the apartment next door to Vera Bishop's, and a new era of family began. It was rich in its confusion and full of love. It was as though Myra and Mrs. Bishop had always been fast friends, and Danny loved them both dearly. In the summer, Danny began a job at the hospital as an orderly and bumped into Jordan, who was visiting a relative. She confided that she had dated a couple of guys but no sparks flew. One look at her and Danny knew he was still physically attracted to her — whatever drew Shaun to her was still in play. She picked him up from work one evening in her father's van. Jordan's dad was a carpet installer and the van floor was carpeted in the back. When they stopped at a park on the shores of Lake Ontario to look at the lake and chat, one thing led to another and the back of the van was barely enough room for what was unleashed. There was a welcome familiarity to it all and they more or less became an item again, although both of them knew something was missing.

When the last year of high school began, Ali was nowhere to be found. Danny learned that Jennifer's father's career had taken off and that the Glessings had moved into a new palace amongst other palaces on the Bridal Path in Toronto, where the big money lived. Ali began attending a new school, and he saw her only once that entire year, by accident. Danny had been standing outside the Royal Alex Theatre in Toronto with his two moms and saw Ali and Brendon drive by in her BMW. They were laughing, and that saddened Danny for a moment. Mrs. Bishop followed her son's eyes and squeezed his hand as if to say, "It's all right." And it was. Ali was happy, and for the most part so was he.

The last year of high school flew by and athletic scholarships came at Shaun Bishop. He accepted one to the University of Toronto so he could stay near Myra and Mrs. Bishop, who clearly needed him in their lives in a big way. Myra, of course, couldn't have been more proud that he had decided to head into medicine. "My son the doctor" — four words at the top of the wish list for most Jewish mothers.

Sadly, it was three years later, when he was finishing his undergrad, that he saw a picture of Ali in *The Toronto Star* above an engagement announcement. Mr. and Mrs. J. D. Glessing were happy to announce the engagement of their daughter, Jennifer, to Brendon Jones. It was a bit of a jolt. Sure, Danny tried to rationalize that Alison deserved an opportunity to live a life she had only dreamed about in her teen years the first time around, but then there was the longing for her that remained in his chest. There was no doubt that she was physically attracted to Brendon, and maybe there was some racial stuff in the mix as well that made Shaun Bishop an oddball selection for her physical mate. The laws of physical attraction were so complex. Were races more naturally attracted to their own kind? he wondered. Pretty good argument for that assertion, by and large. This was a question he had wrestled with from the get-go. He knew Alison was above racism in humanitarian terms, but that was an intellectual discussion. This wasn't about logic or some philosophical stand—this was more attached to basic biology. Female cardinals sought out the nicest red males a bucket of seed could attract. *There you have it!* Danny laughed as he pulled on the thread. *Cardinals are racist pigs!* Humour was such a saving grace.

This journey that Bernard had asked them to embark on was to jump back into a physical pot that boiled with not only biology but also ambition and want. How could Danny find fault with Alison when the pull of the material world was having its own effect on him, as well? His academic career was on track, and he maintained Shaun's body, with the result that he succeeded in both track and field and basketball. At that point in time there was no room in his life for the demands of a complicated relationship. However, less than a year later, Danny saw a birth announcement in the same paper. Brendon and Jennifer Jones were proud to announce the birth of their son … Daniel.

Myra and Mrs. Bishop were concerned for Danny and took him out for dinner that night. Jordan met them at the restaurant, and her tall, well-built body looked fabulous as she walked through the door with a sensual glide. The dinner went well, and Shaun Bishop left with her. She took him back to a place she shared with a girlfriend who was out for the evening. She had begun to undress when Danny felt a little compromised.

"Jordan, I need you to know …" he began, but Jordan cut him off. She was looking for signs of commitment now that Jennifer was officially and irretrievably married with a child, but Shaun Bishop still had that look on his face that said he was in love with someone else.

"I know, I know. It just isn't going to happen for us, not like it was. I can live with that, Shaun. You love me enough in your own way. I don't know what it is with you and Jennifer that you'll never get over, but it's good enough for me that she's over you."

"Yeah. I guess you're right," Danny said contemplating the finality of her words.

"So?"

"So I guess you want to get married, huh?" he asked timidly.

"If you insist." Jordan shot back. She was all over him, and it felt wonderful and wrong at the same time for Danny, but the wheels were in motion and he really had no more excuses, except he wasn't doing a thing until there was an MD after his name.

At long last, Danny and Jordan moved in together. Over the next four years his athletic pursuits were abandoned to the demands of medicine. He insisted on being at the top of his class, and there was only one student, a Chinese woman, who consistently bested him in that regard. The intern thing seemed absolutely ridiculous. Being asked to work shifts that sometimes closed in on a twenty-four-hour period was like some sort of fraternity hazing. It was plainly unsafe, and there had been more than a few close calls where decisions made in a fatigued stupor threatened a patient's life. It was dumb, just plain dumb.

There was an insidious undercurrent in the culture of modern medicine, a "boys' club" arrogance that began to appear in many of his classmates. Many doctors strutted around with a posture of infallibility and condescension that nearly put Danny off the entire damn profession. Patients were all too often excluded from discussions about their own prognoses and other information concerning matters of life and death. More than once Danny had witnessed unnecessary surgeries with fatal outcomes. If it hadn't been for a genuine desire to help people, and meeting a few like minds who also shook their heads in disbelief at the big business of medicine, he would have packed it all in.

The monumental ignorance that remained in modern medicine amazed Danny at times, as did the status so many fools were afforded simply because there was an MD after their name. He also saw how people checked their own intelligence at the door when they handed themselves over to a doctor. No wonder some MDs had a God complex; it was socialized into them by their own patients. Despite all that bothered him about the profession, Danny finally decided to specialize in oncology.

The numbers spoke for themselves. Cancers were on the rise in a world wired to industry that sucked on the fumes of the combustion engine and threw chemicals into foods to make them look fresh and last longer on the shelves. It didn't seem to bother people that respiratory disease was dramatically higher in the corridors of major highways, where many commuters chose to live out of *convenience.* The only real convenience was that funeral cars transporting the dead could make it to the cemeteries in a jiffy … if a police escort held the traffic back. And when the procession passed, everyone sat in cars kicking out fumes, surrounded by other cars doing the same, wondering what the poor son of bitch in the hearse died from … nah, couldn't have been the fumes!

Medicine agreed with Shaun Bishop and the years flew by. He was moving into his field of oncology as a resident at the Princess Margaret Hospital. It was a normal morning on rounds when he saw something on the patient roster that had the effect of a body blow. At the bottom of the "newly admitted" chart, scrawled in permanent marker, was the name … Alison Truman.

25

THE SOUTH

Savannah, Georgia, 1848

As Harding's carriage rumbled out of sight, two well-dressed men sauntered down the street as though out for an evening stroll. They stopped in front of the Harding house, where one lit a pipe and watched Mrs. Harding turn out the oil lamp in the parlour window. They casually continued on around the block and a few minutes later reappeared at the same spot and looked around again. One man slipped down the side of the house to the back, while the other looked up the road and snapped his fingers. Within seconds a horse and buggy pulled up across the street. The driver tipped his hat to the man out front, who then headed up the walk to the front door at a brisk pace.

***

Dust settled around Harding's carriage as it pulled up on the side of the road on the outskirts of Savannah. The lights from the Smitherim plantation could be seen in the distance as Harding got out and shook some of the road from his coat. Matthias looked at Harding's men with admiration: Matheson, with the arms of an ox from lifting and repairing heavy canvas sails most of his adult life, and Ferguson, as canny a second in command as one might find. Like most of the core crew of the *Belle* they worked well as a team, and loyalty and mutual respect was what had saved them all on many an occasion.

"I am grateful to you all for helping me."

Matthias's words were met with a curious look from Ferguson. "We're no helpin' *you*, cheeky breeks. It's the lassie we're here to help." Ferguson patted Matthias on the back, acknowledging the young man's worry, then he looked to Harding for some kind of a plan.

Harding stood staring at the huge, high-pillared Smitherim home, which exuded wealth and privilege with its long carriageway circling in a leisurely fashion to the shelter of the great portico. A clutter of buggies, carriages, and horses were out front indicating that a gathering of some sort was underway. The Captain pulled a six-inch telescope from his inside pocket, extended it to its full length, then squinted through the glass.

"I can't see anything from here. They must be meeting in a room in the back of the house. All right, wide circle around the perimeter of the property to the woods behind the house, stay low, and keep your wits about you for anything that moves."

Harding led the way, circling around the side of the property at a safe distance until they'd reached the cover of the trees and quietly looped around to the back of the plantation house. There was indeed a gathering of men visible through one of the large rear windows that revealed the great hall of the mansion. Harding scanned the room with his telescope and recognized many inside as men of standing in the community. They were also, to his knowledge, mostly slave owners or businessmen who benefited from the plantations worked by slaves. There was another figure, nearer the centre of the room, in a seated position, but too many men stood with their backs to the window blocking Harding's view.

He handed his telescope to Ferguson. "Keep a close eye on me, Ferguson. Matheson, you scan my perimeter. If you see anyone coming at me, shoot to distract, not kill."

Harding moved slowly along the side of a large barn, then into the shrubs under the window. The interior of the great hall must have been getting warm as windows were opened at the bottom for ventilation. The immediate benefit to Harding was that he now could hear everything that was being said.

"The woman is obviously not going to talk, Smitherim, and I for one will not be a party to any more affronts to her dignity." The voice was familiar to Harding, probably someone he had done business with over the years.

"We should wait until the other woman gets here. She will be bound to crack when she sees this one," another voice called out. Harding cringed at the man's words. The "other woman" was very likely Elizabeth.

"Why can't we have them all arrested for conspiracy? We know they've been helping our slaves go north, so surely we don't have to resort to such uncivilized behaviour," a more reasonable voice implored, before being cut off by a more venomous tone.

"Oh, get a hold of yourself, man. You all know why we're here! We're here because this woman, and more like her, would take away our right to the very labour we need to survive, and they must be punished! What they have done is akin to common thievery. They have stolen our property!" The voice had a whiny tone familiar to Harding. It was the voice of Jacob Smitherim, and his words were met with reluctant huffs and puffs of approval.

"Though what you say is true, Jacob, we should act within the law!" There was a smattering of support for this man's position, as well as a few grunts and harrumphs.

Harding rose until he could see into the room. There were a few men with their backs to him, but from the low angle he did see what was positioned in the middle of the room. There was a mass of blond hair sticking out from under a hood, and blood on a crisp white blouse. The face was obviously covered to protect everyone's identity, but the skirt was unmistakably one of Elizabeth's creations. It was what Anna had been wearing when she disappeared. Worst fears realized, Harding sank back down into the bushes and listened.

"I, for one, will have no more to do with this type of carry-on." The reasonable man's voice drew some support, and a number of men fell into line behind him as he strode across the room and out the front door. Coaches clattered off moments later, and Harding stuck his head up once more for an assessment of numbers. There were now only five men left, including Smitherim, who walked over to Anna. Her head was slumped forward as though she had fainted or was unconscious.

Given his height, Jacob Smitherim's portly shape was as much an achievement as it was a testament to a life of excess. He had no control over the way he looked at women and his face gave him away. It was the face of an animal drooling over flesh it wished to devour. His wispy red hair hung like cobwebs over full mutton chop sideburns. The floor creaked under his weight as he took two steps, pulled Anna's head back to get a clear sightline down her slightly opened blouse, and grabbed her breast, looking up at the other men.

"Well, these German women are a well-built lot, I'll give them that!" he cackled, attempting to cover his lust with humour.

"Mr. Smitherim, a little more decorum would better serve our cause." These words came from a wealthy farmer Harding knew as a deacon in the Methodist Church. "I believe she has said all she is going to say. I will wait another half hour for the other woman, and if she has not appeared by then we can safely assume the investigations of this evening are concluded and this one should be safely returned."

"Yes, yes!" Smitherim said, annoyed at the timidity of his allies. "She will be returned after she's been taught a lesson to take back with her as a warning. While we wait for the other woman, might I offer you gentlemen a brandy or whatever suits your taste?" Smitherim snapped his fingers and servants entered, tending to a long table that had been laid out with glasses, libations, and pastries.

Harding cut back to the cover of the woods.

"Anna's there," he said sadly, observing the blood wash out of his friend's face.

"Has she been harmed?" Matthias gulped.

"Hard to say. She looked as though she had fainted but she must have been hit, judging from the blood I saw on her hood and blouse."

"Her hood?"

"Her head has been covered to protect the identities of her abductors and her whereabouts. All right, there are only five men left, I have no doubt we could take them, but if we wait a few minutes I think we may have only Smitherim and his servants to deal with. They keep talking about another woman who may or may not show up. If she is not here soon, more have stated that they will leave. If that happens, Smitherim might think he has the freedom to do as he pleases with his hostage."

"From what I hear of him, he's a sick man capable of ..." Matthias reined in his imagination in order to stop the shudder running through his bones.

"Don't worry, we'll be on him before he has a chance to do any more harm."

Harding sat low, and everyone else followed suit, except Matthias, who grabbed the telescope from Ferguson and gasped at the sight of Anna tied and blinded. It was clear Ferguson had seen her but hadn't wanted to worry Matthias.

A buggy rumbled down the road at a good speed and turned sharply into the plantation, leaving clouds of dust that rose in the black night sky like steam.

"This could be the other hostage. Wait for me here." Harding made his way back to the window as the carriage pulled up in front of Smitherim's mansion. The driver ran into the room and caught his breath before speaking.

"The other woman will not be coming," the man huffed, out of breath. "I am not sure what went on in that house but the screams were loud enough to wake a dead man. I left for fear of being implicated."

"That's it! Something has gone wrong and we must get back to our homes before we are discovered. I trust you will see to the safe return of the woman, Jacob?" one of the men asked.

"I will tend to her immediately," Smitherim responded, with an odd inflection.

Everyone left in a hurry, and when the house was quiet, Smitherim dismissed his servants and walked slowly towards his hostage, dragging a chair that he positioned in front of her. He sat down, savouring his power, and gently lifted the bottom of her skirts with his riding crop, revealing her shapely legs, then lifted them even farther to gaze up her long, white thighs to the frills of her undergarments.

There was the sound of a click behind him that sounded like the door latch. Without turning he shouted at what he assumed was a servant cleaning up. "You are dismissed for the rest of the night." He continued his inspection until he heard another click, only this time it was right behind his ear.

"I said …" He turned and looked down the barrel of Harding's cocked pistol. Matthias and Ferguson stood on either side of the Captain.

"I suppose all of your would-be lovers are tied and blinded in order to stomach your affections!" Harding growled.

Matthias ran to Anna's side and pulled the hood from her head, revealing bloody marks on her face and one very black eye. He looked at Smitherim's riding crop, and the blood on the end of it sent him into an uncontrollable rage. Matthias swung out with all his might at Smitherim, who took the full force of Matthias's fist to his temple and dropped heavily to the floor. Matthias's face was insane with anger as he kicked the man hard in the belly. Harding and Ferguson were attempting to pull him off when they all froze at the sound of another carriage pulling up in the front of the house. There was some spirited shouting outside, then a thud just beyond the door to the parlour. Harding cocked the gun again and whispered to Matthias and Ferguson to remain behind him out of any line of fire.

Just as they started to move, the door burst open and Matheson walked in.

"You lot ready to leave yet? The carriage is at the front door."

"What about Smitherim's men?" Harding asked.

"Only saw the one, Captain, and he fell over like a stone after the gentlest touch I could muster," Matheson replied with a wink.

"Let's get out of here," Harding ordered.

Ferguson and Matthias carried Anna, and Matheson led the retreat. Smitherim groaned some pained words that had something to do with justice being served for such an invasion of his home as he coughed up a little blood.

Back on the road towards town, Anna began to slowly come around. She winced in pain as she began to feel the sting from the bruises to her face and chest.

"You're safe, Anna, you're safe." Matthias rocked her in his arms and stroked her hair, matted with sweat from being under the hood. She started to cry but the cry soon turned to anger.

"It was Smitherim wasn't it?"

"You saw no one?" Harding replied.

"No. I was grabbed from behind as soon as I stepped out your front door, and that hood was pulled over my head. They bound me like a hog and threw me into a carriage. They know about Elizabeth and me and the safe houses to Montreal… they call it the Underground Railroad. They also know about the Pastor and his wife, but they don't know where any of the safe houses in Savannah are yet, or anywhere else for that matter … I don't think. That's what they kept asking me about over and over when they hit me. *Where are the safe houses? Where are the safe houses? Who else is involved?* Then they'd hit me again and again when I said I didn't know. I'm glad I didn't know any names or I fear I would have told them. They kept hitting …" Anna started crying again, and Matthias held her tighter.

"They know about Elizabeth. God, I wonder if she was the 'other woman' they were waiting for?" Harding began to fret.

"If it was Mrs. Harding they were expecting, something must have gone wrong, Captain. I have no doubt Atkins interfered with their plans a wee bit." Ferguson spoke with a measure of confidence, for the Captain's benefit.

By the time they pulled up in front of Harding's house the Captain was coiled like a spring, and he flew out of the moving carriage to the door with Ferguson and Matheson at his heels. Matthias waited with Anna, not wanting her to get caught in any type of scuffle. But a moment later Ferguson gave him the all-clear and Matthias helped Anna into the house.

Upon entering, their eyes opened wide to the sight of two men tied to chairs in the parlour with gags in their mouths. Atkins sat behind them holding the ends of two ropes that were connected to nooses around the men's necks. Elizabeth held her hand over her mouth when she saw Anna's bloodied blouse and moved quickly to her side while instructing Matthias to help her to the kitchen where she could tend to the wounds.

When Matthias returned, the Captain stood across the room staring at the prisoners.

"Remove the gags, please, Atkins."

"Aye, sir." Atkins pulled wads of rags from the mouths of both men, who coughed and spat bits of rough cotton fibres covered in saliva. The Captain assessed the two men as he began pacing the floor.

"So, you would enter my home and kidnap my wife."

"Your wife and the German girl are part of a conspiracy, sir, to remove other people's property."

"I see, and so you have defenceless women beaten to an inch of their lives as some kind of, what would you call it, justice? Retribution?"

"We had no idea that would happen, sir. He should not have…"

"He? Ah, yes, dear Mr. Smitherim. You know he's quite mad, don't you?"

"If you're going to hand us over to the law, get it over with. It won't do you any good … the law is on our side, you know. There is an act before Congress making it illegal to aid slaves who would escape their masters."

"Is the law on the side of beating up women as well?" Harding continued.

"If they have anything to do with the Railroad, they had it comin'."

"I see. Now to the matter at hand: if a man entered your home and attempted to kidnap your wife … would he have anything coming to him? If, for example, I killed you right now for breaking into my home, whose side do you think the law would be on?" Harding aimed and cocked his pistol. Atkins's eyebrows shot up into his forehead as he moved gingerly out of the line of fire. Ferguson put his head down and held back a grin. The room fell silent except for a peculiar dripping sound. Urine ran off the edge of one of the men's chairs onto the wood floor below. Harding fired and the other man screamed.

"I am shot, oh, please mercy! Don't kill me. Don't kill me!" The man began to weep while the other produced even more urine.

Elizabeth ran into the room with worry on her face, only to be signalled by Ferguson with a wink to get back to the kitchen. Ferguson turned back to the men and saw the bullet hole in the wall and the light trickle of blood down the man's arm. The Captain was a crack shot and had just grazed the man's biceps with the lead. Atkins and Matheson were now on to the game.

"You'll probably be dead from blood loss soon. I may have hit a major blood vessel. If you tell me who else is in this with Smitherim, I will get you to a doctor, otherwise I will let you die and simply tell the law I killed an intruder … which is the truth, really, isn't it?"

"Yes sir, it's the truth," one man whimpered, wet with his own urine.

Atkins threw the rags at him. "Put that under your boot and sop your dirty business up, ya big Nelly!"

The man followed orders, red with embarrassment, while the other one, bleeding ever so slightly from his arm, sang like a canary. He named names, revealing that the people involved were pretty much a Who's Who of Savannah. There were some businessmen, plantation owners, officers of the law, and even clergy involved in protecting the slave trade. Harding acted as though he were simply disgusted by what he heard, when in fact he was more than a little fearful for their safety.

Elizabeth and Anna had made themselves enemies of a good portion of the town. Anyone who would be sympathetic to the cause was probably operating in a clandestine manner to avoid personal damages. When the man had said every name he could remember, Harding ordered Atkins to cut them loose.

"Get out, and don't let me see your faces around my house again," Harding barked at the two men.

"But what about a doctor? I'm going to bleed to death!" the man cried, clutching his bloody arm.

"You had better move quickly, then," Atkins said as he pulled the ropes off of both men with two quick moves and pushed them out the front door. Leather hit dirt, and they ran so fast they were out of sight in seconds.

When Atkins came back in, Harding looked at him with gratitude. "I don't know what I would have done without you tonight, Atkins. A job well done."

"Least I could do for you and your missus," Atkins replied.

"How did you best them?" Matthias inquired

"Well, I put Mrs. Harding's iron skillet to good use on the one that came in the back kitchen, and the other caught a good swift kick in the weddin' tackle when he came through the front door to see what was going on. It really wasn't much of a struggle, Mr. Dopp, although the one I kicked screamed like a baby. I don't believe the pair of them to be overly familiar with the rigours of a good fight. By the time they came to their senses I had them unable to move. No sir, they were not fightin' men at all."

"That's what worries me," Harding muttered. "If the rank and file are caught up in this, I don't believe it's going to be safe here any more for any of us, Matthias, at least not without constant protection, and that's certainly no way to live."

"I'm sorry, Captain. Once more I have complicated your life."

"No, Matthias, it was two good women with an ideal sense of justice who complicated our lives, and I must say I can't argue with their motivation. We may have bested these fellows on the first round, but we are greatly outnumbered, and apparently the rule of law isn't on our side. Mr. Ferguson, have the *Belle* pulled out to harbour and moored, then post guards round the clock. If this is, as they say, a battle of property, they might wish to a have a run at ours. Mr. Atkins, if you would be so kind as to bed down here that we might have a measure of security until we leave. Matthias, how long will it take you to conclude business in Savannah?"

"Well, I might be forfeit a deposit on the house I have agreed to purchase. But many of my orders are from other cities. I believe when the *Branden* arrives I could conclude business relatively soon."

"Could you conclude your business from elsewhere, say, a more northern port?"

"I believe I could. What about the banks here? Did I not hear mentioned the name of one of the bankers with whom I do business?"

"You did. That account should be closed in the morning, and actually I would deal with a northern banker more favourable to abolitionists if I were you. I think we should leave preemptively, no later than two days from now. That should give us just enough time to properly provision the ship and conclude business. Things are only going to get worse. I shall look into the selling of my house, as well."

After Ferguson and Matheson left, Harding helped Atkins prepare a makeshift bed for the night. Of course this was not done until Elizabeth had given the floor in the parlour a good scrub with carbolic soap to dispatch the smell of urine. Anna's face when cleaned up looked as though it wouldn't be scarred, but her bruises were becoming colourful enough to draw attention. The remainder of the night was uneventful, much to Atkins's disappointment.

At dawn Harding went down to the Pastor's house, and he was aware that he was being followed at a safe distance. He didn't go in but instead continued down the street, ducking in between a few houses then circling to the rear of the McLean home. After one knock the door was opened. Harding told Mrs. McLean he was being followed and was quickly given entrance.

The Pastor was visibly shaken when informed that his complicity in the Underground Railroad was known to a now-united group of wealthy plantation and slave owners. He sat down in horror on hearing of Anna's beating and the attempt to kidnap Elizabeth Harding. Though the Pastor was irritated by Harding's level of knowledge, he took heed that he must very carefully inform any and all he knew whose hearts had led them to assist slaves in escaping the injustice of their lives.

Harding looked at the Pastor, took a deep breath, and told him the names of men in his own congregation who were in league with Smitherim. The Pastor was winded — it was as though all of his sermons had been rendered meaningless. The knowledge that one of his own deacons, one under his tutelage, could defend the inhuman treatment of one man to another had knocked him down a peg or two in the matter of his own self-importance, which was considerable. His sermon would have noticeably less thunder that morning, and an air of humility that his congregation had never heard before.

When Harding returned, it was Matthias's turn to tend to business. Atkins, at Harding's suggestion, accompanied him, and as they had been told to expect, they, too, were shadowed. As they walked they formulated a plan, and so they turned down the same street where Matthias and Harding had followed their wives the day before. They ducked into the alleyway, and as soon as their shadow passed he was grabbed from behind by Atkins and rendered unconscious with a single blow. Matthias and Atkins then continued on at a quick pace to the Heinyl home.

Heinyl agreed to assist Matthias in concluding his business in town and recommended a good lawyer from the synagogue who was well respected in the community. With that matter concluded, Matthias got right to the point.

"There are those in this town who seek to help the slaves. Should any of your people be involved in this thing they call the Underground Railroad, I would advise you to be careful. My wife was badly beaten last night for information."

Matthias's Aunt Esther appeared out of nowhere. It was clear she had been listening to the conversation.

"Your wife. What does she look like?" Matthias described her, and Esther said, "I believe I know your wife and the woman she often works with. We have worked together. How is your is good wife today, Matthias? I do hope she has not come to any serious harm."

"She is bruised and shaken. I'm afraid we will be leaving soon."

"Leaving? Oh, Matthias! I feel as though we have only just found you again, and now …. Where will you go?"

"We are not sure yet."

"Might I suggest Montreal? You have more relatives there, believe it or not, and they are involved in the textile industry, in which you have some expertise. I know we would not, then, truly be losing you."

"More relatives?"

"Our other son is there with his wife and family. In fact, they are involved in settling many of the slaves in Montreal, and farther east, to the port of Halifax."

The penny dropped, and Matthias looked at his aunt. "Did my wife know you were my aunt?"

"No, we don't use names when we move from place to place. But how did you know, Matthias? Why was it that you decided to warn us about the current danger to abolitionists?"

"I know all too well that, as Jews, you were persecuted in Hamburg. I guess I thought people who had been wronged might hold sympathy for others who are being wronged."

"You've much of Miriam in your heart, Matthias."

"I'll take that as a compliment, Aunt Esther. I hate to be rude, but I must tend to business. I am afraid I am going to have little or no time to get to know you all."

Esther walked over and embraced him. "We know you, Matthias." She kissed him on the cheek, and Mr. Heinyl opened the door.

As Matthias walked down the street he looked back and saw Esther watching him though the window. She looked so like his mother he was moved to tears.

Atkins gave him a stern look. "Now is not the time to be losing any of our resolve, Mr. Dopp," he lectured.

"There is no resolve lost here, Mr. Atkins. Anna's bruised face is my resolve!"

When the address of the lawyer was found, Matthias and Atkins waited on a wooden bench until Mr. Rothstein opened his office door and invited them in. Rothstein was a thin man with a meticulously groomed beard, and he was elegantly dressed, right down to imported fine-leather boots that marched crisply across the wooden floor. Matthias was about to explain his business when Rothstein cut him off.

"Are you of any relation to Gert Dopp?"

"I am his son, sir."

"Ah, then our business is concluded. Your father was responsible for putting my family out of business in Hamburg. I believe I might be shunned should I be found to be in business with the son of Gert Dopp." Rothstein was polite, but there was much unsaid that his face couldn't hide.

"I understand, Mr. Rothstein. It would seem my father has done much to distance himself from those in the House of David. I have only just learned that my mother was a Jew and met my Aunt Esther."

"And how do feel about this new information?"

"I loved my mother. Never was there a more sweet and generous soul. As regards being Jewish, I have no knowledge of any group of people being worth less or more than any other group. In fact, I think I have a distaste for those who would make such claims. Good day to you, Mr. Rothstein, and I am indeed sorry for any unjustified pain my father may have inflicted on your family, and that we will not be able to do business."

"*May* have inflicted? *Unjustified*? Do you think for a moment what your father did to us was justifiable?" Rothstein's aloof demeanour began to crack with shards of anger.

"I don't know, Mr. Rothstein. I have only just met you and am not in possession of all of the facts. I can tell you that the more I learn of my father, the more I would be willing to believe there must be truth in accusations such as yours. I believe what I have been told by my aunt and Mr. Heinyl regarding my father's actions and his cruelty to my mother." Matthias stood his ground and Rothstein retreated.

"What you say is an exceedingly wise position for one so young, Mr. Dopp."

"Oh, I make no profession of wisdom, Mr. Rothstein. I have only seen pain inflicted on others by those who profess to be wise, or worse, have the audacity to presume to inflict the will of their gods on others. Regardless, sir, I am taking up your valuable time. I regret we cannot do business. Good day to you."

Atkins looked a little surprised by the young Dopp's words, and in particular the words about gods. Though he found himself in agreement with Mr. Dopp, he wondered how such words might have sat with his God-fearing Captain.

"Please sit down, Mr. Dopp," Rothstein asked politely.

"I don't wish you to be shunned by your own people, sir," Matthias responded.

"I don't much care for many of them anyway." Rothstein smiled. "I have found as many scoundrels amongst my own as I have outside. I am in agreement with your position, and now have a very defensible argument from which to do business with you. Please sit down, and accept my apologies for dressing you in a father's suit that apparently doesn't fit the son."

The discussion that followed was concise. Rothstein had excellent business skills and made many suggestions that Matthias readily embraced, one of which had to do with the *Branden*. As soon as she hit port no one would need to know who owned her cargo, and Rothstein was certain that, for a small fee, silence could be bought, at least until the goods were sold. Rothstein, for a fair price, would take care of everything in a managerial role. In the matter of the house purchase, Rothstein was sure he could retrieve the deposit through assisting in its eventual sale … for a fee, of course. Rothstein also had contacts in Montreal, which to Matthias was now looking like the place to call home.

The southern American colonies were no place for Anna's strong abolitionist beliefs when there were family and business contacts in Montreal and a country that not only was abolitionist politically but in fact helped provide homes for runaways. He could stay and fight, but he thought about that uphill climb. Racism in Savannah had an economic side he knew would not go away overnight. Slavery was about affluence and comfort that, as Anna had observed, even religion had been reshaped to defend. No, this fight was one he sensed was going to take far too long.

After stopping at his bank and completing the transfers of funds to another institution, Matthias and Atkins headed back. When they reached Harding's street, Atkins noticed that he and Matthias had picked up two more men who now followed at a safe distance. These ones looked a little tougher than the first.

"The opposition is beginning to get bothersome," he muttered under his breath as they approached the Harding house.

The Captain watched through a slit in the curtains, hand just out of sight … holding a pistol.

It was time to make their getaway on the *Belle*, and they decided to make their move under cover of darkness. The two men posted on the street would need to be removed in order to make it to the ship without incident. Elizabeth and Anna packed trunks with only the possessions of most importance in order to travel as light as possible, while Harding and Atkins formulated a plan of escape. The selling of the Harding house and contents was to be handled by a neighbour.

A direct but casual approach to the men watching them was deemed an effective course, and to that end Matheson and Atkins snuck out the back door and circled around. Ferguson and Harding went out the front door and sauntered towards the two men, who watched from a block away. The plan was that by the time Harding and Ferguson reached them Atkins and Matheson would be coming up from behind — surround and overpower. But the best plans, when flown into uncertain winds, can come crashing back into one's face in a hurry. Harding and Ferguson had just stepped outside when two more men approached from the other end of the street behind them, apparently with the same strategy in mind. Anna and Elizabeth were now vulnerable. There was no doubt in Harding's mind that Smitherim wanted the women.

"These fellows are out in numbers tonight, Captain. Perhaps we'd best get back to the house to cover the lassies."

"Read my mind, Mr. Ferguson." Harding spun around and saw his wife waving frantically through the curtains. "Something's up."

Harding's pace picked up, and he and Ferguson made it into the house just as the strangers stopped in front of the walkway, as though they were taking up position for the night. One of them tipped his hat politely with a smug look on his face. Harding's blood began to boil but he smiled back.

"The beggars are carrying pistols, Captain," Ferguson said out of the side of his mouth. Harding shook his head in acknowledgment, and when they entered the house Matthias rushed to them with a look of desperation.

"Anna is missing. She slipped out the back as we watched you leave."

"What? Your wife's strong head might leave her to the mercy of Smitherim yet. Do you have any idea what she's up to, Matthias?"

"None."

"God help us."

26

ILLUSIONS

Toronto, 1999

Danny looked at the name on the "new arrivals" clipboard and shook himself back to reality. It couldn't be Alison. After asking for her chart at the nursing station he learned that this Alison Truman was an elderly woman, and whoever she was, her prognosis was not good … the cancer was everywhere.

The primary site was very probably her lungs, given the shape they were in, but there were metastases at the liver, brain, and possibly the bones in her legs. He called radiology and went down to look at the X-rays. After a cursory glance, he knew this patient wouldn't last a week.

He took a deep breath and went back upstairs to look in on the woman. In the hall upstairs he saw her. She looked as gorgeous as ever, and she was walking towards him with the loveliest young boy, with curly blond hair, holding her hand. She stopped in her tracks when she saw Danny and a warm smile crept over her face. Danny walked slowly to her until they stood facing one another.

"Hi, Danny," she said, quietly and affectionately.

"Good to see you, Ali." And it did feel good. He couldn't believe the warmth that flushed into him in her presence.

"I'd like you to meet Daniel. Daniel, this is Danny." The little boy shyly hid behind his mother.

"Your mother's name … wouldn't be Alison, by any chance?" Danny asked with genuine sympathy

"How bad is it?" Ali asked with a pained expression.

"Bad. She's got about a week," Danny said softly.

Ali's tears welled, then began to roll down the cheeks of Jennifer Glessing. Her little boy didn't see them at first, but when he glanced up his face was puzzled.

"Is the old woman we're going to see already dead, Mummy?"

"No, Daniel." Ali swept the child up into her arms and held the little soul for a moment, then kissed the top of his head and put him down. "Can you take us to her room?"

Danny nodded and led the way. The room was dim, but Alison Truman, Senior, was wide awake. When they entered, she looked up at the blonde with the sweet little boy.

"Well hello there, little fellow. What's … your name?" Her voice was scratchy and her breathing laboured and shallow. The little boy hid behind his mother's skirt, clearly frightened by the gaunt, witch-like face that spoke to him.

"I'm sorry, Mrs. Truman, he's a little shy. His name is Daniel," Alison offered.

"He's love … lovely," the old woman replied, looking at Jennifer Glessing. "Do I know you?"

"I was visiting someone here, and when I saw your name I thought I might stop in. Your daughter, Alison, she was one of my teachers, a friend … "

The elderly woman seemed happy to have visitors, and it seemed to Danny that Ali wished to engage her, to see what the old woman might have to say this time. There was wishful thinking in the mix for sure, but Ali was there for some kind of closure.

Danny heard a page for Dr. Bishop, and for some reason it took a moment to dawn on him that that's who he was. It was amazing how quickly he lost himself and his current reality in Ali's presence. He quietly backed out of the room to the nurses' station to deal with the matter that required Dr. Bishop's immediate attention.

When he returned to the room a half hour later, Jennifer and her little boy Daniel were gone. Mrs. Truman looked up at the sturdy young man with the white jacket and the name tag that said "Dr. Shaun Bishop."

"How are you feeling, Mrs. Truman?" he asked gently.

"How … the hell … do you … think … I'm feeling. I'm … dying … for … Christ's sake," she croaked.

"Can I get you anything?" Danny asked sympathetically.

"Nope." Mrs. Truman turned her head the other way. Danny's audience was over.

The following day when Danny arrived he saw Alison, alias Jennifer, again in the hall outside Mrs. Truman's room, only this time she was alone. She saw him and headed his way.

"Hello, Dr. Bishop."

"Here for some more punishment, Ali?"

"Actually, no. She wanted to talk to me yesterday and tell me how smart her daughter the university professor was. Hell, I had to stick around for that! She's never given me a compliment in her entire life. I've come back to see what else she has to say."

"Are you going to confront her?"

"I don't know."

"Just a heads-up, Ali. She's pretty rough. If you need to say something, I don't think you have much time."

Ali nodded and headed into the room. Danny went to the nurses' station, where he learned that Mrs. Truman had been in and out of consciousness most of the night. Danny hoped the loss of consciousness might have been a stepping stone out of the pain. When he looked in on Ali, Mrs. Truman appeared to be having a conversation with someone in the ceiling. Her eyes were open and she was clearly engaged, just not with anyone in the room that he could see. Ali, tearful but curious, looked to Danny for an answer.

"Could be the brain metastases are inciting some delirium … maybe the morphine."

Ali shook her head in acknowledgment then pulled up a chair. "Or maybe she's looking over the fence," she replied. "Don't forget, you've seen over the fence yourself, Mr. Blum. I'm going to sit with her awhile, if you don't mind." She sat down and tried to hear what her mother was saying.

Danny took his cue and slipped out to do the rounds. It was later in the day when he passed the room and looked in again. Ali was still there, sound asleep in her chair, and her mother was staring at her. When Mrs. Truman saw Dr. Bishop, her eyes suggested that she wanted to say something, so he went to her bedside.

"Who the hell … is she?" Mrs. Truman said, waving her finger in the direction of Jennifer Glessing.

"I think she knew your daughter."

"Oh." The old woman's eyes closed.

A shift nurse came in and gave Dr. Bishop an odd look, as if to say, "This isn't your patient," then went about her chores. She checked the vitals, changed the IV bag, and as she left she whispered to Dr. Bishop, "She'll be lucky to see the morning."

Danny turned to see that Ali was awake and had heard.

"I guess I'd better call home. I'm going to stay."

"Let me buy you a coffee and something to eat. I'll stand watch with you, Ali." Danny reached for her hand and she readily accepted it, then paused to stare at her hand in his. The extension of the hand was a simple courtesy, but the touch ran deep and caught both of them off guard. Alison dropped the hand as if it were a hot stone.

"Sorry, Ali. I didn't mean to upset you. Would you rather I left you alone?"

"No, Danny, I need you here, I think, but I have to keep my eye on the ball. I'm here for my mother."

"Absolutely. I'll get the coffee. This could be a long night."

Before Ali could respond, her mother's voice cut into the moment.

"Alison … is that you? Get me… my blanket … will you? I'm cold." Mrs. Truman's eyes were closed.

"Yes, it's me, Mother." Ali folded the blanket under her mother's feet, then sorted out the rest of the bedding, tucking in the dying woman like a little girl. "There you go, snug as a bug in a rug."

"Thank … you, dear." Mrs. Truman drifted off again.

"I'd like that coffee, Danny," Ali said, resuming her post in the chair. "That's the third time she's called me Alison."

"Back in a flash."

Danny slipped out the door. He thought what was happening had to be a drug-induced delirium, but that was the doctor in him talking. Ali's mother had actually called her "dear." Where had she been in that moment? Here, or elsewhere, or both? Had Mrs. Truman been zoning in and out of two realities? He remembered the old man in the ICU who had said he'd seen the shadows in the light.

When Danny returned all was as he had left it, except Ali now held her mother's hand. Danny gave her the coffee and sat near the window on the opposite side at the foot of the bed, not wanting to intrude. Moments later the old woman started to talk again.

"Where is … Ali… why isn't … Ali … here?"

"I'm here, Mother," Ali responded.

"Wh … where?"

"I'm here, Mother. And I know all about Avril," Ali ventured.

The old woman's face darkened and she looked uncomfortable. Her eyes opened and she looked at Ali.

"Who … the hell … are you?" Mrs. Truman asked.

"A friend of Alison and Avril," Ali replied.

The old woman looked angry for a moment, and then curious. "Oh?" She closed her eyes and drifted. A few minutes later she spoke again.

"Why … isn't … Ali here?"

Ali took a deep breath and went for it. "I came back to tell you I forgive you, and that I know all about Avril." Her voice was shaking with emotion.

Her mother began to cry, then her eyes suddenly opened.

"Who the hell … are you?" The old woman squinted at her. Ali began stroking her mother's hair, and Mrs. Truman looked even more confused. "Ali?" she called out towards the ceiling. Her eyes were closed and tears again streamed down her cheeks. "Ali's … dead."

"No I'm not, Mother," Ali said tearfully, but there was no cognition in her mother's face, she was adrift again, tethered by a thin lifeline to the physical world. The room fell silent. The sound of beeping machines from other rooms became audible; in fact, the world outside of that room was strangely alive in contrast to the silent watch within. It had become a surreal transfer station where consciousness was beginning to shift with an intermittent phasing in and out of physical reality.

About an hour later Ali felt her mother's grip tighten on her hand. The old woman's body began to shake and her feet thrashed as though she struggled with some unknown force. She gripped Ali's hand even tighter and Ali winced with the pain of it. The old woman took a deep breath, then fought to speak.

"Forgive me … Ali," Mrs. Truman begged with a pathetic tone.

Ali burst into tears and shouted, "I forgive you, Mom, I for ..." Before Ali could finish her words, her mother gazed at her as her chest slowly deflated and air wheezed out of her mouth like someone blowing on a blade of grass. Her hand went limp, and when Ali looked into her face it was as though air left her face, too. Her cheeks and eyes sank and one eye half closed, while the other was fixed and dilated, devoid of life. Even her head appeared to sink deeper into the pillow, as though life had somehow kept it afloat on the surface. Ali wept uncontrollably and lowered her head to her mother's chest.

"She didn't hear me. She didn't hear me."

"Speak the words again, Ali, and quickly. She might not be far from her body," Danny instructed.

"I for … forgive you, Mom. I forgive you," Ali sobbed into her mother's chest.

Danny stood behind Ali and gently rubbed her back for a moment until he sensed his touch wasn't welcome. Maybe privacy was the issue, maybe he was the issue … it didn't matter. It was Ali's mom who was dead. It was Ali's grief.

Danny quietly left the room. He tried to look in on a couple of patients but was too emotionally distracted so he headed down to the cafeteria again and grabbed a coffee. A good fifteen minutes later he slowly strolled back to the room. Mrs. Truman's face had sunk even farther and Ali was gone.

Two days later, Dr. Bishop and Jordan saw Jennifer, her son Daniel, and her husband Brendon at the funeral. There were a few folks there that Ali recognized and wanted to speak with, but she couldn't say anything close to what she wanted and needed to say as Jennifer. Sadly, her mourning and grief were to be completely in isolation — no funny stories of a life lived, no exchanged memories from old friends, in fact, no audible evidence that her mother had ever existed. She looked over at Shaun, Jordan, Mrs. Bishop, and Myra, who looked back sympathetically. Mrs. Bishop made the move, unable to stand still in the face of such pain. She pushed through all the awkwardness and went to Jennifer and held her tight while whispering in her ear.

"I am so sorry, child. I don't think I have ever felt pain as complex as yours. I need to tell you something — she heard you, and you know she did. Somewhere inside of you, you know this to be true. Look for it. The knowledge of it is in the love of your spoken words. You also know that if you felt love at that moment she would feel it on the other side."

Jennifer wept on Mrs. Bishop's shoulder until her son tugged on her hand.

"Mummy? What's the matter, Mummy?"

Jennifer looked down at her son and wiped her eyes. "Mummy's okay, Daniel, just a little sad." Ali looked at Mrs.

Bishop. "Thank you, Mrs. Bishop. Would it be okay if we spoke again sometime?"

"Why yes, child, I would like that."

Brendon picked up his son and put his arm around Jennifer. As their late-model Volvo wagon pulled away, Jennifer looked at Danny from the passenger window and mouthed the word "Thanks." Danny stood frozen, sensing an awful finality in the moment.

***

A couple of weeks later, after a particularly trying day, Shaun Bishop flopped on the sofa in his apartment and kicked off his shoes. He reached forward, grabbed the remote, and flipped the television on. A talk show was on with the guy from the San Diego Zoo and a parade of different critters. He didn't have the focus to watch, his head was too busy processing his day.

It had been the usual mix of good and bad. Some of his patients were responding well to treatments … some were not. The difference he wanted to make as a doctor was a constant struggle and minimally effective at best, he thought. For every medical intervention, more often than not there were prices to pay. On many occasions the time that was bought wasn't good time. It was time for families to watch treatments fail; to see loved ones lose their dignity a piece at a time; and to finally hope for death because what was going on was not a life worth living.

It was the cases where complete recovery had occurred that were the opiate. Such cases were the equivalent of hitting the ball out of the park. It happened, it felt amazing when it did, but there were so many games and even more innings where medicine struck out. There was the frequent tease of the foul ball that looked promising only to curve over the line, taken by a fateful breeze. Destined to cross the foul line from the beginning? Who knew?

Maybe it was presumptive, even egotistical, to think that man could intervene with nature with any consistency. Verhoevan had intervened and, from what Danny had seen, attempts to alter natural courses only resulted in complications. Rescuing Myra from the depths of her loss had been a worthwhile venture, and for that, Danny was grateful for Bernard's challenge. The trade-off in that case, though, had been his loss of Ali. He still longed for the image of the nerd he'd met that first day at the university, but even without the image of her, Danny now understood, with a knowing he had never held, that Ali would always be Ali. The problem was, Ali was now in love with someone else.

The material world was a powerful realm and deep, in its own way. His love of Mrs. Bishop had been undeniable from the get-go, as was his attraction to Jordan. As he was thinking of Jordan, he heard her stir in the bedroom. He listened to the toilet flush, followed moments later by the rustle of bedcovers. He smiled at the thought of her and how her love for him had been steadfast through the school years. Though they both lived with the knowledge that a piece was missing from their relationship, nonetheless, her presence in his life was enriching and meaningful.

He switched the TV off and shuffled down the hall to the bathroom to brush his teeth before bed, and as he was scrubbing away, he glanced down at the wastebasket and began casually reading the side of a ripped, empty box. As he was about to spit out the toothpaste, it dawned on him what he had just read. He reached down to grab the box to make sure he had read it correctly. Written across the top of the box in bold print were the words “Pregnancy Test.” Danny rifled through the trash and there it was — the stick.

He took a deep breath and looked at it, and it indicated positive for the presence of human chorionic gonadotropin—hCG. This, of course, meant that a fertilized egg had successfully implanted itself in the uterus. Danny swallowed the toothpaste.

The Shaun side of him was happy in the thought of a genetic line continuing; Danny was unsure and conflicted. It was one more brick in the wall that separated him from Ali. He and Jordan had been taking precautions, but somehow nature had won.

Shaun crawled into bed and lay on his back, eyes wide open. He looked over at Jordan, whose face was pushed into her pillow. She stirred and opened one eye and knew.

“I guess you looked in the trash,” Jordan said sleepily.

“Yup,” Shaun replied.

“So, how do you feel about our situation?”

“I’m not sure, Jordan.”

“Mmm. Me neither. Let’s talk in the morning before I go to work.”

Shaun rolled on his side and stroked her hair. “Okay, honey,” he said softly. She pulled in closer and pushed her face into his chest.

Light was streaming in the window when Shaun opened his eyes. The smell of coffee wafted in from the kitchen and he heard the shower running. He stumbled out of bed in his T-shirt and boxer shorts and felt his stomach rumble. In a flash the peanut butter was out, the toast was toasting, and Shaun held a warm mug of coffee in his hands when Jordan came out of the bathroom wrapped in a towel.

"Throw some toast on for me, too, will you, sugar?" she said as she streaked into the bedroom.

"Already done," Shaun replied.

A few minutes later she emerged ready for work and looking fabulous in an expensive grey skirt with matching jacket and a soft cream silk blouse. Jordan was a stunning woman with exquisite taste and a wardrobe to match. She was a shrewd businesswoman, moving up in a national women's clothing chain that owned the retail outlet she managed. As he watched her walk towards him, he couldn't help but think her face was already radiant with the pregnancy. She grabbed the other piece of toast from the toaster threw it on a plate, then poured a coffee and sat across from Shaun.

"So, what do you think? Do we abort or have this thing?" she opened, rather casually.

"Jordan, I don't know what to say. Part of me is afraid and part of me is delighted. Do you want to be a mother?"

"I don't want to do this alone. If I have this child it will be because both of us are willing, and I don't think I want to do this unless we are married."

"You didn't answer the question. Do you want to be a mother?"

Shaun and Jordan locked eyes. Jordan was clearly wrestling with her thoughts. Her eyes welled, and Shaun reached for her hand.

"I, um … I want this child as much as life itself," she finally blurted out. The professional façade dropped into a flood of maternal instincts and her mascara ran. "Oh, God. I did not want to be so pathetic." Jordan ran to the bathroom.

Shaun wanted to run after her, but Danny was glued to the seat. He loved Alison, but he also loved Jordan. Something clicked. He loved Jordan and she was pregnant. As he searched himself for answers, he realized he wanted the child, and she needed to hear the words. He got up and went to her. She was at the mirror wiping runny mascara when he came through the door.

"Jordan, I love you, and this child has been conceived in love. It will be raised in love, and I want this … probably as much as you do. Something wonderful has happened to us—we have created life. And as for the second part of your criteria for having this child … well, no child of mine is going to be a bastard in the eyes of the law."

Jordan looked at Shaun and tears flowed again, only this time the floodgates opened. These, Shaun sensed, were not tears of sadness but tears of joy from carrying new life in her womb and hearing the words that she had longed to hear.

Ali had clearly chosen a path, and it was time for Danny to walk down the one that had appeared in front of him. It was a path that could not have been more clearly marked.

27

AGAIN

Savannah, Georgia, 1848

Matthias wasn't a superstitious man, invested in the whimsical, but he wondered, were he and Anna to be refugees for the rest of their lives, running from those who would take his life, one step ahead of a hungry inevitability that must be fed? What of fate? Was he supposed to have died in the flames that consumed his father's body? Destiny and predetermination were interesting ideas, but trying to figure out what was predetermined and what wasn't was just too akin to fear.

So Matthias sat, waiting to hear from Anna, or about her. It was unsettling, but he refused to be fearful of what he didn't know. Smitherim was like a petty version of a Som, the source of his power his ability to make people fear him.

Atkins and Matheson had returned to the Harding house when they saw they were outnumbered on the street. Before exposing themselves to further hazard, Harding suggested they stay put for a time to see if Anna might return, and so they sat watch for what seemed like an eternity.

"All right, we don't know where Anna is." Harding broke the silence. "We do know this house is under surveillance by at least four men, and they are still in view, so there's a good possibility she's still a free agent. We can't weaken our defences here by splitting up, and we can't risk her returning to an empty house. I suggest one of us go to look for her and the rest of us turn this place into a fortress. I don't think Matthias or I have any option but to stay, so it has to be one of you three."

Matheson, Atkins, and Ferguson looked at one another. Ferguson appeared to have been wordlessly elected spokesman.

"I think, Captain, that …"

Ferguson turned towards the front door as a curious sound increased in intensity. Matthias had heard the sound before, outside the cathedral in Hamburg, and it unnerved him. It was the sound of a crowd, and it was getting louder. His thoughts ran immediately to images of a huge bonfire, with him as kindling. Harding went to the window and saw a crowd heading up the street towards his house. In the vanguard Pastor McLean and his wife walked proudly. Next to the Pastor was a man he recognized as the rabbi from the local synagogue. Harding spotted Anna, surrounded by Orthodox Jews as well as members of the congregation from his own church. There must have been close to one hundred people!

Pastor McLean and Anna headed up the pathway to Harding's front door. Harding opened it and Anna rushed in.

"Anna, you're safe!" Matthias closed his eyes in relief.

"I am, and so are we all, for the moment. We won't be *slipping away* tonight, we'll be leaving in the presence of a rather large crowd, as you can see. No one would dare abduct a woman with so many witnesses. The danger to you all was my fault, so I sought help in the only place I could. It was the Pastor's idea to invite the congregation from the synagogue, as well, to make the crowd even more imposing. He also said we need to act quickly before any countermeasures can be assembled."

A carriage and a wagon approached from the other end of the street and the crowd moved into position, creating a corridor from the house to the transport. The Hardings' belongings were placed in the wagon, along with one chest belonging to Matthias and Anna. Smitherim's men were denied proximity by a wall of serious-looking church folk who faced outward with pitchforks and rakes at the ready, like the quills of a porcupine. A few of the more serious-minded held rifles and pistols.

Within a minute the refugees were ready to go. As Matthias went to get into the carriage he bowed a grateful bow to the crowd and saw a face that reminded him of some unfinished business. He walked to the man with his hand extended.

"Rabbi, I owe you an apology for my response to you some months back. Mine were the words of confusion, not of my heart."

The Rabbi looked at Matthias and nodded his head in acknowledgement. "Apology accepted, Matthias, son of Miriam."

Matthias grinned at the Rabbi's words. "That's me all right, sir, and proud of it."

Matthias made his way back to the carriage and felt someone grab his hand and put a rather large envelope in it. He looked back into the face of Esther.

"Just a little travelling money, should you need it. Don't be proud … pay me back once you get established. We would love to come to visit one day. The names and addresses of your relatives, along with letters of introduction, are in the envelope. I'm sure they will see to lodgings for you and the Hardings until you get established. Be well, Matthias."

Matthias leaned over and held his aunt, then kissed her on the forehead.

"Be well, Esther. I wish we'd had more time."

Harding pulled Matthias into the carriage, and before it thundered off Mrs. Harding leaned out and shouted, "God bless you all!"

Smitherim's men were pushed back as they tried to ascertain which road the carriage would take. In fact, they were pushed well down the street before they gave up and took off down the only available avenue of retreat to report to Smitherim.

"Will the punts be at the old river warehouse?" Harding asked Ferguson over the roar of the carriage wheels.

"They should have been there for two hours by now. I dearly hope they haven't grown impatient and left seeking further instruction."

Once Harding gave the drivers the destination, the carriage, followed by the wagon, headed northwest under the cover of night. Atkins faced the rear in the back of the wagon looking out for any signs of pursuit. Matthias held on to Anna, occasionally smiling at her and shaking his head.

"What is it, Matthias? Why do you keep smiling at me?"

"Can't a man enjoy looking at a beautiful woman?" Matthias replied, causing her to look embarrassed in the presence of Mrs. Harding and the Captain. "Actually, I'm smiling because I think my good wife may have saved us all," he said proudly.

Anna put her head on Matthias's shoulder and gazed out of the open window.

***

Smitherim was pacing the floor in the carriage house of a wealthy merchant minutes away from the Harding house. He was a serious man when it came to vindictiveness, and his sadistic nature sought satisfaction from a woman he had so nearly tasted. His men burst through the rear door, out of breath.

"They have fled with their belongings in a coach and a wagon," the lead man huffed.

"Fools. How could you let this happen?"

"They assembled a crowd that kept us at bay. It was impossible to get anywhere near them."

Smitherim smacked his riding crop on his thigh repeatedly as he paced the floor, extracting a measure of satisfaction in the pain. It kept his senses focused.

"All right, we know Harding has moved his ship from port. He's a good businessman and a sailor and he would certainly not leave that ship behind. He's either heading southeast to the Ogeechee or north to the Savannah River. Do we know which way the *Southern Belle* sailed?" Smitherim addressed his question to a well-dressed man who man who sat sipping whisky from a small silver flask.

"I believe she's heading north, sir. As we supposed, she did leave harbour. My man observed her sail and thought at first she moved in a southerly direction. He hired a small fishing boat and followed her out under sail and was able to see her backtrack a few hours later with a nor'west heading into the Atlantic. She had no cargo I am aware of, so I can hazard a guess there was no financial gain to be made from a crossing, which means it was clearly a ruse. As we know it is the young Dopp's wish to head north … my guess is she is moored off shore, north of port somewhere, awaiting her captain and his passengers."

Smitherim looked at the man, and one side of his mouth curled up in a smirk. "Nothing gets by you, Rothstein."

"Only that which has little value, Smitherim … only that of little value." The young lawyer stood and put his hat on. "I bid you good night and good hunting. May no one fall victim to injury this night, unless it serves the well-being of Savannah and her survival. Gentlemen." Rothstein slipped out the back door and closed it very quietly behind him.

Smitherim and his men wasted no time and headed directly to the livery, where it was thought transportation had been hired for the refugees. To learn of a possible destination was his wish, but the man at the livery knew nothing more than that the wagon and carriage had been hired for the evening, as some distance might be involved. When Smitherim put that together with Rothstein's guess that the *Southern Belle* was likely moored to the north of port, he knew where they were going.

There were two possible places to meet boats to take them to the *Belle* that were a not a great distance from Savannah. The northernmost road went to an abandoned warehouse, and the other led to a small enclave of clam and crab fishermen. He placed himself in Harding's shoes and put his money on the abandoned warehouse, a location with no eyes or ears. If they were indeed heading there, Smitherim could prepare a welcoming party downstream, and for the right price there might even be enough vessels to effectively blockade the river.

Time was of the essence. Two wagons full of armed men were quickly assembled and Smitherim led the way in his buggy. Now that he had drawn the German girl's blood, it was only fitting he should be granted the kill for the indignity she had inflicted on him, and it would all happen outside of town. Money could buy silence, and if not, the world would surely not miss the stench of a few fishermen.

***

As Harding's coach rounded a corner it slowed for an area of marsh that occasionally ran across the road at high tide, which meant that even at low tide passage could be precarious and muddy.

The estuarine area of the Savannah River was peppered with low-lying terrain with elevations that ran a few feet above or below tidal norms. The old warehouse that was to be their rendezvous point had been, at one time, a going concern, but a few years of unusually high tides had made commercial use of the building an unreliable proposition. The rotting wooden structure was surrounded by marsh and mudflats and was accessible only by one dirt road and the river.

The horses dug in as wheels sank into muck halfway to their hubs before hitting gravel and pulling back onto hard dirt some twenty yards later. A square black building rose ominously out of the marsh grasses ahead. The carriage and wagon approached, stopping short at Harding's signal to the driver.

"Ferguson, you're with me. I think we'll go on foot from here so as to arrive a little more unannounced, for safety's sake. Atkins and Matheson, you stay here with Matthias and the women, and keep your wits about you. If all is well we'll signal you to come forward. If you should hear gunfire or the like, make your way north to Charleston. The *Belle* has been instructed to harbour there if we don't show up by morning."

Harding and Ferguson, pistols in hand, headed down the road. An unnerving quiet fell as they approached the old warehouse, making them suddenly aware of the sound of their own boots. Harding entered the front door, where he had stood some years before when taking charge of a large shipment of cotton. The door to the office was hanging off one hinge, and long counters where bartering and inspections of materials had taken place were covered in the dust and refuse of time. That such a rundown place had once been a part of his life made him feel old. He was staring into a piece of his world that had withered and died.

Ferguson followed as they quietly headed down the stairs at the back of the building towards the loading dock. When the men reached the bottom, they cautiously looked out in all directions before stepping into the open. The only sound was the river rippling around the pier pilings, and there were no boats in sight.

"Surely they would have waited longer," Harding huffed quietly.

"Hmmm." Ferguson signalled caution as he pointed at two lines wrapped on dock hooks that disappeared into the water. The lines were tensed, as though some kind of weight was on the other end. He quietly walked along the dock, untied the tether, and pulled. There was some resistance, so he hauled harder until the line gave way and a man popped up, catching Ferguson totally off guard with the barrel of a pistol pointing in his direction. The man stood in the bow of a boat and heard Harding's gun cock. Ferguson signalled the Captain to hold fire as he squinted at the man facing him.

"If you're gonnie shoot me, Jack, y'ud better be quick about it or I'll kick ye in the bollocks and take that shakin' pistol out yer petrified wee hand," Ferguson said calmly.

"Sorry, sir. I didn't realize it was you in the dark. Would that be you there, Cap'n?" the man asked, turning to Harding.

Harding knew the voice as that of one of his trusted crewmen, and sighed.

"Aye, Jack Brown, it's me. If you aren't going to kill us, could we persuade you to take us to the *Belle*?"

Jack was a man of average height and average seafaring talents; he was, in fact, average in every way, with the exception of a wager-winning capacity for ale. The two boats came the rest of the way out from under the dock, and more men jumped up to secure the boat topside. Ferguson ran back to signal the carriage and wagon, which quickly pulled up to the warehouse. Jack produced a lantern from one of the boats and the oarsmen stowed trunks and belongings and sat at the ready.

After Matthias had paid the drivers and sent them on their way, he ran down to the dock and climbed into the second boat. He and Anna sat towards the bow with their trunk at their feet, two sturdy-looking oarsmen midship, and Atkins on the tiller. The boats pulled out into the Savannah River and headed downstream. It would be a good thirty minutes before they would see the lights of the *Southern Belle* moored off shore.

A warm breeze blew in from the ocean and the water began to churn brackish with the influx of salt-water on a forceful incoming tide. Matthias had his arm around Anna and gave a deep sigh of relief, having once more escaped the madness of humankind. Harding began to relax with the faint whiff of sea air in his lungs. The plan appeared to be running perfectly, until he squinted at a line of shadows that crossed the river ahead.

"Crab fishermen," Jack surmised dismissively.

"Not that far upstream!" Ferguson said, turning to face the line of boats that crossed their path. A flash of light popped and something whizzed by Harding's ear, thumping into Jack's shoulder and causing him to wince in pain.

"Sure as I am about nothin' else, I am shot!"

28

LESSONS IN LOVE

Toronto, 2000

Never was there a child so anticipated as that of Shaun and Jordan Bishop. The pregnancy was uneventful, apart from wall-to-wall delight. Both Myra Blum and Vera Bishop were like excited schoolgirls, and Jordan's mother, Ella, joyfully joined what Shaun called "the sorority." They shopped for baby things, they each held baby showers, and by the time the nine months had flown by it was as though they had always been family. Jordan had no idea of the connection with Myra Blum other than a suspicion that Myra and Vera might be lesbians, which made Shaun laugh.

Danny loved the richness of this new, complex family: the mother of the soul, the mother of the body, the husband, the wife, the wife's mother and father, and the grandchild of three women. Of course, with such an overwhelming sisterhood the baby had to be a girl. And so at three in the morning on a balmy spring day, a gorgeous little girl was born into a complete mayhem of love.

Shaun Bishop was gobsmacked by the event. As a doctor, he had expected that his medical training and pragmatism might dull some of the shine. As Danny, a soul who had travelled elsewhere and back and who loved two women, he had expected that the event might feel less important to him than to the other first-time fathers he had observed over the years. But the appearance of this little soul he had helped create reduced him to mush, and he found a huge place in his heart that he had never known existed. Once again, the power of the physical universe had been underestimated. Any thoughts he had had of how the birth would affect him were simply ground under foot by the reality of it. The imagining of something in advance had once more been reduced to a meaningless dance.

He wept when he was handed his daughter. He wept on the shoulders of the sorority in the waiting room. He wept at the sight of Jordan holding her baby. Though he sensed the differences in everyone's experience of the event, he was in awe of the exquisite bond this child had created amongst them all. Bringing little Shari Bishop home was a happy day for the young parents, although Jordan seemed a little unsteady on her feet. Shaun was concerned but chalked it up to exhaustion from childbirth. There was a celebratory dinner that night, and the condo came alive with the wonderful noise of family.

Shaun Bishop was smitten with his wife, a truly generous spirit who simply glowed with motherhood. There were roots forming in the relationship that pushed any traces of Ali in Danny's mind to the background. One love was eclipsing another. Happiness ruled in the life of Shaun and Jordan Bishop, and within a couple of weeks of being home Jordan had begun working out again, determined to be as fit and trim as she had been before the baby.

The new mother was beginning to drop things, however—baby powder, dishes, and even the coffeepot on one occasion. Shaun might have chalked such episodes up to Jordan's fatigue turning her into a bit of a klutz, but there was more. He noticed that her workouts weren't lasting very long, that she would quickly be overcome with exhaustion. What was initially weakness in one arm moved to the leg on the same side. By the time Shari Bishop was six months old, Jordan had very little strength at all in her hands, and her speech was beginning to slur. With serious concerns about where her symptoms were leading, Shaun was finally able to get her to agree to an appointment with a neurologist he had gone to school with.

Shaun was sitting in the waiting room with Shari, proudly showing his little girl to any one who even glanced his way, when his colleague, Dr. Beth Wilson, came out to get him. She was a lanky redhead with a bit of a nerdy disposition that reminded him vaguely of Alison. She didn't speak until they had rejoined Jordan in the examination room and the door was shut. Then she looked at them both with a rather long face.

"Well, Beth? Spit it out," Shaun said with a clinical tone that attempted to cover his dread.

"We need to do a full workup. I want X-rays, blood work, an EEG, CAT scan, and lumbar puncture."

"What are you looking for, Doctor?" Jordan asked quietly. "And please understand, I'm the sort of person who needs to know everything. I'll just pull it out of Shaun anyway, so you might as well give me my second opinion first."

Beth Wilson smiled at Jordan with a look that sent shivers up Shaun's spine.

"Okay, Jordan, but this is not cut and dried. The body is a complex organism, and sometimes symptoms can lead us in a number of directions. You are demonstrating hemiparesis, or one-sided muscle weakness. This could indicate possible neuron damage, and that could mean we are entering the domain of MS or ALS or an oddball called Guillain-Barre syndrome. Now, a lumbar puncture will show us elevated levels in proteins, but usually with these diseases an exact diagnosis needs more symptoms present, which calls for a sort of `wait and see' approach. Your reflexes probably haven't degenerated enough to analyze electrical velocities to the muscles … that's not to say this won't occur farther down the road, which is why those diseases are on the radar but not necessarily the cause.

"Another cause for what you are presenting at the moment could be pressure on your brain from a growth. Such growths are often benign and operable, but others can be more complex. I want to cover all the bases, though, and if we are looking for a brain tumour we have to investigate if the brain is a primary site or if it is a metastatic tumour, which means the cells have travelled from another location in the body. Let's reconvene after this battery of tests."

Jordan looked at her baby and her eyes welled up with tears. Dr. Wilson excused herself to tend to other patients after explaining that her assistant would provide the requisitions for all of the tests. Shaun and Jordan sat in silence watching Shari. The wide-eyed new life looked back at them both and grinned. Jordan reached for her and held her to her chest.

Shaun cancelled all his appointments and spent the rest of the day with Jordan and Shari. They agreed to save everyone discomfort by keeping the news to themselves, at least until they knew for certain what they were dealing with, but when Jordan's mother called, Jordan burst into tears on the phone, and within the hour her mother was sitting in the living room, joining the perfect family in a fearful silence while staring at the baby.

On test days the three grandmothers arrived to make breakfast and remained to look after Shari. Shaun made himself available to be with Jordan through all of the procedures. They tried to remain as optimistic as possible, which meant ruling out the more fatal options like ALS or an inoperable tumour. Shaun didn't want to intervene with any of the results and decided to wait until Beth Wilson was ready to put all of the cards on the table. She had promised to expedite the process as much as possible, and so one week, one excruciatingly long week later, they sat waiting for her in her office.

Beth Wilson came in and took a deep breath. "Okay, folks, here's where we are. All of the X-rays showed nothing, which means there are no tumours showing in legs or abdomen. The scan, on the other hand, shows a mass in the brain with no clear boundaries. The lack of clear boundaries suggests a high-grade astrocytoma or a glioblastome multiforme. Jordan, these are hard to remove because they're, well, frankly, they have a complex reach in all directions and places we can't see. This type of tumour is heterogeneous, which means it has a mixture of cell types. One treatment or another might hit some of the cells and not touch others. Shaun, we're now into your field, so you might best explain the options." Beth looked at Shaun, who seemed unable to speak for a moment.

"I will need to see the scans," he muttered. Beth was ready and handed him the envelope. He pulled the images out and studied them from every angle, then studied them again. Finally he looked at Jordan, who searched his face for the slightest hint of a positive sign.

"These scans suck, Jord. There are a couple of options — try chemo and radiation to see how we can reduce this thing before thinking about any invasive procedures like surgery, or surgically remove what we can, then blast blindly with chemo and radiation."

"Can we beat this thing?" Jordan asked firmly.

Shaun looked despondent, and Beth knew it was up to her to be the bad cop.

"With glioblastome multiforme, the average life expectancy is around two to five years. Now, if we are wrong and it's a lower-grade astrocytoma, maybe more."

The drive home was silent. Jordan's mind jumped in every direction, from how many years she would have to see Shari grow to intense anger at being so unfairly robbed. Finally frustration burst out with a visceral shriek of anger, "WHY ME?"

Of course there was no answer to that question, and she wasn't expecting one.

The three grandmothers had put Shari down for her morning nap and were waiting quietly in the living room when Jordan and Shaun came through the door. Jordan looked at her mother and was reduced to a little girl.

"Oh, Mummy," she bleated.

Her mother ran to her and held her in her arms, both inconsolable in the unspeakable. Vera Bishop nudged Myra and the two women went to the kitchen, where Vera put the kettle on. Shaun went through and stared at Shari. The only sounds in the condo were of poor attempts at containing tears until the kettle boiled. Vera made a big pot of tea and got the biscuits. Myra pulled out the mugs while Vera put the place mats down and set the table. The sound of the kettle boiling had somehow called a family meeting to order, and one at a time everyone drifted to the meeting place and sat down. Vera poured and Myra did the sugars and milk, knowing everyone's preferences. Once mugs were in hands, it was Jordan who spoke first.

"All right, so I may have as little as a couple of years, or maybe five. I will not have you looking at me with huge, teary eyes for the rest of my pathetically short life. Right now I'm angry and feeling pretty ripped off, but if I only have a short period of time it has to be the best we can make of it. So until I'm officially saying goodbye to you all, I refuse to see a house of sadness surrounding my daughter. First off, I don't think I want to see anyone here for at least a week, or until I say so. I need some time to myself with my husband and child to feel this territory out."

Shaun looked at Jordan and grabbed her hand. She pulled it away and grabbed his hand with her strong hand, squeezing hard, as though she was barely hanging on to her sanity. Vera signalled the sorority and they got their coats and slipped out the door after hugs and kisses all round.

Jordan and Shaun sat in silence for a good hour before Jordan stood.

"Look in on Shari. There's some breast milk in the fridge if she gets hungry. I'd like to be alone in the bedroom, if you don't mind."

Shaun nodded acceptance, and Jordan went down the hall, quietly closing the door behind her. Once inside, Jordan lay down on the bed and began to cry. She cried until she couldn't cry any more, then she waited for the energy to start all over again.

Shaun heard Shari stirring in the nursery on the Fisher Price monitor and went in to change her and bring her into the living room. He played quietly with her and began to cry at one point, but Shari looked so upset he made an effort not to give in to such dark forces in her presence. He heated up some of Jordan's breast milk as instructed and the kid soon gurgled away on the bottle, breathing noisily through her nose while sucking contentedly. Shaun's thoughts ran the road ahead, which scared the hell out of him, so he pulled back to mindless reminiscences of his old life. Life as a lame lounge lizard had been a lot easier than this, he thought. He longed for it, until he quickly hit the shallow bottom of who he used to be. He had never really loved before Alison, and now he was completely in love with another woman who had carried his child. His love for her had a power he had never known, imbued with the biological success of procreation. His body and soul hummed in synchronicity.

The day passed by at a surreal pace, with every minute feeling like an hour. Shari slept in his arms as he watched the news quietly, until he realized they weren't alone. He looked up and Jordan, eyes red with grief, stood at the end of the hallway, staring lovingly at her husband and child. She joined her little family on the couch and lay down with her head on Shaun's lap. Shaun placed the baby on her chest and they held on to that moment of perfection until the baby needed another feeding. Jordan sat up and the little one latched onto her breast. Shaun put his arm around her and they savoured another little moment of perfection. It became obvious to them that this was what lay ahead—a struggle against time with little oases, precious moments of normalcy savoured like never before, glimpses of a life that was to be stolen.

It was five days later when the sorority was invited for dinner, along with Jordan's father, who fought back tears all night. At the end of that week the rest of the lab work had come through and shown the presence of malignant cells, and now the diagnosis was confirmed beyond a shadow of a doubt. Jordan began collecting and storing breast milk, because breastfeeding was a no-no once chemotherapy began. Regular formula was being slipped into the works and the baby got used to it as well, not seeming to care so long as something warm and sweet came her way, which was upsetting to Jordan … already her child didn't really need her.

Shaun managed a few days a week at his practice and became overwhelmed by the impending deaths of patients that surrounded him. He realized how invested in hope he had been — hope that a treatment would be successful, hope that a few more days of meaningful existence might be gained for patients who fought hard for life. He would come home and notice Jordan getting sicker from the chemo sessions, and at the end of the first round Jordan announced she was done. The moments she had managed to savour were ruined with nausea. She agreed to one round of radiation, which didn't appear to have much effect, and so, at her insistence, all forms of treatment were stopped. Within a month she was feeling reasonably well again and was thrilled to be having little snapshots of joy with her husband and daughter. The sorority was always on call, and the apartment was a noisy place of life that filled her soul day to day.

Life was good for six months, until the morning Shaun got up quietly with the baby to let Jordan sleep in. When he was about to leave for work he went in to awaken his wife and she didn't respond. She was breathing but comatose. An ambulance arrived and she was taken to the hospital, where new scans showed the voracious tumour was taking over. Within a week her breathing became laboured, and the attending physician recommended a respirator. Jordan's wishes, witnessed and signed by a lawyer, nixed such extraordinary means.

Shaun and the sorority were gathered at the bed when Jordan's eyes sprang open. Any promise the tease of her open eyes held was instantly ripped away as her body became unusually still. Ella, with her granddaughter in one arm, held her daughter's wrist as the pulse disappeared. The chain was broken, her Jordan was now adrift somewhere.

Vera looked up and said her goodbyes. "You go on ahead, child," she began softly. "You go on ahead, we won't be long."

Myra was overcome and sat, stunned, on a chair, while Jordan's father looked as though he was about to faint, and Shaun quickly slid a chair under the man before he went down. A doctor came in, knowing they were at the end of the road, checked Jordan's vitals, then disconnected her from the heart monitor and IV. He looked at his colleague and said nothing, but gave Shaun's shoulder a sympathetic squeeze as he left the room and closed the door.

Shaun's chest ripped apart in anguish as he leaned over and kissed Jordan tenderly for the last time, tears flooding his eyes. When he rose, Ella handed him the baby and let loose. Myra and Vera went to her, and they all held on to one another and wailed. Jordan's dad sat silently on the chair, in shock.

The family reconvened at the apartment dining-room table later that day. Vera brought out the tea. Myra put the place mats down, while Ella went to the cupboard for a bag of Peek Freans assorted. Jordan's father sat on the couch; his expression hadn't changed and wouldn't for days. Danny put Shari in the highchair and sat quietly with the sorority, staring at Jordan's creation, her precious gift to the world, who in turn looked back at the faces of her sombre audience with a grin that revealed one bottom tooth coming in.

29

WHERE HEARTS LEAD

Savannah, Georgia, 1848

Jack Brown fell back into the boat as blood oozed from his biceps.

"Everyone get down, stay low!" Harding barked. He looked up and down river, getting his bearings, then yelled at Ferguson, who held the tiller.

"Ferguson, steer to the north side. If I'm not mistaken there should be a channel into the salt marsh before we hit Smitherim's blockade!" Harding then looked back to the second boat, where everyone was already lying low.

"Atkins, follow us into the salt marsh!" Atkins pulled on the rudder and instructed the oarsmen to put their backs into it.

In the distance they heard Smitherim yelling at his men. "After them — they're heading to shore!" With that, the blockade lines were dropped and three rowboats pulled away from the crab boats and headed upstream towards Harding. It looked at first as though the two sides were on a collision course until Harding's boats abruptly disappeared into some bushes that disguised the entrance to a small channel off the river. Smitherim fired a few rounds blindly in frustration but the lead only thudded into mud.

Once in the channel Harding tried to remember the maze that was the salt marsh. The channel drifted northeast amongst clumps of marsh grasses and revealed a labyrinth of small waterways, most of which dead-ended into more clumps of marsh grass. He had played there as a child, venturing in like an explorer with a couple of pals in an old, leaky punt they had found on the opposite shore. With an inordinate amount of tar, that punt had managed to stay ahead of the leaks long enough to become a battleship for a crew of three imaginative lads, one of whom always presumptuously assumed the role of captain. The channel did eventually make its way out to the sea, but memory and the constant change of the salt marsh were conspiring against Harding at that moment.

Smitherim's boat had four oarsmen and quickly passed the other two boats, closing the distance to Harding at an alarming rate. Harding knew he was in trouble and decided to turn into the first side channel for no other reason than to take them out of Smitherim's line of fire. His mind was racing for some plan of action when he spotted the lamp in the bow, full of kerosene and promise.

"Pass me that lantern, Jack."

"Aye, Cap'n."

"Do you have any lucifers left?"

Jack reached behind him for a jar and handed it to Harding.

"Pull into the reeds, Ferguson. Atkins, get your boat behind us … and stay low. Elizabeth, you get into the other boat. How many pistols have we?"

"I have one, Cap'n, but I fear my firing hand is no use, and there is one more in the other boat," Jack replied.

"Right, hand me your gun and get in the boat with the women," Harding ordered. He looked at the two oarsmen in his boat. "Which one of you is the best shot?"

"That would be Blake," one of the oarsmen answered, tipping his head at the man beside him as they hit the reeds and a mound of grassy soil. Blake, a quiet sort wearing a red headscarf, swivelled his expansive shoulders and nodded in agreement with his colleague.

Harding handed Jack's gun to Blake. Atkins passed the other pistol to Ferguson as he pulled alongside, where Elizabeth and then Jack were assisted from one boat to the other. Atkins reached back and pulled one of his knives from its sheath to have it at the ready.

"All right, everyone down low. Blake, Ferguson, no one fires unless I say so. We have only three shots amongst us and they had better be well used."

"Turn left ahead. I hear them!" Smitherim's voice rang out from the main channel. A minute later the prow of his boat rounded the corner and headed directly towards the stern of Harding's boat.

"There they are!" Smitherim screamed.

Harding struck the lucifer and lit the lamp, and before Smitherim could get a shot off Harding threw the lamp into the air and it smashed on the floor of Smitherim's boat, sending kerosene and shards of glass everywhere. Lit kerosene soaked Smitherim's trousers and the fabric soon caught fire. One of his oarsmen got a good dose of it on his shoulder and jumped overboard. Kerosene trickled under seats and alighted under the feet of the other oarsmen, who quickly followed their comrade into the water. Smitherim's coat caught, and it was clear he was reluctant to enter the water. He yelled at one of his men.

"Help me! I can't swim!"

With that, Smitherim reluctantly jumped over the side of the boat and landed feet first in the water. He hit bottom and his boots, laced tight, sank into deep mud. He tried to kick himself to the surface but the muddy bottom sucked hard. He flailed his arms and thrashed in the water, his nose barely breaking the surface.

"I'm stuck. I'm stuck! I'm drowning! HELP!" Smitherim wailed, coughing up muddy water. The more he thrashed, the deeper his feet sank, and his head began to drop beneath the surface. Two of his men swam to him and tried to pull, but Smitherim was so panicked that he hauled one of them under. The man surfaced a few feet away, coughing and gasping for air.

Harding realized his opportunity and gave the order.

"Quickly, pull out into the main channel and hurry before the other boats get here!"

Oars hit water and in moments they were back in the main channel pulling southward. Harding was wracking his memory for the channel that led to the sea when another fork appeared that looked as though it headed back to the river.

"Take the right fork, Ferguson!"

The two boats disappeared from the main channel as the rest of Smitherim's boats rounded the corner from the river towards the fire. By the time they arrived at the scene, Smitherim's men were clawing their way out of the water onto wet mounds of marsh grass. One of the men, while pulling leeches from his arm, pointed in the direction of bubbles emerging from the sediments below.

"He's in the middle there! The man nearly killed us all! He can't swim!"

The lead boat pulled alongside fine wisps of reddish hair floating on the surface, like an exotic sea grass rooted inches below in the pale orb that was the top of Smitherim's head. They hauled on him repeatedly until the muck of the marsh bottom released its prey in a foul pool of stinking bottom rot. Smitherim's eyes bulged and his face was made even more hideous by hungry leeches gorging themselves on his cheeks and neck. His body was pulled on board, but as there were no signs of life his face was covered with a coat, leaving the leeches to their feast.

"What should we do now?" one of the leaders in the second boat yelled.

"We know they're heading to the sea, if they can ever get out of the marsh. Let's get back on the river," a well-dressed man from the first boat instructed. With that, the men from shore were loaded on and paddles pulled until the boats were back on the river heading towards what had been the blockade.

Harding found the way back on to the Savannah River a few hundred yards downstream from the blockade of crab boats, only to be immediately spotted by one of the crab fishermen, who happened to be facing downstream, urinating.

"They're downriver!" he screamed.

Smitherim's men rowed hard to one of the crab boats, where they frantically unloaded his body and all extraneous personnel before hitting the river in pursuit.

The welcome lights of the *Southern Belle* flickered in the distance as Elizabeth tended to Jack's wound with bits of her petticoat that she had shredded to form a tourniquet, and when they finally hit the edge of the sea she reached down and soaked some cloth in the cleaner brine to rinse the wound.

A lookout on the aft-deck of the *Belle* alerted the crew that two rowboats were heading their way, pursued by two more boats that appeared to be closing the gap. The ship's gun had been prepared as a precaution. It flashed, then roared a split second later. Harding heard the ball whiz overhead and turned to see it land square in front of the lead boat some hundred and fifty yards behind them. The cannon was an antique but it made for good theatre, which was accentuated by a round of pistol fire into the air from the decks of the *Belle*. It was a grand display of what those who followed could expect should they desire to get any closer.

In truth, it was all they could expect, because Harding knew it was, very likely, the last of the *Belle*'s meagre supply of ammunition. The safety of those under his charge worried him deeply.

"Well, no doubt that's the last of the powder on board. Let's hope that sabre rattle did the job," Ferguson commented.

Elizabeth looked up from tending to Jack. "They've stopped rowing, John. It looks as though they're talking amongst themselves, boat to boat."

Minutes later they rounded the bow of the *Belle* and pulled up on the starboard side, out of sight from shore. Smitherim's men were still arguing as they turned their boats around, afraid of another volley from the *Belle*. Passengers aboard and boats stowed, the sails went up on the *Southern Belle* and she caught some wind that slowly pulled her away. Harding stood on deck and watched Smitherim's boats disappear up the Savannah River before he finally took a deep breath and relaxed.

Elizabeth had gone below decks immediately with Jack, where Brewster, the ship's cook, who also happened to be the chief of medical services, looked the patient over.

"I see you've slowed the bleeding with a tourniquet, mum," he said politely to his captain's wife.

Atkins and Blake, following Brewster's instructions, laid Jack on a rough-hewn wooden table. Brewster handed his crewmate a chunk of leather strapping and a mug of rum. Jack knew the drill and took a good couple of slugs of the rum before putting the strap in his mouth and biting down hard. He gave Brewster the signal he was ready and Brewster began to dig into Jack's arm with the end of a knife, causing him to screech through his gritted teeth. Elizabeth, ever the sympathetic caregiver, stood by, wiping his head down with a cool cloth and softly assuring him that everything was going to be all right. Brewster explored deep into the flesh and finally grabbed onto the tip of some lead shot with the end of his knife, wiggled it up, and pulled it the rest of the way out with a pair of pliers.

"There we go, Jack me boy," he said proudly, presenting the fruits of his surgery to his patient, who was out cold. *Just as well*, Brewster thought, as he washed the wound down with more rum. "How are you with a needle and thread, mum?" he asked the Captain's wife.

"I've only stitched a wound once before," Elizabeth answered, clearly not wanting the job.

"Once more than me, but no need to worry, mum. Matheson's a good sail man. If he can hold canvas together, ol' Jack's hide should be a cakewalk."

Elizabeth sensed her job was done and knew she needed air badly before her nausea overwhelmed her. She ran on deck and breathed deeply a few times before heading to her husband, whom she saw standing near the stern. He was gazing at the heavens alongside Matthias and Anna. Light cloud cover drifted off, revealing an explosion of stars that filled an exceptionally clear night sky.

"How's Jack?" Harding inquired as his wife approached.

"The bullet is out and Matheson has been commandeered to stitch the wound. I think he'll be fine, but a proper doctor should see him," Elizabeth replied, snuggling in close to her husband.

"We can pull into Charleston if need be, but it'll have to be a short stopover," Harding said thoughtfully as he put his arm around his wife and held her tightly.

She looked up at her good man with a smile that quickly dropped when she saw the expression on his face.

"What is it, John? What troubles you?"

"They were waiting for us," he stated pensively.

"You must be reading my mind," Matthias interjected. "I was just thinking that someone had to have tipped Smitherim off. Did you say anything to the Pastor?"

"The only people who knew anything of our departure from the old warehouse were a few members of my crew … and me. Think of it, Matthias, I never even told you or Anna of the escape route."

"Do you think someone might have seen the *Belle* pull out and put two and two together?" Matthias returned.

"The *Belle* ran a decoy southerly course for anyone who watched her reach the sea. She didn't head north until she was well out of sight. So how, then, did they know we were going north? Who knew of those plans? Whoever knew you were heading north might have been interested enough, for whatever reasons, to be watching the *Belle*," the Captain continued.

"Well, the four of us knew that our destination is Montreal, and of course my aunt and uncle, who gave me contacts there. And that could mean any number of their friends at the synagogue and then … Rothstein." Matthias's voice tapered off.

"You said that name rather ominously," Harding commented.

"Well, Rothstein's family was hurt financially by my father. I thought that was behind us but … maybe not. He is a well-to-do lawyer, and you don't get that kind of wealth unless you're plugged into wealth, which in Savannah …"

"… means the plantation owners." Harding finished the sentence.

Matthias dug for more stones to turn over as to Rothstein's motivation. "He's also in charge of a good chunk of my resources and is selling the house in order to get my deposit back. If anything happened to me he would have no one to answer to with regard to my business affairs, in which he is well entangled. No one else knows."

"Sounds to me as though you need a new lawyer, one with a good deal more accountability," Harding worried. "You might consider a few corrective options before we hit Charleston tomorrow."

They all stood on deck for another hour, talking into the night about what lay ahead in the northern town of Montreal. Harding had an acquaintance with a dredging business there. The town was becoming more of an active port, and to that end over a thousand feet of wharf had been created. The dredging business was working round the clock to allow some of the new big steamships to dock.

Elizabeth was a southern girl and fretted over horror stories she had heard about the snow and cold of a Montreal winter. Fortunately there would there be a Meeting House there, where she could worship with other Quakers. The reassurance of her faith and being by her Captain's side would she tought would surely sustain her. Creating a new life in a new city held a measure of excitement, and her passion for the plight of slaves could be put to good use. Montreal, for both Elizabeth and Anna, was, after all, a place where slaves went to be free, a major terminus for the Underground Railroad. Compassion for fellow beings would continue to give Elizabeth a sense of purpose that would hopefully counter whatever a northern winter might throw at them.

Anna further reassured her friend that with Matthias's relatives in Montreal they would not be alone in a strange land. Matthias looked at Elizabeth Harding's expression of worry and spoke with reassurance.

"Elizabeth, you and the Captain mean the world to Anna and me. We are family. We can take care of one another, wherever the wind may take us." Elizabeth looked deeply into the eyes of the young man and woman and there was no denying her feelings for them. Matthias's words welled inside her and she reached over and kissed him on the cheek, and then held Anna.

"I love you both as my own."

The shared love of friends seemed a wonderful way to end the evening, and the Captain, not wishing to appear to emotional in front of others, bade everyone a good night.

Before turning in, Harding and Elizabeth looked in on Jack in the crew quarters. He had come around and was well into the rum to dull the pain. Matheson had done a tidy job with the stitching and the bleeding appeared to be subsiding. Jack looked up at Elizabeth from his bunk and nodded a grateful smile.

It was the middle of the night when Ferguson knocked on the Captain's door. The Captain was already awake, attempting to comfort Elizabeth, who was violently ill from motion sickness. The seas were kicking up and Ferguson needed a consultation with his captain. Harding dressed and went out on deck with his trusted first mate.

"Any idea where we are?" Harding inquired.

"I reckon we're just south of Port Royal Sound, Captain."

"What say we tuck around the corner of Parris Island and sit this dance out," Harding replied.

"My thoughts exactly, Captain. It looks like there's something pretty serious brewing."

Ferguson went to the helmsman and plotted the new course. The coast was still in sight as the night remained partially clear, although a serious black void in the sky was moving up from the south, devouring every star in its path.

Matthias came out on board and walked carefully over to Harding. He hung onto anything in reach to steady himself as the ship rolled in every direction, struggling with both wind and sea.

"What's up, Captain?"

"We're heading to the leeward side of Parris Island to sit this storm out. Would you inform Anna that Elizabeth is ill, and ask that she might look in on her? I wish to work with my crew until we are out of the worst of this. Getting into the sound can be a little tricky with fickle winds like these. There's a strong offshore that's fighting something even bigger from the south. Until we have a clear winner in that battle, we have to keep on our toes."

Anna was alerted and she spent the rest of the night with Elizabeth, who was a worse sailor than Anna, a fact that Anna found hard to believe. Matthias went back to his cabin and managed, in between the severe movements of the ship, to begin a letter of concern to his Aunt Esther. He now worried for the cargo of the *Branden*, which still had not made it to port, as well as the rather sizeable deposit on the house he had agreed to purchase in Savannah. It was time to have someone looking over the shoulder of Rothstein, as Harding had so rightly suggested. "Accountability" was the watchword, and Matthias reckoned that his Aunt Esther and Uncle Schmul would be his best defence. The Heinyl family was so connected at the synagogue that Matthias estimated half the Jewish community of Savannah would be watching the dealings of Mr. Rothstein by the time they were done.

Matthias had a copy of the ship's manifest, detailing the cargo, that he could enclose. He also included the financial details involving the house and every pertinent detail of his business arrangements with Rothstein. The letter asked his aunt and her dear husband to intervene as a family, and pursuant to that request he wrote a separate letter appointing Mr. and Mrs. Heinyl his business partners.

The calmer waters of Port Royal Sound soon made writing easier and Matthias finished final drafts of all his correspondence. Daylight was straining through the clouds, trying to officially declare morning, when Matthias ventured out on deck. Harding was eyeing his surroundings through the glass of his telescope.

"Captain Harding, I have a favour to ask of you, if you would be so kind."

"Name it," Harding answered, focused on the coastline.

"I wonder if there is a town of some consequence nearby where I might have some correspondence delivered to Savannah."

"Does this have anything to do with our friend Mr. Rothstein?"

"Yes, I think I know how we might make an honest man of him regarding the business that concerns us both."

Harding looked at Matthias and smiled. "You don't waste any time, do you? I was getting ready to drop sail but we could dock at Port Royal in a couple of hours. I have no doubt you could find someone to deliver your correspondence from there as supply ships do a Port Royal to Savannah round trip on a regular basis … and …"

"What is it?" Matthias inquired.

"Well, we can have Jack looked at. We might as well lay over there to sit out the storm. I think we'd be fine for a couple of days before any word of us might reach Savannah, should Smitherim's bunch still be after us."

Harding informed Ferguson of the course change and a few hours later they moored at Port Royal. Rooms were found on shore as Elizabeth clearly needed the stability of land. Crew members took turns on watch while others enjoyed the camaraderie of other crews in the pubs.

There was indeed a ship leaving for Savannah, and Matthias's correspondence was placed in the hands of her captain, a man of good reputation under whom some of the *Belle*'s crew had sailed.

The storm passed quickly, moving out into the Atlantic steered by prevailing westerlies, and on the sunny morning of the second day the *Belle* set sail once more. Jack insisted on finishing his recovery on the *Belle* after the doctor in Port Royal assured him that his wound should not prove any trouble if it was kept clean, and so he found his way back to the ship and sought permission to board, which Harding granted with a grin moments before the sails were hoisted.

The *Belle* was back out on the ocean with favourable winds, winds that would take the Dopps and the Hardings to their new life in Montreal

30

FALLOUT

Toronto, 2003

The next couple of years were a slow climb for Shaun and the sorority, of which Shari had become a full-time member. The three grandmothers delighted in sharing responsibilities as Shaun opened a medical practice that became increasingly demanding. Jordan's father went about his work but never spoke of his daughter, as though such talk would open up the doors of Hell. Professional ambitions aside, little Shari was the light in her father's eyes. Breakfast, most dinners, and weekends were sacrosanct as he sought to balance his passion for medicine with his devotion to his daughter.

It was a normal patient day at his practice, with a mix of good and bad news to work around, and Shaun was scanning a file in his office when he heard a familiar voice talking to the receptionist.

"Could you tell Dr. Bishop that an old friend, Jennifer Glessing, is here on personal business?" Jennifer's voice sliced into his consciousness like a scalpel. Shaun dropped the file on his desk and looked out into the reception area. She looked as cosmetically sound as ever, though somewhat heavier … but her face revealed a darkness he had never seen before.

"It's okay." Shaun nodded to his receptionist. "Jennifer, please come in."

Jennifer turned to Shaun, attempting a smile as she entered the cluttered inner sanctum. It reminded her a bit of her old office as Alison Truman at the university. No attention to interior décor or tidiness, just a blind passion for the work that placed appearances low down on the list of things to fret about.

Shaun closed the door and they faced one another for the first time in years. They studied each other's faces, she looking for traces of Danny and he for any sign of Alison.

"How are you, Ali? How is your life going?" Danny began.

"It's so good to hear someone call me Ali again," she replied as she turned and sat down on the chair facing his desk. Danny went along with the apparent rules of engagement and went to his high-backed leather chair and stared at her over the piles of paperwork and files on his desk.

"I hope this isn't a professional visit?"

"No, Danny, I don't have a cancer … well, that I know about, anyway." She looked at the pictures on the desk and around the room. There were shots of Jordan and Shaun and the baby, single shots of the baby with three different older women. She recognized Myra and Mrs. Bishop and rightly assumed the other woman to be Jordan's mother. Her eyes were drawn to an endearing photo on the wall behind Shaun of father and daughter in profile, laughing hysterically at one another.

"She's lovely, Danny."

"She sure is, Ali." Danny swung around in his chair and smirked at the photograph and drifted in the memory of it for a moment before refocusing on Jennifer Glessing.

"And how's your Daniel doing?"

"Oh … he's a pretty wonderful little guy, although he's not so little any more. I spend most of my life driving him to one sport or another," she said, with the first hint of any happiness Dr. Bishop had seen so far.

"Danny, I was so sorry to hear about Jordan. I wanted to call more than a few times but thought it would have been intrusive."

"You were probably right. I don't think I could have stood a call from Little Miss Perfect with her perfect family, particularly after being dropped like a hot potato. I waited, Ali. I waited and waited, and when I quit waiting I began to have a wonderful life with a wonderful woman who I still love deeply." Danny realized that his words sounded a bit more venomous than he'd intended, and he regrouped. "I can't believe I just said something so nasty to you. I'm sorry. I guess you know there was some hurt."

Ali nodded stoically, accepting the lashing. "Funny stuff … the physical world." She sighed, looking down at the floor. "Certainly took me for a ride."

"And how is Brendon?" Danny asked, adopting a more reasonable tone.

"Oh he's, uh …" Jennifer's face crumpled and tears started.

Danny looked at her and felt no real sympathy until he thought of the tears as Ali's. He reached for a Kleenex and handed it to her.

"What's going on, Ali?"

"Brendon and I are separated … for about a year now. She's ten years younger and blond, and, more importantly, she's got a smaller ass than I've acquired along the way. Brendon is in love with some image he has in his mind, not a real person. After breastfeeding, he began complaining that my breasts were turning into beanbags and he wanted to send me in for a tummy tuck and a boob job. It was all so crass. I had the damn surgeries and thought we had made it through all of that stuff when out of the blue one day he says he's leaving me and he's in love with someone else … end of story. He makes a sorry attempt to see Daniel once a month or so, but for all intents and purposes the son of a bitch appears to have moved on with his life and we are now a minor footnote. I don't get it. How does someone do that?"

"I don't know, Ali, how *does* someone do that?" Danny asked with a serious expression.

"I saw that coming a mile away." Ali shook her head in disappointment.

"Ali, I'm not rubbing your nose in it, I am just as interested as you in how some people can up and walk while others can commit for life. I know that all relationships are different, and that some people just grow apart … we're different souls, from different gene pools, walking through this gauntlet we call life with an expectation of remaining together, without any training or real infrastructure apart from a few marital vows. I guess maybe the miracle is that two people can remain on a parallel course when each is broadsided by events or temptations that knock them out of alignment. But those that do stay together … what's the glue? I'm talking about people who still love each other, not the ones who stay together out of convenience or economics or complacency. Is it a dogmatic belief, like religious fanaticism but more benign? Is it about investing so heavily in the power of your love for someone that it becomes a total non-negotiable, so whatever life coughs up, it can't get through such dogmatic armour? Does there always have to be something physically attractive about the one you love that somehow exudes what you love about them? Ali, I don't have a clue how any of this is supposed to work. I do know that somehow a part of me still needs to see you the way I knew you."

"Oh, not you, too," Jennifer snapped.

"I didn't mean it like that," Danny backtracked. "I meant as Alison, not Jennifer. I guess the complicating piece in all of this is that we are all capable of loving more than one person. But of course because it is love we're talking about here, when one is still invested and the other is divested, the loser has their self-esteem pulled out from under them. I'm sorry you're having that boat of yours rocked again."

"Bernard did warn us," she sniffed.

"So what unravelled for us. What happened?"

"I dunno, I had no idea what I was doing. I was just doing it, Danny. Maybe, and I am ashamed to say this, but maybe …"

"C'mon, spit it out."

"Maybe . . . I'm more sexually attracted to white guys."

"Yikes, not what I wanted to hear. I thought there was some of that socialization and biology stuff in there somewhere. Still, it's a bit of a smack in the head. Okay, then, I have a confession to make, and it's even flimsier than what you've just said. As a musician, I was pretty much done with the blond bimbo look, and maybe that's why I found Alison Truman fresh and interesting."

"Don't sugarcoat it for me … God, Danny, what a horrid thing to say."

"No more horrid than your statement … think about it." Danny looked at Ali, who shook her head.

"We were doomed from the get-go in this world," she huffed.

"Maybe." Danny let the word hang in the air.

"What's that supposed to mean?"

"You said something to me the first time you kissed me as Jennifer. You said, `There you are.'"

"My eyes were closed, Danny, and …" Ali burst into tears.

"And what?"

"Quit cross-examining me, Daniel. I think I liked you more when you were a dumb rock 'n' roll singer instead of this annoying shrink you've become." Ali spat the words out and stood up. "I think I'd better leave, I'm not sure I can take any analysis just now."

"I understand." Danny was about to try another tack when a knock on his door caused him to look at the clock on his desk.

"Ali, I'm sorry but I've got patients to see. If you need me, here's my home phone number." Danny handed her a card from a stack of them on his desk.

Ali took the card and opened the door. A mother stood waiting in reception with a bald-headed eight-year-old child. Ali smiled at them as she made a quick exit.

Danny looked at the child, found his focus, and invited them to come in, ever so grateful that he had some good news to share with them.

The day was long, and it was a pretty exhausted Shaun Bishop who arrived home just in time to relieve grandmother Ella, who needed to get home to her sad husband. Shaun played with Shari for a few minutes then read her a story and tucked the little giggler into bed. He sang "Twinkle Twinkle Little Star" to her, as he often did, while he gently rubbed her little back. She was fast asleep in minutes, and Shaun headed through to the kitchen for the frozen dinner Ella had taken out of the fridge for him. Myra and Vera made a good supply of them every couple of weeks, so the fridge was well stocked. The sorority had decided that this was one doctor who was going to eat properly. In those last days of Jordan's life all the hospital cafeteria food had been sampled and judged "unfit for living things!"

Danny was well into some Chicken Kiev and leafing through a batch of new medical journals when the phone rang. It would be the usual, he thought, Myra and Vera wondering how his day had gone. He picked up the phone and spoke expectantly.

"Hello, Moms, the Chicken Kiev is fantastic."

There was silence on the line for a moment and then a rather distraught voice.

"When I kissed you and said, `There you are,' it was because I knew it was you and I felt totally safe because I knew you loved me," Ali sputtered.

"And you knew you loved me," Danny said dryly.

"Yes … I did," she answered softly.

"A dumb rock 'n' roll singer in a new black disguise."

"Yes … the nerd in the body of a blond bimbo loved the rock 'n' roll singer in the body of a black man."

"Interesting, Ali … so what happened?"

"I didn't call to talk about what happened. I called because I want to know what might happen."

"Can't answer that," Danny said flatly.

"Yes you can, but …"

"But what?"

"I, uh … I have to kiss you, I think."

"Ali, I'm not fucking Snow White. You're not going to wake me from some spell I'm under with a magic kiss. I have a beautiful daughter and a life."

"I'm sorry, I just … I'm sorry to have bothered you, Daniel."

The phone went dead, and Danny stood there stunned for a few seconds before hanging up. The phone rang again and he picked up.

"What now, Ali?"

"Ali?" Vera Bishop began. "Oh dear, Shaun. There's a name I haven't heard for some time. What's going on?"

"I'd rather not talk about it, if you don't mind. The Chicken Kiev is wonderful, the baby's asleep, and I have some research reading to catch up on," he said, shutting the conversation down.

"Well, I won't say a thing unless you bring it up. If you want to talk, you know our number, or come over and we'll make a pot of tea. I'll see you in the morning, son, when I drop Myra off tomorrow. It's her day with Shari. God bless."

They hung up the phones, and Shaun went to look in on his daughter. He stood there staring, then pulled up a chair and watched her short breaths through the crib bars until her gentle rhythms soothed his soul and he slumped over, asleep.

31

IN THE BLINK OF AN EYE

Montreal, Quebec
1849–1851

The *Southern Belle* stopped in the port of Halifax for fresh food and water. It was there that Harding learned the fate of the *Branden*. The captain of another vessel had heard of a Dutch ship that had lost her mainmast and most of her canvas in an Atlantic crossing. She had drifted for days before a steamer carrying lumber to England had stopped and assisted. Most of the Dutch vessel's stores had been depleted, and her crew was in rough but workable shape after a good hot meal. Supplies were provided and a large timber from the cargo hold of the steamship was used to crudely fashion a new mast. The *Branden* had enough canvas for sail and, once raised, she limped to Lunenburg on the coast of Nova Scotia for serious repairs. Word was that she would set sail for Savannah within a week.

The rest of the journey to Montreal was uneventful, other than Matthias's astonishment at the vastness of the Gulf of the St. Lawrence River, gaping like a giant mouth that attempted to devour the sea. Farther upriver, the hum of civilization became more and more obvious as ships of commerce sailed around them in all directions with increasing frequency. Black clouds rose to the heavens from a large steam-powered schooner fitted with paddlewheels that passed confidently by them, not to be seen again until the *Belle* approached the new wharf in Montreal.

The immigrants from Savannah stood on deck, taking in the place they would call home. It was certainly no "northern outpost" as imagined by Elizabeth; it was, indeed, a sophisticated city with substantial architecture rising from the earth that was being broken daily in answer to the ever-increasing population.

Once ashore, Matthias and Harding sought out Esther's son and found the name Heinyl on a large textile mill next to a granary. Günter Heinyl looked at Matthias suspiciously at first, given the family's history with Gert Dopp, but after reading his mother's letter he embraced his cousin. Günter was in the textile business with his own mill, but textiles weren't his love, merely the family business he had been thrust into, much as Matthias had.

Lodgings were found that would do until the Hardings and the Dopps got more established. Matthias accepted some contract work for the mill in Hamburg that his cousin generously threw his way, and correspondence with deposits for the same were sent via steamer to Hamburg. The *Southern Belle* worked regularly as a cargo transport along the river to Quebec and Kingston, but Harding began to eye the new steamships that passed by, with more than a passing interest.

In the first month, Matthias learned of Smitherim's death in a letter from Esther. The plantation owner's involvement in kidnapping Anna, to say nothing of his cruelty to her, had become the gossip of the town. His obsession with Anna leaked out from many sources, and Smitherim's own lust was blamed for his demise by the court of common opinion.

Dear Aunt Esther and Uncle Schmul appeared in person at Rothstein's office, where it was discovered that he had already sold the house in Savannah and recovered Matthias's deposit. This was reluctantly turned over to a new bank account opened in the name of Matthias Dopp, with the Heinyls as appointed business partners. Matthias had no doubt the glare from his aunt's eyes expedited the matter.

When the *Branden* finally made port in Savannah, the textiles were quickly marketed by Rothstein, with Esther and her husband looking over his shoulder to ensure he could get away with nothing. And indeed he proved to be quite shrewd in elevating profit levels so his percentage would add some meaningful weight to his own pocket. The furniture from the Dopp home in Hamburg, once unloaded from the *Branden*, was sent on to Montreal on a British steamship, and by the time it arrived, Matthias had found a home.

The new Dopp home was a huge stone edifice recently vacated by a wealthy merchant who had returned to Europe. Some blocks away, the Hardings had found a more humble structure, in keeping with their Quaker beliefs, and of course the road between the two dwellings was well travelled.

Roots were clearly being planted, as everyone sensed a vibrant future in the city of Montreal.

Matthias and Anna rarely spoke of Matthias's incredible journey. Anna wasn't sure if his had been a temporary madness from a fever, but whatever it had been, she believed the effect on her husband was somehow a positive one. She did eventually stop attending Catholic mass, not wishing to join in the drone of worship as she felt the religious space in her life was taken up by simply loving others to the best of her ability. Loving eventually made more sense to her than listening to a priest tell her how the one called Jesus loved hundreds of years ago. So somehow Matthias's journey had an effect on her over time — noticeable to him, deniable by her.

Mrs. Harding found the Godless couple hard to reconcile with her own beliefs, but the good Mr. and Mrs. Dopp left in their wake was undeniable, and so there was an unspoken truce.

Matthias and Anna bought an old store near the harbour, which they set up with a soup kitchen in the front and a few beds and supplies in the back. It soon became a major destination in the Underground Railroad. Elizabeth Harding worked alongside Anna with a group of like-minded volunteers, including a few former slaves who had settled in Montreal. Matthias cajoled Günter into helping him locate housing and jobs for the former plantation workers, who proved to be valuable assets in a growing city with an insatiable appetite for those not afraid of hard work.

There was a celebratory dinner when Matthias's mother's dining-room suite arrived. Günter Heinyl and his wife were guests, as were the Hardings, and during the course of the evening Captain Harding revealed that he had found a buyer for the *Southern Belle*. She would be put to work by her new owner as a supply freighter servicing some of the ports on the Great Lakes of Upper Canada. A couple of the crew would stay on board under her new captain and former first mate … Ferguson.

Harding expressed his desire to put all of his money in a partnership with Günter Heinyl and Matthias Dopp for the purchase of a brand-new steamship, which he felt sure would make them a tidy profit. A vessel of good size could be completed by spring, giving them plenty of time to round up both freight and passengers.

There was money to be made in immigration, and steam power made Atlantic crossings a far more commercially reliable endeavour. Günter jumped at the opportunity, given his keen interest in the technology, and Matthias was delighted to enter into a business venture with both of them.

Midway through that first winter, Anna found herself with child. The joy was shared with the Hardings and seemed to lift Elizabeth's spirits, which were a little low with the cold. The thought of a child to dote on would hold her until the warm breezes of spring filled the air and made the city acceptably balmy for the southerner.

A daughter, Miriam Elizabeth Dopp, was born in the late fall of 1851. Matthias looked at his love holding their child, and though he hadn't thought it possible, he was aware that he loved Anna even more in that moment. Esther made the journey to Montreal to meet her grand-niece, beside herself with joy yet feeling great sadness for the one who wasn't there — her sister, Miriam.

Matthias came home early one afternoon with an odd look on his face and asked Anna to sit down next to him in the parlour.

"A letter has come from Jorge Hacker in Hamburg. Your family has been found," he began.

Anna looked at him, knowing something was missing.

"And?"

"Your father, brother, and sister were found in the slums of Frankfurt, where your mother died of cholera over a year ago." Matthias watched Anna's face sink into sadness.

"She was such … a good woman. She fought my father the day he took me to Frau Hoffmann and took a terrible beating for it. He loved us, but he was such a miserable drunk. If there is a Hell, it is the like of my mother's life." Anna wept on Matthias's shoulder while he stroked her soft blond hair.

"They have been given enough money to make their way to Hamburg, and John Harding, who leaves in a few days, will bring them back to Montreal."

Matthias looked up as Esther came through the door holding Miriam. She was about to turn around, seeing what was obviously a private moment, when Anna put her arms out for her child.

"There is some of my mother in these eyes," she said, reaching for the child and the thought.

***

The *Northern Belle* steamed into Hamburg harbour and was moored at the main wharf for a few hours when Captain John Harding saw three figures, with rags hanging from their emaciated bodies, staring up at him on deck. He went down the gangplank, and the closer he got the more he realized the presence of a pungent odour from their rags.

"Herr Franz Gruber?" Harding's tone was strong and assertive, and it caused the man to cower slightly.

"*Ja, mein Herr*," he said respectfully, looking at the ground.

Harding smiled at the children. "Wilhelm *und* Greta?"

"*Ja, mein Herr*." They trembled as they spoke, staring at their rag-wrapped feet.

Harding felt such pity that human beings could be reduced to such a state that he was momentarily overcome. Greta's blues eyes shone out from her dirty face as she glanced up at Harding. He took a deep breath, put his arms around the children, and nodded at the father.

"*Kommen*," Harding said affectionately.

He led them to the Harp Inn, where they were escorted upstairs to two rooms with baths for which he had already paid. The proprietor's wife, Frau Freeman, was ready, and after curling up her nose at the stench of them all she quickly took Greta to one room and called for buckets of hot water. Harding helped Herr Freeman bring water from a boiler out back and up the stairs. The water had to be changed for the father and son twice, and Harding sent out for new clothing and had the Grubers' rags burned.

Harding was sitting talking to Herr Frerman when Greta came down stairs with Frau Freeman, who was grinning from ear to ear with the result of her work. Young Greta looked stunningly like her sister Anna, despite her undernourished body. Her clean white-blond hair shone, and Frau Freeman ran to get some of her own perfume to complete the transformation. Herr Gruber and his son came down the stairs moments later looking like self-conscious gentlemen.

Harding sent for a fine carriage and the Grubers were taken to the Captain's favorite eatery and treated to a feast. After a good tuck in, more clothing and personal items to suit their own tastes were purchased in some of Hamburg's finest shops for the journey to the New World. They were escorted to their luxurious berths on the new steam-propelled marvel that would leave in a two days after she was loaded with cargo, coal stores, and fifty-two additional passengers, all emigrating to Canada.

Franz Gruber seemed a beaten man, in Harding's estimation. He had refused any more clothing than what was needed to replace his rags. He clearly delighted in the joy on his children's faces, but there was no joy in him. His first words to Harding were to express regret for how he had let Anna down by accepting money to feed the rest of the family from Frau Hoffmann in exchange for Anna's services. Harding had not known these details and tried to keep his shock from showing.

Franz Gruber had visited Frau Hoffmann to collect his daughter's earnings, and he'd been told that she had fallen in love with a man with the plague and was dead. His wife had died with the agony of thinking she had outlived Anna, her firstborn, whose dignity, youth, and ultimately life had been stolen. She never forgave Franz, who wept as he spoke of the heartache his wife took to her grave. When he'd learned of Anna's good fortune from Jorge Hacker's man, he'd wept more for what his wife never knew.

Late one night in the mid-Atlantic, Franz waited until the ship was quiet. His son opened one eye and asked him where he was going, and Franz simply replied that he needed some air. He walked out on deck and found the seas incredibly calm as he went for his stroll. He bowed gracefully as he passed other passengers.

The coal-fired boilers spat smoke from the red stack into the night sky. Gruber watched the twin screws stir the frothy water that hissed astern. He had some understanding of the side-paddlewheelers he had seen, but the idea of a propeller pushing a ship that size through the water was beyond his grasp. He gazed up at masts barren of any canvas as the ship appeared to magically glide in a straight line towards the New World at a speed he was told averaged around ten knots. The technology was for a new generation, he thought, as he looked for a nice spot away from the eyes of the bridge crew and waited for late-night stragglers to return to their cabins.

Kneeling humbly at the railing Herr Gruber thanked God for the mercy that had been granted to his children and begged forgiveness for his failure to provide for them, and for being responsible for his wife's anguish at the time of her death. In his mind there was only one way to atone for such monumental shortcomings as his, and so he climbed the railing and dropped quietly into the numbingly cold sea. He watched the ship get smaller and smaller, shivering as his limbs quickly tired from trying to stay afloat. He let himself slip under the water but came up again, sputtering salty brine, afraid to die. More resolve was needed as he realized he hadn't considered what drowning was all about.

To make clean work of it he knew what he would have to do, and he steadied himself for the task. The next time he went under, he breathed in deeply and water flooded his lungs. It stung, and he convulsed to spit it out, but he forced himself to suck in more water, overruling his body's reflexes. Instead of thrashing to the surface he pushed himself downward, until he began to see stars, as though he were staring at the heavens. A tingling warmth crept through his body as he sank, deeper and deeper, until the stars slowly went out, one by one.

No one knew Herr Gruber was missing until breakfast the following morning. Engines were brought to a full stop until Harding had ascertained from young Wilhelm that his father had gone out on deck for fresh air in the middle of the night. There was no way he could be found, and indeed no way he would have survived the temperature of the water. The ship was underway again, while two orphans stared into the wake of the *Northern Belle* with a crewman close by … on watch.

Harding considered the subject of good fortune and wondered: would Franz Gruber still be alive if "good fortune" hadn't come his way? His children were the only reason he lived. Knowing their needs were taken care of, maybe death was good fortune to one whose life was filled with such guilt. Harding shuddered at the thought of how a man could face a daughter he had consigned to life as a whore. In this thought, Harding concluded that death might very well have been the least painful option

When the ship docked in Montreal, Elizabeth, Anna, Matthias, and little Miriam were all on the wharf waiting to welcome Anna's family. She barely recognized her siblings in the two young adults on deck, gazing at the New World in front of them. She'd expected to see wonder and joy in their faces, but she saw only expressions darkened with sadness. And … where was her father?

Harding came down the gangplank with a solemn air to quietly inform them all of Herr Gruber's demise. It hit Anna broadside. She had dreamed of showering forgiveness on her father, not thinking for a moment about whether or not he could forgive himself. When Wilhelm and Greta came down the plank Anna ran to them but stopped just inches away, taken aback by their defensive posture. They stood as though she were a stranger who had harmed them. She spoke tearfully, in their mother tongue.

"Come, we will take you home, where we can talk of our mother and father."

Greta shattered into tears, and Wilhelm stopped her from going to Anna, who stood with open arms.

"He would still be alive if we had stayed where we belonged!" he spewed, winding Anna with his anger.

"His reasons for what he did were his, not mine or yours, Wilhelm. From what I am told he wished you both a new start in life. He brought you to the boat, didn't he?"

Wilhelm would have none of it. He and Greta got in the carriage with Matthias and their niece in silence. Greta was thrown off by the child staring at her, which caught the eye of Matthias. He handed little Miriam to her young aunt under the pretense of seeing to a business matter with the Captain before they headed off.

Greta held the child and gently wept, thinking how her mother would have loved the moment. Wilhelm took a seat in the carriage and stared into space, not wishing to engage anyone on the ride into town. However his eyes did open rather widely when he saw the size of the house his sister lived in, and he muttered, "*Mein Gott*," under his breath, causing Anna to smirk.

It took a good month for Wilhelm to tire of being angry and affixing blame as a way of dealing with his grief. The wonder and promise of this New World he found himself in demanded all of his energy — there simply wasn't enough left to devote to anger. Anna took him to help at the soup kitchen, where he realized there were many whose plight was far worse than his own.

Matthias wondered if Franz Gruber had been more afraid to face Anna or the man who had married her, in light of what he had done to his daughter. In actual fact, Matthias and Anna had let go of any judgments, as they now both believed that this single action, the consigning of Anna to Frau Hoffmann's brothel, as horrid as it was, had set a chain of events in motion. Change one thing … change everything, they'd concluded. If Anna hadn't been standing in the door of Frau Hoffmann's that day, Matthias wouldn't have met her, which meant he wouldn't have been late for the cathedral, which was the reason he had escaped his father's fate, and so on. The consequences of their meeting fell like dominoes that landed them in

Montreal, the town where their child, an undeniable happiness in their lives, was born. They believed in the idea that they were destined for one another.

1851–1870

Over the next few years, Wilhelm and Greta learned to speak perfect English and French as they integrated into the vibrant social surroundings of Montreal life. Matthias and Anna had two more children — a daughter, Greta, named after Anna's mother and sister, and a son, John, after Captain Harding.

Life was good in Montreal, the town where they were destined to live out their days. Matthias delighted in his children and every success they achieved, no matter how minuscule, and when his time came he felt his life had been filled with good fortune. Anna still remained the greatest gift any man could have asked for. His love for her transformed slowly with the changes of age, growing deeper and more caring as her touch took on new meaning.

The simple physical manifestation of one human being lovingly touching another he grew to recognize as the ultimate privilege. From that touch he knew well-being, and a love that he carried in his heart everywhere he went. An appreciation of being so loved by another filled him in ways for which there were no adequate words.

Anna's sister Greta fell in love with an acquaintance of the Heinyl family and had no trouble with the idea of converting to Judaism, loving the sense of extended family she felt with the Jewish side of her sister's family. Wilhelm slowly worked his way into the textile business under the kind and fatherly guidance of Matthias, and he was soon welcomed into the Hardings' church. Both Greta and Wilhelm looked upon Matthias and Anna as strange individuals. They were Godless, if religious faith was the measuring rod, and yet they encouraged them to seek some kind of spiritual meaning in their own lives, provided it never harmed those of unlike minds. There was something about Matthias and Anna Dopp that people couldn't understand, with the exception of John Harding.

1870–1875

It was the fall of 1872 when dire news of the *Northern Belle* arrived in Montreal. She had just cleared the Gulf of St. Lawrence and was a day into the Atlantic when a hurricane crossed her path and cracked her superstructure. The water she began to take in overtook the bilge pumps, and Harding, running out of options, turned her around, hoping to make it back to the coast. She made it all right, but with no boilers functioning. One small mast with some stitched, shredded canvas took her to the coast of Pictou, Nova Scotia, where she floundered off shore. The good Captain saw most of his crew to the one rowboat that hadn't been swept overboard.

The craft was filled to the brim and set off for shore in the turbulent seas. Harding and Matheson remained on the *Belle*, waist-deep in water, waiting for the rowboat to return, when the spine of the ship let out a horrifying crack and she snapped the rest of the way into two clean pieces that went under in a matter of minutes. Matheson made it to shore holding on to a chunk of shorn mast and the unconscious body of his captain, who had been severely injured by falling rigging.

Leaving Anna behind with the children, Matthias and Elizabeth Harding left on another steamer and pulled into the old Scottish settlement of Pictou five days later. In the stone house of Mr. Muir, a local merchant, they met Matheson, who sat glumly on guard like a faithful dog outside his master's room. Elizabeth ran in to see her husband, grey and drawn and drifting in and out of sleep. She wanted to kiss him, but Mrs. Muir, who had been tending to him, was present. After a couple of awkward looks she left Elizabeth to be alone with her husband and went out in the hall.

"How is he?" Matthias inquired.

"His head wound is severe and I fear it will take him soon. He is often delirious and frets about needing to summon one he loves to meet him in the light. God only knows what that means." The woman looked fatigued. "I'll make us all some tea."

She had no sooner gone downstairs to the kitchen than Elizabeth poked her head out of the door.

"John knows you are here and wants to speak with you, Matthias." Matthias followed Elizabeth back in.

Harding watched with eyes deep-set in a gaunt, skeletal face as Matthias approached the chair at the bedside.

"Matthias, it is so good to see you," he croaked.

"You as well, my friend, though I must confess I wish you were in a little better state for the trip home," Matthias said, attempting to muster up a little hope.

"I'm quite sure I am about to die." The words scratched their way out of his dry throat, and tears streamed down Elizabeth's face as she held a glass of water up to his lips. He sipped and continued.

"I am not afraid of it, just what I might miss of you all if I leave now. What can I expect, Matthias? You are the only one I know who has already done this."

Elizabeth looked horrified by her husband's words.

"And all this time I thought you never believed me," Matthias said.

"I didn't," Harding continued, "but I'm heading into uncharted waters and you are the only one I know who at least claims to have sailed there before. I sure hope Jacob Smitherim doesn't come to greet me." Harding attempted a laugh that turned into a foul cough.

"It has to be someone you love who has passed … unless there's something about you and Jacob you have neglected to tell me?" Matthias countered.

Harding laughed again, and again the cough followed, only this time his face turned a horrid colour and he appeared to slip into unconsciousness.

"Oh, John." Elizabeth placed her ear close to her husband's face to hear if he was still breathing, and when she had assured herself that he was, she looked at Matthias curiously. "What are the two of you talking about? It surely sounds like the Devil's work."

"Mrs. Harding, you know the two of us better than that."

Mrs. Muir appeared with a silver tray carrying tea and scones, with Matheson in tow. It was some two hours later that Harding began to stir. His feet began to thrash a little under the covers, and Elizabeth ran to his side. Matheson stood with a worried look, as did Matthias. Mrs. Muir turned to Matthias and whispered, "They often thrash around like that just before they die." Matthias went to the other side of the bed. Both he had Elizabeth held one of John Harding's hands. The Captain's eyes opened wide and he began to squint with curiosity.

"Ver … hoevan?" The word fell out with his last breath, which continued on in a diminishing hiss. A shadow drifted over his eyes and he was gone.

Elizabeth wailed in pain, and Matheson went to her and patted her back while she stroked her dead husband's face, as though trying to will him back to life.

The body was prepared for the journey back to Montreal, where Matthias saw to all funeral arrangements. Harding's service was well attended by businessmen of some stature, as well as many who had served at sea with the fair-minded Captain, and the Friends of his Quaker congregation. Before the pastor of Harding's church began the ceremony, a wagon pulled up and Captain Ferguson got out with his first mate, Atkins. The two men went solemnly to the grave, and the words were read as the box was lowered. Ferguson wept openly and quietly with no embarrassment, and Elizabeth went to comfort him.

Elizabeth continued to work for a few years with Anna at the soup kitchen, but the joy had left her life, and on a cold winter's night, after a tenacious flu, her heart gave way.

The body waited in an expensive coffin at the mausoleum until spring when the ground thawed and she could be buried next to her husband. Much of her church's congregation was at the burial service, as well as a few former slaves who had known her kind heart. Matheson, Ferguson, and Atkins appeared, again, out of respect, and back at the Dopp house stories were traded into the night over the Captain's best whisky, which was brought from its hiding place in the pantry.

Anna listened with her bedroom door open as the men got more inebriated. It was the story of Matthias's unconscious body being rescued from the coffin of a dead woman that caught her by surprise, placing more flesh on the bones of her husband's incredible journey.

The next day, when Anna returned to plant flowers at the foot of Elizabeth's grave, she noticed one daisy sitting sweetly on the fresh soil and wondered who had placed it there.

1875–1907

In the years that followed, life began to complete its cycle for many in the Dopps' circle of friends and acquaintances. They observed marriages and births and an increasing number of funerals, which circled around them ominously as a sign that their own lifespans had far more past than future. Word arrived from Savannah of the death of Esther Heinyl. The stress of the American Civil War ten years earlier had taken its toll on many of those who lived in Savannah, and her son Günter swore it was the loss of relatives in that damned war that had weakened her heart. By the time they learned of her death she was long buried, and so Matthias sent a lengthy letter of condolence to Schmul Heinyl, which Günter delivered on his trip to visit his mother's grave and console a grieving father.

Matthias and Anna delighted in their children and grandchildren as they continued to share their good fortune with many. It was a few days after Matthias's seventieth birthday that his health began to fail rather dramatically. Anna was amazed at how calm he was when the doctor told him he didn't have much time. After the children had visited and returned to their own homes one evening, Matthias assured her yet again that he already knew what was on the other side and felt no fear, only a measure of inconvenience that they would be parted for a while. Anna still had difficulty with such talk, though she now believed more of it than she disbelieved.

Matthias realized from Anna's example that the knowledge he possessed was, in some respects, of very little value. The life lived was the gift, the struggle to love … the lesson, the imperfect world … a truly magnificent classroom. As he lay dying, he looked at Anna with the only bit of worry that crossed his face.

"I wonder if Verhoevan's book should be returned to him in Magdeburg. I'm pretty sure it's not such a good thing to have lying around."

With that he smiled at his Anna, and almost as though he were just stepping out for a moment, he casually drew his last breath and died. She stared at her handsome prince, now lifeless. Waves of sorrow began to slowly roll over her until the powerful undertow of grief pulled her under. Even if all Matthias had said was true, her body craved a physical presence that was no more.

On the day of Matthias's funeral the Heinyl and Dopp mills were silent. Many loyal employees attended, and their ranks were populated with European immigrants and a good number of former slaves. At the grave, one black woman remained and placed a daisy on the coffin. Anna saw this from her carriage and suddenly remembered the daisy on Elizabeth Harding's grave some twenty-six years earlier. She quickly ordered the driver to stop, and she sent one of the funeral directors to ask the woman if she might have words with her. The woman reluctantly agreed, and moments later she stood staring at Anna.

"Do I know you?" Anna inquired.

"Not really. I was a child when you last saw me … but you knew my mother," the woman replied sheepishly.

"Who was your mother?"

"She was a slave to Jacob Smitherim. You stopped Jacob Smitherim from beating my father on the street. Before my father died of his wounds he would tell us the story of the young woman who had humiliated the evil man, Smitherim, for all to see. It was our favourite story, and it gave my father some hope for his children, that there were those in the world who saw the wrong."

"Oh my." Anna held her hand to her mouth and studied the woman's face. "I see your mother's kindness in your face. She was one of the first ones Elizabeth and I ever helped escape the madness of Savannah. Please allow me to offer you a ride home. I would love to hear of that brave woman."

The woman was given a hand by the funeral director and room was made for her in the carriage.

"Was your mother's name not Smithers, as many were called from that horrible plantation?" Anna asked.

"Yes, she was Daisy Smithers."

"Is she still living?"

"Oh my goodness, no. She died shortly after Elizabeth Harding. My momma asked me to place a daisy on her grave," the woman said with a sad smile.

"And what is your name?" Anna inquired.

"My name was Sunny Smithers. My father named me Sunny because the day I was born, he said, was the sunniest day the Lord had ever made. But I'm married and have children of my own now. I am Sunny Bishop."

"Well, Sunny Bishop, you have certainly brought some sunshine into this dark day." Anna's eyes welled up, and Sunny reached for her hand.

A week after Matthias's funeral Anna sadly began to sort through some of his possessions. As she was removing his belongings from his office, she found the odd book with illuminated Latin text that Matthias had brought with him from Germany as if it were some important family heirloom. She never understood any of the Latin writing and so it never really interested her, apart from Matthias's attachment to it. On the first page she saw a name that snagged something in her memory …*Verhoevan*. This was the book Matthias wanted returned. Verhoevan … she had heard the name once before … and then it came to her. Elizabeth Harding had told her that the Captain had spoken that name on his deathbed, and she'd wondered if Anna knew what it signified.

Anna began to flip through the manuscript's pages until she found some writing near the back of the book that she could read, and she recognized the hand as Matthias's. It was a list that began with meeting Anna. It was a list of the good fortune that had resulted from their meeting, though some of the entries made her weep. One stated, "The love for her brought me back into my body. It was the only thing strong enough to defeat the Som. Love … my Anna gave me this magic, the greatest gift of all. Greater than all we could ever invent, surely the greatest discovery of any living soul." It was dated the day before Matthias's death and signed, "Matthias Dopp, one who has crossed and returned from the great mystery."

For the last six years of her life Anna tried in vain through correspondence to find out if anyone knew of a man named Verhoevan in Magdeburg, so that she might carry out her husband's final request. She longed for the gaze of unconditional love that used to emanate from the eyes of her Matthias, but she was grateful to have even known such a thing. There was a sadness in sensing her own time was near its end, but most of the sadness she felt was missing a world that no longer existed. She could no longer dream of an earthly future as life slowly whittled her down. She was filled with love for her children, and there was a sweet pain in knowing that she would not be there to watch her grandchildren grow.

She died of pneumonia in a fever that brought about the oddest sensation of drifting out of her body, where for a brief moment she could have sworn she saw Matthias. She longed to drift off again for another good glimpse of him and soon did, never to return.

Her daughter Miriam found the leather-bound book carefully wrapped in a quilt inside a travel case under her mother's bed. Neither her brother nor her sister expressed any interest in it, so Miriam took it home, despite protests from her Orthodox husband, Joshua Sidney Feldman.

On the soil of Anna Dopp's freshly covered grave one morning Miriam found a single white daisy. She noticed a new one every year on the anniversary of her mother's death for the next nine years, and wondered who was bringing them, and why they stopped.

32

WITH TIME REMAINING

Toronto, 2003

Three months had passed since Shaun Bishop and Jennifer Glessing had spoken on the phone. After a long day and a never-ending line of patients, Shaun had come home to dinner with Vera and Myra. Vera would stop in when Myra was babysitting and the three of them would often have dinner together, before leaving Shaun to some quiet one-on-one time with his daughter.

Having played with Shari till bedtime, he had to satisfy her need for not one story, now, but at least two before she would finally drift away into the Land of Nod. He patted her back as he always did when she snuggled into her pillow, then he headed down the hall and poured a scotch. A good, stiff single malt chilled him out sufficiently for what he called an "enjoyable read," although not one member of the sorority understood how medical journals constituted what anyone in his right mind might call "enjoyable."

It was sometime after ten-thirty when Shaun was awakened by the doorbell. He had fallen asleep in his favourite chair and stood up a little stunned. Rubbing his face with his hands in an attempt to pull himself together, he opened the door, and Jennifer Glessing was standing in front of him.

"Jennifer?" he said, still half asleep. "What can I do for you at this hour?"

"You might invite me in for a minute." She seemed rather agitated, so Shaun complied.

Jennifer was no sooner through the door than she grabbed Shaun and kissed him, long and quite seriously, on the lips. Shaun didn't quite know what to do but instinctively kissed her back. The kiss went on and held a million words, and both seemed to lose themselves in the doing of it. Jennifer finally ended what she had started and pulled back, staring at Shaun Bishop.

"Oh Daniel, you're there, you are *so* there."

"C'mon, Ali, we've been through this. I am not Snow White, for heaven's sake!"

"No, you're not, and you're also not Shaun Bishop. You're Daniel Blum, and I'm Alison Truman."

Daniel went for another scotch and socked it back. "Drink?" he asked, realizing that he was drinking alone.

"What, to bring me to my senses or something? I'm here, Daniel. I'm here to say I am in love with you and will wait for you to come around, no matter how long it takes. I guess it's my turn to eat some crow."

"Would this ever have happened if Brendon hadn't dumped you? You've got to admit, I've had good reason to feel like a pathetic second choice, even a convenience. What if some other cosmetically sound Caucasian strolls into your life and you've finished with your black guy phase? Remember, it was you who confessed you weren't attracted to black men."

"Yeah, and you were pretty much done with blond bimbos, isn't that the category you blessed me with?"

"Well … uh, yeah … I guess."

"What did you feel when I kissed you, Daniel? Tell me it didn't feel right."

"It didn't feel right, Ali," Danny shot back.

"Then I don't know anything. Maybe you're right and I'm nothing but a stupid girl wishing for some fairy-tale ending. God, I feel like such an idiot." Jennifer's eyes filled as she strode out the door and slammed it behind her.

Shaun stood staring at the door, trying to process everything that had just happened. He wasn't about to become a temporary fix to some girl he used to know who was on the rebound. He sucked back another scotch, then one more, and went to bed.

The following morning at around six-thirty Shari started chattering and singing, as she usually did. Shaun got up and began their daily ritual. Shari now sat on the living-room floor and looked at her books or played while Shaun had a shower. She'd bring clothes into the bedroom and they'd both get dressed and head to the kitchen, where she helped her dad make breakfast by bringing the bread from the fridge for the toaster and the peanut butter from the cupboard, while Shaun nursed a coffee and got her orange juice. The well-oiled machine was winding down when the doorbell rang and it was Myra, ready for another day. She reached up and kissed Shaun

Bishop on the cheek and whispered into his ear, "Good morning, Daniel, my lovely boy," as she always did.

That morning Daniel stopped his usual rush out of the door and hugged Myra Blum until she hugged him back. "I love you, Mom. More than you'll ever know." He looked at her tearfully, eye to eye, to make sure she saw the sincerity of his statement. "I know this hasn't been easy on you, Mom. You have been so loyal, so constant, all of my life. I don't know how I can ever thank you."

"You just did, my lovely boy," she said.

Shari laughed from her highchair. "My lovely boy. Daddy's a lovely boy!"

Myra smiled at her granddaughter. "He sure is!" She turned back to Shaun. "You tell me about what's troubling you when you get it sorted out," she said as she kissed him on the cheek. Then she went to Shari. "Well now, who is my lovely girl?"

Shaun hurried out the door, and as he started up his new Mercedes S420 he saw Vera Bishop pulling on to the road in her latest old Toyota. He put the pedal to the metal, pulled up next to her at the first stoplight, and honked his horn. Vera looked surprised but reached over and rolled her window down.

"I need to chat with you," Shaun yelled out his window.

"Lunch?" Vera threw back.

"I'll pick you up at noon," Shaun replied.

The morning was too long for Shaun and, needless to say, he felt he was he far too distracted to be of any real use to his patients. By eleven he had cancelled the rest of the lineup for the day. He was in the parking lot of the bank where Vera worked by eleven forty-five. Vera recognized his car but couldn't get away from her desk until five minutes after twelve. She hurried out to Shaun's car and sat looking at him with a worried expression.

"What is going on, Shaun? You never have time for lunch."

"Ali came to see me last night."

"Oh, thank the Lord, I thought there was something wrong with you."

"She kissed me."

"Mm-hmm.

"That's all you have to say?"

"Mm-hmm."

"I kissed her back. I'm still in love with her."

"You never stopped loving her, Shaun. But I guess I should call you Daniel in this discussion."

"Vera, I loved Jordan."

"I know."

"I can't do this to Jordan's parents. Ella would feel I'm betraying her daughter's memory, and Jennifer Glessing isn't even attracted to black guys." Daniel's thoughts were fractured and all over the map.

Vera looked at him and began to smile. "Shaun, Daniel … whatever … look at you. You are so alive at this moment it is a wonder to behold. You are alive because you know you're in love. A piece of you died with Jordan, and even though you've been doing your job and raising your child and being a wonderful father, I might add … the thing that died in you was passion. Without passion for something in life you are not fully engaged. I am so glad to see you like this. Does she love you?"

"She said she did, and it sure felt like she did."

"And what did you say to her?"

"I told her … I told her I wasn't going to be a convenience just because her husband dumped her."

"You what? You men can be so stupid. You know you love her. She came to you and said the same. Now if she came to you even though you said she is not attracted to black men, something was pulling on her that was pretty deep. You got a problem with her wonder-bread-honky-ass thing?"

"Her what? Her wonder bread … honky ass…?" Shaun burst out laughing and Vera started to giggle.

"I have never said such things out loud before, I am so sorry." Then she laughed some more until she got a grip. "Oh, Daniel Blum, you love her, so quit standing in the way of what you've always felt for Ali. Your love has been dormant and, granted, it's all a little complicated, but if it's too simple it's not worth having. You go find that girl, Shaun … Daniel … whatever, and one more thing." Vera was now clearly struggling to hold back tears. "I never said this because I know Jordan loved you, but I just feel in my bones she's pretty all right at the moment."

"Shaun?" Daniel asked, knowing full well what she was thinking.

Vera Bishop reached into her purse and pulled out a Kleenex. "Mm-hmm," she answered as she wiped her eyes and fluffed up her hair. "You go find Ali, Daniel. This is your time now."

"I love you, Vera."

"I know, son. Does Myra know?"

"I think she suspects."

"Mm-hmm, that woman always knows what's going on. Don't ask me how, but she always knows. I've underestimated her more times than I can shake a stick at." Vera reached over and kissed Shaun Bishop on the cheek. "Don't you worry about Ella and Darth Vader. Myra and I can work on them. They'll come around. And one other thing … next time you ask me out for lunch, you better be serious." Vera reached over and kissed him on the cheek. "Now go find that girl."

Danny shook his head in wonder at the woman as she headed back into the bank. He had heard her call Jordan's dad "Darth Vader" before but it still made him laugh. Jordan's dad had indeed surrendered to the "dark side" since his daughter's death. It was so hard for Ella to recover with his gloom facing her every day, and Vera's calling him Darth Vader had somehow made it easier for Ella to separate herself from his darkness. A good part of what made Vera Bishop tick was her steadfast refusal to surrender to the dark side of life. For her, life was a challenge to which she rose with nobility, a gift from her idea of God. There was no such thing as defeat, only the random dues of the bargain that began with the metaphor of Eden: the confines of a perfect existence had been shed for the imperfect world of free will.

When Jennifer had seen him last she had said she was staying with her parents until she found a place. Shaun knew where her parents' home was, having driven by it years ago hoping to get a glimpse of her.

Shaun's shiny black Mercedes with the baby seat in the back caught Mrs. Glessing's eye as it streaked in front of the house then pulled into the circular driveway. Shaun got out and rang the bell and Mrs. Glessing opened the door.

"May I help you?"

"Yes, Mrs. Glessing. I am Shaun Bishop, a friend of your daughter's, and I wondered if I might speak with her."

"Oh, I know who you are. You're an oncologist at Saint Margaret's. You helped one of my friends, Mary Bonnel, though her breast cancer. You went to school with Jennifer … my God, you were the one in the ICU in that horrible time."

"That's right. How is Mary?"

"Why, we're going for a speed-walk in an hour. She is great!"

"I'm glad to hear that, Mrs. Glessing. Might I speak with Jennifer?"

"Jennifer has her own place now, it's a townhouse near where we used to live back in the day. I'll give you her number." Mrs. Glessing disappeared into the house and moments later produced a piece of paper with a phone number on it. "If you'd like, you could use our phone," she offered.

"I can call her on my car phone, but thank you, ma'am."

Shaun turned and hopped back into his car and drove away. He dialled the number and Jennifer Glessing answered. Danny couldn't speak, and finally Jennifer made a wild guess.

"Danny?"

"Directions, I need directions," was all Danny could say.

Ali complied, and twenty minutes later she opened the door to Shaun Bishop, who immediately put his arms around her and kissed her as if it was the most important kiss humankind had ever known. Ali kissed Danny back for a good few minutes before she realized the door was open and kicked it shut with her foot.

"So I guess now *I'm* Snow White, huh?" she asked.

"Well, you are about as white as they come. Actually, Vera thought that if you could love me even though you're not attracted to black folk and I could love Ali even though she was a wonder-bread-honky-ass, there had to be something strong between us. Ali, I'm sorry."

"No, no, no, Daniel, it's me who should be saying I'm sorry."

The next few weeks were interesting, to say the least. Myra and Vera of course welcomed Jennifer and her son Daniel with open arms. Myra confessed that she'd always wanted to know the soul her son had fallen in love with on the other side, and with a little boy named Daniel to boot, Jennifer could do no wrong.

It would take time, but Jordan's mother, Ella, looked as though she would come around, and the sorority would gain a new member. Her husband, whom Ella now called Darth Vader openly, didn't appear to have an opinion, as nothing mattered any more in a world so heavily invested in mourning.

One evening when Ali stopped in for a quiet dinner, while Danny was putting Shari to bed she wandered around the house and spotted the suitcase on the shelf in Shaun's bedroom. She pulled it down, opened it, and carefully took out Verhoevan's manuscript, which she placed on the bed. Danny came around the corner and was surprised.

"Well, you make yourself at home, don't you?" he quipped over her shoulder.

"I figured you'd still have it," Ali answered. "What if someone else gets into trouble? Or what if one of the kids got caught up in this thing, like we did! What are you going to do with this, Danny?"

"Not sure," Danny replied as he watched her flipping through the pages. "I never saw these last few pages before. Someone took a pen and wrote in it, like a family Bible. See? There are names with dates, like a family tree or something. I would say the hand was well familiar with the German language by the way it's written."

"Were there German immigrants in your family?"

"On my mother's side. Thousands of Jews emigrated from Germany. I wonder if it was some relative who brought it over."

Ali looked at the last name on one branch of the list. This one was clearly written in ballpoint instead of pen and ink. "Sid Feldman?"

"My grandfather. Sid Feldman was my mom's father."

Ali followed the trail to the first entry. "Matthias Dopp?"

"Never heard of him."

"Well, he must have been your great-great-grandfather if this is your family tree." Ali flipped to the last page, and on the inside cover was some writing. She flipped the page over to the family tree and compared the ink and the hand.

"Most of this is written in German by the person who signed as Matthias Dopp in 1900. This is probably your great-great-grandfather's handwriting." Ali tried to read it all aloud even though it was in German. "The last entry in his writing is this odd inscription. *Verliebt, ich fürchte nicht, ich bin frei.* Any idea what that means?"

"Sounds important, but most things in German sound important. We should get all of that stuff translated.

"The very last entry is in a different hand and in English. *This book should be returned to Verhoevan in Magdeburg. Anna Dopp, 1907.*"

"So Verhoevan is in Magdeburg."

"I think we have a task to fulfill," Danny realized out loud.

***

The flight to Frankfurt felt odd. Danny and Ali had booked off an entire week together, just the two of them. The sorority, of course, were taking good care of Shari, and young Daniel was staying with the Glessings, who didn't really approve of their daughter going away with someone they felt she hardly knew. Danny had shared the family tree with Myra, who had jotted it all down with some curiosity about the possibility of living relatives. Both Vera and Myra agreed that the manuscript did not belong; even though their experience had been positive, the chord's potential for chaos was overwhelming. The two mothers were intrigued with the familiarity of Daniel and Alison and the obvious bond between them and were completely supportive of their need for time alone.

Once on the ground in Frankfurt they had an hour-long wait for the commuter flight to Berlin, There they rented a small Mercedes C-class. Overcome with fatigue, they decided to grab some welcome sleep in a hotel before continuing on to Magdeburg. Waking up next to one another felt right. Somehow the universe was in sync again, and what had become a labyrinth of human entanglement was at once simple … when eyes were closed.

Ali and Daniel were with one another again, having made it to the other side and back with a love intact. Ali's humour returned, and with it the realization that Brendon had discouraged it. Brendon, Ali confessed, hadn't liked his wife being wittier than him, so she had gradually deferred until, over time, her humour had dried up. With its return came more passion and a reinvestment in her fascination with ancient languages and cultures. Danny sensed he was about to learn more than he wanted to about the history of the Germanic tribes and the evolution of their language, but it was good to have Ali back, nerdy interests and all.

Magdeburg was an unassuming town, and they got a list of old churches and began the search through cemeteries. After an afternoon of wandering through communities of the dead, they sought lodging at an old mill that had been converted into a hotel. The age of the building caught Ali's eye. The original mill wheel sat proudly in the lobby as a centrepiece under a sheet of Plexiglas. When they were checking in, Daniel inquired about any churches nearby for the next day, and the girl on the front desk informed them that there was a small chapel just down the road on what would have been the outskirts of town in the middle of the nineteenth century.

They learned even more about the chapel from Josef Muller, the proprietor of the hotel, later that night over a good German beer. His family had been in the area for generations, and in fact had owned the mill for over a hundred years. He warned them that whatever they were looking for in the cemetery down the road might not exist any more, as there had been severe damage during the Second World War and many of the stones had been destroyed. There were a few that still stood, however, and the largest stone in the cemetery, he told them quite proudly, was that of one of his ancestors. He added a moment later that, oddly, there were was another name on the stone monument that bore the name of his relative. No one knew who the other man was, except he too had been a Franciscan Brother.

Ali looked at Daniel and lifted her eyebrows. "Was your ancestor's name Verhoevan?" Ali asked Herr Muller, whose jaw dropped.

"No, why do you ask?"

"Oh, we're just following up on a little history," Ali answered.

"I see," Muller said with a serious expression. "No, Verhoevan was not my ancestor, but that is the other name on the stone. My ancestor's name was Vasquez, Henri Vasquez. So, how is it you know the name Verhoevan?"

Ali's memory served her well. She remembered much that she had scanned in the book Dr. Walters had produced on their visit to his home.

"He is mentioned in the writings of a Franciscan Brother by the name of Pietro Brebeuf, who was a musician of some repute in the mid-1800s. Verhoevan was his mentor and apparently a brilliant composer. Your ancestor was, I believe, a valued colleague of Verhoevan's in the Franciscan brotherhood," Ali answered, omitting the good stuff.

"So why the interest in an old grave? Surely you didn't travel all the way from Canada to look at the gravestone of a couple of old priests."

"No, not at all," Danny began. " We, uh, we're …"

"… a couple of pipe organ nuts," Ali jumped in, "and this guy Pietro Brebeuf wrote some pretty nice music in his day. He is said to have been a magnificent performer who played most of the great pipe organs of Europe in his time. So, I guess you could say we're fans of his, and in one of his books he mentioned his mentor, Verhoevan, who was buried in Magdeburg. We thought while we were here we'd see if we could find him, for fun."

"Well, you have. I would be glad to show you where they rest in the morning, if you wish. Would nine o'clock suit you?"

"That's a date," Ali replied

They retired for the evening and talked like excited kids as they got ready for bed. They had found Verhoevan! Ali was in bed first and looked up at the body of Shaun Bishop as he undressed..

"I need a fix," she said softly.

Danny hopped in and kissed her, then ran into the bathroom to brush his teeth. By the time he returned Ali was out cold, which ended any further ideas Danny was having. Jet lag had caught up with both of them, and Danny soon followed Ali to Dreamland.

***

The next morning, over a typical German hotel breakfast of cheese, fresh bread, cold cuts, and strong coffee, Ali and Danny decided that their trip to the graveyard with the proprietor would be a recon mission. Muller met them at nine and they all crammed into his Opel. They had driven only a few kilometres when an old stone chapel came into view. Josef Muller pulled off the road and began to expound on the history he knew. There had once been a monastery attached to the west side of the building, but it had been destroyed during World War Two. In the aftermath, the church had changed denominations a few times and now was rarely used. The old chapel, currently owned by a local congregation, was maintained primarily for its historical value and the occasional small wedding.

To the east side of the church sat the remnants of an old graveyard that ended abruptly at a modern brick wall. The cemetery had once extended well over into the other side, where a series of small shops now stood on ground that Muller believed held the remains of many monks. He pointed to a monument standing straight and proud and quite close to the church. It was a large chunk of white granite with black flecks, monolithic in design and resembling an arch-topped door. The stone was some two feet thick and six feet high, sitting on an equally imposing mount of the same granite that sat a foot above the ground.

They walked past ancient-looking memorials that lay broken or cracked, names worn off by the erosion of time and poor limestone. It was clear that whoever had built Verhoevan's monument had been told to make it one of substance. The top of the stone was carved with a design of vines and simple plants that appeared to be an artist's attempt to make it complement the humble surroundings. Large hinges and a keyhole were carved in relief, and in bold print arched around the top of the door were the German words:

Verliebt, ich fürchte nicht, ich bin frei.

Danny looked at Ali, whose eyes opened wide. "The last words that Matthias Dopp wrote in the book," he whispered. Ali nodded.

Midway down the door of stone sat two names and a date, carved as deeply and purposefully as the epitaph above.

Henri Vasquez　　　*Peter Verhoevan*
1848

Daniel and Ali were both more than a little moved, standing over the mortal remains of one they had met who had died a century and a half ago. It brought home the surreal nature of all that had happened to them. Danny immediately thought of those who were called "mad," who dreamed of flying through the air or breathing under the sea. Verhoevan had found the means, the technology, for something so incredible that it was more than humans could handle. It was technology that surpassed the capabilities of the species that designed it — like a jet fighter capable of pulling Gs in a dive that no human pilot could bear without the loss of consciousness. He grabbed Ali's hand and they stood quietly for a moment. Danny glanced down and inspected the soil around the stone. The grass was moist, and disturbing it wouldn't be too obvious, he thought.

"I suppose it is always good to remember those who have gone before us, *ja*?" Muller said, almost to himself. "Come, I have a surprise for you. As you might already know, we have a wonderful pipe organ in one of our churches here in Magdeburg. I am told the organist rehearses today, and I have received permission for us to go and listen."

"How fantastic. Oh, Daniel, isn't this wonderful?" Ali was so over the top that Danny began to laugh and joined in the ruse.

"Unbelievably kind, Herr Muller! Unbelievably kind of you!"

"The least I can do for our guests from Canada. I love your country. It is my wish to see your Rockies and canoe on one of your beautiful emerald lakes."

They headed back to the car and Danny caught Ali rolling her eyes at him. Muller stopped as he opened the door.

"She calls you Daniel, and yet the name in the register and on your credit card is Shaun Bishop?" Muller looked politely puzzled, but he was actually more worried about getting ripped off with a phony credit card, Danny deduced.

"Don't worry, Herr Muller. My credit card is good and does not bear all of my names. My middle name is Daniel. She has a girlfriend named Shaun and refuses to call me the same thing."

Muller laughed and got in the car. Ali gave Daniel an impressed nod for quick thinking as they opened their doors.

The organ rehearsal was not a great experience. In fact, even Muller wrinkled his nose at more than the occasional bad note. The organist flailed away on the same passage of Bach's Brandenburg Concerto Number Three, but his left hand just couldn't keep up with his right, and it sounded as though his feet on the pedals were working on another piece of music entirely. It was very disappointing to Herr Muller, who had sought to impress his guests.

As Ali explained in an attempt to offer some consolation to their host on the way back to the hotel, many churches spent all their money on exceptional organs and had little left to hire an exceptional musician to play them. However, the organ itself was indeed fabulous, and what a treat to hear its power and to be given such a grand tour!

The afternoon was spent in bed, doing what might be expected of reunited lovers. Somehow Ali and Daniel also managed to plot a course of action for that night. A spade was needed, one with a thin edge. They went out in the late afternoon and bought one from a local hardware store, then threw it in the trunk of the rental car. They enjoyed a late dinner at a Japanese restaurant and walked around town as they awaited the cover of night.

It was good and dark after a couple of pints of the local brew. The grave of Verhoevan and Vasquez was far enough away from the road and out of the reach of passing headlights. They waited for the road to quiet then got the spade out of the trunk and headed over to the grave. Ali carried Verhoevan's manuscript and watched as Daniel sliced through the moist soil. He went beyond the metal end of the spade and kept shoving until he was halfway up the handle. Prying the spade against the angle, a slot was ready.

"Dr. Walters would shoot us for doing this to a book that has survived so long," Ali said with some remorse.

"Don't you think we're doing the right thing?"

"Of course it's the right thing. It was the dying wish of your ancestor, and we already know the trouble and pain this manuscript has caused Verhoevan from all those who have suffered from its power. Do it for Verhoevan, to save him any more grief."

"Mmm, but would you ever have loved me if it hadn't been for this thing?" Danny asked with a more than serious expression.

"Probably not, but the fact is I do love you, and maybe we should talk about this someplace where we won't get arrested for defiling a grave."

Danny slid the manuscript behind the spade and then slowly pulled the spade out, allowing the earth and sod to slip back into place. He walked the sod down until the ground appeared to have successfully swallowed Verhoevan's manuscript.

Unbeknownst to the couple, as they walked away from the cemetery, the door of an Opel opened quietly in the shadows across the street. Herr Muller got out and walked straight to the small disturbance in the grass.

***

There was a wonderful sense of closure now for Danny and Alison, with one exception. It was also time to bury the names of Alison Truman and Danny Blum. Danny Blum, according to acceptable norms, lay rotting in a cemetery in Montreal, and Alison Truman was nothing but a pile of ashes in an urn. To speak of their journey would be an affront to the rules of the world they lived in. Danny had a million questions for Bernard, and Ali was deeply curious about her mother, but that was a lifetime away.

A year later, Dr. Shaun Bishop and Jennifer Glessing moved into a new home together. One of Joel's country songs was playing loudly on the radio of a truck as it pulled into the driveway. Some of the biggest names in Nashville had enjoyed hits with Joel's songs, and every so often he would call to say "Hey" with his newly acquired southern accent. It felt good to him that he now had two people he could talk of strange things with on his visits … after the children were in bed, of course.

The Bishop-Glessing-Blum-Truman family was now an even bigger beautiful mess. Jennifer became a card-carrying member of the sorority. Young Daniel became a loving big brother to his funny little sister, Shari. Mr. and Mrs. Glessing began unwittingly learning lessons in love from Vera and Myra, and any uppity edges they'd had were soon rounded off by the affectionate consideration that came their way. It took Jordan's mom a while to come around to the idea of a white woman mothering their grandchild, but Jennifer was sensitive to her needs, and the sorority slowly worked its magic.

Jordan's father was getting tired of the Darth Vader handle and a smile would break through the dark side of the force on occasion. He got to hear his own name on the days he wasn't dedicated to grief, and Shari began to fill the hole in his heart. Myra still whispered, "Daniel, my lovely boy" in Shaun's ear, loving every challenge of her crazy mixed-up extended family. Of course the sorority were all hoping for a new child from the new union, and the pressure was on.

Jennifer soon saw only the man she loved in Shaun, and for his part he doted on his wonder-bread-honky-ass. There was an expression carved into the stone mantle over their fireplace, a remnant of an incredible journey.

Verliebt, ich fürchte nicht, ich bin frei.

They gladly translated it for anyone who asked:

In love, I fear not, I am free.